THE NOMINATION

Books by William G. Tapply

Brady Coyne mystery novels
*Death at Charity's Point * The Dutch Blue Error*
*Follow the Sharks * The Marine Corpse * Dead Meat*
*The Vulgar Boatman * A Void in Hearts*
*Dead Winter * Client Privilege*
*The Spotted Cats * Tight Lines * The Snake Eater*
*The Seventh Enemy * Close to the Bone*
*Cutter's Run * Muscle Memory * Scar Tissue*
*Past Tense * A Fine Line * Shadow of Death*
*Nervous Water * Out Cold * One Way Ticket*
*Hell Bent * Outwitting Trolls*

Other novels
Thicker than Water (with Linda Barlow)
First Light (with Philip R. Craig)
Second Sight (with Philip R. Craig)
Third Strike (with Philip R. Craig)
*Bitch Creek * Gray Ghost * Dark Tiger*

Books on the outdoors
Those Hours Spent Outdoors
*Opening Day and Other Neuroses * Home Water Near and Far*
*Sportsman's Legacy * A Fly Fishing Life * Bass Bug Fishing*
*Upland Days * Pocket Water*
*The Orvis Guide to Fly Fishing for Bass * Gone Fishin'*
*Trout Eyes * Upland Autumn * Every Day Was Special*

Other non-fiction
The Elements of Mystery Fiction: Writing the Modern Whodunit

THE NOMINATION

A NOVEL OF SUSPENSE

WILLIAM G. TAPPLY

Skyhorse Publishing

Skyhorse Publishing books may be purchased in bulk at special discounts for
sales promotion, corporate gifts, fund-raising, or educational purposes. Special
editions can also be created to specifications. For details, contact the Special
Sales Department, Skyhorse Publishing, 307 West 36th Street, 11th Floor,
New York, NY 10018 or info@skyhorsepublishing.com.

www.skyhorsepublishing.com

10 9 8 7 6 5 4 3 2

Library of Congress Cataloging-in-Publication Data

Tapply, William G.
  The nomination : a novel of suspense / by William G. Tapply.
    p. cm.
  ISBN 978-1-60239-990-7
  1. Police--Massachusetts--Boston--Fiction. 2. Boston (Mass.)--Fiction. I.
Title.
  PS3570.A568N66 2011
  813'.54--dc22

                                2010012390

Printed in the United States of America

To my five kids with love,
Mike, Melissa, Sarah, Blake, and Ben

PROLOGUE

He'd expected to be one of the first ones there, but even at seven in the morning, with rain spitting from gray clouds and a chilly March breeze coming off the Bay, they'd already begun to gather. They stood in scattered clusters around the parking lot and on the sidewalk with placards on their shoulders and naïve enthusiasm on their faces.

The place had opened one year after that monstrous Supreme Court decision, one of the first of its kind, and they'd been killing babies here ever since. Today marked the thirty-fifth anniversary of the day it destroyed its first innocent life. The television cameras would be here today, they were saying.

He'd overheard their excited, disorganized planning—if you could call it that. They'd form a human barricade. They'd lie down across the entrance to the parking lot. They'd wave their placards and chant their slogans, and they'd try to get themselves arrested and dragged, bodies gone limp, heels digging in, to the police wagons.

And nothing would change. The babies would continue to be murdered.

He recognized a couple of preachers working the crowd, patting shoulders, whispering their canned words of wisdom and encouragement into eager ears. He'd heard them at meetings, their pious, high-pitched passion invoking God and Jesus and Gandhi and

Martin Luther King and the Bill of Rights. Humility and passive resistance. The meek shall inherit the earth. Turn the other cheek.

It was all bullshit.

Despite thirty-five years of slogans and placards and demonstrations, Dr. Devil was still violating God's laws, as bold and self-confident as ever. Nothing had changed.

And again today, after the placards had been waved and the slogans had been chanted and the human barricades had been dragged away and the television cameras had shot their footage and the reporters had gotten their stories, Dr. Devil would once again march on into the building and continue committing murder, as he did every day.

He allowed himself a silent chuckle. Today these lemmings would see how things *should* be done.

He pressed his elbow against his side and felt the solid, comforting, deadly weight in the pocket of his windbreaker.

Today Dr. Devil would die.

"Wouldn't you like to hold a sign?"

He turned his head. A white-haired man with a red face and a clerical collar showing under his jacket was standing beside him. He was carrying an armload of cardboard signs tacked to rough wooden stakes.

"Sure," he said. "Thanks. God bless."

The preacher smiled, handed him a placard, and moved away.

He propped the placard against the wall without bothering to glance at its slogan.

The crowd was swelling. He guessed that close to a hundred people were here now, and the leaders were trying to organize them, moving from person to person, waving their arms, shouting instructions.

A woman approached him. "He'll be here soon," she said, her eyes shining. "Let our voices be heard."

"Amen, sister," he said.

Around quarter of eight, four police cruisers and two vans arrived. The officers left them parked at the curb and took up stations around the parking lot and along the pathway to the clinic. They folded their arms and assumed their practiced bored expressions.

Five minutes later excited murmurs passed through the crowd.

Somebody said, "Channel Eight's here!"

The crowd was milling around, and the police moved among them, pushing and prodding them to open an aisle from the parking area to the front door of the building.

There was some excitement out by the entrance to the parking lot. He craned his neck and saw two officers dragging a middle-aged white man and an overweight black woman toward a police van that waited with its back doors open.

"Here he comes!"

He wedged his way toward the front of the crowd and saw a black Volvo station wagon nose its way into the parking lot. He stood on tiptoes. He wanted to see Dr. Devil's face.

"Baby killer!"

"Murderer!"

Placards bobbed in the air, and the chants filled his ears. Camera flashes sparked in the gray, sunless morning air.

A minute later he saw the familiar white hair and sun-crinkled face looming over the crowd. The face of the Devil, and the Devil was smiling. Dr. Richard Bryant, all six feet five inches of him, director of the San Francisco Woman's Reproductive Center.

Reproductive. These abortionists did have a fine sense of irony.

A woman had been riding in the Volvo with Dr. Devil, and now she was walking beside him, headed for the clinic. A patient, he supposed. Another rich suburban woman, come here to have her "procedure," their favorite euphemism, performed by the best baby-killer in the business.

She looked a little Chinese or Japanese or something. Around the eyes, mainly. But her hair wasn't right. Brown, not black, and curly, almost kinky, parted in the middle and pulled back in a loose ponytail. She was taller than most Asian women he'd seen. She was beautiful, in an offbeat, exotic way, and she moved with the self-confident grace of a celebrity, someone who'd been coddled and admired all her life. He wondered if he had, in fact, seen her on TV. A lot of showbiz people lived in the Bay area.

She wore tight black pants and a black jersey over a thin black jacket. All black. The color of death.

Her dark eyes darted from side to side as the protesters waved their signs and yelled their pitiful slogans at her. She didn't look nervous or scared, though. She looked like she hated everybody as much as they hated her, and she didn't mind looking them straight in the eye.

He understood how these entitled suburban women thought. Babies wrecked their bodies, smudged their beauty, crushed their egos.

He hated them all, these selfish, narcissistic women who valued their looks and the shape of their bodies and their self-indulgent freedom more than human life. He hated them almost as much as he hated Dr. Devil himself.

"Excuse me," he muttered, shouldering his way toward the front of the crowd. A cop was standing there facing them, holding his nightstick across his chest to keep the aisle from the parking lot to the clinic door open. He edged away from the cop, murmuring "excuse me" and using his elbows to wedge himself into position.

He eased into the second row of protesters. Now he had a clear view of the open pathway where the baby-killing Dr. Devil and his patient would pass, shielded from full view by the short bald man and the elderly woman standing in front of him. He reached into his coat pocket, gripped his weapon by its cold handle, and slid it out. He held it flat against his thigh. Its weight felt serious in his hand.

Now Dr. Devil and the tall woman were approaching, and the voices around him became deafening. Dr. Devil ignored them all, as he had been doing all these years. He gazed straight ahead, intent on the sanctuary inside the clinic, smiling that bemused holier-than-thou smile of his. The woman beside him with those searching black eyes looked more alert than frightened.

He slid the revolver up to his chest and held it inside his open jacket.

Dr. Devil was about fifteen feet away now, moving slowly in his direction, working hard to appear casual and relaxed, ho hum, another day at the office. He was speaking out of the corner of his mouth to the woman beside him. Only his eyes, still grimly focused on the clinic doorway, betrayed his fear.

You better be afraid, Dr. Baby-Killer.

The woman's eyes kept darting around. If she was afraid, she hid it well.

He'd get her, too.

He eased the weapon out from his jacket, shifted his position.

Another two steps and they would be directly in front of him.

His thumb found the hammer, cocked it. He held the revolver in his right hand, bracing it against his hip and aiming it through the space between the man and woman standing in front of him, using them for a blind. From this distance, he couldn't miss. He looked at the baby-killer and the woman with the Asian eyes. In about fifteen seconds he would pull the trigger and keep pulling, and he visualized the cries and the spurts of blood, the two of them falling, big black puddles on the wet pavement . . . one more step, come on, his finger caressing the trigger, and then Dr. Devil's torso, with the Asian woman right at his side, filled the space between the two people, and as he braced his elbow against his hip and tensed his muscles to pull the trigger, he was aware of the woman moving between him and Dr. Devil, her head turning, her eyes stopping, suddenly staring at him—

Then everything happened too fast for his brain to keep up. A flashing movement, a sudden sharp pain in his wrist, balance gone, reflexively yanking the trigger, hearing the explosion of the gunshot, falling backward, his finger snapping with a hideous crack like a pencil breaking, and the sudden exploding pain shooting up to his armpit, the gun gone from his hand, his back smashing onto the pavement. A claw, an iron vise, grabbing, squeezing his scrotum, the weight on his chest crushing him, driving the breath from his lungs, the pain searing his finger and the unspeakable fire burning in his groin, his stomach convulsing, the gray sky above him swirling . . .

It went black and fuzzy, and when he was able to focus again, he was looking into a pair of big dark almond-shaped eyes. She had one knee on his chest. Her face was close to his and her forearm was pressing against his throat so that he could barely breathe. Her other hand was squeezing his testicles. It hurt like hell, but he knew it could hurt more. She was doing it just hard enough to keep him under control. She'd done this before. She was some kind of professional.

She narrowed her eyes and opened her mouth as if she was going to speak to him. Then suddenly her head jerked up. Her forearm left his throat, and she looked up, her eyes wide and her arm out straight with her palm raised like a traffic cop at the man who was aiming the camera at her, and she was yelling, "No! No! Please don't!"

CHAPTER

1

Patrick Francis Brody sat on the wooden bench facing the Boston Inner Harbor with his scuffed old leather briefcase on his lap. He'd swear it was still the dead of winter. The knife-sharp east wind blew off the water at him and sliced through his topcoat, through his suit jacket and his shirt and his undershirt, through his muscles and skin, and penetrated to the marrow of his bones. The April sun that ricocheted off the water was pale and empty of warmth.

He'd only been there ten minutes, and already he was freezing his ass off. He hunched his shoulders inside his spring-weight topcoat and shivered. Bad decision, that thin, unlined topcoat. He'd been wearing it for a couple weeks now back in D.C., where the cherry blossoms were ablaze and the endless acres of lawns had turned that amazing lime green that made your eyes hurt. It was spring back in Washington. Two hours ago, a couple hundred miles ago, it had been spring.

Behind him rose the sweeping glass facade of the John Joseph Moakley United States Courthouse. The building had won several awards, and Pat Brody, who had spent a lot of time in courthouses all over the country, had to admit that it was impressive, architecturally, not that he really gave a shit. It was what the people inside the courthouses did that impressed him, although not always favorably.

Brody glanced at his watch. Twelve noon on the dot. He turned and looked back toward the courthouse, and sure enough, punctual as hell, there was Judge Larrigan, strolling down the wide path, looking around.

Brody lifted his hand. Larrigan spotted him, waved, smiled that million-dollar one-eyed smile of his, and started toward him.

As cynical as he was—and Pat Brody didn't get to be a special assistant to the president of the United States by being naïve—he had to admit that Judge Thomas R. Larrigan was a pretty impressive specimen. Well over six lanky feet tall, with a thick shock of black hair sprinkled with dignified gray, a wide, lopsided, fun-loving grin, and, of course, that black eye patch. He moved like an athlete, oozed self-confidence. Fifty-nine years old, Brody knew, but he looked about ten years younger. Mature, but not old. Experienced, but not over the hill.

The right look didn't hurt. It didn't hurt at all. Larrigan had it.

The son of a bitch had his suit jacket hooked on his finger and slung over his shoulder. His tie was loosened at his throat, and his cuffs were rolled halfway up his forearms, as if it was the middle of July. Shirtsleeves on a day like this. Jesus.

Brody couldn't stop shivering.

Then Larrigan was standing in front of him. "Mr. Brody?" he said.

Brody looked up and nodded.

"Hope I didn't keep you waiting," Larrigan said. "Lawyers, you know?"

"You're right on time. I just got here."

Larrigan sat beside him on the bench and folded his jacket on his lap. "Nice day, huh?"

"I'm freezing my balls off, you want the truth."

Larrigan grinned. "You get used to it." He shifted so that he was half turned and looked at Brody out of that one sharp blue eye. "I got your message. Pretty mysterious. Don't know why you wouldn't want to get together in my chambers where it's warm. So what brings you to Boston?"

"Do you know who I am?" said Brody.

Larrigan nodded. "Of course I do."

"Then I thought you might've figured out why I'm here, Judge."

"Maybe I did," Larrigan said. "But maybe I'd rather hear you say it, just the same. I've been trained to withhold judgment until I've heard all the evidence, you know?"

"Okay," said Brody. "Here it is, then. Supreme Court Justice Lawrence Crenshaw has informed the president of his intention to retire at the end of the term. You've heard the rumors." He made it a statement and looked up at Larrigan with his eyebrows arched.

"Rumors," said Larrigan. "Sure, I've heard talk. It's true?"

"It's true," said Brody. "And you, Judge, are on the president's personal list."

"Personal list," said Larrigan. "What does that mean?"

"It means," said Brody, "that the president's staffers are studying and evaluating dozens of men and women. Eminent attorneys and jurists from all over the country. A dozen or more of them will be invited to the White House for interviews. Those candidates are on what we call the staff list. You are bypassing all of this, Judge. The president wants you to know that. That's why I'm here. It's why you weren't asked to make the journey to Washington. You're on the president's personal list. His is a very short list."

"So what does this mean, exactly?"

Brody cocked his head, smiled, and nodded.

"Oh," said Larrigan.

"The president asked me to come here today to ask you—informally, of course, strictly off the record for now—whether, if you were officially asked, you'd be willing to serve your country as an associate justice of the United States Supreme Court."

Larrigan leaned back against the bench, tilted up his head, and laughed.

Brody frowned. "I don't—"

"I'm sorry," said Larrigan. "It's just, like every lawyer in the country, I've fantasized about someone asking me to be a Supreme Court Justice ever since I started filling out applications to law school, and in all my fantasies, not once did I imagine it would happen on some random April day in Boston, sitting on a wooden bench during noon recess with . . . excuse me, Mr. Brody, but with a man who is pretty much anonymous. I visualized the Rose Garden, the president himself, television cameras . . ." He shook his head. "I do apologize. I know you're one of the president's most trusted aides. It's just that this seems terribly . . . I don't know . . . clandestine."

"No offense taken," said Brody. "I appreciate your candor. It *is* clandestine. I'm sure you understand why at this point the president must keep himself removed from this process."

"Ah, yes." Larrigan smiled. "The process. So what exactly is the process?"

It was interesting, Brody thought, how the eye behind the black patch crinkled at the corner just like the sharp blue one did. He wondered vaguely whether the eye socket behind that patch was empty, and if so, what it looked like. Angry red scar tissue? Or was there a cloudy, sightless eyeball there that still moved in unison with the functional one?

Brody folded his hands on top of the briefcase on his lap. "The process has already begun," he said. "Our meeting here today—this clandestine get-together, as you call it—is evidence of that. It actually began before the president even took office." He paused and looked at Larrigan, who was peering steadily at him. That single blue eye blazed with intensity. He suspected that Thomas Larrigan had no trouble intimidating lawyers. "Here's where we're at. At some appropriate time within the next month or two, Justice Crenshaw will formally announce his retirement. By then we will have leaked a list of the president's possible nominees to the press. The Fourth Estate, in their own relentless way, will vet the names, dredge up what they can, and the list will shake itself down. Of those names, only two or three will be serious contenders. The rest will be stalking horses. The president must appear to be considering a representative demographic and philosophical sampling of possible candidates—conservatives, liberals, moderates, women and men, gay and straight, African-Americans, Native Americans, Hispanic Americans, disabled Americans—"

"One-eyed Americans," said Larrigan.

Brody did not smile. "Marine lieutenant, decorated Vietnam veteran. Bronze Star and Purple Heart. Suffolk Law School. Night classes, no less. Blue-collar, up-by-your-own-bootstraps, American dream stuff. Intrepid prosecutor, tough on criminals, elected twice as crime-busting District Attorney, once as state Attorney General, well-respected Federal District Court judge, loving family man." He paused. "Not to mention, occasional golf partner of the president. Your wife and the First Lady were college classmates. He likes you. Trusts you."

Not to mention, Brody chose not to say, you are the closest person with anything remotely resembling acceptable credentials we could find to match the profile that the researchers distilled from the focus groups and opinion polls. The profile of a man who could complement—cynics would say "compensate for"—the president's perceived character. The profile of a strong, confident, sturdy, vigorous man. A man of conviction. A man who knows who he is and what he stands for and doesn't mind who else knows it.

Unlike, lately, the president.

"And sure." Brody smiled. "That patch over your eye doesn't hurt at all."

"Fair enough." Larrigan grinned.

"You would be the first Vietnam vet on the Court. The president absolutely loves that idea."

"Then—"

"It's early times," said Brody.

Larrigan nodded.

Brody liked the fact that he didn't seem too eager. "The fact that you've played golf with him, that your wives are friends," he said, "those things don't count for much. With the staff, in fact, they're seen as negatives. They link you too closely with him. The whiff of nepotism."

"That makes sense," said Larrigan.

"Don't get me wrong," said Brody. "You're exactly what the president is looking for."

"He likes my, um, my demographics."

"He likes your record, Judge. He likes what you stand for. He thinks you'd make a terrific Justice of the Supreme Court. He likes everything about you. And he thinks you can win the consent of the Senate."

"What you mean is, I wouldn't embarrass him."

"Well," said Brody, "that, of course, we'll have to verify. We have scrutinized your record as a prosecutor, as a judge. It appears impeccable."

Larrigan smiled. "Meaning I've managed to avoid any controversial rulings. Let's face it. That's my record. That's what I stand for."

Brody shrugged. "We found no red flags. You're a moderate. A centrist. Your record will cause no problems."

"But?"

"There are no buts, Judge. Your personal life, what we know of it, should cause no problems, either." Brody narrowed his eyes. "I need a direct answer, Judge, before this goes any farther. If asked, would you accept the president's nomination to the Supreme Court?"

Larrigan combed his fingers through his hair. "It's an awesome question." He fell silent.

Brody waited. He huddled in his thin topcoat and gazed at the Inner Harbor. A few sailboats were skimming over the gray, choppy water. Seagulls wheeled overhead with their wings set, riding the air currents.

After a minute or so, Larrigan swiveled back to face him. "Of course I'd accept. It's the ultimate honor, the ultimate challenge for any lawyer."

"Good." Brody cleared his throat. "I just need to ask you a few questions, then. Eventually, of course, if you're his final choice, you'll be asked a great many questions."

"I understand."

Brody snapped the latches on his briefcase, flipped it open on his lap, and removed a manila folder. He slid out a sheet of paper and squinted at it. "First, some issues that, according to our research, have never come before your court. Please confirm this. Abortion?"

"No. I've never had any case involving abortion."

"Or violence at an abortion clinic, malpractice involving abortion, anything of that sort?"

"No. Nothing like that."

"And when you were a prosecutor?" Brody was frowning down at his notebook.

Larrigan shook his head. "I prosecuted murderers mostly. Some drug stuff."

Brody peered up at him. "What is your position on abortion, Judge?"

Larrigan looked up at the sky for a moment, then turned to Brody. "How do you mean?"

Brody shrugged. "Simple question. Are you for it or against it?"

"I've never had a case brought before me that involved abortion."

"If you are nominated, you will be grilled."

"You mean, what are my personal beliefs?"

"I mean," said Brody, "have you ever revealed your opinion on abortion in any forum? Your public statements as well as your legal opinions are all fair game."

"I've never revealed my opinion," said Larrigan. "I try to avoid public statements on any legal or political issue. I'm a judge. It's the law, not my personal opinions, that matters. I don't believe a judge should even *have* personal opinions. We find answers to difficult questions in the law, the Constitution. We deal with cases, not issues."

"What about gay marriage?"

"I have no personal opinion," Larrigan said. "If the question came before me, I'd consult case law, seek precedent."

"You'd consider yourself a strict constructionist, then?" said Brody.

"Judges don't make law," said Larrigan. "Legislators do that. Judges merely apply it to specific situations."

Brody nodded noncommittally. "What about abused women and children, deadbeat dads, the sanctity of marriage? The president is very big on family values, you know."

"So am I," said Larrigan. "You are talking about legal matters. Crimes. I have a record on abuse. I prosecuted dozens of cases when I was an A.D.A." He shrugged. "I'm against breaking the law."

Brody smiled. "We know. Just checking. You are tough on abuse. Your decisions reflect a solid commitment to family values, women's rights, children. Not radical, but solid. That's good stuff." He glanced into his notebook, then looked up. "There'll be more of this. Every case you've ever prosecuted, every closing argument you've ever delivered, every decision you've ever handed down, every quote you've ever given a reporter, every country club you've ever joined, every gardener you ever employed, every woman you ever danced with, all of it will be dredged up. The media has no compunctions, and the Senate takes its advice and consent function very seriously."

"Sure. I know how it works, Mr. Brody."

"I need to ask you a harder question."

Larrigan smiled. "You want to meet all the skeletons in my closet."

"Yes. Now. Today. There must not be any surprises down the road."

"I inhaled when I was in law school." Larrigan grinned. "Drank beer in high school a couple times, too. Never got caught."

"Twenty years ago," said Brody, "I would've shook your hand and said, oh well, too bad, thanks just the same. Today, those things are not a concern."

Larrigan folded his arms and frowned. "I'm an alcoholic," he said quietly.

Brody nodded. "We know that. It's very much to your credit that you are forthright about it."

"I've never tried to make it a secret."

"You've been dry for sixteen years," said Brody. "The president believes that fact can work to our advantage. What you've done is heroic, Judge. You've overcome a very common and terrible disease and risen to the top of your profession. It makes you human and . . . interesting. A kind of role model."

"I never thought being an alcoholic would work to my advantage for anything."

"Did you ever do anything, um, regrettable in those years?"

"Lots of things that I regret," said Larrigan. "I suppose I embarrassed myself and my friends and family more than once. But I was never arrested for DUI, never hit my wife, never ended up in the wrong bed, never a public nuisance, nothing like that. I wouldn't have been confirmed for the seat I presently hold if I had. I sought help, and I got it, and I've been dry all this time." He cleared his throat. "Of course, I'm still an alcoholic. Always will be. Nobody is cured."

"You understand," said Brody, "the scrutiny will be a lot more intense when the Senate Judiciary Committee holds its confirmation hearings. More scrutiny than you've ever had before. Your friendship with the president and the senators and congressmen from Massachusetts will not protect you. Probably intensify the scrutiny, in fact."

"There's nothing."

"What about when you were in Vietnam?"

"I'm proud of my record." Larrigan's forefinger went to his eye patch. It was no doubt a meaningless, unconscious gesture, but Brody had the odd sense that Larrigan was staring at him right through his patch. "It was a crazy, nightmarish time, of course, those last months in Saigon before the evacuation. I saw friends, men under my command, die. I saw innocent civilians, women and children, die. I was responsible for the deaths of many of our enemies. I lost my eye in combat. The nightmares still come back sometimes." He leaned forward and fixed Brody with that unnerving one-eyed gaze. "You know that I spoke out about the war after my discharge."

Brody nodded. "We do know that. What you did, the way you went about doing it, was admirable. You served your country honorably as a soldier, and then you came home and served your country as a citizen."

Larrigan smiled. "I never thought of it that way."

"The president does." Brody shut his notebook, shoved it into his briefcase, and snapped it shut. "If you are nominated, you can expect your entire life history to be made public. Are you prepared for that?"

"Yes. Of course."

"Good." Brody stood up. "For now, the president must have your assurance that our meeting today will remain confidential."

"What about my wife?"

Brody shook his head. "I'm sorry."

Larrigan stood up, too. "I understand."

Brody held out his hand. "You'll be hearing from us. The president wants me to tell you that he's very much looking forward to seeing you again."

Larrigan gripped Brody's hand. "Please tell the president that I am greatly honored."

—⟨∙⟩—

THOMAS LARRIGAN WATCHED the little man with the big briefcase walk down the wide pathway and disappear around the bend. It took all his willpower not to leap in the air and click his heels together.

Justice Thomas R. Larrigan. Oh, yes. It had a nice ring to it. It sounded good.

What lawyer didn't dream of someday sitting on the Supreme Court? He wanted it. Of course he wanted it. If Brody only knew how badly he wanted it . . .

Surprises, Brody had called them. Skeletons—that was Tom Larrigan's own word. Shit, who didn't have skeletons? Nobody who'd spent three years in Southeast Asia during the war. Certainly nobody who'd been a drunk for twenty years. If you looked close enough, you'd find a skeleton in every closet in America. If you looked close enough, you wouldn't find anybody who'd qualify for the Supreme Court.

Old dusty skeletons, long dead. Skeletons can't tell stories.

Larrigan reached into his pants pocket, took out his cell phone, and pecked out a number. When the voicemail recording invited him to leave a message, Larrigan said, "Meet me at five-thirty. You know where. I've got some news. Semper fi."

He snapped the phone shut, shoved it into his pocket, turned, and strode back into the courthouse.

—⟨∙⟩—

DURING THE FORTY-FIVE-MINUTE limo ride to Hanscom Field in Bedford, where the anonymous private jet waited to take him back to Andrews A.F.B., Pat Brody transposed his cryptic handwritten notes into his laptop, then shaped them into an eyes-only memo to the president.

He concluded with these words: "You are right. Larrigan's perfect. Almost too good to be true."

Brody liked everything about Thomas Larrigan. He liked his record as both a prosecutor and as a judge. He liked the way he insisted on putting the law above his personal views. He liked the man's life story. American dream stuff. And he liked his appearance and his personality. He was handsome and likable. Charismatic, even. He'd play well in the media.

The president needed someone exactly like Larrigan. The reelection campaign was looming, and he needed a slam dunk. He needed something that would make everybody in both parties stand up and cheer. He needed an appointee that the Judiciary Committee would approve unanimously and enthusiastically.

The president desperately needed some good wound-healing, bipartisan, no-controversy, polls-spiking, feel-good publicity, and this Judge Larrigan should give him just that. To oppose the appointment of this perfect nominee would appear mean-spirited and partisan. It was a no-lose situation for the president.

Pat Brody couldn't figure out why he felt vaguely uneasy about the judge. He *was* perfect.

He sighed. He'd been in the political game too long. He was too damned cynical.

Brody had earned his Ph.D. in history, and in all of his studies, not even to mention his fourteen years in public service, nobody yet had been perfect.

Somewhere along the way the rules had shifted. Now a one-eyed alcoholic federal district court judge who'd never handed down an important decision in his career, never made a decision with constitutional implications, a plodding jurist at best, but an attractive man—okay, a charismatic man with an interesting personal history and a spotless but bland professional history, and a good golf swing—such a man looked like the perfect Supreme Court appointee.

A Bronze Star and an eye patch and a blank slate on every controversial issue of the day. That was the ticket. It was all about perception.

The times they were a-changin', all right, and Pat Brody supposed he just wasn't keeping up.

Like his daughter kept saying: Nobody listens to the Kingston Trio anymore, Dad.

The president would be pleased, though. That, he reminded himself, was what counted.

Pleasing the president. That was Patrick Brody's job.

That evening Pat Brody was sitting at his desk in his windowless basement office almost directly underneath the most powerful office in the world. Brody's own little workspace was dim, lit only by the single fluorescent bulb on the desk lamp and the glow of his computer screen.

He had delivered his memo to the president, debriefed him, and chatted for the allotted five minutes.

The president had seemed pleased. "So far so good, then," he had said. "Do what needs to be done."

And Brody understood his meaning: "Don't tell me anything else. What I don't know I can't be responsible for. But don't let me make a mistake."

Brody typed in his password—an utterly random eight-digit number that he changed daily, memorized, and wrote down nowhere—hit the "write letter" icon, and typed in the six-digit address, also random, that he had also memorized.

His fingers hovered over the keyboard as he stared up at the ceiling. Then he wrote:

Blackhole: Your professional services needed for deep backgrounding, utmost discretion, time of the essence, usual extravagant fee for OYO job well done. Meet Bellwether, regular place, Thursday 01:00 for details. Read and delete.

He signed it: "Shadowland."

He read it over, clicked the "send" icon, deleted it from his "mail sent" file, then opened the "deleted mail" file and erased it from there, too.

Brody knew that somewhere out there in cyberspace this e-mail would continue to exist even after it had been deleted at both ends, and that, in theory, it could be recovered and traced back to his and Blackhole's computers. That was highly unlikely, but should it happen, and if it were then decrypted, which was unlikely bordering on impossible, it would still take a lot of other knowledge to make any sense out of the message. Minimal, acceptable risk. Nothing was absolutely without risk.

He paused, stretched and yawned, then wrote another e-mail:

Bellwether: Need for Patchman scrutiny confirmed. Meet Blackhole OYO, usual place, Thursday 01:00, specify assignment per previous instructions. Read and delete. Shadowland.

Again he sent the mail then deleted it from his computer.

Brody checked his own incoming mailbox, found no important messages, logged off, and shut down his computer.

He leaned back in his chair, cradled his neck in his laced fingers, and smiled up at the dark ceiling.

Pat Brody loved this shit. He loved the Byzantine complexity of it all. He loved pulling the strings, making things happen. He loved the fact that he was Shadowland.

Somewhere out there two men—or, for all he knew, two women, or one of each, or whatever—were reading his words in virtually untraceable secrecy. "Blackhole," whoever that was, did the important jobs that official government agents could not do. He—or she—got his or her assignments from another ghostly character, an intermediary known to Brody only as "Bellwether."

He communicated with them in the anonymity of cyberspace, safely insulated from the president and his immediate circle. Whatever services they rendered, they did OYO—"on your own." Nothing could be traced back to the white mansion on Pennsylvania Avenue, never mind to the Oval Office within it. They were free to use any method that promised to work. The end justifies the means. Introductory Machiavelli. Raison d'état. Realpolitik.

Their OYO activities were, in the delicious jargon of bureaucratic survival theory, "plausibly deniable."

Pat Brody didn't want to know what they did or how they did it. If Brody didn't know, there was no way the president could know. And if the president didn't know, he couldn't be blamed. He might be accused of naïvete, or of ignorance, or even of failing to maintain sufficient control of his staff. That was the worst-case scenario. But in the final analysis, with the proper degree of spin, what the president didn't know could do him no harm.

If Blackhole, or Bellwether, or Shadowland himself—if any one of them should get careless, all of them would be sacrificed, no questions asked. Brody would become the victim of the president's self-righteous indignation. He would be "the man I thought I could trust," the maverick, the loose cannon.

Blackhole and Bellwether . . . they would simply disappear.

Everyone understood how it worked.

The system had always been there. Nixon had exposed it to public attention. Reagan had refined it, perfected the illusion, mastered the art of plausible deniability. Their successors—hello, Dick Cheney—with the benefit of personal computers and cellular telephones and other technology, and with their cynical scruples, had made it into an art.

Fuck up and your head rolls. That was part of Brody's job description.

The president needed to be sure that nominating this Larrigan—or even announcing his possible candidacy—created no problem. The one-eyed war-hero judge could be an attractive feather in the president's political cap.

Of course, he could also be a disaster.

It was Pat Brody's job to avert disasters. That's why he had activated Blackhole.

—⁀⁀—

JESSIE CHURCH WAS sitting in her anonymous Honda Civic across the street from Anthony Moreno's dingy little bungalow in Mill Valley on San Francisco Bay. Jessie's camcorder was braced on the window ledge, and her Canon EOS with its 600-millimeter lens sat on the seat beside her. She was sipping bottled water and sweating under the unrelenting midday sun, waiting for the poor schmuck to do something stupid.

Anthony Moreno had found an orthopedist willing to testify that Mr. Moreno's work-related back injury, quote-unquote, would forever prevent him from performing his job, which was driving a bus around the streets of Oakland, and that Mr. Moreno should therefore, in accordance with the contract negotiated between the bus drivers' union and the city, be entitled to full retirement benefits plus workman's compensation.

The city's insurance company assumed that both the orthopedist and Anthony Moreno were lying—anybody could fake a back injury, and it was not exactly unheard of for a doctor to help out a friend, so they hired BSI—Bay Security and Investigations—to get the goods on Mr. Moreno.

Today was Thursday. Jessie had been on the case since Monday, and so far the most back-breaking thing she'd seen Moreno do was squat down to retrieve his newspaper from his front stoop, which he did, carefully, every morning at 7:15. He opened the front door, stepped out onto the stoop, slowly bent his knees, keeping his back straight and one hand on the wrought-iron porch railing, picked up the paper, and slowly pushed himself upright.

She'd recorded that performance each time. The man was either one hell of an actor—and playing, as far as he knew, for an imaginary audience—or a man with a bad back.

Moreno stayed indoors most of the time. For all Jessie knew, he was moving furniture and doing jumping jacks in there, but he kept the curtains drawn all day long.

Tuesday after supper, with the help of his cane, he'd hobbled out to the Dodge minivan under his carport. Jessie followed him to the Sons of Italy hall a few blocks from his house. She guessed he'd normally walk there, but now he drove. She couldn't follow him inside, of course. It was a private club. But the square one-story building had four big floor-to-ceiling windows facing the street. So she found a place to park from which, through her 600-millimeter lens, she could see what was going on inside. There were a few pinball machines and a pool table and a little dance floor. But all Anthony Moreno did was sit at a table and drink a couple of beers. He used his cane whenever he stood up. He didn't shoot any pool or dance with any of the women. He just sat there stiffly and sipped his beer. When somebody spoke to him, he turned his head slowly to look at them without twisting his body.

Maybe Moreno was performing for her, although there was no way he could know he was being observed. Jessie was too good for that. But as far as she could tell, Anthony Moreno behaved as if he really did have a bad back.

She'd stick with it through the weekend, then file her report. If they wanted her to keep at it, well, it was their money.

She found herself shaking her head at the irony of it, though. Jessie Church, the heroic bodyguard who'd saved the abortion doctor's life, and look at her now, a little over a week later, on a crummy insurance stakeout, and it wasn't even going to pan out. The only assignment Jessie found more distasteful than insurance work was to follow husbands around so she could photograph them sneaking their blonde receptionists into motel rooms.

But she'd asked for the Moreno job. That damn picture of her taking down that guy at the clinic had appeared in the newspaper, and even though they'd used her invented name, Carol Ann Chang—Chang being the most common Asian name in the Greater San Francisco phone book, the Smith or Johnson of Asians—she decided she better lay low for a while, if it wasn't too late already.

After she nailed the wacko at the abortion clinic, she'd taken a few days off to wait for the insane ringing in her right ear to subside. It could've been worse, of course. The .38 revolver had discharged barely a foot from her head. Luckily, it was aimed straight up.

No luck involved, actually. Jessie had the guy's wrist in her grip, and one second after he'd yanked on the trigger she'd snapped his finger.

It was just a minute after that the damn photographer took her picture.

When she went back to the office after her mini-vacation, Del, her boss, told her that Sharon Stone had called. Sharon had seen the story in the *Chronicle* and wanted Jessie to bodyguard her on a trip to Europe in June. Del was pretty excited.

"Awesome opportunity, Jess," Del had said. Del was the only person in her new life who knew her real name. Sometimes she wondered if that had been a mistake, but she trusted Del, and he made out her paychecks to Carol Ann Chang, and she deposited them in bank accounts in the name of Carol Ann Chang. Her credit cards, her driver's license, the lease on her apartment, her fake Social Security card—her entire new life in San Francisco was Carol Ann Chang's life, not Jesse Church's.

But now, with her picture circulating on the Internet and in national publications, she wasn't at all confident that a fake name was enough.

"I'm not working with Sharon Stone," Jessie told Del.

"Aw, jeez, Jess," Del said. "It'd be great for you, great for the company. Sharon loves you. She wants to get together for lunch, go over a few things with you before we do a contract, but it looks good. I got it all set it all up, tomorrow, one-thirty—"

"No," Jessie said.

"Aw, Jess. Do this for me."

"No bodyguarding."

"But Sharon—"

"You gotta get somebody else, Del."

"You don't get it," he said. "She's asking for you. You specifically. I mean, she wouldn't've called in the first place if she hadn't seen—"

"No," said Jessie. "You're the one who doesn't get it. Listen. I don't care who it is. I don't care what she pays. I don't care what it will do for business. I'm sorry. I'm not doing it. Get somebody else."

Del blinked. "Hey, come on, babe. Sharon's really a down-to-earth person. Great sense of humor. Smart as hell. You'll like her."

"Don't call me babe," said Jessie. "How many times've I got to tell you?"

He'd leaned forward, folded his hands on top of the desk, and peered at her over the top of his wire-rimmed glasses. "I'm sorry, kid," he said. "I didn't realize that abortion clinic thing shook you up so bad. That nutcake came a whisker from killing you."

"I'm not shook up," she said. "That's not it. And don't call me kid, either."

He rolled his eyes, then leaned back in his chair. "I need you to do the Sharon Stone thing, Jess. Whaddya say? Please?"

Jessie laughed. "Did you actually say please?"

Del grinned. "Don't tell anybody, for God's sake."

"The answer's no anyway," she said.

"Listen," he said. "I'm the boss, remember? I own this fucking business? You're the employee? You're supposed to take the jobs I assign to you?"

"Fine," she said. "I quit, then."

Del peered at her for a minute. Then he took his glasses off his face, pinched the bridge of his nose, and said, "Howie Cohen, huh?"

Jessie nodded.

"Something happen?"

"No," she said. "Not yet."

"But they didn't use your real name in the paper. You were Carol Ann Chang, kick-ass hero, in that story."

"It's the picture that worries me," she said.

He stared at her for a long moment. Then he nodded. "Okay. I hear you. I got an insurance thing in Mill Valley, if you want it."

"I'll take it," said Jessie.

"Be careful, huh?"

"I'm always careful."

He shook his head. "I know you are. That's why you're the best. That's why you'd be great with Sharon. This is such a fucking waste, babe. Waste of an awesome client, waste of a great talent, waste of an unbelievable PR opportunity. But, hey, I don't blame you for wanting to keep a low profile for a while, and if that's what you're thinking . . ."

He let it dangle there like a question, hoping, of course, that his flattery plus the logic of it would change her mind.

She looked at him, smiled, and shook her head.

"I mean it," he'd said. "Be careful."

Del was right, of course. Her talents were wasted on insurance and divorce stakeouts. You didn't need brains or resourcefulness or strength or quickness for that work. You didn't need to be able to scan a hostile crowd and spot the one guy with the handgun. You didn't need to be able to move quickly enough to disarm him before anybody got hurt. All you needed for stakeout work was patience.

Having Sharon Stone for a client would be huge for Del. Jessie felt bad, having to turn him down. It sounded like a lot of fun, actually, traveling around Europe with Sharon, staying in high-class hotels, eating in the best restaurants, hobnobbing with famous people. They'd make a striking pair, Sharon's classic sexy blonde, Jessie's exotic brunette.

But there would be cameras everywhere they went. Jessie Church, no matter what name she used, couldn't risk any more exposure, if it wasn't too late already.

So now she was slouched in her old Civic, waiting for Anthony Moreno to make his mistake, quite content to be invisible and anonymous.

People magazine. The morning talk show at the local CBS affiliate. The newspapers and radio stations. Even some guy claiming to be a Hollywood agent. They all wanted to make Carol Ann Chang a star.

They should see her now, in her green Oakland A's cap with the visor pulled low and her wraparound sunglasses and grungy old Hard Rock Cafe T-shirt. Glamorous as hell.

Before she'd stopped answering her phone, she told them all the same thing: Please, I'm no hero. I was only doing my job, what I've been trained for, what they pay me for. Millions of people go to work every day and do their job, and nobody hounds them for interviews or wants to take their pictures. Their phones don't keep ringing so persistently that they have to stop answering. They don't feel they must wear sunglasses and caps with the visors pulled low over their foreheads whenever they go to the supermarket.

Go do a story about a schoolteacher or a social worker or a beat cop or an EMT. They're heroes. They save lives every day. They deserve publicity. They'd probably welcome it.

Don't write about me. Please.

They had, of course. They'd written about Carol Ann Chang, the reluctant hero, and they'd reprinted the *Chronicle* photo that showed her kneeling beside the guy she'd just defeated, barely in the nick of time, saving the doctor's life. She had her arm raised up and she was looking straight at the camera, and her mouth was in the shape of the letter O, as if she was shouting, "Wow!" or "Yeow!"

From the photo, you'd think Jessie was exulting at her conquest of the assassin.

In fact she'd been yelling at the guy with the camera. "No! No! Please don't!" *Please don't take my picture*, she meant.

Now Jessie Church was spooked.

Four years earlier she'd quit the Baltimore cops. She drove across the country, about as far as you could get from Howie Cohen and his crew without crossing an international border, to make herself a new, anonymous life in San Francisco. She'd changed her name, bought the fake documents from her old friend Jimmy Nunziato in Chicago, got the job at BSI, and found a nice one-bedroom apartment on 24th Street in Noe Valley near the farmers' market. She liked the neighborhood and had made some friends, though she didn't let anybody get too close. She liked working for Del. She liked being Carol Ann Chang. Life was pretty good. Once in a while she even found herself relaxing.

Howie Cohen was behind bars. "Safely behind bars" was the way the newspapers put it, whatever "safely" meant, and after four years of doing investigations for Del Robbins, Jessie had almost managed to convince herself that the Howie Cohen thing really was in the past.

But now, with her picture in the paper, it had started up all over again. Howie Cohen had loyal friends and relations and business associates with long memories everywhere. In her eighteen months of undercover back in Baltimore, Jessie had gotten to know them all way too well.

Then she'd betrayed them.

Cohen was locked away. So maybe it was stupid to wake up ten times a night imagining somebody was creeping around in her bedroom. Maybe it was neurotic to mistrust every guy she passed on the sidewalk or saw standing in a checkout line or heard on the other end of the telephone. Maybe she was paranoid. Probably she was. Nothing stupid about it, though. Paranoia kept you alive.

Bodyguarding Sharon Stone was the last thing she needed.

What she needed was witness protection, except they didn't do that for undercover cops after they testified at the trials of men who kidnapped runaway children in American cities and sold them to rich Middle Eastern pedophiles.

What they did for undercover cops after they testified was take them off the street and assign them to a desk.

Jessie had lasted two months on the desk in Baltimore. She probably could've tolerated the dreary walls and the mindless paperwork and the lousy coffee and the sexist jokes for several more months. She was adaptable and patient. She had a high tolerance for boredom.

What she couldn't tolerate was the powerful apprehension that she was being watched, followed, stalked, and that sooner or later, at his whim, Howie Cohen would reach out through his prison bars to wreak his revenge.

When she'd stepped down from the witness stand and glanced at Cohen, sitting there beside his lawyers, a paunchy sixty-year-old guy with a bald head and big ears and horn-rimmed glasses, he'd smiled at her, pressed his two fingers to his lips, then wiggled them at her.

Kissing her off. Telling her she was dead.

That awful smile still haunted her dreams.

So she quit the cops, packed her stuff, which wasn't much, into her Civic, and headed west. She left no forwarding address. Couldn't, since she didn't know where she was going.

She ended up in San Francisco and presented herself to Del Robbins, the president of Bay Security and Investigations in Oakland. Del talked with her for about ten minutes, made one phone call, and hired her on the spot.

Perfect, Jessie had thought at the time. For an ex-cop there was no more anonymous, behind-the-scenes job than private investigating. The whole job was about not being noticed or recognized.

Unless you save a public figure from being assassinated in front of a mob of people and reporters, that is. And unless some lucky cameraman is there to shoot you kneeling beside the creep with one hand squeezing his balls and the other arm raised and a look of triumph on your face, and the photo is so good that it gets reprinted in newspapers across the country and makes the rounds on the Internet.

So now Jessie Church was looking over her shoulder again. Some Cohen friend or relative or business associate or customer was bound to spot that newspaper photo and recognize her, phony name notwithstanding. Sooner or later, inevitably, Howie Cohen would send somebody to track her down and kill her.

So far, it hadn't happened. Not yet. Nobody could tail Jessie Church without her knowing it.

But it would happen soon.

She guessed it was about time to think about loading up her Civic again. Time to change her name again, change her habits, change her look. Get a job in an office somewhere. Couldn't be worse than sitting in a car waiting for Anthony Moreno to make a mistake.

⌒⌒

JUDGE THOMAS LARRIGAN hung up his robe, slumped into his desk chair, and sighed. Another long, tense day on the bench. He rubbed his good eye, stretched his arms, then quickly jotted some notes on a yellow legal pad. He had to hand down an admissibility ruling when court convened the next morning. It raised a couple of tricky questions, and Larrigan didn't want to blow it. Not now. Not with a Supreme Court nomination on the horizon. It wouldn't look good if an appeal was granted because Judge Larrigan had misapplied the law.

But if he erred, he knew enough to err on the side of the victim; in this case, a two-year-old girl whose skull had been fractured by an unemployed pipefitter while her mother lounged on the sofa in the same room watching the Home Shopping Network. The search of the apartment had turned up a stash of marijuana, an assortment of barbiturates, and two grams of cocaine. The problem was, the warrant had neglected to mention drugs, and they hadn't been in plain sight when the police entered the apartment.

Larrigan would, of course, rule the drugs admissible. His problem was to justify that ruling with case law. Then, even if he were overturned on appeal, his reputation would not be tarnished. These days, a jurist's reputation hinged less on his even-handed application of the law than on what he seemed to believe.

Larrigan believed in the fair application of the law. He believed justice should be blind.

But he also believed that the war on drugs should be fought aggressively and that criminals should be punished. He had the reputation of being a tough judge. He'd nurtured that reputation. He'd earned it. That reputation had put him on the president's short list for a seat on the Supreme Court.

It had been a week since Pat Brody had come to Boston. Larrigan wondered what would happen next.

Nothing, probably. As Brody had told him, there were hundreds of names, hundreds of top-notch judges and lawyers. Even if he was on what Brody called the president's "personal list," even if he'd played golf with the president a couple times, Larrigan knew he was still a long shot.

Still, he couldn't help wanting it, tasting it . . .

He swiveled around in his chair to stare out his office window. Black roiling thunderheads were building out over the harbor. They'd burst open any minute, he figured. Just in time to rain out his late-afternoon golf match in Belmont with Jonah Wright, which was disappointing. Larrigan enjoyed golf, and he liked playing with Jonah. The man had a flamboyant, erratic game. He hit the ball a mile, usually into the rough, which set up both his occasionally spectacular recoveries over, around, and under trees and his more frequent double bogies. Wright tended to sink long serpentine putts and miss two-footers.

He was a challenging opponent but, of course, no match for Larrigan's steady, methodical game, and even giving three shots a side, Larrigan rarely lost to him. For that matter, Larrigan rarely lost to anybody. When he played the president, he beat him, too. Larrigan believed that the president admired the fact that the judge didn't hold back, that he was a competitor, that he refused to lose.

But that's not why Larrigan didn't want to miss his weekly match with Jonah Wright. Jonah was a well-positioned State Street investment banker, a Boston power broker, an ally. Larrigan hadn't figured out how yet. But sooner or later Jonah Wright would be able to do him a favor.

Of course, when the Supreme Court appointment went through, Larrigan wouldn't need any Jonah Wrights ever again.

Meanwhile, he did not intend to burn his bridges.

He glanced at his watch. Four o'clock. They'd planned to tee off at five. Nine quick holes, just the two of them sharing a cart, and back in the clubhouse before seven. Gin-and-tonics for Jonah, iced tea for Larrigan, then a Bibb lettuce salad, club steak, and baked potato. Coffee on the veranda, a chance to catch up, see who was who and what was what these days in Massachusetts politics, and home by eight-thirty or nine, in time to tuck the kids in before holing up in his office to write up his ruling on the admissibility of those drugs.

No way it wasn't going to rain. No golf today.

Amy would get flustered if he showed up before nine. Amy didn't care what he did or who he did it with as long as he gave her his schedule and stuck to it. Amy didn't do well with surprises. Maybe he'd drive out to the club anyway, sit in for a rubber or two of bridge, have supper with Jonah.

The intercom buzzed. He turned back to his desk and pressed the connecting button. "What's up, Arlene?" he said.

"Mr. Brody's on line one," came Arlene's voice.

"Brody? The—"

"He's calling from the White House, Tom. I'm sitting here trying not to wet my pants."

Larrigan smiled at the image of Arlene Bennett, his plump white-haired secretary who'd become a grandmother for the second time back in January, wetting her pants. "Nothing to get worked up about," he said. "It's probably just the president again. You know how he keeps pestering me."

"Yes, that man is a nuisance, isn't he?" Arlene chuckled. "Want me to get rid of him?"

"I'll handle it, thanks." Larrigan disconnected from Arlene, took a deep breath, picked up his telephone, and pressed the blinking button on the console. "This is Judge Larrigan," he said.

"It's Pat Brody, Judge. How are you?"

"Just fine, Mr. Brody." Larrigan paused. He wasn't going to let Brody hear his eagerness. "How can I help you?"

"You can help me by saying hello to the president. Is this a convenient time?"

"Sure. Of course." Damn, thought Larrigan. That definitely sounded eager.

A moment later he heard: "Tom?" It was that familiar raspy voice.

"Hello, Mr. President."

"I just wanted to say hello, Tom, and to tell you that I'm hearing nothing but good things about you."

"Thank you, sir. I'm deeply honored."

"I expect we'll be talking again soon," said the president. "Things are moving pretty fast down here. You're still good with this?"

"Yes, I am. Of course."

"That's fine, Tom. Great. We'll have to get out, play some golf one of these days. Okay, then. Pat Brody needs to speak to you again."

"Thank you, sir," said Larrigan. "I—"

But the president was no longer on the line.

Brody talked to the judge for nearly fifteen minutes, and by the time he finished, Larrigan realized that receiving a phone call from the president still left him a long way from donning the robes of a Supreme Court Associate Justice.

As Brody put it, he'd leaped the first hurdle. The list of possible nominees had grown significantly shorter.

First, the FBI would intensify its "background check." If they found anything in Larrigan's personal or professional history that might embarrass the president or raise eyebrows on the Senate Judiciary Committee, his name would be eliminated from consideration. Assuming he passed muster with the FBI and became the president's nominee, Larrigan would be formally presented to the Washington press corps at a Rose Garden ceremony as soon as Justice Crenshaw made his official retirement announcement, whenever that happened to occur.

Then would come the press, digging and prying and nosing around for a story, an angle, a hint of scandal. And the president's opposition in the Senate would unleash their own hounds.

Of course, said Brody quietly—and, Larrigan thought, with a hint of ironic skepticism—he would pass with flying colors, and next thing he knew, he'd be a Justice of the Supreme Court. For life.

The best job in the world. Respect, power, security. Immortality.

Brody concluded: "Sit tight and don't talk about it. No interviews, on or off the record. If you've got a vacation lined up, take it. Preferably someplace where the media can't find you. And for God's sake, don't do anything . . . controversial."

"I understand," said Larrigan. "But it sounds like you're not—"

"The president is not ready tell the world what he told you today, Judge. You understand."

In fact, Larrigan wasn't sure what exactly the president had told him. "Sure," he said. "Of course I understand."

"We'll be in touch with you, then." Brody hesitated. "Congratulations, Judge."

"Yes. Thank you."

Larrigan replaced the phone on its cradle and shivered. It was happening. It was really happening.

He swiveled around to gaze out his window again. While he'd been on the phone with the White House, the black thunderheads had rolled off to the west, and now the afternoon sun reflected in the windows of Boston's skyscrapers. The city looked bright and clean. Just like Tom Larrigan's future.

He hit the button on the intercom, and Arlene's voice said, "I want to hear all about it. Did you talk to him?"

"I can't tell you much, but yes, he and I had a pleasant chat. For now, I want to continue the moratorium on all interviews. And—"

"Tom," said Arlene, "this is me."

"I know. I'm sorry. You can probably figure it out, but I'm sworn not to say anything to anybody."

"My God," Arlene whispered.

"Oh," said Larrigan with a chuckle, "I'm not God yet. Not by a long shot. But maybe, one of these days." He paused. "If you utter a peep to anybody, young lady, you'll feel God's wrath, I promise you."

"Have I ever disappointed you?"

"Never," he said. "Anyway, I was supposed to play golf with Jonah Wright today. Call him and tell him I've got to cancel, please. Then you go home."

"Okay. Is—?"

"I've just got some things to clean up here. You have a nice evening."

"Yes, you too. This is very exciting."

"Not a peep," said Larrigan.

He waited until Arlene had left, then picked up his cell phone and called Eddie Moran.

"What's up?" said Moran.

"I just got off the phone with the White House."

CHAPTER

Eddie Moran pecked out the number on his cell phone, wedged it between his ear and his shoulder, and lit a cigarette. The traffic on Route 1 hummed steadily past the parking lot where he was sitting in his rented Camry, most of it heading south to Islamorada, Marathon, and Key West.

The phone rang three times, and after the voicemail recording, Moran said, "Call me," and disconnected.

He put the phone on the seat beside him and waited, and before he'd finished his cigarette, it rang.

He checked the number on the screen. Larrigan. He hit the "send" button and said, "Semper fi."

"You secure?"

"Of course I'm secure."

"Where are you?"

"Key Largo." He hesitated. "In Florida."

"I know where Key Largo is, for Christ's sake."

"Did you know they named this place after a movie? That Bogart movie? I mean, when they made the movie, there was no place called Key Largo. So they—"

"Jesus Christ," said Larrigan. "Did you find her?"

"She's working in one of these tame dolphin places. Tourists go there and pay seventy-five bucks to swim around with the fish. Can you believe it?"

"Dolphins are mammals, Eddie."

"Sure. Whatever." Moran cracked the window and flipped his cigarette butt out onto the pavement. "She gives this slide show before each swim. I caught her act. She does a nice job. It was kinda interesting. Bunny always liked animals. Had cats. I remember how her place always smelled of cat shit." Moran blinked away a drop of sweat that had dribbled into his eye. "So, anyway, yeah, I found her. She's looking good. So now what do you want me to do?"

On the other end of the line, Larrigan hesitated. "I've got to know what she remembers, how she feels," he said, "if there's any chance she'll . . ."

"It's gonna take a while. I can't just walk up to her, say, Hey, it's me, Eddie Moran. You remember old Tommy Larrigan, dontcha? Well, guess what?"

"For Christ's sake, Eddie, be discreet."

"Have I ever let you down?"

"Not yet. And you better not this time."

―⁌ひ⁍―

EDDIE MORAN SPENT the rest of the afternoon sweltering in the rented gray Camry. Every once in a while he'd switch on the ignition and turn the air conditioning on high, let it blow out the hot air, but he couldn't leave the motor running all day. So mostly he sat there with all the windows open, and every once in a while a puff of hot salty breeze would blow through.

He'd parked strategically in the supermarket lot on Route 1. Every road on the island attached itself to Route 1, he'd learned. Route 1—the same Route 1 that traced the crooked coastline of New England—was the spine of the Keys. People down here oriented themselves by the mile markers along the roadside. It was, "Second left after mile marker thirty-four," or, "You come to a Japanese restaurant on your right, then look for mile marker fifty-nine."

So he waited there at the corner of Route 1 and the side street that led down to the dolphin place on the ocean, close enough so he could see every face in every car that came along that side street. Sooner or later, Bunny Brubaker would have to pass directly in front of him.

He sweated and drank orange soda and ate beer nuts and smoked cigarettes and pissed in a plastic milk jug. The Marines had taught him how to blank his mind against the passage of time, how to remain alert without thinking about anything. Boredom was a state of mind, and Eddie Moran had learned to master it. He just watched the faces go by, registering everything, thinking about nothing.

Finally he spotted her. She was driving a maroon Volkswagen bug, braking for the stop sign right in front of him. Automatically he glanced at his wristwatch and jotted the time into the notebook on the seat beside him. 7:48 PM. The previous note read, "1:22. Called T. L." He'd been sitting there a little more than six hours. That wasn't bad. Plenty of times he'd sat outside an apartment building all night and nothing had even happened.

When she pulled onto Route 1, heading south, he got a glimpse of her license plate. He hastily scratched the number into his notebook, too.

Bunny's old VW Beetle had a roof rack and a big plastic daisy stuck on top of the antenna. Considerate of her. He had no trouble hanging four cars behind her and keeping the daisy in sight.

She was a few years younger than Eddie, which put her somewhere in her early fifties now. But she still had nice tits. He'd noticed that right away, when she was talking about how smart dolphins were and how well they were treated in their caged-in pool and how the place wasn't a zoo but a "habitat." Nice hair, too. Eddie Moran liked long hair, and Bunny Brubaker wore her auburn hair long and straight down her back, the same as she had in the old days. From where he'd been watching her, he couldn't tell if she dyed it, or if there was any gray in it.

Bunny Brubaker had been a real dazzler back then. She still looked good. If anything, a little thinner than she'd been back then.

Thirty-five years. He wondered if she'd even remember him.

The real question, of course, was what she remembered about Larrigan.

Up ahead he saw the right directional begin to blink on the maroon VW. She turned off onto a narrow side road, and he followed. There were no vehicles between them now, so he crept along, keeping plenty of distance between them. When she pulled into a driveway beside a little square flat-roofed modular house pretty much like all the other little square flat-roofed modular houses on the street, he kept going. The road ended half a mile later in a turnaround by the water. He stopped there for the length of time it took him to smoke a cigarette, then turned and headed slowly back up the street.

He took it all in as he drove back past her place: scraggly unkempt gardens, one shutter hanging loose on the front of the house, carport crammed with plastic barrels and cardboard boxes and green trash bags. An old sailboat was parked on a trailer beside the driveway, its hull green with mildew.

Hypotheses automatically formed in Eddie Moran's mind. The boat hadn't been in the water for a year or more. It belonged to some guy who wasn't around anymore. He figured Bunny wasn't much for yard work or home repair herself and probably couldn't afford to hire someone to do it for her. Or maybe she just didn't give a shit how the place looked. She didn't have her trash picked up or go to the dump very often. The house looked like it had maybe four or five small rooms—cheap and small, about right for a single woman who made a living giving the same speech about how great dolphins were over and over again.

Back on Route 1, from the parking lot of a Burger King this time, he was able to watch the end of Bunny Brubaker's dead-end street. He ate a chicken sandwich, large fries, chocolate shake, and kept an eye out for a maroon VW with a plastic daisy on the antenna until one in the morning. Then he drove back to his motel.

He followed the same routine the next day. Bunny left for the dolphin place at nine-fifteen in the morning. She got off work at seven-thirty in the evening, drove past the supermarket parking lot where Moran was parked, turned south onto Route 1, and went home.

On the third evening, the maroon VW turned north onto Route 1. Tonight she wasn't going straight home.

Eddie kept a discreet distance—Larrigan's favorite word, "discreet"—between them. Three or four miles north, she pulled into the gravel parking lot beside a low-slung rectangular building. The neon sign over the door identified it as Jake's Conch Hut. From the street, Eddie could see that it had an outdoor bar with three open sides and a thatched roof. He turned into the lot and parked in the far corner. He waited ten minutes after Bunny went to the bar, then went over to the bar himself.

The bar was shaped like a semicircle, and Bunny was seated at the far end. Two guys and a woman were at the near end. That was it. Jake's Conch Hut did not appear to be Key Largo's most popular hangout.

Moran hitched himself onto a stool, leaving two empty ones between himself and Bunny Brubaker.

The underside of the thatched roof was festooned with old fishing nets. A stuffed tarpon hung on the one wall behind the bar, and a television mounted on a bracket was showing a baseball game with the sound muted.

The bartender, a kid in his twenties with a neatly trimmed black beard and hoops in both ears, swiped at the bar in front of him. "What'll you have?" he said.

"Bud in a bottle," Moran answered.

He took his pack of cigarettes from his shirt pocket, picked one out with his lips, and placed the pack on the bar in front of him. He fished his Zippo from his pants, lit up, and put the lighter on top of the cigarettes.

He glanced over at Bunny. Up close, he could see the lines at the corners of her eyes and mouth. But she still looked great. Nice skin, wide, sexy mouth, white even little teeth, and those big blue eyes. She could pass for about forty, Eddie thought. She was gazing up at the television and sipping from a glass of white wine. Christ, is that all women drank anymore? White wine?

In the old days, Bunny drank beer from a bottle.

A pack of cigarettes and a lighter sat by her elbow.

The bartender slid a bottle of Bud and a frosted mug in front of him. "Wanna run a tab?" he said.

Moran nodded.

Out of the corner of his eye he sensed Bunny giving him the once-over. He poured beer into his mug, took a long draught, dragged on his cigarette, stubbed it out in an ashtray, gazed up at the television, sighed, took another drink, and casually glanced at her.

Just in time to catch her hastily shifting her eyes up to the TV.

A couple minutes later he tapped another cigarette from his pack, picked up the Zippo, flicked it a few times, tapped it on the bar, flicked it again, blew on it.

He turned to her. "Excuse me, Miss. My lighter's out of fluid. Do you mind . . .?"

She smiled. A really great smile. "No problem," she said.

She slid her lighter across the polished top of the bar to him. It was one of those cheap plastic throwaways. He lit his cigarette with it, then leaned toward her, holding it in his palm. "Thanks a lot," he said.

She plucked the lighter gingerly from his hand, as if she was afraid to touch him. She was frowning, cocking her head, looking at him.

He smiled. "My name's Eddie," he said.

"Jesus," she whispered. "It *is* you."

"Huh?"

"You don't remember?"

He pretended to study her face. Then he started shaking his head. "Bunny? Holy shit. Bunny Brubaker? Is that really you?"

"It's been a long time, Eddie," she said softly.

"God," he said. "You look terrific." He picked up his cigarettes and beer and moved to the stool beside her. Up close, he could see the fine cross-hatching of lines around her mouth and the puckery softness of the flesh on her throat. But those tits still looked great, the way they pressed against the front of her white short-sleeved shirt. She was wearing the same khaki-colored shorts she'd worn when he'd listened to her dolphin speech, and her bare legs, wrapped around her barstool, were brown and smooth.

"You look good, too," she said.

"I don't believe it," he said. "Small world, huh?"

"Yeah," she said. "I always say. Small world."

The bartender came by, and Moran ordered another Bud for himself and another glass of wine for the lady.

She plucked a cigarette out of her pack with her long finger-nails.

Moran picked up her lighter, flicked it, and held the flame for her. She touched his hand, steadying it as she bent to the lighter, looking up at him, those nice blue eyes smiling at him, the front of her shirt opening, giving him a glimpse of cleavage.

Her eyes flickered for an instant. Her hand dropped away from his and she straightened on her stool. She took a long drag from her cigarette, tilted her chin, blew a long plume of smoke at the ceiling. A little smile played on her lips. "Sergeant Eddie Moran," she said. "So what brings you to Key Largo?"

He shrugged. "Quick getaway. Little fishing, little diving. I'm headed back tomorrow. What've you been doing? Still with the Red Cross?"

She shook her head. "I got my fill of that over there. When I got back I joined a band. Had some fun for a while."

"What kind of band?"

"Oh, you know. Good ol' rock 'n' roll. I played the guitar and sang. I had a good voice. Janis Joplin."

Moran nodded.

"I was like her," she said. "I could belt out a song, man. I had that Southern Comfort sound. Sexy, everybody said. I could give every guy in the place a hard-on, just singing 'Summertime.' I could play the guitar, too. I could really play." She shook her head. "People used to say I even kinda looked like Janis."

"You were much prettier than her," said Moran. "You still are."

"Well, that's sweet." She drained her wineglass in two gulps. "This is awfully weird, you know?"

Moran nodded. "It is. Who'da thought, after twenty-something years . . . ?"

"More like thirty." She smashed her half-smoked cigarette into an ashtray and kept grinding it. "I got a divorce."

Moran nodded. "I kinda figured you would. It never really seemed real, though, did it?"

She smiled quickly. "I need another drink."

Moran lifted a finger to the bartender, who brought a fresh glass of white wine for Bunny and another bottle of Budweiser for him.

She picked up her glass and sipped. "So how about you? What've you been up to?"

Moran waved his hand in the air. "I was a cop for a while. Up in Massachusetts. Now I'm . . . well, kinda freelancing. Security work, mostly."

"The old Marine training, huh?"

"Oh, nothing like that," he said. "Boring, safe stuff. Just trying to make a living, you know?"

Bunny was staring off somewhere beyond Moran's shoulder.

He touched her arm. "Hey. Something the matter?"

She shook her head. "No. Nothing's the matter. I was just remembering . . ."

"Remembering what?"

She turned to look at him. "You know," she said softly.

"That was a long time ago," he said. "I don't think much about it anymore."

She looked up at the silent television for a moment, then glanced at her wristwatch. Abruptly, she picked up her cigarettes and lighter and shoved them into her purse, which had been lying on the bar. "I gotta get out of here," she mumbled. "I get up early for work." She fumbled out a couple of bills and put them in front of her.

"No," said Moran. "I got it."

She looked at him evenly for a moment, then nodded. "Okay. Thanks." She picked up the bills and stuffed them back into her purse.

They sat there for a minute. He sipped his beer.

Then Bunny swiveled off her barstool. "I really gotta go."

"Well," said Moran, "it was nice seeing you again, huh?"

"Yeah," she said. "Nice." She shook her head. "You're right, you know? All that *was* a long time ago."

Moran nodded. "Long time, Bunny. They were good times, though, huh?"

She shrugged. "If you call war a good time, I guess we had a good time."

"Imagine," said Moran, "bumping into each other like this."

"Like you say, small world." She touched the back of Moran's neck. "So you coming or what?"

"Huh?"

"Don't you want to come home with me?"

He turned to look at her.

"You married or something?" she said.

He shook his head. "Nope. Not me."

"Doesn't matter, anyway," she said.

"I gotta get a plane out of Miami tomorrow afternoon."

"So I won't see you again, that what you're saying?"

"I guess so."

"So what?" she said.

He shrugged.

"Listen," she said. "I never worry about tomorrow until it gets here. And by then it's too late anyway."

"That's how it was over there," said Moran. "You never knew nothing."

"Live for today," said Bunny. "That's what we always said."

"It worked, didn't it? I mean, it got us through."

"It still works," she said. "It still gets me through."

"Okay," said Moran. "I'd like to go home with you."

⎯⎯◌⌒◌⎯⎯

HE WOKE UP when she plopped down on the bed beside him. Her ass pressed against his hip, separated only by the sheet and the shorts she was wearing. "I gotta go to work," she said. "There's coffee in the kitchen. Be sure to turn off the pot when you leave."

She still looked good to him in the morning. That sleek auburn hair, still damp from her shower, those nice tits, those smooth muscular legs. He reached toward her, tangled his fingers in her hair.

"Don't," she said, jerking her head back. "I can't be late."

He moved his hand, trailing the backs of his fingers over her breast.

She hunched her shoulders, twisting away from him. "Please," she said softly.

He let his hand fall onto the bed. "I'll call you next time I come down," he said.

"Sure. That'd be nice." She stood up, hesitated, then bent and kissed him on the cheek. "You still got it, Eddie Moran," she said. "It was nice to see you again." Then she quickly turned and left the room.

A minute later he heard the VW chug out of the driveway.

He slid out of bed, pulled on his pants, and padded into the kitchen. He poured a mugful of coffee, took a sip, lit a cigarette.

The previous night he'd followed her VW home from the bar at Jake's Conch Hut. She drove too slow, the overly cautious way people drive when they've had two or three glasses of wine. She parked in front of the house. He pulled into the driveway, got out of his car. She came up to him in the dark, put her arm around his waist, leaned her hip against him. He slung his arm around her shoulders and she turned, moved against him, pressing her pelvis hard against his. She murmured something in her throat that he didn't understand. Then she was kissing him, grinding at him, those nice tits soft and pillowy on his chest, her hips moving against him, her tongue in his mouth.

After a minute, she kind of sighed and pulled back. She took his hand, led him into the carport, which reeked with the sweet rot of old garbage. The side door to the house opened from the carport into the kitchen.

It was cool inside, blasted by the air conditioner that had been running all day. She didn't bother turning on any lights. Just led him through the dark into the bedroom, pushed him onto the bed, knelt between his legs.

He sat there on the edge of the bed, his pants down around his ankles, while she worked on him with her mouth and her fingers. He reached down, touched her hair, stroked her shoulders, remembering all those times half a lifetime ago, over there where you never knew if you were going to be alive the next morning, where it always felt like a one-night stand.

Just about the time he thought he was going to explode she pulled away. She tugged his pants all the way off and helped him pull his jersey over his head. Then she stood up and undressed herself, and they crawled under the covers. Her skin was still smooth and youthful against his, and he ran his hand down her sleek back, from her neck to her butt, remembering the feel of her skin, and it almost seemed like he could remember thirty-five years ago through his fingertips.

She pushed him flat onto his back, then slithered atop him, her favorite way, straddled him, put him inside her, and rode him until he couldn't hold back.

"Okay, oh fuck, okay, yeah," she murmured when he came. "Oh-*kay!*"

And about a minute later she was snoring beside him, bubbling quietly and rhythmically.

He'd lain awake for a long time, listening to her breathe and wondering if he should tell Larrigan that he'd gone home with her, that she'd given him a great blowjob, that he'd spent the night with her, that she still had skin like a teenager and really nice tits, and that he thought they'd come at the same time, if she hadn't been faking it.

When he went to sleep, he still hadn't decided what he should tell Larrigan. Hell, it was none of his business. Bunny had always been Eddie Moran's girl.

Now, the next morning, with her sober and maybe a little regretful or embarrassed or something and off to tell the tourists about dolphins, he went to work. Methodical, one room at a time. Desk drawers, kitchen drawers, bureau drawers, cabinets, closets, bookshelves.

He found the shoebox behind a pile of sweaters on the shelf in her bedroom closet. A thick layer of dust covered it. Clearly the box had not been touched in a long time.

He took it down, opened it, looked inside. It was a random jumble of old photographs, different sizes, some in color, some black and white, curled and creased, faded and discolored. Moran guessed there were a couple hundred photos in that shoebox.

He dumped them out on the bed and sat there sipping his coffee, looking at the photos one at a time.

She looked a hell of a lot better than Janis Joplin back then. Bunny Brubaker with her electric guitar, wearing very tight jeans and a T-shirt. A little heavier and curvier then, but always with those nice tits, the way he remembered her.

Bunny stretched out on a blanket in a little bikini, leaving nothing to the imagination. Bunny at various ages with other people—a young teenager, before Moran knew her, with an older couple, Mom and Dad, maybe. With a serious young man with a receding hairline and rimless glasses. Bunny with a bunch of women about her age. Bunny holding an infant.

Bunny's life in a shoebox.

And, yeah, there were some shots of Bunny and Eddie together. Her in her crisp Red Cross uniform, him in his camo pants, no shirt, both of them holding bottles of beer, grinning drunkenly into the camera. And the two of them in bathing suits on the beach, palm trees in the background.

Looking terribly young, except for that weariness in their eyes. A long time ago.

And photos of Bunny and Eddie with Larrigan and his girl, that scrawny Vietnamese chick, Larrigan's little hooker. A child, really. Couldn't have been more than thirteen or fourteen. No tits, hardly any hips on her. Looked malnourished. Eddie never really knew where Larrigan had found her. He liked 'em young, that was for sure. Li An. That was her name.

Larrigan had a big bush of curly black hair in those old photos, and a floppy mustache and sideburns half way down his face. Back then he still had two eyes. In several of the shots, he wore a drunken shit-eating grin and his arm was slung possessively around the shoulders of his little native chick, that Li An. A couple shots of Li An and the baby.

Old Larrigan. Who'da thought he'd ever be nominated for the Supreme Court?

Moran hadn't gotten Bunny to say much. She didn't want to talk about it, and he figured he better not push her. Last thing Larrigan would want was for Bunny Brubaker to suspect something.

But there was no doubt she remembered all of it.

He thought of taking the photos, then thought better of it. After seeing Eddie Moran, Bunny might decide to go to her shoebox, fish out the old pictures, and reminisce about the old days. Best for now if she found them right where she kept them. Best not to arouse any suspicions.

So he put all the photos back into the shoebox and wiped all the dust off it. Bunny wouldn't notice the absence of dust on the box if she happened to take it out of her closet. But she'd certainly notice finger smudges on a dust-covered box.

He replaced the shoebox exactly where he'd found it on the closet shelf behind the pile of sweaters.

Then he went through the dumpy little house again, to make sure he hadn't missed anything. Which he hadn't. Eddie Moran was a pro.

He ended up in the kitchen. He turned off the electric coffeepot. He thought of leaving Bunny a note but couldn't think of anything to say.

He went out through the side door, holding his breath as he hurried through the stinking carport, climbed into his rented gray Camry, and headed north on Route 1 for the airport in Miami.

He'd have to give some thought to what he wanted to tell Larrigan before he called him.

Simone Bonet sipped her herbal tea and gazed out through the big window at the bright rushing ribbon of water beyond the meadow at the foot of her hill. The afternoon sun was warm here in her glassed-in west-facing porch, and she had pushed the blanket off her legs. She had to be careful of overheating.

Soon the new leaves would fill the gaps in the maples and willows and the pretty stream would disappear behind the foliage, but now, in the middle of April, although the rising sap and swelling buds were turning the branches pink and yellow, the trees were still skel-etal, and from her little house huddled against the Catskill hillside, Simone could still see the stream running milky and swollen with snowmelt.

Simone loved the leaves, the way the thick summertime foliage hugged her in and protected her in her little sanctuary. But she loved her view of the moving water, too.

In the Catskills, the streams were called Kills. A Dutch word, she'd been told, meaning stream or creek or river.

Simone had heard that some earnest group of animal lovers had staged a demonstration against the name of one of the creeks—the Fishkill—because they believed it promoted violence against trout. How empty their lives must be, she thought.

The newspaper clipping lay flat on the table beside her cup and saucer. The crease across its middle had started to rip from all the times she had folded and unfolded it in the past few days, trying to make up her mind.

"Abortion Doc Assassination Foiled!" blared the headline.

Jill, her best friend, her nurse, her housemate, and her lover, had brought home the paper from the dentist's office. Simone had no interest in the news, subscribed to no newspapers or magazines, didn't own a television. She'd paged through the newspaper because she rarely saw one, idly, without any interest or curiosity.

Simone Bonet didn't care about abortions or assassinations, foiled or otherwise. She no longer cared about issues or policies, wars or catastrophes, heroes or celebrities. She'd had her fill of all those things.

She was only interested in the inevitable, comforting passage of the seasons, the leafing out of the trees, the blooming of the lilacs, the arrival of the migrating songbirds, the gentle unfolding of whatever life she had left.

At least, that's how she'd felt until she saw the photo.

It wasn't the headline that had grabbed her attention.

It was the photograph of the young woman kneeling beside the abortion clinic assassin with her arm raised. Her face was alive with emotion. Simone read triumph and something like terrible agony in her expression.

The name was wrong, of course. Carol Ann Chang. Chang was a Chinese name, and anybody could see that this young woman wasn't Chinese. But her age, that was about right, Simone judged. And her eyes, Vietnamese, not Chinese, they were Simone's.

The sharp nose, the wide mouth, the curly hair, they could certainly be his.

This was May. Even after all these years, a mother would recognize her baby. Her name should be Jessie Church, not Carol Ann Chang. Simone felt it with absolute certainty. This was her child.

Simone picked up the newspaper. Her right hand trembled, causing it to flutter. It was getting worse. She took the paper in her other hand and skimmed the story again. The world-famous doctor, outspoken defender of a woman's right to choose, director of the Woman's Reproductive Center in San Francisco, celebrating its thirty-fifth anniversary on that morning a few weeks earlier, the crowds, the demonstrations, the foiled assassin—a random, anonymous fanatic—and the hero, the bodyguard, Carol Ann Chang, a private investigator employed by Bay Security and Investigations of Oakland. She had subdued the armed fanatic with her bare hands and then refused to be interviewed for the article.

Good for her. She was smarter than Simone had been when she was that age. No good would ever come from compromising your privacy.

The doctor, Richard Bryant was his name, had been quoted at length. Ms. Chang was a hero, he said. She'd saved his life. He'd never seen anybody move so fast or incapacitate anybody so quickly and decisively.

Simone touched the face on the photo with her fingertip, gazed up at the sky, and drifted into that place where truth would separate itself from expectation and hope and despair . . . and she felt she was right.

This was her May, and this newspaper photograph was the omen that Simone had been waiting for, fearing and expecting for all these years.

Another wave of dizziness rolled through her brain. She squeezed her eyes shut. She hated the double vision the most, and the awful vertigo that accompanied it, the sensation of falling even when she was secure in her wheelchair.

The dizziness passed a moment later. She blinked her eyes experimentally, then opened them. She realized that she had been crying.

She pressed the buzzer on the lanyard around her neck, and a minute later Jill came out onto the porch.

Jill bent down, pushed Simone's long pigtail to the side, kissed the side of her neck, then knelt in front of her. She peered into Simone's eyes, then reached up and gently touched her cheek. "You've been crying," she said. "Did you have a spell?"

Simone nodded. "Just a little one." She smiled. "I am fine."

"Do you want to try to walk a little bit?"

"Maybe later," said Simone. She reached for Jill's hand and held it in both of hers. "Bring me my stationery and a pen, would you please? The one with the green ink. And then check the Internet, see if you can find an address for this, um, Carol Ann Chang for me." She handed her the newspaper.

Jill folded the paper and slid it into the hip pocket of her pants. "Are you sure you want to do this?" she said.

"I am not sure about anything," Simone said. "But I do feel strongly that she is the one." She shook her head and smiled. "I *am* quite sure that after I finish writing the note, I will be ready for my massage."

_ೂ ೄ_

THOMAS LARRIGAN WAS parked in the far corner of the McDonald's lot, as close to the shadows as he could manage with all the flood-lights on the tall poles surrounding the lot. He sipped the coffee he'd bought at the drive-through and fumed. He'd said seven-thirty, and here it was, nearly quarter of eight, and Moran still hadn't showed up. As if his time was more valuable than that of a United States District Court judge, soon to be Supreme Court justice.

He checked his cell phone again. No messages.

Then, without warning, the passenger door opened, the dome light went on, and Moran slid into the front seat.

"Shut the damn door," said Larrigan.

Moran shut the door, and the dome light went off.

"Do you have to do that?" said Larrigan.

"Do what?"

"Sneak up on people?"

Moran chuckled. "It's what I do. I sneak up on people. It's what I'm good at."

"You're good at being late, too."

"Somebody's gotta watch your ass, Judge. Or don't you mind if you're seen in my company?"

"I definitely mind," said Larrigan.

"So what's up, you gotta meet in a fucking McDonald's parking lot?"

"Bunny Brubaker," said Larrigan.

"What about her?"

"You should've taken those pictures when you had the chance."

"I explained it to you," said Moran. "She probably doesn't even know they're there. That box was way in the back of her closet. But if she ever noticed they were missing, she would've put two and two together. She's no dummy. It would've blown both of us. This way, we know more than she does. That's always how you want it to be."

"You said she wouldn't be a problem."

Moran shrugged. "She didn't want to talk about it. It was a long time ago. Another lifetime. She hadn't touched that box of pictures for years. She's into dolphins, for Christ's sake."

Larrigan reached into his jacket pocket, pulled out the letter-sized envelope, and held it up for Moran to see in the glow from the parking lot's floodlights. "This came to my office this morning." The envelope was addressed to Judge Thomas Larrigan, Federal District Court, Boston, MA. It was postmarked Miami, FL.

Moran looked up at him with his eyebrows arched.

Larrigan slid the newspaper clipping out of the envelope and handed it to Moran. "Read this," he said. Larrigan himself had pretty much memorized it.

It read:

JUDGE CRENSHAW TO RETIRE

Supreme Court Justice Lawrence Crenshaw will announce his retirement from the seat he has held for the past thirty-two years, effective at the end of this term.

A source close to the Justice said: "Justice Crenshaw has informed the president of his intention to step down. He will make his formal announcement at the end of the current session."

Justice Crenshaw celebrated his 86th birthday in February. He has been in failing health.

According to Beltway insiders, the search for a replacement has already begun. Leading contenders for Justice Crenshaw's seat include Maria Anna Alvarez, Circuit Court judge in San Diego; William Howard Raymond, former Virginia Attorney General; and, Thomas R. Larrigan, Federal District Court judge in Boston.

White House sources declined comment.

Moran glanced at it, then folded it and handed it back to Larrigan. "So it ain't a secret," he said. "Congratulations, I guess, huh?"

"Take a look at this." Larrigan handed Moran a photograph. Actually, it was a photocopy of a photograph. "Look familiar?"

Moran glanced at it and nodded. "It's like those from Bunny's shoebox. There's you and your Vietnamese chick—what was her name? Li An?"

"Yes," said Larrigan. "Li An."

"And me and Bunny." Moran laughed. "We're all looking pretty drunk, wouldn't you say?"

"Yes, we are. We're not looking very dignified."

Moran frowned. "How'd you get ahold of this?"

Larrigan didn't answer. He took the note out of the envelope and handed it to Moran.

Larrigan had memorized the note, too. It had been eating at him all day.

There was no date or return address on the top.

"Dear Tom," it read. "Now it all makes sense. Congratulations. And then Eddie Moran just happens to show up after all these years. Nice to see him again. He's still cute. I'm guessing that the *National Enquirer* or *Hard Copy* or *Geraldo* might enjoy our story along with some photographs from those happy days. I bet one of them would give me $50,000 for it. Maybe all four of us could go on TV together. Have a tearful reunion, talk about old times. What do you think?"

She had signed it: "Bunny."

Larrigan studied Moran as he read the note. His lips actually moved. If you didn't know better, you might think that Eddie Moran wasn't very bright.

Larrigan knew for a fact that Moran was extremely bright. Unprincipled, devious, amoral. Borderline sociopathic. But plenty bright.

Moran folded Bunny's note and handed it to Larrigan.

Larrigan put it back into the envelope. "Well?" he said.

"I probably shoulda taken the damn pictures," said Moran.

"She expects me to give her fifty grand."

"Extortion's illegal, Judge." Moran was grinning.

Larrigan snorted. "Yeah, we'll have her arrested. Good idea. A public trial. Just the ticket."

"You want to pay her off?"

"You think that'll shut her up?"

"Probably not," said Moran.

Larrigan gripped the steering wheel with both hands, squeezing as hard as he could, as if he could strangle it. All that was thirty-five years ago. Nobody who hadn't been there could have any idea what it was like. You could watch all the movies, read all the novels and memoirs and history books, and you still wouldn't have a clue.

They were just kids, and they all thought they were going to die. They had all resigned themselves to that. It was the only way they could keep going.

You did whatever you had to do to stay alive, and you hoped that tomorrow, not today, would be the day you died. You killed so you wouldn't get killed. You set huts on fire, and sometimes you slaughtered women and children and old men, because if you didn't, they might kill you.

Larrigan himself had not done that. But he knew, if he'd been in the right situation, he would have. In a heartbeat. Without giving it a second thought. And without remorse.

The only other way was to blow your brains out. Plenty of boys did it that way.

That's how it was. Unless they'd been there, they had no right to judge.

But, of course, they would.

He turned to Moran. "Only four people know, and two of them are sitting in this car and one of them most likely died a long time ago."

"Leaving Bunny," said Moran.

"Get those fucking photos, Eddie."

Moran looked at him. "You really think Bunny's gonna—?"

"Do what you have to do," said Larrigan.

—◌◌—

BLACKHOLE SAT IN his nondescript Subaru and watched the judge's Lincoln Town Car, parked in the corner of the McDonald's lot, through his zoom lens. When the unidentified man opened the passenger door and slid in, he snapped one picture in the brief flash of the dome light. Hard to say if the man's face would show up, although the computer techs could do wonders with blurry, under-exposed digital photographs. Not that it mattered. Blackhole had already photographed the license plate of the Ford Explorer the man had parked on the other side of the lot. Identifying him would be no problem.

The two of them sat in the front seat for twelve minutes—from 6:42 to 6:54 by Blackhole's watch. From where he watched, he couldn't see what they were doing. Then the stranger opened the passenger door, stepped out, and went back to his Explorer.

Blackhole snapped several photos of the judge's friend in the light from the parking lot floods. He looked to be somewhere in his fifties. Five-ten, about one-seventy-five. Thinning hair, bony face. Bulky around the shoulders. He walked with his arms held a little bit away from his body. Wrestlers carried their arms that way on account of their overdeveloped upper bodies. But this man wasn't awkward or muscle-bound. There was a smooth efficiency to the way he moved. Graceful, almost, like a confident, well-conditioned athlete.

Most people, civilians, they wouldn't take a second look at this guy, and afterward, they wouldn't remember him, or if they did, they wouldn't be able to describe him. He was nondescript, ordinary. He blended in—which, of course, was the whole point.

Blackhole knew the type, though. He knew a lot of men who carried themselves like this one. They were highly trained. Former SEALs or Special Forces, civilians now, still valued for their partic-ular skills. Dangerous men. Men without normal compunctions.

Blackhole himself was one such man.

The Town Car and the Explorer started up, flashed on their headlights, and headed for the parking lot exit at the same time.

The judge turned left, which, Blackhole knew, would take him home. The Explorer turned right.

Blackhole was briefly tempted to follow the Explorer. But his orders were to stick to the judge, so that's what he did.

Perhaps that would change now that he had finally come up with something worth reporting. Blackhole's job was to gather intelligence, not to judge it or interpret it. But he knew that Federal District Court judges didn't meet highly trained, dangerous men in the shadowy corner of a McDonald's parking lot unless they were up to something.

Eddie Moran drove slowly past the little square modular home. It was nearly three in the morning, and this was his fifth trip past the place since he'd gotten to Key Largo late that afternoon.

On his first pass, Moran had observed that the trash still hadn't been cleaned out of the carport. Nor had the boat's hull been scraped or the shutter repaired or the lawn cut or the gardens weeded.

Now, after five trips past her place, the maroon VW with the daisy on the antenna still hadn't showed up.

Bunny Brubaker, he figured, had gotten lucky. She was shacked up for the night.

He smiled to himself, remembering his night with her. If she was shacked up, he thought, it was definitely the guy who'd gotten lucky.

I could do it now, he thought. She's not coming home tonight.

Nope. Can't take that chance.

So he drove the rental—it was a Chevy sedan this time, rented under a different name with a different credit card from a different Miami rental agency—back up Route 1 to his motel. Not the same motel as last time, either.

‒‒‒ʕ‑ʔ‑‒‒

THE NEXT MORNING he thought about going to the dolphin place, but he couldn't risk Bunny spotting him. So he looked up the number in the motel directory and called it on his cell phone, and when a guy calling himself Carlos answered, he said, "May I speak with Bunny Brubaker, please?"

If Carlos said he'd go get her, hang on a minute, Moran would hang up. If he said Bunny was busy, could he take a message, he'd make something up.

What Carlos said was: "She not here."

"When do you expect her?"

"I don't," said Carlos. "Bunny don't work here no more."

Moran sighed. "Damn. That's disappointing."

"Sorry, man."

"Look," said Moran. "I'm her cousin Joey, see. We used to be real close. I haven't seen her since she moved to Florida. I finally get down here, first thing I want to do is see Bunny. I talked to her, it was only a couple weeks ago, told her I was coming. I just got in this morning, tried calling her house. No answer. She mentioned that she worked there. I figure, she's at work . . ." He sighed. "You don't know how I could reach her, do you? Maybe she took another job . . . ?"

"Can't help you. Bunny told me nothing."

"Is there anybody there who she might've told what she was doing?"

"No," said Carlos. "Just me. She quit, that's all. Called last week. Told me she wasn't coming back. Too bad. Bunny a real nice lady, hard worker, good with the kids."

"Well, okay," said Eddie. "Thanks anyway."

"Sorry, man."

⁓

HE LEFT THE Chevy at the turnaround at the end of her street and walked back. It was a little after noon, the best time to commit a burglary. That's when houses were empty and most of the neighbors would be out, and in the midday heat of the Florida Keys, those who were home would be huddled inside with their air conditioning turned up high and their curtains drawn against the sun.

Besides, normal law-abiding citizens always assume that burglars work at night, which is, of course, fallacious. But it's what they assume. They're more likely to notice a stranger in the neighborhood after dark than at noontime.

All the burglars Moran knew, which was quite a large number, worked in the middle of the day.

He strolled up the street, a middle-aged guy in khaki pants and a blue short-sleeved shirt and a straw hat, neither tall nor short, fat nor skinny, an average-looking white guy with sunglasses and a forgettable face, although Bunny thought he was still cute and women seemed to remember his deep brown eyes and the tiny star-shaped scar on his cheekbone and the hard bulk of his chest and shoulders when he slipped out of his shirt.

"Well, officer, I remember a man. He was wearing a straw hat and sunglasses. No, that's really all I remember about him."

He assumed he was being watched. It was always best to operate on that assumption. He turned up the path to her front door and rang the bell. If by chance she was home and answered the door, he'd grin and say, "Hey, surprise! I'm back in town. Thought I'd take a chance, see if you were home."

Of course she didn't answer the bell.

He stood there, shifting his weight from one foot to the other, feigning impatience for whatever eyes might be watching him.

Then he shrugged, walked back to the street, hesitated, shrugged again, putting on a show for his imaginary audience, and went up her driveway, into the carport, around the smelly trash barrels, to the back door. Out of sight, now, from all eyes.

He had his tools with him, but first he ran his hand over the ledge above the door, then lifted the doormat. No dice. Probably she'd hidden her spare key somewhere in the chaos of the carport, but Moran figured it'd be quicker just to pick the damn lock.

It took him four minutes. He was a little out of practice.

When he opened the door and stepped inside, the heat almost blew him back out. It must've been a hundred-and-twenty in there. Well, okay. That confirmed that she'd been gone for a while. When she'd been living there, he recalled, she kept the AC on all day.

He went straight to the bedroom, opened the closet door, fumbled behind the pile of sweaters, and took down the shoebox.

He dumped the photos out onto the bed.

Fifteen minutes later he left the house, strolled back to his car, and drove a couple of miles down Route 1. Then he pulled to the side of the road and took out his cell phone.

When Larrigan answered, Moran said, "She's not there and those photos aren't there, either."

"What do you mean?"

Moran explained that Bunny had quit her job, left her house, and taken the photos of her and Larrigan and Eddie and Li An, Larrigan's Vietnamese girlfriend, with her to wherever she'd gone. "It doesn't look like she moved permanently," he said. "Hard to say if she took a lot of clothes with her. But as near as I can remember, everything else was the way it was."

"So now what?" said Larrigan.

"Up to you."

"Find her."

"It's gonna—"

"Goddamn it, Eddie. Do what needs to be done. Get the damn pictures."

⸺◌◌⸺

JAKE IN NEW York told Moran it would take ten or twelve hours to get what he needed—if he could get it. No guarantees. So Moran spent the day in his motel room alternating between his Elmore Leonard paperback and the television.

It was nearly ten that night when his cell phone chirped. Moran had been dozing.

"Yuh," he mumbled.

"It's Jake."

"Get anything?"

"She's been in Davis, Georgia, for at least the past two days, including yesterday afternoon. Before that Jacksonville, and before that West Palm Beach. She's heading north."

"Credit card?"

"Nope. That would've been easier. ATM card. She used it three days ago and then yesterday, same place in Davis. Maybe she's still there. Worth a shot, anyway."

"Well, good," said Moran. "So where the fuck is Davis, Georgia?"

"Christ, Eddie, I gotta check the map for you?"

"No, I guess I can—"

"Well, I did, anyway. It's a few miles northwest of Valdosta, just over the line from Florida."

"I know where Valdosta is."

"Just tryin' to give you your money's worth."

"You did. Thanks."

⸺◌◌⸺

HE GOT UP at six the next morning, drove to Miami, returned the Chevy sedan to the rental place, and caught a flight to Atlanta.

There he switched planes, and he landed at the Valdosta Municipal Airport a little after two in the afternoon.

He rented a Dodge minivan with one of his many credit cards under one of his many names. The girl at the Budget desk gave him a map of the area, and he found Davis. It was about twenty miles outside the city, the third exit north off I-75.

Moran found the town and spent the afternoon driving around, orienting himself.

Davis turned out to be a nondescript little Southern town, mostly red-dirt farms, a few residential streets lined with big old houses with wraparound verandas, trailers and shacks scattered along the back roads, a couple of rib joints, and several roadside taverns. What passed as a business center was a couple of strip malls.

There were three banks. Bunny Brubaker had used her ATM card twice at one of them.

There were two motels, and at eight-thirty that evening he spotted the maroon VW with the daisy on the antenna and the Florida plates parked outside the motel nearest the bank she'd used. It was a run-down sixteen-unit flat-roofed boxy structure tucked into a little grove of scrub oak on the main drag heading west past the second strip mall.

What a brilliant fucking detective I am, thought Moran. Less than twenty-four hours ago I had no idea where she was. She could've been anywhere.

Now I've got her.

He drove back into town, found a Burger King with a drive-through, and ordered a Whopper, fries, and coffee. When he paid the girl at the window, he kept his sunglasses on and the brim of his straw hat pulled low so she wouldn't see his face. He ate in the parking lot, lit a cigarette, and sipped his coffee while the light faded from the sky. Then he drove back to the motel.

The red neon sign out front read, unimaginatively, MOTEL. The VACANCY light was on.

Her VW hadn't moved. There were two other cars pulled up in front of the motel.

Bunny Brubaker's car was nosed up to unit seven, near the end. The other two occupied units were one and three, judging by the light that glowed in the windows behind the pulled drapes where the cars were parked.

He pulled the minivan in front of unit eight, beside Bunny's VW, got out, and walked up to unit seven.

He could hear television voices inside. He tapped softly on the door.

A moment later the door opened until it pulled tight against the chain. Bunny looked at him through the crack.

"Oh, Jesus," she whispered.

"Hi, Bunny. Surprise, huh?"

"Yeah. Surprise. What do you want?"

"I got a message from a mutual friend."

She peered at him through the cracked-open door. "How'd you find me?"

Moran chuckled. "It wasn't easy."

"Nobody—"

"It doesn't matter, does it? I'm here and we need to talk."

She nodded. "Okay. So talk."

"Aren't you going to invite me in?"

"No, I don't think so. Talk to me. What's he got to say?"

"Bunny," said Moran, slapping a mosquito that was drilling into the back of his neck, "the bugs're driving me nuts out here. Leave that door open like that, you're gonna have a swarm of 'em in there. Let me in. I don't get it, anyway. You don't seem happy to see me."

"Tough about the bugs," she said. "What's the message?"

"Fifty grand."

"Got it with you?"

"Come on, babe," said Moran. "It's a little more complicated than that."

"No, it's not. I know what he wants, and he knows what I want. It's simple."

"Well, if you want what you want, just let me inside for a minute so we can talk private and I don't get lifted up and carried away by these goddamn bugs, okay?"

She stared at him for a moment. Then the door shut. He heard the chain rattle, and then the door opened again. "Okay," said Bunny. "Come on in."

She was wearing running shorts and a pale blue T-shirt. Bare feet. Her auburn hair tied back with a rubber band, long smooth brown legs, those nice tits bulging under her T-shirt.

She went over and sat on one of the twin beds that practically filled the room. He noticed that she kept her left hand hidden behind her. "You can turn off the TV if you want," she said.

He turned the TV sound off, leaving the picture flickering. He sat on the other bed, facing her. "You're looking fine, Bunny," he said, reaching out and touching her leg.

She twitched and moved her leg. "Don't," she said. "I don't trust you."

"Why not? I bring you good tidings of great joy."

"You—you messed with my head. He sent you down to find me. You didn't tell me the prick was up for the goddamn Supreme Court."

"Yeah," he said. "I felt bad about that. You're a good kid, and we go way back, you and me. It would've been nice if we'd just happened to run into each other. But . . ." He shrugged and grinned. "What's it matter? We had fun, didn't we?"

She cocked her head, then smiled. "Yes. We had fun. We always had fun." She shook her head. "But we're not going to have fun now. We're going to do business now. Did you bring the money?"

"Depends."

"Depends on what?"

"You got the pictures?"

She frowned. "Christ, I don't know how to do this." She looked up at the ceiling for a moment, then pulled her left hand from behind her back. It was holding a short-barreled revolver. A .38, Moran guessed.

"What's that for?" he said.

"A single girl can't be too careful."

"You don't need that. Jesus. I don't like guns."

"Me, neither," she said. "But I'd like it less if I didn't have one. So you got the money?"

"Not in my pocket. Show me the pictures. Then we can do business."

"The money first."

He pretended to ponder his options, then shrugged. "Okay. You're the one with the gun. The money's in the car. Parked right outside."

"Let's get it."

He nodded, stood up, and turned for the door.

"Wait," she said. "I'm going with you."

He stopped, and when she came up behind him, he turned quickly and slammed his fist into her stomach, just under her ribcage. The air exploded from her, and she collapsed onto the floor and rolled onto her side, her knees drawn up to her chest.

He picked up the revolver where it had fallen to the carpet and tossed it onto the bed. Then he crouched beside her. "The photos," he said softly. "Where are they, Bunny?"

"Fuck you," she gasped. She was having trouble breathing, and tears brimmed in her eyes.

"Aw, come on, babe. Don't make it difficult."

"I haven't got them," she whispered.

"I hope that's not true," he said. "I'd really feel bad if that was the truth. I need those photos." He reached for the TV and turned up the sound to full volume. Then he knelt on the floor beside her. He stroked her hair, moved his hand down her back, patted her ass softly. He put his mouth by her ear. "Okay, sweetheart. Let's talk."

"They're not here," she said. "Honest."

Eddie Moran shook his head, sighed, and grasped her breast. He squeezed it and twisted it until Bunny screamed. Her scream mingled with the television noise, and he was pretty sure no one outside the motel would notice.

⌒⌒

HE TOSSED HER room methodically, and when he didn't find the photos he combed through her VW. No luck.

Eddie Moran was confident that he was more proficient at finding things than Bunny Brubaker was at hiding them. She'd told the truth. She didn't have those damn pictures with her.

It was too bad he'd had to kill her. She was a good kid. Always had been. But he'd had no choice. From the moment he knocked on her motel room door, she was a dead woman, whether she handed over the photos or not.

He'd twisted her breast and she'd screamed and twisted and bucked against him. She lashed out wildly, catching him across his neck with her fingernails, leaving three parallel gashes running from his ear to his collar.

"Aw, shit, Bunny," he'd said. "That hurts."

Again he smashed his fist into her solar plexus. She gagged and puked and curled into a fetal ball, and he knew he'd knocked the spirit out of her. He'd moved his hands to her soft throat, stroked it, watching the terror in her eyes. His thumbs found her larynx, pressed until he could feel it collapse, and he'd watched her face turn red then blue then purple. Her back arched, and a great shudder vibrated in her chest, and her eyes bulged before they rolled up into her head.

Now he stood in the middle of the room, examining his work, trying to see it the way the cops would see it. All the bureau drawers had been pulled out and dumped on the floor. He'd dragged the mattresses off the twin beds, tipped over the upholstered chair, spilled everything out of her suitcase.

Bunny's body lay crumpled in the corner.

Her revolver was in his pants pocket. He'd taken all the cash and plastic cards and loose papers from her purse and stuffed them into his jacket pocket.

He shrugged. Too bad. It was a waste.

He shut off the television and switched off the lights in the room. He cracked open the door and peered outside to be sure nobody was hanging around.

He slipped out of Bunny's room and shut the door. He went to his rented minivan and fumbled in his duffel for his baggie of Mexican weed, which he took to her VW and tucked under the front seat. His gift to the local redneck cops. Make the scenario easy for them to understand.

He wiped his prints from Bunny's revolver and tossed it into the Dumpster out back. If the cops found it, it'd give them something else to think about.

Then he climbed into his minivan and headed back to the Valdosta airport. As he drove through the Georgia night, he remembered the single word Bunny Brubaker had gasped as his thumbs had begun to press into her larynx.

It had sounded like "Seymour," which didn't mean a damn thing to Eddie Moran.

_____ ✺ _____

OUTSIDE THE BIG windows of the sunporch, mist blanketed the valley and a soft rain filtered down from the low gray clouds. It was a fuzzy black-and-white photograph, a Japanese ink drawing, beautiful, but stark and foreboding, too, Simone thought.

Or maybe that was her disease. She'd been having a lot of dark and foreboding hours lately.

From the big speakers, Beethoven's *Pastorale*, the ineffably beautiful Sixth Symphony, washed over her.

Two weeks, no reply. She'd included her address and her phone number in her letter.

Perhaps she'd been wrong. Perhaps Carol Ann Chang in San Francisco wasn't her May after all.

She'd been so certain of it.

Wishful thinking, probably.

For all those years, Simone had not allowed herself to think of May, whose adopted name was Jessie Church, to wonder what kind of woman she'd become, to imagine a reunion. Then the newspaper photograph had unleashed all of her repressed longings and regrets.

It would've been better had she not seen that photograph.

She felt her eyes growing watery. Her thoughts were so muddled sometimes, her moods so uncontrollable. The frustrating part was that even as she was aware of the confusions and the irrational fears—and the hopes, too—she just didn't have the energy to concentrate on them, sort them out, solve them with logic.

She blinked away the tears and huddled under her afghan, drifting on the music . . .

A touch on her shoulder snapped her awake. She reached up and placed her hand over Jill's.

"You were napping," said Jill. "Do you feel okay? Do you need some medicine?"

Simone turned her head, looked up at her, and smiled. "I am all right, dear."

Jill reached down and touched Simone's cheek with her fingertip. "You've been crying again."

"It is nothing."

"It's happening more often," said Jill. "The symptoms. I'm going to call Dr. Mattes."

"Yes," said Simone. "I suppose you should."

She saw the flicker of concern in Jill's eyes. If Simone agreed to see the doctor, Jill would know that the symptoms were getting worse.

Jill tried to smile, then handed Simone an envelope. "This came for you. I thought you'd want to see it right away."

The large padded manila envelope felt heavy in Simone's hand. It had been addressed in a loose, careless feminine scrawl, and it had been sent by certified mail. The word "personal" was scrawled across the bottom and underlined twice. No return address.

It had been postmarked in Valdosta, Georgia, four days earlier. Simone didn't think she knew anybody in the entire state of Georgia.

"I'm sorry," said Jill. "It's not from . . ."

Simone nodded. "I guess not."

"What about a nice hot cup of tea, then?"

"Thank you, dear," said Simone. "Tea would be lovely."

After Jill left the room, Simone opened the envelope and withdrew a single folded sheet of white stationery and a handful of photographs. She put aside the photos and unfolded the note.

She glanced first at the signature at the bottom.

"Bunny."

Bunny Brubaker was the only "Bunny" Simone knew, but that had been over thirty years ago.

"Dear Li An," Bunny's note began.

Li An! An avalanche of memories washed over her.

Simone quickly read the note. "It's been a long time," Bunny had written. "I've been trying to live the quiet life in Key Largo. I've thought of you often, followed your career. I read the gossip, of course. I didn't believe a bit of it.

"I figured it would be best if I did not try to get in touch with you. It would only remind us of back then, and I figured it was better for both of us to leave all that behind us. What happened is ancient history, and I never saw any reason to dredge it up. Best if you and I just went our separate ways.

"However, I wanted you to have these photos. Something happened recently that inspired me to dig them out.

"Now, I think, we need to talk. Here's a number where I'm staying. I'll wait to hear from you. In the meantime, please keep the photos in a safe place. They're all we have left of those days."

Simone placed Bunny's letter on her lap and absentmindedly smoothed it flat. She gazed up at the ceiling for a moment, then picked up the handful of photos and thumbed through them. Her tremors were bad today—or maybe it was the photos, not the disease, that caused the trembling—and she quickly put the photos down.

Her eyes blurred. The memories were still vivid, the pain still palpable.

How young they had been. How innocent. How desperate. How frightened.

How utterly corrupt.

Thomas Larrigan. Bunny Brubaker. Eddie Moran. All of that had been thousands of miles and one long lifetime ago. So far from this quiet place that had become her sanctuary.

She picked up one of the photos and looked at it again. It showed Thomas and Eddie and Bunny. And Simone herself. Li An, back then. So young, Simone thought. I was a mere child among these adults.

Thomas was holding little May—she couldn't have been more than a month old—cradled in one arm. His other arm held Li An close to his side. They were all smiling.

Simone touched this photo lightly with her fingertip, tracing the outline of the sleeping baby's tiny face.

A tear fell onto the photograph, and Simone realized that she had been silently weeping. Such a maelstrom of emotions she was feeling. Sadness, loss, anger, yes, but those almost-forgotten moments of love and joy had come storming back, too. All the emotions that she'd succeeded in repressing for all these years. They had never really left. They'd been waiting for release.

Her chest ached with an awful foreboding. First it was seeing May's picture—Carol Ann Chang, which Simone knew was not her real name, but it was, she felt certain, her face—in the newspaper.

Now this.

She picked up Bunny's note and reread it. "I think we need to talk," she had written.

No, no, thought Simone. *I do not want to talk. I do not want to think about any of that. I cannot bear feeling it all over again.*

But she knew she had to do it. Fate had taken the decision out of her hands. Two pictures of May within a week of each other. First May the grown woman, strong and beautiful. Then May the infant, small and helpless.

Simone did not believe in coincidence. There was a purpose to everything. It was time to confront her destiny, while she still could. She understood now that she could no longer escape it.

She picked up her cell phone and pecked out the number Bunny had written.

A female voice, unmistakably southern, answered. "Motel. How may I help you?"

"May I speak with Bunny Brubaker, please?" said Simone.

"Is she a guest here, ma'am?"

"Yes, I believe so," said Simone.

"Y'all have a room number?"

"Sorry, I do not. Is there a Ms. Brubaker registered there?"

"I'll check. Just hold on for a minute, please."

A moment later the woman returned. "I'm sorry, ma'am. No Brubaker registered here."

"You are certain?"

"Yes'm."

"Well, thank you."

Simone disconnected. She looked again at the postmark on the envelope. Four days earlier. Bunny had said she'd be there, waiting for her call. For some reason, she had changed her mind.

Simone let out a long breath. She realized she was vastly relieved. She didn't want to talk to Bunny Brubaker. She didn't want to think about those times.

She looked again at the one photograph that showed all of them. She laid it on her lap. Then she slid Bunny's note and all the other photographs back into the big envelope. *I should probably burn all of it*, she thought. *No good can ever come of it.*

Then she thought, *No, I will save them so I can show them to May.*

When Jill came back with two mugs of steaming herbal tea, she said, "Are you all right?"

Simone handed her the envelope. "Put these away for me, please, dear."

She watched as Jill went to the rolltop desk against the inside wall of the sunporch, opened the bottom right-hand drawer, and placed Bunny's envelope in there along with the other documents—the contracts, the citizenship papers, the birth certificate, the marriage certificate—and the handgun wrapped in its oily cloth, and the box of bullets.

Simone noticed how Jill hesitated whenever she saw the gun. Jill hated guns, said it was dangerous to have one in the house, and Simone supposed she was right.

But she felt better, knowing that the gun was handy.

Jill came back and sat down beside the wheelchair. "Dr. Mattes will be here tomorrow afternoon."

Simone nodded. "Good. He is a nice man."

Jill pointed at the photograph on Simone's lap. "What's that?"

Simone handed it to Jill. "It is from a very long time ago."

Jill looked at it. "I recognize you. Who are the other people?"

Simone waved her hand. "Just some people I knew. Would you mind putting it on the table beside my bed?"

Jill took the photograph into Simone's bedroom. When she came back, she said, "What can I do to make you comfortable?"

"Oh, I am comfortable enough." Simone smiled. "Come, dear. Sit with me and tell me if you think spring is really going to come this year."

Thomas Larrigan found Eddie Moran right where he said he'd be, leaning his back against the railing of the footbridge that crossed the Charles River near the Esplanade. Moran was smoking a cigarette and watching the joggers and the inline skaters go by as if he didn't have anything better to do on a sunny Friday afternoon in early May.

Larrigan walked onto the bridge. "So," he said. "Did you get them?"

"The photos?"

"What the hell do you think? Yes. The damn photos."

"No."

"What do you mean, no?"

"No means no," said Moran. "I didn't get the fucking photographs. She didn't have 'em."

"Bunny?"

Moran nodded.

"You searched her house, and you—?"

"Don't ask," said Moran. "Bunny Brubaker ain't going to bother you anymore, leave it at that. But the photos weren't where they were, and she didn't have them, and I don't know where the fuck they are."

"You killed her?"

Moran shrugged.

Larrigan shook his head. "Jesus."

Moran flicked his cigarette butt into the river.

"Okay," said Larrigan. "But we've still got to get those photos."

Moran watched a blonde jogger with a cocker spaniel on a leash cross the bridge. "I've been thinking about this whole thing," he said. "Maybe we ought to reconsider before it's too late. Maybe you oughta just tell the president to withdraw your name from consideration."

"What do you mean, too late?"

Moran shrugged. "What I've been doing. You know what I mean?"

"What you did to Bunny?"

"For example."

"Had to be done, didn't it?"

"My point exactly," said Moran. "It had to be done. And more things'll have to be done. No end to it. You could quit now. It'd be over with."

Larrigan rolled his eyes. "And what do you think would happen then?"

"He'd nominate somebody else." Moran shrugged. "You'd get your life back."

Larrigan rolled his eyes.

"You don't think so?" said Moran.

"If I were to pull out now," said Larrigan, "the media would be all over my ass. I could make up any excuse I wanted, wouldn't matter. They'd smell something, and they wouldn't let it go 'til they found it. We've got to finish what we started. You've gotta hang in there, Eddie. Don't crap out on me now. We can do it. It's gonna be worth it."

Moran looked at him. "You think so?"

Larrigan grinned. "Sure."

"Okay, then," said Moran. "You're the boss."

"So how are we going to get those photos?" Larrigan said.

"Well," said Moran, "does the name Seymour mean anything to you?"

"Seymour who?"

"I don't know. Just that name. Seymour. Or something like that."

Larrigan frowned for a minute. "One of the clerks on the civil side is named Seymour. Robert, I think."

"Yeah," said Moran. "Probably not him."

"So what's with this Seymour?"

"Something Bunny said."

"What are you thinking?"

"I'm thinking," said Moran, "that maybe Bunny had a friend named Seymour, and maybe he's holding the photos."

"Okay," said Larrigan, "I guess you better figure out who this Seymour guy is, huh? Do what you need to do."

Moran nodded. "Just wanted to be sure we're on the same page."

⸙

BLACKHOLE SAT ON a bench on the Cambridge side of the river with one leg crossed over the other, reading the sports page of the *Herald* and watching Thomas Larrigan and Eddie Moran talking on the footbridge. He couldn't hear what they were saying, of course, and using a camera with a long lens to record their meeting would've been too risky.

But Blackhole could read body language. Larrigan's spoke volumes. He was the boss. In charge. He was cool, relaxed, determined.

The judge was wearing sunglasses to hide his eye patch. Trying to be anonymous. Blackhole smiled. What he actually looked like was a guy with a black eye patch whose picture had been in the papers, wearing sunglasses and trying to look anonymous.

The other guy, the one Blackhole had identified as Edward Moran, he was the shaky one, which was a little surprising. As Blackhole had suspected, Moran had been career Special Forces— Southeast Asia, Afghanistan, the Middle East, Africa. Whatever he was up to now should be a game of patty-cake compared to what had gone down in those places.

Larrigan had been in Southeast Asia at the same time as Moran. That was the connection. So far, that was all Blackhole had been able to get.

As Blackhole watched from behind his newspaper, Moran shrugged and nodded, and Larrigan gave him an encouraging pat on the shoulder. Then Larrigan headed back to the Boston side of the river. Moran waited for a minute, then turned and came Blackhole's way, toward Memorial Drive on the Cambridge side.

Blackhole gave Moran three minutes. Then he folded his newspaper, tucked it under his arm, stood up, and headed back to his vehicle, which he'd parked half a block behind Eddie Moran's Explorer.

— ⚬⚬ —

OLD HABITS FROM her undercover days. Looking over her shoulder. Keeping an eye on her rearview mirror. Parking her car in a different place every night. Sticking a hair in the door latch. Studying every face, making eye contact, interpreting the reaction.

Now the old habits had paid off.

Jessie Church spotted him Friday evening after her fifth day on the Moreno stakeout. He was parked directly across the street from her apartment in a white late-model Ford Focus with California plates. The numbers and letters on the plates told Jessie that it was a rental from the airport.

It was possible that a man alone in a parked rental car—this guy was in his thirties, with thinning sandy hair and wraparound sunglasses—was a tourist, sitting there at seven o'clock on a Friday evening waiting for his wife to finish shopping. There were lots of great shops and boutiques on 24th Street in Noe Valley.

But Jessie doubted that's what he was doing.

She drove past him, and he didn't even look at her. She kept going, watching in her rearview mirror. The white Focus didn't pull out and follow.

She figured he knew what she looked like and where she lived, and he was waiting for her to appear at her front door, unlock it, and go inside. That's how he would identify her. He wasn't paying attention to the cars on the street or the shoppers and dog-walkers on the sidewalks.

She drove around for a while until she was positive he wasn't following her. Then she stopped at a mini-mart, bought a bottle of water and two bananas, and exited through the side door. The Focus had not pulled in, nor was it parked outside.

An hour later she returned to her neighborhood in Noe Valley, turned onto 24th Street, and once again drove past her apartment.

The Focus had moved down the street half a block. Same guy in the driver's seat, still wearing his sunglasses even though the street-lights had come on, watching the front door to Jessie's building through the car's rearview mirror.

Jessie kept going. She drove aimlessly around the city, ate the bananas, sipped from the bottle of water, and thought about it. Del knew some San Francisco cops. He could convince them to roust the guy in the Focus, bring him in, sweat him.

But he'd have a story that would check out, and they'd have to let him go, and the next guy Howie Cohen sent around would respect Jessie's professionalism more than this one.

She could hole up in some cheesy motel for a few days, then go back and see if the guy in the Focus was still there.

But even if he wasn't, even if Cohen's man gave up and went back to Baltimore—or Chicago or New York or L.A., he could live anywhere, Cohen had associates, men who owed him favors, all over the world—she knew that wouldn't be the end of it. A man serving twenty-five to life in a federal penitentiary in Maryland had all the time in the world.

They'd started the easy way. They'd recognized her picture in the paper. They wouldn't be surprised or deterred by the fact that she was using a phony name. They'd found her address, and staked it out, and if she hadn't been paranoid, expecting them, looking for them, and if she wasn't a professional trained in observation, that would have been good enough.

Next time there might be two or three of them, a team, and they would be more proficient at their job, and if Jessie sniffed them out, too, others would follow.

If Cohen had his way, there would never be an end to it until Jessie Church was dead.

She'd have to find a way to deal with that.

For now, though, she had the immediate problem of the guy in the Ford Focus.

She needed to buy herself some time.

She pulled over to the side of the road, fished her cell phone from her purse, and hit Del's number on the speed dial.

When his voicemail answered, she said, "Sorry if this is a problem, but I need a break. You've got to get someone else for the Moreno stakeout tomorrow. I'll be good for Sunday. Get back to me if there's a problem."

She sat there for about five minutes with her phone in her lap before it rang.

"What the hell's going on?" Del said when she answered.

"Nothing," said Jessie. "I've been sitting in front of that guy's house for five straight hot boring days, that's all. I need a day off."

"Something's going on," said Del.

"I just want to spend my Saturday at the beach. Don't try to make something out of nothing."

"I know you, Jess," he said.

"No, you don't," she said. "I'll be back on the job bright and early Sunday morning. See ya." And she disconnected before he tricked her into admitting anything. The last thing she wanted was to get Del involved in this.

She drove back to her neighborhood, found a place on the street, and walked the two blocks to her apartment on 24th Street. The Focus was back where it had first been parked, directly across from her building.

She acted nonchalant, even though every nerve in her body was zinging. She strolled up the street, pretty sure the guy had finally spotted her, fumbled in her purse for her key, unlocked the front door, and went inside.

Her apartment was on the second floor. The hair in the door latch was still there. Even so, she took her little automatic .32 purse pistol out of her bag before she went inside.

She turned on the lights, because that's what he'd expect her to do, and if she didn't, it wouldn't take half a brain for him to figure out that she'd made him. She went to the front window and peeked down through the blinds. By the light of the streetlight, she could see that the guy in the Focus was talking on his cell phone.

A minute later, the headlights went on and the Focus pulled out of its slot and drove away.

He wouldn't try it here, tonight, in her apartment. There were cleaner, easier ways.

He'd be back bright and early the next morning, in a different vehicle probably. Now that he'd found her, now that it was inevitable, he'd stick with her, biding his time, in no hurry. He'd wait for the right situation.

How about tomorrow? thought Jessie. *Suppose I pick the time and the place?*

She slept, fully dressed, in the armchair in the corner of the living room facing the doorway, with the lights turned off and her Sig Sauer 9mm Parabellum, her serious weapon, in her lap. She knew that the faintest scratch on the door, the softest footfall on the doormat, the quietest whisper in the hallway would wake her up instantly. She trusted her training.

—◌◌—

JESSIE WOKE UP at six, as always, without any help from an alarm clock. She felt good. Alert, strong, well-rested. She'd thought about her plan, looked at it from every possible angle, tried to imagine where it could go wrong. She'd slept on it, and now that she was awake, she believed it was still a good plan.

She went to the front window, looked down to the street, and saw no white Ford Focus parked in front. She felt a pang of disappointment. Now that it had started, she wanted to keep it moving.

He'd be back.

She made a pot of coffee, ate a muffin, had a glass of orange juice, poured a mug of coffee.

Then she went back to the front window and looked down at the street. She smiled.

He'd exchanged the white Ford Focus for a shiny new blue Toyota Camry. He was sitting there across the street with his window rolled down and his elbow on the ledge, sipping from a Styrofoam cup and pretending to read the newspaper that was propped against the steering wheel. Same sandy hair, same bland, forgettable face, same wraparound sunglasses.

Okay, good, thought Jessie. *Today's the day*.

She packed her daypack and got dressed—khaki walking shorts, black T-shirt, hiking boots.

At seven-thirty she filled her travel mug with coffee, slipped on her sunglasses, pulled on her Oakland A's cap, slung her daypack over her shoulder, and left her apartment.

When she emerged onto the sidewalk, she darted her eyes behind her sunglasses at the man in the Camry. He was casually turning a page of his newspaper. He gave no sign that he'd noticed her.

Jessie strolled down the sidewalk to where she'd left her Civic. She stopped a few times to say good morning to some neighbors, pet their leashed dogs, agree that it was indeed another beautiful day in California.

Just a carefree young woman on a Saturday morning, off for a hike but in no hurry. Lived in the neighborhood. Carol Ann Chang was her name.

She got into her car and headed down 24th Street.

In the mirror she saw the blue Camry following along. He had, of course, scouted out the area and located the place where she'd left her car overnight.

He stayed about half a block behind her all the way through the city to the Golden Gate Bridge.

The Saturday-morning traffic on the bridge was light. He kept four or five cars between them. A few times she lost him in her rearview mirror, but then she spotted him again.

She turned on her directional signal a quarter of a mile before the Stinson Beach exit. She wanted to be sure he knew what she was doing. A moment later, his directional began flashing.

She followed the winding road into the parking lot at Muir Woods. At quarter past eight on a Saturday morning, the lot was already filling up.

Jessie got out, slipped her daypack onto her shoulders, sauntered over to the building where she paid her three-dollar visitor's fee, and then lingered there until the blue Camry pulled into the lot.

The guy in the wraparound sunglasses got out and stretched his arms, looking around casually, letting his eyes slide right past her. He was wearing sneakers, blue jeans, and a lightweight blue windbreaker zipped halfway up over a plaid shirt. Jessie noticed the slight bulge over his left hip at his waist, though she doubted anybody else would.

She waited for him to pay his fee, then began strolling along one of the well-worn pathways into the ancient woods, and despite her jittery, nerved-up mood, she was, as always, awed by the grandness of the ancient redwoods and the vast stillness of the forest. Some of the trees were a thousand years old and reached 250 feet into the sky. The understory, perpetually shaded by the high canopy of foliage, was sparsely vegetated—mostly moss and ferns and a scattering of shrubs, and some old fallen trees silently rotting away beside their big stumps.

There was no chitter of birdsong, no buzz of insects. Just that awesome shady silence.

There weren't many other people on the trails yet. Now and then Jessie spotted somebody or heard the echo of laughter or voices. She walked slowly, pausing often to look up into a tree or to bend to examine a fern or a wildflower or a mushroom, watching out of the corner of her eye to make sure the man in the windbreaker hadn't lost her.

He was there, fifty feet or so behind her, keeping pace, as slow and as casual as she, biding his time, waiting for the right time and place to make his move.

Whenever the opportunity came along, Jessie chose the less-traveled trail, and after half an hour, the voices and the laughter faded and she was certain that the two of them were quite alone.

She figured he was having the same thought and had started looking for his opportunity.

Pretty soon she found what she was looking for—a narrow, little-used trail that angled away from the main pathway and twisted steeply up to a ridge. Here the trees were sparser and not so tall, and the undergrowth was thicker. Head-high evergreens and thick shrubbery crowded against the edges of the trail.

Jessie climbed the path to the ridgeline, then stopped and listened.

She couldn't see him, but she could hear him coming along behind her. The bushes scratched against his nylon windbreaker and his sneakers scraped against the roots and fallen leaves in the trail. He was moving purposefully now. He was no longer maintaining his distance from her, no longer pretending to be just another hiker admiring the redwoods.

Now he was trying to catch up with her.

How would he do it? When he got to where she could see him, would he call to her and wave and grin sheepishly and tell her he thought he might be lost? Would he suddenly cry out and pretend he'd sprained his ankle?

She didn't figure he was stupid enough to think he could sneak up behind her.

However he intended to play it, when he felt he was close enough, he would simply pull out his weapon—she guessed it would be a .22 automatic with a suppressor—and shoot her three or four times in the chest. When she went down, he'd shoot her once more in the head.

He wouldn't say anything. He'd just smile, point his gun at her, and shoot her.

When you fired a .22 handgun with a suppressor, it sounded like a rubber band snapping against the palm of your hand. A sound the woods would absorb.

. He'd make sure she was dead, he'd tuck his gun into his belt under the windbreaker, and he'd retrieve the ejected cartridge cases. Then he'd follow the trails back to his rented blue Camry in the parking lot. He'd head directly to the airport, making one call on his cell phone along the way. He'd disassemble his gun and throw the parts into different Dumpsters along the way. He'd turn in his car, buy a plane ticket with cash, and fly home, wherever that was.

Jessie had a different plan.

She lingered at the ridgeline until she glimpsed the guy coming up the trail behind her. When she was pretty sure he'd spotted her, she started down the other side of the ridge where the trail began to descend, then slipped off the trail into a thick stand of young evergreens. Paralleling the trail, she crept silently back up the slope to the crest of the ridge where the trail curved sharply around a boulder the size of a Volkswagen.

Jessie crouched on the uphill side if the boulder right next to the path and listened. He was coming fast now. He'd lost sight of her, and she sensed panic in his movement. He'd be scanning the trail far ahead of him, trying to glimpse her, to get her back in his sights.

She took off her daypack, then removed her cap and her sunglasses and put them into the pack. She snapped on a pair of latex gloves. She set the pack on the ground behind her where it wouldn't get in the way.

He was close. On the downhill side of the big boulder. In a minute he'd walk right past her. She could hear him panting. He was out of shape, sweating probably, stumbling against the roots in the trail, moving awkwardly.

Excellent.

Suddenly he was standing right beside her, pausing to look around and catch his breath, so close she could reach out and touch him.

He was taking deep breaths and peering down the twisting trail ahead of him. He wiped his wrist across his forehead—and that's when Jessie made her move. One quick step and she was behind him. Her left forearm levered against his throat under his chin and snapped his head back. A cry died in his chest. He gagged and clawed at the arm that had closed off his windpipe. She increased the pressure and dragged him backward away from the path into the underbrush.

All of Jessie's weight was focused on her bone-hard forearm wedged against his throat. He was gasping for air. Tiny strangulated cries gurgled and died in his chest.

Without decreasing the pressure on his throat with her left forearm, Jessie curled her right arm around his body to where she'd seen the lump under his jacket. She traced the outline of the bulge with her fingers. It was, as she'd thought, a square handgun, an automatic.

The gun was the confirmation she needed before she did what had to be done.

After a minute, the man went limp in her arms. Jessie let him slump to the ground. She straddled his chest and moved both hands along the sides of his neck until she found the soft places behind the hinges of his jawbones just under each ear. She dug her fingers into the thin layers of skin and muscle and drove them hard against the carotid arteries. She could feel the vessels pulsing rhythmically, pumping blood into the man's brain.

She pushed hard, focusing all of her strength on her fingers, compressing both arteries, shutting them down. Unless you constricted both carotids at the same time, you wouldn't do much harm.

Constrict them both, and you could do lethal damage.

She felt the man's blood vessels balloon and flutter under her fingers as his heart fought against the blockaded arteries, tried to force blood through to the brain.

After about two minutes, he let out a little sigh and went still.

She moved so that she was kneeling beside the man and looked down at him.

He lay there on his back. His eyes were half-lidded and unfocused, staring blankly up at the California sky. His mouth hung open, and foamy mucous dribbled over his chin. His skin was pale and shone with sweat.

Jessie picked up his wrist and found his pulse. It was racing, erratic, panicky. He was not dead. Not quite.

She let his arm fall to the ground.

If a heart attack didn't follow the stroke, and if medical help came soon enough, the man's life might be saved, although the stroke would probably leave him paralyzed, brain damaged, speechless, vegetative. Jessie was no doctor, but her training had been thorough.

She sat back on her heels and hugged herself, and then she felt the sobs rising in her chest, the tears welling behind her eyes, her stomach clenching. She shut her eyes tight and forced herself to breathe slowly.

After a few minutes, the horror at what she'd done, the regret, the sadness, the overpowering sense that she was living in a sorrowful place and time—all those feelings passed. No matter how civilized the world might appear, the fittest always survived. Kill or be killed. No mercy.

She'd had no choice. It was done.

Jessie reached inside the man's windbreaker and pulled out the pistol that he'd tucked into his belt in front of his left hip. It was, as she'd expected, a .22 automatic with a long suppressor screwed onto the end of the barrel. A professional killer's weapon.

She retrieved her daypack and shoved the automatic into it.

She found the man's sunglasses in the path where they'd fallen. She picked them up with a stick and dropped them onto the ground beside him where he now lay, twelve or fifteen feet off to the side of the path, half hidden in the underbrush.

She knelt beside him to search him thoroughly.

She fished his wallet out of his hip pocket. The name on his driver's license was Leonard P. Lesneski, from Richmond, Virginia. She didn't bother counting his money. A couple hundred dollars, it looked like.

Stuck in with the bills was a plastic magnetized key card. For his hotel room, Jessie assumed.

She put the wallet, with all its contents, back into the man's hip pocket.

Then she went through his other pockets. His cell phone was in one pants pocket. Jessie left it there. In the other pants pocket was a ring of keys and, separate from the key ring, another key with a plastic tag attached to it. This would be for the rental car. Jessie kept the car key and put all the other stuff back into his pocket.

She finally found what she was looking for tucked in his shirt pocket. She didn't know exactly what it would be—an old photograph, perhaps, or a printout of descriptions and directions, or at least an index card with her address on it.

It turned out to be a photocopy of that damn newspaper clipping with the picture of her at the clinic.

Finding the photo in his pocket assured Jessie that she had killed the right man. She wouldn't have lost too much sleep if he hadn't had her picture in his pocket. The .22 automatic was good enough. But it was better this way.

She sat on the ground beside the man and thought it through.

They'd find Leonard Lesneski—his damaged or dead body— eventually, of course. Maybe this morning, maybe not for a few days. A middle-aged man, not in the best of shape. They'd ID him by what they found in his wallet. He'd been climbing a steep side trail when the clot smashed into his brain. He'd staggered and stumbled off the path and crashed into the bushes.

Poor guy. Bad luck to have his stroke all alone in a remote corner of Muir Woods National Monument on a pretty Saturday morning in May.

They'd link the rented blue Camry to him without too much trouble—it would be the only car left in the lot after closing time that evening.

She doubted if they'd figure out that poor Mr. Lesneski's stroke had not been spontaneous. But if they did, if some sharp-eyed coroner noticed bruising on the sides of the anonymous man's neck, and if the autopsy report speculated that he had been assaulted by somebody proficient in the deadly arts, the case would frustrate the investigators and soon find its way to the bottom of the pile. No suspects, no clues, no witnesses, no crime-scene evidence. Jessie had made certain of all that.

If life were a television show, they'd relentlessly track her down.

But this was the real world. Jessie Church knew how things worked in the real world.

Whether the man lived or died—either way was okay with Jessie—it would take a while for the information to filter back to Howie Cohen in his cell in F.C.I. Cumberland.

Cohen, of course, would understand exactly what had happened to Leonard P. Lesneski. Howie Cohen knew what Jessie Church was capable of.

She'd bought herself some time. That was all.

She stood up, peeled off her gloves and stuffed them into her daypack, put on her sunglasses and green baseball cap, and hunched the pack onto her shoulders. She paused to survey the area with her cop's eye. There were no anomalies. Whoever eventually spotted the man in the bushes would trample the path and the grass and the bushes and destroy any trace of Jessie Church before the police decided to consider it a crime scene, if they ever did.

Jessie turned and headed back through the silent woods to the parking lot. She passed a few hikers along the way, exchanged smiles, said, "Nice day for it." Just another Saturday hiker.

As she'd expected, the parking lot was packed with vehicles when she got back to it. On a perfect California Saturday in May, Muir Woods National Monument, just fourteen miles north of San Francisco, was always mobbed.

The lot was full of cars but empty of people. Those who had arrived early enough to park here were already hiking in the woods. It was still too early in the morning for them to begin returning to their cars.

Those who arrived after this lot was full would have to park in one of the satellite lots.

So there was nobody around to see the young woman with the sunglasses and the cap pulled low over her face and the daypack on her shoulders unlock the blue Camry, look into the front and back and under the seats, then pop the trunk and remove the small carry-on-sized suitcase, the leather briefcase, the laptop computer, and the camera case. There was nobody to notice that she left the key in the ignition before she shut the doors, or to see her carry the suitcase and the briefcase and the laptop and the camera case to the undistinguished gray Honda Civic on the other side of the lot.

Jessie Church had no illusions. As far as the police were concerned, she figured she'd gotten away with murder.

But Howie Cohen would know.

Simone sat in her wheelchair watching the evening shadows spread over the meadow and seep into the valley outside the porch windows. Her hands wrestled with each other in her lap. The tremors were bad today.

Jill was standing behind her, brushing Simone's long hair in soothing, rhythmic strokes, and one of Jill's soft, tinkling New Age CDs was playing over the speakers. Jill was humming along with the music.

Dr. Mattes had not tried to soothe her. Simone had made it clear to him long ago that she had powerful intuitions and that she would always know if he dissembled or equivocated or tried to hide or distort any speck of truth from her.

So he told her the truth.

"Your disease is progressing, Simone," he said after he'd finished examining her a few hours earlier. "Pretty much as we've expected.

The spasticity in your legs and arms. The tremors. The sensitivity to heat. The sudden dark moods. The moments of confusion. They're getting intense, and more frequent and more frightening, aren't they?"

Simone had nodded.

"I'll leave some prescriptions with Jill," he said. "They will help with your symptoms. But . . ." And then the dear man had shrugged and smiled and left the thought unspoken.

Simone knew the rest of it without being told. She would become increasingly confused. She'd begin to lose her memories. Gradually but inexorably her body would betray her and she'd descend into a nightmare of dark, disconnected thoughts and wild random images.

Soon she'd become too much for Jill to care for, and inevitably . . .

Well, that was her fate.

Eleven years ago, when the double vision had started, Dr. Mattes had delivered his awful diagnosis. Primary progressive multiple sclerosis. The disease would develop steadily, he told her, with few remissions. There was no way to predict how rapidly it would consume her body, but there was no cure, no miracle, no escaping her fate.

The onset of this particularly acute form of the disease, he'd told her, typically first appeared in people over forty. Simone believed that she'd not yet had her fortieth birthday back then eleven years ago. But maybe she was older than she thought. Maybe fate had sent this disease as a clue that might help her piece together her childhood, to trace her life back to her birth.

Impossible. She couldn't be that old. That didn't match her memory. Besides, her skin was still smooth, her face unwrinkled. There was not a single strand of gray in her glossy black hair. She knew without ego or narcissism that she was still the beautiful, mysterious, fascinating Simone who made the movies and became the cult star and then suddenly retreated into permanent reclusion.

Simone reached a hand up to her shoulder. Jill stopped brushing and gripped it.

"Are you all right?" said Simone.

"You know I'm sad," said Jill.

"Are you crying?"

"Yes. I'm sorry. Please don't try to give me courage."

"I wish I had extra courage to give," said Simone.

As she had requested candor from Dr. Mattes, so also had Simone demanded of Jill that she always be truthful and straightforward.

When Jill had first come to live here in their retreat in the Catskills, the young nurse had been a passionate lover. As Simone's disease had progressed, their love had deepened, but their lovemaking had diminished, until now all that was left were gentle kisses, soft caresses, heartfelt conversations, and comfortable silences.

Sometimes Simone wanted to ask Jill why she didn't find a more satisfying lover. She was young and fiery. How could she be satisfied with bathing and cooking for an invalid?

But Simone knew the answer. Jill loved her. She didn't have any choice. That was her fate.

"I have decided it is time to call Ted Austin," said Simone.

Without letting go of Simone's hand, Jill moved around to the front of the wheelchair. She knelt beside it, took Simone's other hand and held them both in hers. She looked up into Simone's eyes. "Are you sure you want to do this?" she said.

Simone felt her eyes brimming again. It was happening with increasing frequency lately. Sudden, uncontrollable, unprovoked weeping, of course, was a symptom of her disease's progression, as Dr. Mattes had explained.

"I had hoped," said Simone, "that I would hear from May. I had hoped to persuade her to come here and spend time with us so I could tell her our story, face to face. That would have fulfilled my obligation." She paused. "It has been a month. If she was going to respond to my note, she would have done it by now."

"Maybe Carol Ann Chang isn't your May," said Jill.

"She is," said Simone. "I am certain of it."

"Making a book of your life will be painful for you."

"Yes," said Simone. "But it is my legacy. I must do it now, or it will be too late."

⁓

ON HER WAY home from Muir Woods, Jessie took the exit to Sausalito. She drove to the houseboat village, parked her car, and retrieved Leonard P. Lesneski's .22 automatic from her daypack. She quickly disassembled it, shoved the parts into her pockets, then got out of her car and began to saunter casually around the piers and boardwalks.

Here and there she slipped a part of the gun from a pocket and dropped it into the water.

Then she drove to Oakland, stopped at a Salvation Army deposit bin, and threw all the clothes from Lesneski's suitcase into it.

She opened his briefcase. The notebook she'd seen him writing in was there. There were some names and phone numbers that might be worth checking. Jessie stuck the notebook into her glove compartment. She emptied the rest of the briefcase into a Dumpster behind a seafood restaurant.

The empty briefcase went into another Dumpster. The suitcase into a different one.

She decided to hang onto the camera—it was a Nikon, a really nice camera—and the Apple laptop, at least for now. She wanted to see what information she could get from them, and anyway, she could always use good equipment.

⁓

JESSIE WAS BACK outside Anthony Moreno's bungalow at seven the next morning with her long-lensed Canon and her video camera and her notebook on the seat beside her.

It was another long day under a hot sun, but Jessie was grateful for the boring routine. It gave her time to refine her plan.

When she got home that evening, she made herself a gin-and-tonic, opened up her laptop, took out her notebook, and wrote up her weekly surveillance report.

Then she took the envelope from her desk drawer where she'd stuck it when she'd received it a few weeks earlier. At the time, she hadn't given it much thought. After the disaster at the clinic and all the ensuing publicity, Jessie had received dozens of letters, mostly from men who claimed to be handsome and wealthy, swearing they wanted to marry her.

Well, this note was a little different. It was handwritten in green ink. The penmanship was unquestionably feminine, elegant but slightly tremorous, as if it had been written by an old woman. The postmark was from Beaverkill, New York.

Jessie slid the note from the envelope and read it again.

"My Dear Ms. Chang," it said. "I have reason to believe that you are my daughter by birth, and that your real name is Jessie Church. I would like to verify this. I beseech you to respond. I enclose my address and telephone number. I anxiously await your reply. Sincerely yours, S. Bonet."

Well, nothing personal, but Jessie really didn't care. She'd always known she was adopted. She'd never had any interest in tracking down her birth parents. In fact, given the choice of knowing who they were or not knowing, she'd opt for not knowing. She'd done fine so far, not knowing. Anyway, her life was too complicated as it was.

On the other hand, she'd checked this S. Bonet's address in her Atlas and found that Beaverkill, New York, was a tiny town in a lightly populated mountainous area north of New York City.

A long way from San Francisco, and maybe far enough from Howie Cohen.

—◦◦—

SHE GAVE DEL her weekly report at their regular Monday morning meeting.

He read it, then looked up at her. "So you think this Moreno's legit, huh?"

"I'm sure he didn't make me," said Jessie, "if that's what you're asking. He behaves exactly like a man with a serious back problem who's having a lot of discomfort and should not be driving a bus."

"They signed us up for two weeks."

She shrugged. "Get somebody else. I've had it."

"Give it one more week," he said. "Come on."

Jessie shook her head. "I need a break, Del. I'm going to take some vacation time. Anybody can do a stakeout."

"If I refused, you'd threaten to quit, right?"

She grinned. "Absolutely. And if you still said no, I *would* quit."

"Well," said Del, "fine. Whatever. I guess you've earned it. Got any plans?"

Jessie shook her head. "Probably just turn off the telephone, hang around the house, sleep late, lay out on the beach, a day at a spa, maybe drive down to L.A. or San Diego, visit some friends. I just need to relax."

"How long will you be gone?"

"I don't know."

"You better come back, Jessie," he said. "I need you."

"Sure," she said. "I'll be back."

She hated lying to Del. But what he didn't know he couldn't tell anybody else.

After leaving the office, Jessie made the rounds of her banks. She had spread her money among several modest-sized accounts, all in different banks scattered around the city, all in the name of Carol

Ann Chang. It was a precaution from her undercover days when it was quite literally a matter of life and death that mysterious deposits and withdrawals should not call attention to themselves.

When she was finished, she'd withdrawn a little over eighteen thousand dollars in cash from five different checking and savings accounts, leaving enough in the checking accounts to pay her bills, and enough in all of them to keep the accounts open.

Back home, she wrote checks for all of her bills, including the rent, even though it wasn't due for another three weeks, and she paid the entire balances of her two credit cards.

She figured that would give her at least two months before some computer flashed a red flag on her telephone or electricity account, or her landlord tried to get hold of her, or debt-collectors started checking and figured out that Carol Ann Chang was no longer living at 4175 24th Street in Noe Valley in San Francisco.

By then she'd be long gone and, she hoped, hard to find.

～ை～

TED AUSTIN CAME out from behind his desk with his hand extended. "Mac," he said. "Good to see you."

Mac Cassidy grasped Austin's hand. "You too," he said. "It's been a while."

"How're you doing?"

"Okay." Mac shook his head. "It's been hard."

"And your girl? Katie? How's she bearing up?"

Mac shrugged. "I worry about her. She doesn't say much." He forced a smile. "We're getting there. It takes time."

Austin released Mac's hand. "You didn't have to wear a necktie on my account, you know."

Mac shrugged. "I almost forgot how to tie it, to tell you the truth. I'm not much of a necktie guy, as you know." The full truth was that Mac Cassidy had avoided occasions that required him to wear a tie since Jane's funeral a little over a year ago.

"I like the beard," said Ted. "The Hemingway look, eh?"

Mac touched his face. "The gray, you mean."

Austin smiled. "It gives you character."

"Anyway," said Mac. "Congratulations. You got Simone. Quite a coup."

Austin nodded. "I've been hounding her for years."

"So why'd she agree now?"

"Dunno. But I can tell you this. Suddenly it's urgent. She wants to get it done right away." Austin slapped Mac's shoulder. "You up for it?"

"Yes," said Mac. "I think so."

Austin arched an eyebrow.

Mac nodded. "I'm up for it."

"Good. What about coffee?"

"Sure. Please."

Austin waved his hand toward the sofa in the corner of his office. "Grab a seat. I'll be right with you."

The walls of Austin's comfortable Manhattan office were covered with framed book jackets—the big sellers, the prizewinners, the books that became films—several dozen of them, but still, Mac knew, just a fraction of the books that Ted had midwifed for his authors.

Ted Austin was one of New York's big-time literary agents. Publishers respected him and authors trusted him. Mac knew he was lucky to have Ted representing him.

The covers of all seven of Mac Cassidy's ghost-written auto-biographies hung on the agent's office wall. His first had been the Jackie Gleason story, which the egotistical funnyman had reluc-tantly allowed them to call *And Away We Go*, an unintentionally ironic title, as Gleason had died shortly after the book came out. Mac Cassidy's name had appeared nowhere in that one, not even in Gleason's acknowledgment page—which Mac had also written. Jackie had taken full credit, but the industry knew that every word had been penned by Cassidy, and after *Away*'s sixteen weeks on the

Times bestseller list, boosted, no doubt, by the news of Gleason's well-timed death, Mac and Ted Austin had found themselves in the enviable position of picking and choosing their projects.

They'd turned down Brando because he balked at the "with Mac Cassidy" credit that Austin demanded, and they'd been unable to reach an agreement with the elusive Hepburn. Mac and Austin could now laugh at their decision not to go after Lee Iacocca when they'd heard he was in the market for a ghost.

There were six after Gleason. Sports figures Julius Irving (*Doctor J*) and Lee Trevino (*Swinging from the Hip*); political luminaries Bob Dole (*A Life to Give*) and Barbara Bush (*Mrs. President*); entertainment personalities Bruce Springsteen (*The Boss*) and Jay Leno (*Cracking Wise*).

In the process of researching the books, Mac Cassidy had interviewed hundreds—make that thousands—of people. He'd always done it honestly and with class, and he'd made a lot of friends, earned a lot of trust.

So now it would be Simone, the Garboesque woman known to the world by that single name, the reclusive millionaire—or maybe she was broke, no one was quite sure—the former film beauty, the mysterious cult icon. Simone had once been the envy of every middle-aged American woman and the wet dream of every red-blooded American male, the source of periodic speculation in the supermarket tabloids. Simone's sexual partners? Simone's wealth? Simone's origins? Simone's age?

Since Mac had received Ted Austin's call three days earlier telling him about the Simone project, he'd prowled the Internet and looted the library, consuming every word he could find about her.

Simone always had been an enigma, from her first memorable role as a Mafia don's traitorous Eurasian concubine in the otherwise forgettable 1986 film *This Side of Daybreak*. After that there had been a film or two every year for twelve years.

And then, without explanation, she had walked away from it, away from the public life. She had, effectively, disappeared. No explanation. No forwarding address. No more photo shoots or public appearances. She just quit.

Which, of course, only enhanced her mystery.

Simone, as it turned out, had never appeared in a critical hit or a box-office smash. She'd never played opposite Redford or Newman or De Niro or Harrison Ford. Mostly she'd played supporting roles, not leads. If she were a man, she'd have been called a "character actor." In truth, she'd never been cast in a complex role or played against type, never been nominated for an Oscar or a Golden Globe.

She had been, simply, one of those actresses who always seemed to just play her own fascinating self: elusive and manipulative, desirable and unattainable, mysterious and seductive and utterly, incredibly beautiful.

For those twelve years of cult stardom, she'd allowed herself to be photographed for the fashion and entertainment magazines. She'd even endorsed a shampoo. But never had she sat for a personal interview. When she allowed herself to be quoted about a film, or a role, or the talents of her director, or the foibles of her fellow actors, she'd been unfailingly bland and uncontroversial. She never said anything critical or nasty, and so she got the reputation for being a poor interview.

Her blandness, Mac surmised, was calculated to keep the hard questions away. She'd consistently refused to discuss her past or her private life. The only Simone quotes on the subject he'd been able to find were, "I don't talk about that," or, "You know better than to ask that question."

Which, of course just sparked new speculation.

Now, after over twenty years of mystery, Simone would speak. She would speak to Mac Cassidy.

He felt a hand on his elbow.

"Here's your coffee," said Austin.

"Oh, thanks." Mac accepted the mug.

The two men sat across from each other.

"She's got MS," said Austin.

"Simone?"

He nodded.

"That's why she quit making movies?" said Mac. "That's why she's become a recluse?"

"Apparently."

"Is she prepared to talk about her disease?" said Mac. He smelled a hook for the book. Simone could do for multiple sclerosis awareness what Mike Fox had been doing for Parkinson's.

"She says she's prepared to talk about everything," said Austin. "But I sense some skittishness. She'll need some hand-holding."

"That will be my pleasure," said Mac with a grin. "She's a gorgeous woman."

Austin nodded but did not smile. "You know, Mac," he said, "it's not too early to begin thinking about our next project."

"Assuming I do a good job on this one," said Mac.

"Assuming you do a *great* job. Which I'm confident you will."

Mac shrugged. "I haven't honestly given future projects much thought." He waved his hand in the air. "There are a lot of things I should've been doing lately that I haven't thought about."

"Understandable," said Austin. "I've had a few conversations, but frankly, with you, um . . ."

"Out of commission," said Mac.

"Yes. All right. With you out of commission, I was reluctant to pursue anything."

"First things first," said Mac.

"Well, yes," said Austin. "First Simone." The agent sat back in his chair. "I know it's been a tough year for you, my friend."

Mac nodded. It had been a very tough year.

He kept returning to the railroad tracks in Concord, less than a mile from their suburban Massachusetts home, where Jane had been walking that foggy March evening a little over a year ago. He'd sit there near where they said it had happened, trying to understand.

He kept seeing the face of the cop at the door, how he'd refused to meet Mac's eyes, how he mumbled, "Um, are you Mr. Cassidy?"

And Mac just nodding, knowing instantly that something terrible had happened, barely hearing the cop's words: "The seven o'clock commuter train from Boston . . . where the tracks curve, down there along the river . . . couldn't stop in time." Trying to imagine what she had been thinking and feeling at the moment when the train suddenly was upon her. Trying to understand why she was there on that moonless March night standing on the tracks. Endlessly replaying their last moments together, their mundane argument, their hurtful parting words.

Trying not to think the obvious.

They'd called it an accident. Mac wanted to believe that's what it had been. A tragic, senseless accident. That was infinitely preferable to the alternative.

"Local Woman Killed in Train Accident." Headline in the local paper. The investigation had absolved the conductor. The local woman, Jane Cassidy of Chester Street, had apparently wandered onto the tracks, perhaps disoriented by the fog.

Nobody's fault, they said.

Suicide. The obvious thought. The thought that he tried not to think. The thought that he thought all the time.

A tough year, indeed.

Guilt, anger, shame, loss, bewilderment. And the other feelings, the harder ones to acknowledge. Relief. Release. The feelings that circled back to the guilt.

And there was Katie, the fifteen-year-old child-woman who refused to talk about her mother, refused to go to therapy, refused to cry, who cooked and vacuumed and washed and ironed and got A's in her classes and had taken a sudden liking to classical music.

Katie, whose simple announcement that fateful day—"Me and Laurie are heading for the mall. I'll get something to eat there."—had set it off.

"No," Jane had said. "No, you're not."

"Why not?"

"I don't need to give you a reason," Jane said.

Katie turned to Mac with that smile he couldn't resist. "Daddy? Please?"

"Is your homework all done?"

"Well, yeah. Sure."

"I made dinner," said Jane, "and now, Goddamn it, we're going to eat it. For once we're going to sit down together like a normal family."

Mac, trying to lighten it up: "Nowadays it's not normal for families to sit down together."

"She is not going anywhere," said Jane. "Do you always have to take her side?"

"I wasn't taking—"

And Jane suddenly standing up, her chair toppling backward, tears bursting from her eyes, saying, "I don't care. You can do whatever you want. The hell with you, both of you." Grabbing her jacket and striding out of the house, the door slamming behind her.

An hour later she was dead.

Katie blamed herself.

Mac blamed himself.

And they blamed each other, too.

Mac looked at Austin and shrugged. "Yeah, it's been a little rough."

"You understand," said Austin, "it's going to be tight. Beckman wants the book by the end of November. They want it to be the lead title in their spring catalog. We're working up the contract. You won't be disappointed. I don't want to wait 'til it's signed. I'll front you the advance. I want you to get started right away."

"I can do that," said Mac. "It's really up to Simone. We'll see what she's got in mind for her book."

Austin sat forward and tapped Mac's knee. "It's not *her* book, Mac. It's *our* book. No. Think of it this way. Think of it as Beckman's book."

"Don't treat me like a novice, Ted," said Mac quietly.

"I'm sorry. It's just . . . well, you know Beckman. He wants the dirt, the glitz, the gossip, and I'm pretty sure that's not exactly what Simone has in mind. But, hell, she spent twelve years in Hollywood. She's got to have stories. And how'd she get there from Paris, for God's sake? That's a story right there. And why'd she quit? People want to know that stuff." Austin shook his head. "I'm sorry, Mac. You're a pro. You know what sells books as well as I do."

"I do," said Mac. "I'll get it."

"Not just what she wants to tell you. She's got to give you some juice, too. The mystery of Simone. Where she came from, how she got to where she is, who she fucked along the way. And who fucked her, literally as well as figuratively. Her tragic childhood, her abusive parents, whatever."

"The juice," said Mac.

"Yeah. Absolutely. Get the juice."

Mac smiled. "Trust me."

"Oh, I trust you," said Austin. "It's just that . . ."

"I understand," said Mac. "People are wondering. They wonder if I've lost it. You're probably wondering yourself. Hard to blame you."

"I wasn't thinking that," said Austin.

"Well," said Mac, "don't worry. I haven't lost it. Go get that giant contract done."

Austin smiled. "Good. I've got faith in you. Give Simone some of that old charm. Get her to tell you stories. That's all we need here. A few good juicy stories."

Mac nodded. "I'll do my best."

"Your best," said Austin, "has always been awfully damned good."

Mac noticed Austin's choice of verb tense. "Has always been" was not quite the same as "is." A writer, he knew, was only as good as his next book.

—⟨•⟩—

EDDIE MORAN NOTICED a bulge in the pocket of the jacket when he started to put it on. He remembered the last time he'd worn it. It was the night he'd found Bunny in her motel room in Georgia.

He emptied the pocket on his desk. There were balled-up bills, ones and fives. There were a couple of debit cards, an ATM card, and a bunch of ATM receipts. Jake in New York had traced Bunny from Key Largo in the Florida Keys to Davis, Georgia by her ATM visits.

One scrap of paper was a green post-office certified-mail receipt. The name Simone Bonet and the address, a post-office box in Beaverkill, New York, were hand-printed on it in ink. They meant nothing to Eddie Moran.

He smoothed out the bills and tucked them in his wallet. He cut the debit and the ATM cards in half and dropped the pieces into his waste basket. He ripped up the receipts and tossed them, too, and he started to throw away the green post-office receipt when he found himself pronouncing the name written on it. Simone Bonet. Simone.

He remembered Bunny, her eyes wide, her face red, gasping the word, "Seymour."

Out loud, Eddie Moran said, "Seymour. *Simone.*"

It took Mac Cassidy a little over four hours to drive from his house on the north side of Concord, Massachusetts, to Simone Bonet's rambling old farmhouse in the rolling Catskill foothills of Beaverkill, New York. You couldn't see her house from the winding country road, and he drove past the unmarked driveway the first time before he figured he'd gone too far and rechecked the directions she'd given him on the telephone.

She'd had a shy telephone voice, softer than he'd expected, with the hint of an accent he couldn't quite place and the formal diction of someone whose native language wasn't English, and he had to listen hard to hear what she was saying—which, he thought, might have been her intent.

He'd rented the only two of her films he'd been able to find. Her voice had been stronger in the films, but the accent and the diction were the same. Cassidy guessed that her disease had weakened her and affected her voice. Even so, hearing her on the telephone had quickened Cassidy's pulse. It was the sexiest voice he'd heard in a long time.

For the past year—since Jane—he had resisted even thinking about women. The idea of sexual intimacy caused bile to rise in his throat. It literally made him sick. He understood this was some kind of guilt mechanism, but that didn't help him deal with it.

He'd felt it when Simone spoke to him on the telephone, the sudden clenching sensation in his stomach, the need to swallow repeatedly, and he'd felt it all over again watching her on film.

Objectively, Simone had been, well, an adequate actress. In both films she'd played the third corner of love triangles, the mysterious temptress with shady connections. Standard roles without much nuance. The films were trite, and she didn't actually do much or say much in them.

But you couldn't take your eyes off her.

The dirt driveway to Simone's house wound downhill through a mixture of second-growth birches, oaks, and pines. A tumbledown stone wall paralleled one side, and here and there the woods opened into overgrown meadows and rocky old pastures. Cassidy surmised that this had once been farmland.

After nearly a quarter of a mile the terrain opened up and flattened out, and her house appeared, perched on a plateau. Beyond it, the land resumed sloping down to a distant valley, and on the other side of the valley there were more hills, all painted in the pink and yellow and lime-green pastels of spring. It was a gorgeous setting. Except for a white church spire rising above the treetops in the valley, there wasn't another sign of human habitation in sight. It was pretty much what he'd expected. Simone's reclusiveness had become the last element in her legend.

He parked beside a big old Jeep Wagoneer in the gravel turnaround in front, grabbed his briefcase from the backseat, and went to the door.

There was no bell or knocker. He hesitated, then rapped with his knuckles.

A young woman opened it almost immediately. He guessed she had been watching him from the window.

"You must be Mr. Cassidy," she said. She held out her hand. "I'm Jill Rossiter. Simone's nurse."

He took her hand. "I'm Mac," he said. "Please don't call me Mister. It makes me feel old."

Jill smiled. She was tall and lanky, blonde and quite beautiful. She wore a white T-shirt with a picture of a sunflower on it, snug-fitting blue jeans, and sneakers. "Mac it is, then," she said. "Come on in. Simone's out on the deck enjoying the sunshine. She's been looking forward to meeting you."

He followed her through an open living area. The inside of the house had the bones of an old New England farmhouse, but it had been completely remodeled. There were big exposed beams and wide-plank floors and lots of glass. The furnishings were leather and stainless steel and maple, with earth-tone area rugs, and the walls were hung with an eclectic collection of primitive oils and pastoral watercolors and black-and-white photographs.

The back of the house was a big sunporch, with slate floors, glass walls, and skylights. Jill led him across the porch, out through double glass doors, down a short ramp, and onto a wooden deck. Simone was sitting in a wheelchair facing the valley and the distant hills. Jill touched her shoulder and said, "Simone, Mr. Cassidy is here."

Simone twitched, and Mac figured she'd been either day dreaming or sleeping.

He knew she was ill, knew she was wheelchair-bound, but even so, he was shocked at how small and frail and tired she appeared. In her films, Simone had simmered with life and strength and sexual energy.

He moved around so that he was facing her and said, "Hello, Simone."

She looked up at him. She seemed to study his face for a moment before she smiled and said, "Hello, Mac Cassidy. I am happy to meet you. Ted Austin speaks very highly of you." She turned her head and looked back over her shoulder. "Jill, dear, please bring Mac some coffee. We are going to get started right now before I become tired again."

Jill, standing behind Simone, caught Mac's eye and gave him a quick nod.

"Coffee would be great," he said. "Black, please."

Jill smiled, turned, and went back into the house.

Mac pulled a wooden Adirondack chair around and sat in front of Simone. "I'm very enthusiastic about this," he said. "Everybody's thrilled that you've agreed to do it."

"It is something I feel I need to do," she said softly. "But I am apprehensive. I have changed my mind a dozen times since I called Ted."

He nodded. "I understand."

"Tell me about you, Mac Cassidy."

"Me?"

"If I am to confide in you," she said, "if I am to tell you all of my secrets, I need to know some of yours."

He flapped a hand. "I'm not important."

"To me you are," she said.

"Well, okay," he said. "I've ghostwritten quite a few books. I began as a newspaper reporter many years ago, wrote a couple of long profiles that—"

"Ted vouched for your credentials," she said. "I want to know what moves you, what frightens you, what you love."

"I love my daughter," he said before he could stop himself. "I . . . I love my wife."

Simone's hand reached toward him and settled lightly on his knee. "There is a sadness in you," she said. "I sensed it the moment you stepped into the room."

"My wife—Jane—she died a little more than a year ago. A train hit her. I still don't understand what happened."

Simone held his eyes with hers, encouraging him, and Cassidy found himself telling her the whole story.

When he was done, Simone said, "You blame yourself, then."

He nodded. "I suppose I do."

"You must find the answers to your doubts and questions," she said.

"I don't know," he said. "I just—I'm not sure I could live with what I might learn."

"You are an expert in unlocking other people's secrets," she said. "Making sense of their lives. You must do that for yourself. Only then will you be able to move on."

At that point Jill came into the room and put a tray on the coffee table. It held a mug and a carafe and a glass of orange juice and a plate of cookies. She handed the juice to Simone and poured coffee from the carafe into the mug. "Can I get you anything else?" she said to Simone. "I thought I'd run out for the mail and pick up some groceries while you had company." Simone turned to Mac. "Is there anything you need before Jill leaves?"

"I'm wondering if you have any scrapbooks or photo albums or old letters or documents or—"

"I didn't keep scrapbooks," she said. "I was never very interested in preserving the past. You can't preserve it. Even if you wanted to. You can only remember it."

Mac shrugged. "If you have anything at all, it would help."

"What about those photos?" said Jill.

"Of course," said Simone. "Bring that envelope from my desk, will you?"

Jill went into the sunporch, and a minute later she came back out holding a manila envelope. She handed it to Simone.

Simone held it in her lap. "There are some photos in here from a time in my life that I will tell you about. Also a couple of documents from that same time." She handed the envelope to Mac.

Inside the envelope were eight or ten black-and-white snapshots of a very young Asian girl in various poses with a couple of somewhat older people, obviously Americans. The photos were curled and faded and poorly exposed, probably taken with a point-and-shoot camera. There were also a couple of official-looking documents printed in an alphabet Cassidy didn't recognize, with signatures in ink that was so faded he'd need a magnifying glass to read them. He held them up to Simone. "What are these?"

"I will tell you about them," she said. "They are part of my story."

He nodded. He didn't want to push her. He sensed her skittishness about the whole thing. "May I take them?" he said. "I'd like to photocopy them. I'll return them to you."

"You can have everything," she said. "I have taken one photograph for myself. I keep it on the table beside my bed."

Cassidy slid the envelope containing the photographs and documents into his briefcase and took out the new battery-powered tape recorder he'd bought for her and a twelve-pack of tapes.

"I want to show you how this thing works," he said.

―⟨⟩⟨⟩―

Two HOURS LATER Mac was back on the road. He wanted to get home in time to have supper with Katie, even though he'd told her he might be late. Talking with Simone had made him feel anxious, as if some new disaster was lurking just beyond his peripheral vision.

When your wife gets killed by a commuter train, you understand that anything can happen to anyone, any time. You can't count on anything. Nobody is ever safe. The knot of anxiety he felt whenever he couldn't actually see Katie and know that she was all right was a constant reminder of that.

It had gone well with Simone, though. They'd decided that the best way to get started would be for her to tell as much of her story as she could remember into the tape recorder he'd brought for her. She tired easily and napped frequently, and this way she could speak to the tape for short periods of time whenever she felt up to it. No purpose would be served for Mac to be present whenever she was able to talk. She didn't need him to prompt her. Anyway, at least now, at the beginning, he didn't want to start asking hard questions. Simone thought she'd feel less inhibited if she were alone, and besides, he could do better things with his time than wait around for her to feel well enough to talk for a while.

He'd visit periodically to give her suggestions and pick up the tapes. On his end, he'd begin to line up interviews he'd need to conduct. He'd try to get copies of her other films. He'd touch base with his contacts in Hollywood, track down the actors and directors and others who'd worked with Simone, who might have stories to tell him. He'd look at the photos, try to determine if they could be enhanced enough so they could be reproduced for the book. He'd get somebody to translate the documents she'd given to him. Then he could ask Simone about them.

There were some medical people he needed to talk to about multiple sclerosis. At this early point in the project, he believed that Simone's disease might turn out to be a central theme in her story.

He planned to drive out to her house every week or so to spend an afternoon with her, perhaps ask her to elaborate on something he'd learned through his research, but mostly to get a sense of her.

Already he was convinced that she was a complicated and secretive person with important stories that she might be unable to remember or, if she did recall them, unwilling to tell. Mac Cassidy's job was to help Simone unlock her subconscious mind where painful memories tried to hide and convince her that she needed to release them.

He glanced at his watch, then fumbled his cell phone from his jacket pocket and speed-dialed his home number. It rang five times before his own voice answered. "You've reached the Cassidys'," he heard himself say. "It looks like nobody's home. Please leave a message and we'll get back to you."

The Cassidys', he'd recited when he made the new recording, unable to say, *Mac and Katie*, unable to specifically omit Jane.

"Hi, kiddo," he said to the voicemail, forcing joviality into his tone. "It's me, your old man, and it's a little before four. I'm on the road, heading home. My ETA is six, and I've got a hankering for pizza. How's Grapelli's sound to you? See you then. I love you."

When he disconnected, he realized that the knot in his stomach had tightened a notch. It was five after four. The bus always dropped her off at 3:25, and she never missed the bus.

Don't worry about it, he told himself. *She's fine. Relax.*

But he couldn't see her and touch her, didn't know where she was, and so he didn't know that she was all right.

—◦◦—

"ALL RIGHT, MAC Cassidy, my new trusted friend. You left a few hours ago, and I have had my third nap of the day, and now I am sitting here in my wheelchair with your tape recorder for company. I shall try to tell you what you think we must have for our story. As you will soon understand, much of this is painful for me to recall and to make public. However, I am not ashamed. My life is what it is, and it is time to tell it, although I cannot imagine that anybody truly cares. I do hope you make some money from this. I am telling it for other reasons.

"I have asked Jill to bring me here into my sunporch and then to leave me alone. I think if she were nearby I would feel inhibited. I know I would feel inhibited if you were here. This is better. I sense your presence, and it is comforting. You are a dear, sad man, and now I can tell you that had I not felt good karma when you visited me today, when we met for the first time, when I touched your hand and looked into your eyes, I had planned to call Ted and tell him that I had changed my mind, that I had decided not to do this. But your karma is good. So let us begin.

"It is very pretty here right now. Spring is the best time of year, don't you think? The afternoon sun is shining on the hillside. A few minutes ago, two deer walked through my garden. "All right. I am wasting your tape. It is hard to begin, so I am babbling. I am taking a deep breath, dear Mac Cassidy. All right.

"Although I am a citizen of France, I was not, as I have allowed the public to believe, born in Paris.

"My mother was a peasant, a native of Annam, which was a province of what was then called French Indochina—Vietnam, of course, as it has always been properly called. She lived in a village northwest of Saigon. That village no longer exists. I do not know what its name was. You would never have found it on a map even when it did exist.

"When the Japanese occupied Indochina, my mother, then a young girl of no more than five or six, fled her village with her family. They made their way to Saigon where she was put to work in a factory run by the Japanese. When the war ended and the French occupation returned, my mother was taken into the home of a French diplomat as a maid. There she learned how to speak French, and she learned manners, and she acquired ambition and a taste for luxury. She remained with that family for many years as a maid and the French diplomat's mistress, for that was how it worked if a young woman wanted to keep her job, and inevitably she became pregnant. When her condition became obvious, the diplomat's wife banished my mother from their house.

"She returned to her village pregnant and poor and alone and unhappy. I was born there. I have never known the year, never mind the date, of my birth. Sometime around 1960, as well as I can figure. My name was Li An. I didn't become Simone Bonet for many years. That part of my story comes later.

"My early childhood memories are few and confused. I mainly remember being hungry and ill. I remember heat and rain and biting insects, and in my head I carry pictures of enormous oxen and skinny yapping dogs and flooded rice fields. I have no memory of being held or rocked or sung to by my mother. She died when I was quite young. I see her face still. It is the face of a tragic old woman. Her hair was long and dull and tangled, her eyes large and dark and frightened, and her skin was pale and gray and stretched tightly over the bones of her face. As well as I can figure, she was not much past thirty when she died.

"Am I boring you, Mac? I hope not. In my mind, I see you smiling at me, encouraging me to go on, pretending you are fascinated. Well, this is my story. I cannot tell you a better one. I shall continue.

"After my mother died, I lived with relatives. Cousins and aunts. I remember very few young men in our village. Most of the boys went to battle before they became men. My country was always at war. There were the French, of course. Also the Vietminh, the nationalists of Ho Chi Minh. The people of my village had no politics, did not understand or care about politics. We had no leisure for politics. Everybody worked hard to grow enough food to eat.

"My cousins told me stories about my mother, and I assume they were true, how she had returned from Saigon to the village in disgrace, how she had been refused comfort by our local Catholic priest, how I had been born with her disgrace in my blood. It was from my cousins that I pieced together my mother's story. I wish I remembered her better. I wish I could find love for her in my heart. But I did not truly know her. I have no sense that she loved me. She is a phantom to me.

"Oh, Mac. I was a peasant girl, half French. My people hated the French. They oppressed and exploited us. Life was hard for everyone. For me, it was especially hard. I do not tell you this for your sympathy. But perhaps it helps to explain me and who I became. I was an orphan and a bastard child and an outcast. The older women in the village were not unkind to me. But I was an extra mouth to feed. I was always ill. I could not work like the other children, and I needed care.

"Whether it was from kindness or from the desire to get rid of me I do not know, but one of the women, whose brother had found work in the city, managed to tell lies and get me enrolled in a Catholic school in Saigon. I cannot tell you the year. I suppose I might have been eight or nine. I lived with many other girls. We slept on straw pallets in a large hot room.

"I worked in the kitchen where, for the first time in my life, I had enough food to eat. I especially remember the bread, that over-powering aroma in the very early morning when it was baking in the big stone ovens. And the soup, with bits of chicken or fish in it, and the oatmeal and the milk and the eggs. It was wonderful. It was the first time in my life I did not feel hungry all the time, although I remained a very skinny child.

"I was taught by French nuns. I remember them being kind and patient. I believed they were saints in their great black gowns. I learned to read and write, first in French, then in English. I learned some music and geography and arithmetic. And religion, of course.

"It was, in a way, a good time for me. But I was not a happy child. The other children mocked me because I looked different from them. I was a mixture of European and Vietnamese, and I imagined that the nuns did not approve of me, blamed me for my mother's sins, although they were always kind.

"All of this is the truth as well as I can remember it. It is difficult for me to recall and painful for me to recount. It reminds me of those childhood feelings, the burden of shame that I could never escape, my fears, my illnesses, the emptiness where my mother should have been. The lack of love, the resentment I always felt from her. It was—it has always been—a hole in my soul. I hated her.

"There, Mac. I have said it. I have never spoken of my hatred for my mother before. I never acknowledged it. But there it is. Telling you this story has enabled me to confess that to you. For me it is a revelation. For your book, I suppose it is not important. But, yes. I hated my mother. I still hate her for giving me birth and then for abandoning me. It is irrational, I know. But there it is.

"I am suddenly tired, dear Mac. I suppose it is my disease. Or perhaps it is because I find telling you this painful and difficult. I will try to continue my story for you later. Now I must nap again."

_____

A HALF HOUR after he'd tried to call Katie, his cell phone rang.

He glanced at the screen. It was his own home number.

He pressed the button and said, "Honey? That you?"

"Hi, Daddy. I'm sorry. I was in the bathroom when you called and I didn't hear it ring and I didn't notice the light blinking 'til just now, and . . ."

"It's okay, kiddo." Mac chuckled as he felt a wave of relief wash over him. Katie was okay. For now, anyway. "You're entitled to go to the bathroom, for heaven's sake."

"I know how you worry," she said.

"I don't worry," he lied.

"Yeah, you do," she said, "Anyways, I made some chicken cacciatore when I got home. I hope that's okay?"

From one of Jane's old recipes, no doubt, Mac thought.

"It sounds great," he said. "We'll do the pizza thing another time."

"Drive carefully," said Katie.

"I always do."

"Seatbelt buckled?"

"Of course."

"Well, you shouldn't be talking on the phone and driving, so I'm going to hang up now. Love you. Bye."

"Bye, honey," he said. "I love you, too."

Jessie spent two days getting everything ready.

Deciding what to bring had been a challenge. She figured she'd never be back to her apartment, so what she left behind would be gone forever. She didn't want to clean out the place. She guessed that sooner or later Howie Cohen would send some other assassin to sit in a car across the street, and after a few days, he'd break in to see what he could learn. She wanted him to see the apartment of someone who'd gone on vacation and would be back.

Fortunately, Jessie Church was not a sentimental person. That's why she was good at undercover work. Possessions were replaceable. So were friends. If you didn't get too close to people, you could walk away from them.

She left behind all of her books, all of her framed photographs, all of her paintings, and all but a dozen of her favorite CDs, which would keep her company on the road. She left most of her clothes hanging in her closet. She left her television and her audio system. She left her file cabinet the way it was, packed with old receipts and statements and tax forms, all in the name of Carol Ann Chang. Nothing there would suggest where she had gone.

She ended up bringing only the clothes that she could stuff into her backpack. She packed her Sig Sauer 9mm Parabellum and her little backup gun, a Colt Mustang .380, along with her cameras and her laptop computer and a few boxes of cartridges, everything carefully wrapped and cushioned, in her small duffel. The Sig was on top where she could reach it if she needed it.

She was leaving behind thousands of dollars worth of stuff. Nothing that couldn't be replaced. No regrets. It was just stuff.

She went to the post office and filled out a form instructing them to hold her mail. She'd pick it up when she got back, she wasn't sure exactly when, she said. She chatted up the woman behind the counter, telling her that she hadn't had a vacation in a long time, that she planned to drive down the coast, visit some friends in San Luis Obispo, spend some time in L.A., maybe continue on down to Coronado, she wasn't sure. She was playing it by ear, she said, no schedule, no deadline, just getting away from it all for a while, and the woman had chuckled and said she sure wished she could do that.

Howie Cohen was no dummy. You had to be pretty smart to keep an international child sex operation going for nearly twenty years, the way he had, and even though it was Jessie who had taken him down, she had no illusions. He'd made an uncharacteristic mistake, underestimated her, let his guard down with her, trusted her, and it had cost him twenty-five to life. It was an aberration, and she knew he'd never let it happen again.

She didn't like what she'd had to do to get the goods on him. But she didn't regret it.

So she knew he'd assume that she had killed the first assassin he'd sent, and he wouldn't necessarily believe the evidence and the stories she was leaving behind about taking a vacation. He'd quickly guess that she was on the run, and he'd probably assume that the last direction she'd be headed would be south. Howie Cohen understood misdirection as well as Jessie did.

That left north, east and west. It was a big country, a big world, and Jessie intended to lose herself in it.

First Jessie Church had become Carol Ann Chang. Now she was entering her second personal witness protection program.

—⌒⌒—

JESSIE WALKED OUT her front door after supper on Thursday with her backpack over one shoulder and her duffel strap over the other. She strolled down 24th Street to where she'd left her car. She stopped on the sidewalk and talked with a few people she knew, smiling happily, yes, she was off on a little vacation, heading south, following the coast, no big plans, mainly just get away, relax, pamper herself.

She drove with the carry-on-sized duffel on the passenger seat where she could reach into it if she needed to get her hand on the Sig nine and still keep her eyes on the road. She headed northeast, and a little less than four hours later she parked her car against some bushes on the shadowed side of the lot and paid cash for a room for one night in a cheap motel on the outskirts of Reno. She was wearing her sunglasses and her Oakland A's cap, and she kept her face averted from the surveillance camera. When she registered, she signed her name S. Stone, left the phone and address lines blank, and made up the numbers on her car registration.

The clerk, a skinny bald man about seventy years old, was absorbed in a *Law & Order* rerun on the little television on his counter. He didn't even glance at the form. He took her money and gave her a key and mumbled, "It's around back. Just leave the key on the dresser when you leave."

In her room, she took off all her clothes, went into the bathroom, and cut her hair short. She hacked up the hunks of hair into small pieces and flushed them down the toilet. Then she applied Clairol blonde coloring according to the directions on the box, including her eyebrows.

An hour later, when she looked at herself in the mirror, a different Jessie Church looked back. From now on she wouldn't wear her A's cap. Anyone who noticed her would remember the short-haired blonde.

—✦—

"Hello, Mac. It is evening here. It has been a warm sunny day, and I am sitting out on my deck with a blanket over my lap. I'm sipping a mug of tea, and the sun is just sinking behind the western hills. It is very peaceful, and the air smells sweet. Soon it will become chilly and Jill will wheel me inside.

"Your tape recorder is sitting on the table beside me, winding around silently. I have been screwing up my courage all day. I am trying to confront my past. I know our book means so much to you. But I think I already regret ever agreeing to do it. Now I do it for you. You and Ted Austin. I hope our book will make you rich.

"I have been telling you about my boring childhood. I cannot imagine that you will include any of this in your book, but you encouraged me to just ramble, and I know that is what I am doing.

"I left the nuns' school in Saigon when the American soldiers began to arrive. I simply walked away one afternoon. And I never returned. Things had changed at the school. Food became scarce. The nuns were all afraid of what was happening in our country. I was no longer happy there. I was just a skinny girl, eleven or twelve years old, I think. I had tiny little breasts and no womanly curves. But I was taller than the Vietnamese girls, and my skin was fairer, thanks to my French father, and I suppose I would have been considered attractive.

"Mac, I was an absolute virgin when I left the school. No one had ever touched me. I had never even touched myself. I had looked at the other girls. I wondered if they experienced the strange feel-ings that haunted me. The only men I knew were priests, and they were not fully men. I was very naïve. The nuns sometimes spoke to us of sin. But I did not understand what they were saying, because they did not speak plainly and I had no experience, no source of knowledge.

"A woman in the city—Mai Duc was her name—found me on the streets. She brought me to her house and fed me and offered to let me stay with her. She was, of course, a madame, and her house a bordello, although I did not understand that. She was kind to me, and I instantly loved her.

"Mai Duc taught me about my body and about men's bodies. She was gentle and patient. She gave me much pleasure, and when she felt it was time, she arranged for a man to take my virginity. He was an American, and wealthy, I'm sure. I later learned that men paid Mai Duc a lot of money to be with very young girls, especially those who were still virgins. I recall that this man had white hair and wore sweet-smelling cologne, but I have no other memory of him.

"I had no particular feelings about any of this. I don't remember much about it. I was doing what I needed to do to survive. I would do anything Mai Duc wanted me to do. I had no morals about it, no personal feelings. I had no sense that I was doing anything wrong. If Mai Duc wanted me to do it, then that was the right thing.

"After that first man I began to work for Mai Duc. I used what she had taught me, and the men paid her. She bought me clothes and gave me a place to sleep and food to eat, and I was comfortable and happy. She showed me beauty tricks and sex tricks, and she showed me how to use condoms and how to be clean, and I felt no shame.

"Mai Duc took the place of a mother for me. She loved me and cared for me and I happily obeyed her. I knew she was using me to make money for herself, but that did not seem in any way incom-patible with the love I felt she gave me. In Vietnam, the children always worked for the family. Mai Duc was my family. She taught me to be proud to be Vietnamese.

"There were many Americans in Saigon at that time, and every week there seemed to be more of them. They were gentle, innocent men—boys, really—and when they were drunk, as they often were, they were generous and undemanding. It felt good, being honest and businesslike. There was no lying, no shame for me. You are probably disgusted with me, Mac, but those were perhaps the happiest years of my life.

"I know that must sound strange to you. I was a prostitute. It seemed to be my calling. But, yes, it was a good time for me. The American men were mostly homesick and lonely and frightened. And young. They were not all that much older than me. I believe my youth was attractive to them. They were so young and inexperienced. They liked the fact that I spoke English, that we could converse. They liked to tell me about the girls they knew back home. I think they saw me as innocent, like the girls they idealized from their childhood. I gave them comfort. It fulfilled me. Their pleasure was my pleasure.

"Those American boys—now I cannot remember a single one of them as an individual. But when I was with one of them, he was all I thought about. And when he left me, soon there was another, and then another. They all became one for me, one collective boy for me to love and comfort.

"Mac, I should feel ashamed, I know. But I don't. This is my life. Will these memories be good for your book, this confession of mine?

"You see? I am thinking of it as your book. That makes it easier for me to speak honestly. Anyway, I do not expect that I will see your book. My disease is progressing. I hope we will finish while I am still able.

"It is growing dark, Mac. Stars are glittering in the sky above me, and a cool breeze is blowing through the valley. I am very sensitive to temperature. So I think I will call for Jill to come and take me inside for a hot bath. I will talk with you more tomorrow."

—⸝⸝—

"HELLO, MAC. IT is raining this morning. I am sitting in my sunporch, except there is no sun. Jill has opened some windows for me, and I am smelling the moist air and listening to the raindrops spatter softly on the leaves of the trees outside. It tugs me all the way back to the time when I was a young girl in my village, when my mother was still alive, when the rain came violently and suddenly and lasted for what seemed like forever and the village was all mud and nothing was ever dry. This soft rain today smells the same as those smells in my memory.

"The rain makes me feel sad. All these memories that talking to your machine brings back to me.

"I did not keep track of the passage of time when I was comforting American boys in Saigon and being loved and cared for by Mai Duc. It was not long. A year or two, I think. Much was happening in the city, but as I have told you, I did not understand politics, nor did I have any interest in the war. I do not think I could have told you who was fighting against whom, or why. My job was to be with the boys. Others had their jobs. Time passed. I cannot mark it by events, because I knew little of events.

"There was, I recall, much violence in the streets of Saigon. Vietnamese people were killed by Vietnamese police. There were explosions and gunfights and much death. Every day there seemed to be more young American men in the city. And money. There were bars and dance halls and prostitutes on every street. There was marijuana and heroin for everyone. I liked the marijuana. But I did not try the heroin. I saw what it did to other young women. Anyway, Mai Duc forbade the heroin. She supplied us with the marijuana. It was to share with our boys. Marijuana and rice wine and American beer.

"One day Mai Duc called me to her office, which was a room in a Saigon hotel, part of her suite. She had a desk and file cabinets and two telephones and a typewriter and a television set. Mai Duc was very rich. She was one of the most powerful people in the city. She employed a number of policemen, whose job was to protect her interests and keep her and her business safe.

"There were, I remember, two very comfortable upholstered chairs in her office. Mai Duc's special customers, I knew, sat in those chairs. But on this day she asked me to sit in one of them.

"She sat behind her desk, and she did not smile at me. I guessed that I had done something wrong, that she would tell me she no longer wished to be my mother. These were fears that haunted me in those days. I did not fear the soldiers or the explosions. I was afraid of displeasing Mai Duc.

"Mai Duc seemed to me to be a very wise and old woman, but thinking back, I suppose she was younger then than I am now. She smoked little black cigars, and there was one in an ashtray beside her elbow on that day. She picked it up, puffed it, and looked at me through the smoke. 'Li An,' she said, and her voice was gentle, telling me she was not displeased with me. 'You are my favorite child. And I know you love me. So you will do what I wish.'

"I said nothing. She was not asking for my agreement. She never asked for my agreement. Only my obedience, which I was happy to give to her.

"'A young man,' she said, 'an American boy who has been with you, who was pleased by you, has come to me. He is an important man, an officer, and he wants you.' Mai Duc held up her hand as I began to speak. 'No, my child. Not as the others have had you. This man wants something different, and I have agreed. You will be for him alone. He has rented a room for you. There you will live. You will be with no other men. Just this one. Do you understand?'

"I told her I did understand. Other girls, I knew, had such arrangements. They were taken care of well. 'If it will please you, my mother,' I said.

"'Whatever this young man chooses to give you, you may keep,' Mai Duc told me. 'If there are problems, you may come to me. I know you will please him.'

"'I will do my best,' I said.

"Mai Duc smiled. She came to me from behind her desk and hugged me. Then she said, 'Now I will bring this young man to you. He is waiting in the next room.'

"And that was when I met Thomas.

"I am tired now."

"HELLO, MAC CASSIDY. It is evening now. I stopped this morning without saying good-bye to you. I wondered if I could continue. I felt that I had told you too much already, that I should keep my secrets to myself as I have kept them all these years. I know this is for our book. But you can understand that it is you to whom I speak, and even though we have only met one time, talking with you so intimately, telling you my secrets, makes me believe that we are friends. I speak to you as a friend. I want my dear new friend to like me, and I fear that these stories of mine will prevent you from liking me.

"Since this morning I have been thinking of you and your book, and as painful as this is for me, I want to be honorable. My life has not been very honorable, Mac. But I do think of myself as an honorable person. I agreed to tell you my story. So I shall.

"Besides, in a strange way, telling you my stories, putting them outside of myself, sharing them, feels like a burden is being lifted from me, as if this life of mine, these hard memories, they are no longer mine alone. They are yours, now, too, whether you want them or not, and some day they will belong to everybody who might read our book.

"Now the rain has stopped, and it is beautiful and peaceful here in my valley. Jill has wheeled me out onto the deck so I can smell the freshness of the damp earth and hear the evening sounds. This time of day is sad for me. It means another day in my life has passed, and I know my remaining days are limited. But it is lovely, too. As the sun settles behind the hills a soft velvety color seems to wash through the trees. The chirping of crickets and the singing of night birds mingles with the distant tinkle of water bubbling through the brook. It fills the air with quiet music. Bats and swallows swoop around snatching insects. So peaceful. The only peace I have ever known in my life, Mac, has been here, in the quiet solitude of this house here in my valley, although the peace is outside of me. It does not truly penetrate my heart. My soul has never felt peace, and I suppose it never will.

"But as I have said, I am hoping that telling you my story might help me to find peace before I die. That is what I am beginning to feel. The pain of speaking these words to you is purging me. I do not know if that will continue. My memories grow more painful as I proceed with my story. We shall see. If talking with you fails to bring me peace, well, Mac, you will have your book, anyway.

"There is one other person who I want to hear my story. I am feeling that if I tell it and you write it and Ted Austin gets it published, she will see it, and then she will know. I think of her and it gives me the courage to continue. It gives this difficult thing we are doing purpose. I will soon explain that to you. Please be patient with the way I ramble.

"So I met Thomas. How can I tell you about Thomas? He entered Mai Duc's office that day, stood before me, held out his hand to me, looked directly into my eyes, and said to me, 'If this arrangement is not agreeable to you, Li An, then it will not happen.' He spoke very formally, as if it was a speech he had memorized and practiced. I am certain that Mai Duc required him to say this, but I believed he was sincere, and I believe it to this day.

"Mac, he had eyes the color of the summer sky and hair as black as night. He had a wonderful tan, of course. Thomas always had a tan. His face was the color of strong tea, almost as dark as mine, and except for tiny crinkles at the corners of his eyes, his skin was as smooth and as soft as mine, too. And when he smiled, his teeth flashed. He was quite young, but to me he seemed very wise and mature, more a man than a boy.

"I had, of course, been with many American boys. It never mattered to me how they looked. There were dark-skinned boys and fair-skinned boys, boys with crooked teeth and pock-marked faces, fat boys and skinny boys, handsome boys and homely boys. I noticed these things, of course. But that did not affect how I felt toward them or how I treated them. Mai Duc had taught me that my own beauty and cleanliness were very important, but that the beauty of men had no significance, although many of the boys acted as if it did have significance. Handsome boys behaved differently from those who were not handsome. But whether they were beautiful or ugly, in their souls they were all lonely and frightened. I was aware only of their gentleness and their sadness and their need for my comfort, and even though I was just a child, I felt wise and motherly toward them. So the fact that Thomas was handsome was of no particular interest to me. I knew that he was lonely and frightened, too.

"He was staring at me, smiling. 'Do you remember me, Li An?' he said.

"I did not remember him. There had been so many boys. But Mai Duc said that I had been with him, so I smiled at him and said, 'Yes, I remember you.'

"He said nothing. He was waiting for my decision, still holding his hand out to me.

"So I took Thomas's hand, bowed my head, and said, 'The arrangement is agreeable to me.'

"And so it was done. I belonged to Thomas Larrigan. I was, as near as I can figure it, not yet thirteen years old.

"I must stop now."

10

Eddie Moran parked on the fourth level of the parking garage on Summer Street and waited a couple of minutes in his car to be sure he hadn't been followed. Then he walked down the stairs to the third level, where he found Larrigan right where he said he'd be, sitting in his big Lincoln. The garage was dimly lit by yellow bulbs in steel cages, and from somewhere in the shadows came the slow, rhythmic echo of dripping water. It was seven o'clock on a Thursday evening and, for the moment, there was no traffic on level three, no cars starting up, no clatter of high heels, no voices, no chirps of remote openers, no businessmen with briefcases striding toward their vehicles.

You had to give it to the judge. This was a pretty good place to meet someone you didn't want to be seen with.

Moran opened the passenger door. He noticed that the dome light did not go on when he opened the door.

Larrigan didn't even turn his head when Moran slid in beside him. "Don't slam the door," he said.

Moran pulled the door shut.

"So," said the judge. "What've you got?"

Moran took the paper out of his pocket and unfolded it. It was the photo he'd downloaded from the Internet. He handed it to Larrigan.

Larrigan took a miniature flashlight from his jacket pocket, looked at the photo, then looked at Moran. "She's gorgeous. Who is it?"

"You don't recognize her?"

"No. Should I?"

"You fucked her plenty of times."

Larrigan laughed. "I never fucked this woman. I think I'd remember a beautiful woman like this. Who the hell is she?"

"Her name is Simone. How she looked about twenty years ago. Simone Bonet. Ring a bell?"

Larrigan frowned at the picture, then stared up at the roof of the car. "Yeah, maybe. The name sounds familiar. Not the face, though. Somebody appeared before me in court sometime? Some lawyer? I can't place her."

"The name 'Seymour,' remember?"

"Seymour." Larrigan frowned. "Oh, right. What Bunny said when you . . ."

"She was saying 'Simone.' She wasn't exactly articulating too clearly."

"Yeah," said Larrigan. "Great. That's good work, Eddie, but so what? I don't get it. This Simone some friend of Bunny's or something?"

"You might say that," said Moran. "Take another look."

Larrigan squinted at the picture. Moran saw him blink, look again. His eyes widened. Then he whispered, "Holy shit. You think this is . . . ?"

"It's Li An," said Moran.

"She survived?"

"Evidently. She's a lot older in this picture than last time you saw her, wouldn't you say? You don't get older if you don't survive."

"All these years, I just assumed . . ."

"You hoped," said Moran. "But it didn't happen that way. She survived, and she became a movie star, and she's still alive."

"It's her," said Larrigan softly. "I see it now." He looked at Moran. "What're we going to do?"

"You mean, what am *I* going to do?"

"You are a prick sometimes, you know that?"

"Just so you remember," said Moran, "I'm in this as deep as you are."

Larrigan shrugged. "So what do you suggest?"

"I found a certified-mail receipt in Bunny's purse, addressed to Simone Bonet. I think Bunny was trying to say that Li An's got the photos. So I guess I better go get 'em."

"I guess you better. You think that will take care of it?"

Moran shrugged. "I been thinking about it. Who knows how many of the guys we knew back then remember you and Li An? But it was a long time ago, and stories are just that. Stories. If Li An is still pissed at you—and why wouldn't she be?—she might want to go to the media and tell her story. But without those photos, what has she got? Nothing. You just deny the whole thing. Just a story. Rumors. Gossip. Exaggeration. Faulty memory. Some broad, looking for a little attention. There's always gossip with public figures, and you're gonna be a very public figure, if all goes well."

Larrigan was nodding. "Get the fucking photos, we're in the clear."

Moran nodded. "Maybe she's got photos of her own, too. Get them and get Bunny's from her, and I'd say we're in good shape."

Larrigan turned his head and looked at Moran. "What'll you do?"

"With Li An, you mean?"

"Yes."

"We'll have to see how it plays out," said Moran.

—⟡—

BLACKHOLE, INFINITELY PATIENT, infinitely watchful, was parked across the street from the exit to the parking garage. Moran had driven in a little before seven, nine minutes after Judge Larrigan arrived.

The judge's car pulled out at 7:22. Moran's vehicle emerged five minutes later.

Blackhole let a couple of cars get between them. Then he entered the slow flow of traffic behind Eddie Moran.

Bellwether had doubts about this judge, and Blackhole was now convinced that those doubts had substance. An upstanding judge with nothing to hide would not be meeting in a parking garage with a shadowy character like Eddie Moran unless he had secrets.

Blackhole's job was to learn those secrets.

—⟡—

"GOOD EVENING, MAC. Jill has tucked me in for the night. I am in bed now, and I will go to sleep soon. I am sipping a glass of sherry and feeling relaxed and brave. I will tell you of my life with Thomas Larrigan while I have this courage.

"The sherry reminds me. One of Mai Duc's rules was that we should not drink alcohol. We had wine for the boys, and we were allowed to smoke marijuana. Mai Duc believed marijuana made us more sensitive and responsive without dulling our minds. She wanted us to be alert and vibrant and focused on our work, and she believed that alcohol made us dull.

"But when I went to live with Thomas Larrigan, alcohol became a part of my life. Thomas insisted that I drink with him, and he was always drinking when he was with me. Wine, beer, rum, gin, vodka. It did not matter to Thomas, as long as he had a glass or a bottle in his hand. When I would tell him that I did not want to drink, he would become angry with me. And so I took a glass or a bottle, too. At first I only pretended to drink, or took just tiny sips, but gradually I began to drink with him. It didn't take much to get me drunk. I was such a skinny little girl. Sometimes it was fun, being drunk with Thomas. But too many times the alcohol changed him.

"Mac, I did understand how it was for the American boys in my country, being in a war they did not understand, fighting against an enemy they could not see and who was much more clever and vicious than they were. They all believed they were going to die. I understand about courage, and I know many of them were courageous. Perhaps Thomas was, too. But he was afraid of dying every minute I was with him. Alcohol gave him a way of forgetting. Many of the boys used heroin or opium, but as far as I know, except for the marijuana, Thomas relied on alcohol for his courage.

"I lived in three small rooms in one of the old Saigon hotels. By the standards I know now, it was squalid. But back then, in that city during that war, my rooms were luxurious. Thomas expected me to be there for him whenever he appeared, and since I never knew when he would arrive, I simply lived in my rooms. There was very little for me to do when Thomas was not there. I had a radio that played American rock and roll all day, and I had some books. I quickly learned that alcohol helped make the time pass.

"Thomas was a Marine officer stationed in the city. I never did know exactly what his job was. He was a soldier, that's all I knew. He never talked about it with me. With me he wanted to drink and make love. He did not want to talk.

"Sometimes he took me away for little holidays. We went on boats and we went swimming and we went for rides in his Jeep. Sometimes his friends came with us. In particular, his friend Eddie, who was not an officer but who worked with him, or for him. Eddie had an American girlfriend, a Red Cross nurse, or a nurse's aid, named Bunny, who was a few years older than me. Bunny was seventeen or eighteen, I think. She became my friend. Sometimes Eddie and Bunny would come to my rooms and we would all get drunk. Sometimes all four of us would get into Thomas's Jeep. Eddie would drive and Bunny would sit up front with him. Thomas and I would sit in the back with a bottle of gin while Eddie would drive around the city streets or into the countryside.

"At first, dear Mac, I was content with Thomas Larrigan. He brought me presents—clothes and jewelry and food and alcohol. He treated me tenderly most of the time. He was amusing. I enjoyed Eddie and Bunny, and we laughed often. Of course, we were drunk most of the time. But we thought we were all having fun, and we weren't thinking about death.

"It is hard to forget the bad things, though, no matter how much you are drunk. I understand that. You can push it aside, but a bad thing lingers there in the shadows of your mind like a predator, ready to leap out when you are not expecting it. That happened to me sometimes. And I suppose it happened to Thomas. The alcohol did not always make him happy.

"Sometimes he would be sad and frightened, and when he got that way, he would became angry with me. I never knew when that would happen. It was always sudden and unexpected.

"I am remembering one time, Mac. It is not easy to remember. Eddie and Bunny were with us. We were on a beach, all alone, just the four of us on this long beautiful sand beach. We had taken off our clothes to swim, and afterwards all four of us were lying naked on a blanket drinking cold beer under the hot sun. I was lying on my back with my eyes closed, and Thomas was beside me. On the other side of him was Bunny, and Eddie was on the other side of her. I think I had been dozing, because Thomas's voice at first seemed far away. He was saying, 'Look, Li An. Look at this.'

"I opened my eyes. Thomas was straddling Bunny, who was naked and on her back. Bunny had her eyes shut tight, and Thomas was moving his penis between her breasts. He was holding her breasts in his hands, squeezing them around himself. 'Your tits are too small,' he said to me. 'You can't do this. Bunny's got nice big ones.'

"And in a very small voice Bunny was saying, 'No, no. Please, no.' When Bunny said, 'No, no' to Thomas like that, she sounded like a child.

"Eddie was sitting up on the other side of Bunny. He looked at me and gave his head a little shake, and I understood. He couldn't do anything. Thomas was his superior officer.

"Thomas turned to me. 'Watch,' he said. And he held his penis in his hand and put it against Bunny's mouth. 'Take it,' he said to her.

"Bunny was shaking her head back and forth. Her mouth was forming the word 'No,' but no sound was coming out.

"Thomas slapped her face. He hit her very hard. It sounded like a gunshot. 'I told you to take it,' he said, and he grabbed her hair and held her head still and forced himself into her mouth.

"Eddie had turned away. He was sitting with his back to us, hugging his knees. Bunny was making noises in her throat and Thomas was holding her cruelly by her hair.

"'Please, Thomas,' I said. 'Let me. I will do it.' I reached to him and touched his shoulder. Suddenly he whirled around, and there was craziness in his eyes.

"'Shut up,' he said. 'I told you to watch.'

"But I saw the tears on Bunny's cheeks and heard the way she was gagging. 'Please, Thomas,' I said, 'let me do it,' and I tried to pull him to me.

"I didn't see it coming. It felt like I had been hit on the side of my head with a rock. I fell backwards onto the sand. It took me a minute to realize what had happened. He had punched me with his fist.

"I refused to cry. I lay there, feeling the dizziness and the pain in my head and the sickness in my stomach, listening to Thomas groaning and Bunny making noises in her throat, and after a few minutes I felt Thomas lie on his back beside me and I heard Bunny crying quietly.

"That was the first time Thomas hit me, Mac.

"Oh, remembering is painful, dear gentle Mac. You see? Now I am crying. I will now cry myself to sleep. Good night."

—◦◦—

"Dear Mac. I am finding that the more I talk to you this way the easier it is. Even what I told you last night, as hard as it was, it feels good, now, getting it out of my head where it has been lurking all these years. I am telling you my secrets, and I feel that you are not judging me or condemning me, and so I find it easier not to judge or condemn myself. I do not know if I could do this while looking into your face. But your little tape recorder is becoming my trusted friend. It does not frown or look away from my eyes. It just keeps turning around faithfully.

"Will you be able to look at me after you hear these things? Will I see pity in your eyes, or contempt, or disappointment? I'm not sure I could bear your pity, Mac. But I feel your kindness. I felt it when we met, and I feel it still.

"I am afraid of giving these tapes to you. It is becoming easier to speak these words. But the thought of your pity remains very painful to me. I could not bear it if you judged me harshly. Well, I trust you.

"It is evening again. The whole day has passed, and I have not been able to summon up the courage to continue telling you my story. I have been thinking all day about Thomas, remembering that first time he hit me, wondering how it was that I so quickly became accustomed to having him hit me, and even accepted it as his privilege. He had bought me and paid for me, and that meant that he owned me. He could treat me kindly or cruelly, as he wished. And he did treat me both ways. When he was kind and tender and generous, as he often was, I was grateful, because I knew he had no obligation to treat me that way. And when he hit me, what could I do? Sometimes I thought of going to Mai Duc and telling her how Thomas was treating me, telling her that I did not like it. But she had always been kind to me, and I did not want to disappoint her, so I said nothing to her.

"And so I began to welcome the times when Thomas was not there, when I could be alone in my rooms with my radio and my books. And as time passed, I did have more and more time alone. Bunny visited me sometimes. She, too, was lonely and frightened. Her work was difficult and dangerous. She saw horrible things every day.

"Sometimes I wouldn't see Thomas for a week or more. The war was changing, and I think his work was changing, too, although he never talked to me about what he did.

"I never knew what to expect when he showed up. Often he would already be drunk when he arrived. He would insult me and hit me, and, as I have told you, I could do nothing except allow it to happen. But sometimes he would bring me flowers and wine, and he would make love very tenderly to me and I could feel the sadness and fear in him. His war was not going well. I could comfort him, and I did, and it gave me pleasure.

"One afternoon he showed up with flowers. He was already drunk, and he was acting very happy. He told me to put on my prettiest dress. He was taking me someplace special.

"Eddie and Bunny were in the Jeep outside. Everybody was acting funny, as if they all had a secret they were not sharing with me. Eddie drove us to a part of the city where I had never been. We stopped in front of a brick building and went into an office where a little Vietnamese man was sitting behind a desk. He wore a white suit with dirty smudges on it, and he was bald and smoking a cigarette. There was a picture of President Johnson on the wall and a tiny little American flag sticking out of a holder on his desk. The man jumped up when we entered and began talking in rapid Vietnamese. He kept looking at me, and I realized I was supposed to translate.

"The man was asking which was the lucky couple. I translated, and Eddie took Bunny's hand and said, 'Tell him it's us.'

"I did. Eddie gave the man some money, and the man took out a book and read from it very fast—too fast for me to catch all the words. But he pronounced them man and wife and produced a document which all four of us signed and which Bunny folded and put into her purse.

"Then Thomas took my arm and said, 'Tell him to do us.'

"I looked at him, and I must have frowned, because he smiled and squeezed my arm. 'Tell him, Annie,' he said. Annie is what Thomas called me when he wasn't angry with me.

"'What about Mai Duc?' I said.

"'I have already talked to her,' he said, which meant that he had given her the money that she required.

"You see, Mac? Thomas never asked me to marry him. He asked Mai Duc. That was how it worked, and I understood. I never did know why he wanted to marry me. But I knew that he did not need my consent. And so I told the little man to marry us, and Thomas gave him money, and he repeated the same words he had said for Bunny and Eddie. Then we all signed an official document, which I put into my purse.

"That should be an interesting fact for your book, Mac. Simone was married.

"No. Correct that. Simone *is* married, has been married all these years.

"Do you really think anybody cares about this? Well, you can write it into your book or not. These stories are my gift to you, my dear friend. You can do with them what you want."

"Jill has come with my tea. I want to be with her now."

11

Four days after he visited her, Mac Cassidy called Simone. Jill answered the phone.

"It's Mac Cassidy," he said. "I wonder if I can talk to Simone?"

"I'm sorry," said Jill. "She's napping. I don't like to interrupt her. She doesn't have much energy. Is it important?"

"It can wait," he said. "I just wondered how it was going."

"With your book, you mean?"

"Yes."

"She's been talking into the tape recorder whenever she's awake. She's got five or six tapes filled."

"She hasn't finished, has she?"

"I don't think so. She doesn't tell me anything about it. She won't allow me to be near her when she talks to you." Jill laughed quietly. "That's how she puts it. 'I'm going to talk with Mac now,' she'll say. 'Please leave us.' I'm getting jealous." She hesitated. "It's taking a lot out of her. Emotionally, I mean. She's more withdrawn. She tires easier."

"I don't want to jeopardize her health," he said.

"You've got to understand Simone," said Jill. "Whatever she does, it's what she wants to do, what she believes she should do. Otherwise, she wouldn't do it. You or I, we have no control over it."

"I was thinking of driving out to see her—the two of you—on Saturday. I could pick up the tapes she's finished, and I'd like to ask her some things."

"Well," Jill said, "it's not like we have this busy social calendar. I'm sure she'd love to see you. I can't promise you that she'll last very long."

"It's getting worse?" said Mac.

"She sleeps more and more. After an hour or so, even just sitting on the deck, she has to nap."

"I'm very sorry," he said.

Jill didn't say anything.

"I'd like to talk with you sometime," he said.

"Me? Why?"

"Your insights will be important for the book. You know her better than anybody."

"I don't know," she said. "I don't think I'd be comfortable with that."

"I'll ask Simone about it," he said. "Is that all right with you?"

"I can't stop you from asking her, but it goes against my grain to . . . to divulge private things."

"Sure. I understand." He paused for an awkward minute. "Well," he said, "please tell Simone that I'll be there Saturday around noontime. I was thinking of bringing my daughter for company. It's a long drive. Would that be all right?"

"Of course," said Jill. "We'll have lunch. I'm sure Simone would love to meet your daughter. So would I."

"Katie," said Mac. "Her name's Katie. She's fifteen."

"Katie's a sweet name," said Jill.

_ɔ·ɔ_

"IT IS EARLY morning, Mac. Although I nap frequently and am always tired, I seem to be awakening earlier and earlier. So Jill has wheeled me out on my deck. I have a heavy blanket over me, and I am sipping tea and watching the sky turn from purple to pewter. Soon the sun will rise, but it has not yet. The air is filled with birdsong and insect buzzing, and it smells moist and cool and sweet. Two rabbits were munching grass right beside the deck a few minutes ago. Often deer wander into my yard around sunrise on a spring morning. It is a wonderful, magical time, my favorite time to be awake. The rest of the world is asleep, and I believe I have the advantage over them because I have already begun my day. It makes me feel virtuous, even though I accomplish nothing.

"I developed the habit of early rising when I lived in the convent school in Saigon. Then I was awakened before dawn to work in the kitchen preparing the day's bread. Even when I worked in Hollywood I arose early. That, I discovered, was the best time to learn my lines. My mind has always focused best before the sun comes up.

"So this morning as I sit here in the cool damp of this springtime dawn with a thick blanket covering my legs, I am remembering clearly the events that led to my leaving Vietnam. It was about survival. I always did what I had to do to survive. Surviving was foremost in my mind for much of my life. Lately thoughts of survival have preoccupied me again, although now survival seems somehow less important to me than it did when I was younger. Now I am prepared not to survive. It is actually a big relief.

"I told you how Thomas and I were married. I gave you the legal document that the nervous Vietnamese man in the dirty white suit gave me that day. I wonder if you looked at it and understood what it is. Were it not for events that followed, that civil wedding of ours would be of no importance.

"The fact that we were married did not change the way Thomas and I lived. I continued to stay in my hotel room and he continued to work in the city. Bunny often came to stay with me. As time passed, Thomas came over less and less often. When he did show up, he was either already drunk or he quickly became drunk. He hit me regularly. I got used to it. He rarely hurt me, and I understood that he needed to do something with his anger and fear. It was not personal with him. Hitting me was safe for him. He had paid Mai Duc for the right to hit me.

"That first time on the beach he punched me with his fist, but after that he only slapped me. I suspect that was his agreement with Mai Duc. She allowed him to slap me but forbade him from hitting me with his fist. Usually he had no particular passion for it. Here was Annie, his property, and she needed to be slapped now and then. That was all.

"I look back and am amazed that I accepted being hit as his right and my duty. But I belonged to him. What did I know?

"Well, Mac, like my mother and my mother's mother, I got pregnant. If I had followed Mai Duc's rules, it would not have happened. But I was drunk much of the time I was with Thomas, and so was he, and we were careless.

"I did not know what to do. I told Bunny, of course, and she said she could arrange an abortion. She knew American doctors who could do it safely. But the idea of an abortion frightened me, Mac. I had been educated by the Catholic nuns, who taught me that abortion was murder.

"I knew I had to tell Thomas. He was my husband and my child's father. I did not know how he would react. I was afraid. But I decided I would tell him, and then I would do whatever he wanted. If the decision was his, it would free me of sin and responsibility.

"I will speak more of this later, Mac. The sun has risen and the dew had dried from the grass. Already it is warm. The magic time of my spring day has passed. I don't feel like talking anymore."

—⚭—

"THIS MORNING I was speaking to you of my pregnancy, Mac, and how I had to tell Thomas. I feared his anger, of course. I believed he would either hit me and demand that I abort the child or else simply abandon me.

"I had learned to judge Thomas's moods. Sometimes he was gay and laughing, and he'd take me out. We would visit a restaurant, go dancing. When Bunny and Eddie were with us, we might drive out into the countryside and Thomas and Eddie would tell us about the fighting and show us the destruction. Then when we returned to my rooms, we would make love, Thomas with me and Eddie with Bunny. The four of us often ended up in the same bed, but after that time at the beach when Thomas hit me for the first time, he never tried to touch Bunny. Afterwards we would all fall asleep naked together. We were good friends, like a pair of married couples— which we were—and I sometimes fooled myself into thinking that we had a future, that we would always be together.

"Other times, of course—most times—Thomas was angry or depressed when he came to me, and then I tried to soothe him. Sometimes that's what he wanted, and I'd hold him and caress him and whisper to him as if he were a child. At other times he had to hit me.

"Anyway, Mac, I waited for the evening when I sensed a happy mood to tell him that we were having a baby. He came in with wine and flowers and food. I prepared the food, and after we ate he turned the radio to a station that played American music and took me in his arms and danced with me. We ended up laughing, I remember, and trying to sing along with the music. Then we sat on the sofa and poured more wine, and that's when I told him. 'Thomas,' I said, 'I have some news.'

"He smiled, and I think he knew then what I was going to say. 'We are having a child.' I said it as simply and quickly as I could. I braced myself for his anger. But it didn't happen. He looked at me for a moment, and I thought I saw tears in his eyes. Then he hugged me. 'I am very happy, Annie,' he said.

"That night after we made love Thomas talked to me in a way he had never done before. He told me how frightened he was to be in my country. He told me of the friends he had lost to the war, how his responsibilities were changing, how he expected one day to be killed himself. He wanted the child, he said. He wanted to leave a child in the world when he died, and he was pleased that it was my child. He would grow to be a strong and beautiful man, Thomas said, for he assumed the child would be a boy. With me for a mother and him for a father, said Thomas, how could the child not be extraordinary?

"If he survived the war, Thomas told me, he would bring me to America where our child would be safe and healthy. We would send him to the best schools. Everything was possible in America.

"Mac, I cannot tell you how happy I felt that evening. It did not seem possible that this man loved me and wanted to spend his life with me, that I would have his beautiful child and we would care for him together.

"During my pregnancy, Thomas changed. He stopped hitting me. He was still often depressed, and sometimes I saw his anger. He did not stop drinking entirely, but he was drunk less often. He began to take an interest in my health. He worried about what I ate and about my sleep. He insisted that I stop drinking and smoking marijuana.

"When the time came, he took me to a Catholic hospital and I gave birth to a daughter. She was beautiful. I thought she looked more like Thomas than me. She had his coloring, and except for her eyes, it was hard to see my Vietnamese mother in her appearance. Thomas, I knew, was disappointed we did not have a boy. But he was tender and loving toward our girl, whom we named May after Mai Duc, but spelled the American way.

"Oh, Mac. Things never remain the same, do they? The war in my country was growing fierce. All around Saigon battles were waging. Villages were being destroyed. Young men—Vietnamese from the north and the south, and Americans—were being killed. I understood little of the war. I knew that Vietnamese were fighting against Vietnamese. I knew that the United States thought it was terribly important that the South should win. Thomas sometimes tried to explain it to me. When I asked him what was the sense of all the killing, of his risking his life, of the American government sending its boys to Vietnam to be killed, he talked about democracy and freedom, but I could tell he was uncertain and confused himself.

"After May was born, Thomas found a new place for us to live. It was in a different part of the city, an apartment with two bedrooms, one for May and one for me. I know it was expensive. I once asked him why we could not all live together like a family, but Thomas refused to explain. He continued to live separate from May and me and visit us when he could.

"I am tired again, Mac. Telling you my stories is not easy. If this is boring, well, you do not have to put it in your book, do you? But it is my life. I think most people's lives are boring.

"I will talk to you more tomorrow. It has been pleasant, remembering this part of my life. It was a contented time when I cared for my baby and Thomas treated me with love. It all changed, of course. That is one thing I know for certain about life. Nothing ever stays the same."

JESSIE STOPPED FOR the night in a little no-name town off the Inter-state a few miles east of Billings, Montana. She rented a motel room, this time registering as Julia Roberts. The woman who gave her the key looked up and squinted at Jessie when she read the name off the form. Jessie shrugged and smiled at her, as if to say, "Nope. Not *that* Julia."

She had a cheeseburger and a Coke at the bar in the roadhouse next door to the motel, where an all-girl hillbilly band was playing and folks were drinking longnecks and doing the two-step on the little dance floor. Several handsome young cowpoke types tipped their Stetsons at Jessie and asked her if she cared to dance. She declined politely, and they didn't pester her.

Back in her room, she called Jimmy Nunziato in Chicago on her cell phone.

When he answered, she said, "Hey, Nunz. How you doing?"

"Jessie Church," he said. "Jesus Christ. After that Cohen thing I thought you probably died or something."

"Nope. I'm fine."

"Where the hell are you?"

"Nowhere," she said.

"Ah, shit. I get it. So I guess I know what you're after, right?"

"That's it," she said.

"When do you need it?"

"Um, how'd Friday work for you?"

"Friday would be fine," he said. "You want the works?"

"Yep. This is gonna be for a while. You still got a photo you can use?"

"On my computer somewhere. I never throw nothing away."

"I'm blonde now. It's cut short. Can you do that?"

"Sure. Hard to picture you, short blonde hair, though. Anything else? I can give you big ears, fat cheeks . . ."

"Just the hair will be fine," said Jessie. "And my age. I'm thirty-four now."

"Thirty-four," he said. "No shit."

"Time flies when you're trying to survive, huh?"

"So where do you want to pick it up?" he said.

Jessie had already checked her road map and done some researching on her laptop. "There's a place called Deer Creek, a little east of Peoria. Know it?"

"Hell, no," he said. "But I can find it. Peoria's maybe a three-hour drive from here."

"There's a Motel 8 there right off the Interstate. Let's make it seven in the evening, in the front parking lot. I'm in a gray Honda Civic, California plates. You'll recognize me. I'll be the blonde with the short hair."

"Okay," he said. "I'm there."

"It'll be good to see you again, Jimmy," she said.

"You too," he said. "Not that I'll recognize you."

⸺ ৩৲ ⸺

"HELLO, MAC. I am sipping some iced tea and waiting for Jill to return from her trip to the post office.

"There is one thing I do not want you to misunderstand. At first I had no particular feelings for Thomas Larrigan. He had made a bargain with Mai Duc, and my feelings did not matter anyway, which I understood. I knew what my duty was, and I did it. It never occurred to me that I had the right to hate him or to love him. My feelings were irrelevant. I was available to him, and he could make love to me or slap me, as he wished. I was grateful when we made love and I was unhappy when he hit me. But I accepted whatever happened.

"After May was born, the hardness in my heart that had protected me for so long melted away. I loved my baby, and I found myself unable to control my feelings for Thomas. I allowed myself to love him, Mac. I could not love my child without loving her father. It began to matter to me how he treated me. I actually dreamed about the future. I thought about the war ending and Thomas taking May and me to America and how we would have more children.

"It was weakness. I understood that even then. It made me vulnerable. But I could not help myself.

"I loved watching her grow, Mac. I spoke only English to her. I sang lullabies to her and told her stories. She was a beautiful baby, and I never tired of being with her. I spent all my time with her. I had never been so happy.

"Everything changed one day a few weeks after May's first birthday. It was the rainy season. May and I had not been out of our apartment for almost a week, and Thomas had not come by for longer than that. The war was bad and close by, and Bunny was working twelve or fourteen hours every day, so I rarely saw her, either. May and I were running out of food, and I had finally decided that I had to take her out to get food, even though it was pouring rain, when Thomas showed up. When he came in the door I could see on his face that something was wrong. It was not just his normal anger or sadness, although I saw those things, too. And it was not just that he was drunk, although he was. It was more than that, and I should have been smart enough to be more careful with him.

"But May was hungry and we had been alone for a long time. So when he came in, rain dripping off him, I said, 'Thomas, will you please get some food for us? May is hungry and we do not have any milk.'

"He ignored me. He took off his wet slicker and threw it on the sofa and went to the refrigerator. He looked inside, then slammed the door so that the whole apartment shook. 'Where is my beer?' he yelled, and his voice was so loud and angry that May started crying.

"'We do not have any beer,' I said. 'I told you. We are out of everything. Will you buy some food for us and some beer for you?'

"'Make her shut up,' he said, for May was screaming now, and at the sound of his voice, she cried even louder.

"'She is hungry,' I said. 'She cries because she is a baby and her stomach hurts.'

"Suddenly Thomas went to May and picked her up and began shaking her. 'Shut up!' he yelled at her.

"Of course, she cried harder. He was yelling at her and shaking her.

"I started scratching at him and hitting him. 'Leave her alone,' I said. 'Please. Hit me, but be gentle with our child.'

"He turned to me, and I saw hatred in his eyes. I had never seen such hatred in Thomas Larrigan. 'Okay, bitch,' he said. 'I will hit you, then.' He put May back into her crib, and then he reached into his holster and took out his gun. His sidearm, he called it. It was big and square, and he held it by the barrel and raised it over his head like a club and came at me. As I backed away from him, feeling for the wall behind me with my hands, I touched the handle of the broom that I used to sweep the floor. It was an old straw broom, and the bristles had been worn down so that they were short and very stiff. As Thomas came at me, holding his gun over his head, I grabbed the broom, and with all my strength, I shoved the bristle end into his face.

"Mac, he screamed like a bull, and I saw that one of his eyes was gushing blood where the bristles had stabbed into it. And then he was on top of me and . . . and then it felt as if a giant machete had split my head in half. I felt myself falling into a black bottomless hole, and I could not stop myself. It was as if my legs had melted and my head had floated away, and that is all I remember.

"I will tell you the rest of it next time, Mac. These are my true nightmares I am sharing with you now. I have tried to forget them for a very long time. It is very painful to speak of them. Please be patient with me."

Mac Cassidy was in his first-floor office downloading informa-tion about Simone and her films and the people she'd worked with when he heard the front door slam. He looked at his watch. Three-thirty. Like clockwork.

Then Katie called, "Daddy? I'm home."

"Hi, honey. Come on in, give me a hug."

A minute later she came into his office. She was looking more and more like Jane every day. She had Jane's sharp blue eyes, Jane's reddish-blonde hair, Jane's high cheekbones and pointy chin. She had a grown-up body, he couldn't help noticing. Jane had large breasts and had always complained that her butt was too big. Mac always told her that her butt was perfect, and he was being sincere.

Now Katie seemed to be growing into Jane's body.

She was wearing a knee-length gray skirt and a flowered blouse buttoned to her throat with a thin gold chain around her neck.

No other jewelry. No make-up. It was how she always dressed for school. Matronly, almost.

Katie had no body piercings, not even her ears, never mind tattoos.

Mac had noticed how the other freshmen girls dressed. How could you not notice? Low-cut jeans, high-riding T-shirts, bare bellies, more often than not with a jewel glimmering out of their navels. Lipstick, eye shadow, purple hair. Nose rings, studs in their eyebrows and lips and tongues.

He found none of that offensive, but he didn't think it was particularly attractive, either. So why did it bother him that his Katie dressed and groomed herself like a business executive?

She came over to where he was sitting, hugged him from behind, and kissed his cheek. "Are you getting a lot of work done?"

"I'm doing a lot of work," he said. "I don't know if any of it will turn out to be worth anything."

She sat in the other chair in his small office with her knees pressed together and her hands lying quietly in her lap. Perfect posture. "Working on the new book?"

He nodded.

"How's it going?"

Just like Jane, he thought. Jane had always asked how his work was going. About all he could ever think to tell her was that he'd written four pages today, or he'd revised a chapter, or he'd spent a frustrating day trying to dig up some arcane but vital bit of information, or he'd written nothing but did some good thinking. He never did figure out how to make a day sound interesting when he'd devoted it to scouring the inside of his head for words that matched up with the images and ideas he wanted to express.

People who didn't know better seemed to think that the writer's life was romantic and fascinating. The wives and children of writers quickly learned otherwise.

"It's going fine," Mac told Katie. "How was your day?"

Most kids, he knew, would say, "Oh, fine," or, "It sucked as usual," or, "Margie dissed me in front of everybody, and I hate her."

Not Katie. Katie went methodically through her day at school, class by class, what they were studying, the history quiz she got back, A-, she made a couple stupid mistakes, the big bio test coming up, what she had for lunch, her French teacher was out sick again, kids are gossiping that she's pregnant, she's not even married, the interesting discussion they had in English about Lady MacBeth . . .

His daughter was a mystery to him.

When she finished her recitation, she stood up, smoothed her skirt against her legs, and said, "Well, I'm going to change and get dinner started. I thawed some pork chops, and I thought we'd have rice and green beans."

You're fifteen years old, he wanted to scream. *You should be on the softball team. You should be riding around in some horny senior boy's car. You should be gossiping with the other girls. You should be trying out words like "bitch" and "bastard" and "shitfaced." You should be experimenting with beer and marijuana and sex. You should be doing forbidden things and lying about them. You should not be rushing home from school every day to cook dinner for your father. What's the matter with you?*

Well, he knew exactly what was the matter with her. Her mother had been run down by a commuter train, and Katie Cassidy believed it was her fault and intended to make sure nothing like that happened to her father.

He no longer knew what to say to her, how to deal with her. He'd talked to Miss Richards, the guidance counselor, and Dr. Wagner, the psychologist Miss Richards had recommended. Both of them assured Mac that this was a "stage" that Katie needed to go through, that he was lucky she hadn't reacted in the opposite way, by rebelling. This was Katie's way of grieving, they said, and it gave her life structure and meaning. Many kids would run away from home or attempt suicide. Katie was trying to be the best person she could be. She was trying to replace Jane, to fill that emptiness for her father.

No, it wasn't necessarily a normal response to what had happened. But it wasn't self-destructive, and who's to say what's normal, anyway?

Therapy would help, of course, but Katie had to be willing or there'd be no point to it. Mac had raised the subject with her several times. Her response was always the same: *I'm fine, Daddy. Really.*

And so she told him about her day at school and he told her about his day at his desk, and she cooked and cleaned and did her homework, and he earned the money and paid the bills, and sometimes in the evening after Katie had loaded the dishwasher, they sat in the living room and watched some dumb reality show on TV and made fun of it.

It didn't seem like a healthy relationship. But Mac didn't know what to do about it. It was working, more or less. It was getting them through each day.

She started to leave his office.

"Honey?" he said.

She turned. "Yes?"

"I've got to drive out to the Catskills in New York on Saturday. I wonder if you'd like to come along?"

She shrugged. "Okay."

"I've got to meet with Simone—she's the subject of my book, remember?"

Katie smiled. It was a smile of patience, of tolerance. It was the sort of smile a loving parent might bestow upon a cute child. A condescending smile. "Of course I remember," she said. "The movie star."

"I thought you might like to meet her," he said.

"Sure," she said. "Great."

Some day, Mac wanted to say, *you should say no. Some day you should get angry with me. You should yell at me, tell me I don't understand you,*

and you should lock yourself in your room and call your best friend and tell
her how your father is unfair and stupid.

What he actually said was, "Terrific. We'll have a fun day."

And Katie smiled and nodded and went upstairs to change out of
her school clothes before she made dinner.

———

IT WAS HAPPENING in the Rose Garden, right outside the building
where Pat Brody's office was located, but Brody was watching it on
his television, live on CNN.

Old Justice Crenshaw had just finished his two-minute statement
to the cameras and microphones, explaining in his soft, quavery
voice that he had been hearing all the speculation and thought it
was detracting from the business of the Court and so had decided
not to wait until the end of the session to announce his retirement.

Brody knew that the president had put pressure on the old judge.
The administration needed a quick hit of positive publicity, preferably something that would divert media attention from another
month of bad economic news.

On Monday, three days earlier, the president had called Pat Brody
into the Oval Office and told him he was going to announce the
Larrigan nomination now rather than later. The fact that he didn't
ask made it clear that he didn't want to hear Brody's opinion.

If he'd had a solid, definitive reason to think the president was
making a mistake, Pat Brody would have said something, and he
knew the president knew that.

But he had nothing like that. Oh, he had some doubts. Blackhole had observed the judge meeting in unusual places with an old
Marine buddy from Vietnam named Edward Moran. Moran seemed
vaguely unsavory, and they'd investigated him, but they'd come up
with nothing. And otherwise, there were only the normal sorts of
things that, if you looked hard enough, you'd learn about any man
who'd been on Earth for more than half a century, who'd gone

to war and to law school, who'd worked hard and made enemies, who'd made love to women and raised children.

So when the president told him that he wanted to go public with Larrigan, Pat Brody had kept his doubts to himself, preserving the president's plausible deniability.

Sometimes the president welcomed contradiction and debate from his staffers, and sometimes he wanted agreement and support. Brody was skilled at figuring out which before he said anything. That's how he had kept his job all this time.

This time, when the president said, "Any problem with this?" Brody knew he wanted support, not debate.

"He seems like a good candidate, sir," Brody had said.

"Remember what Churchill said?" said the president. "He said: 'Politics are almost as exciting as war, and quite as dangerous. In war you can only be killed once, but in politics many times.'"

The president was saying that he knew he might be making a mistake, and he was willing to live with it. So Brody just nodded and smiled. "You've got to be a cat. Nine lives."

"Right," said the president. "So we'll just have to take the chance of getting killed one more time." He'd flashed Pat Brody his famous grin. "Keep up the good work, Pat."

So now, as Pat Brody watched on the television set in his office almost directly beneath the Oval Office, the president introduced the tall judge with the eye patch as an American hero, a distinguished jurist, a worthy successor to Justice Lawrence Crenshaw, a personal friend, and a worthy golfing adversary.

And Thomas Larrigan thanked the president, shook his hand, moved to the microphone, and delivered a little speech that emphasized how honored he was to receive the president's confidence, how humbled to be given the opportunity to carry forth the distinguished legacy of Justice Crenshaw, how committed to serving his country, and, his punchline, how determined he was to continue trying to beat the president at golf.

It was quite a good speech, Brody thought. It hit all the right notes of humility and confidence, with the pitch-perfect hint of self-deprecating humor.

He recalled something Will Rogers had once said: "I tell you folks, all politics is applesauce."

Nobody was perfect. Not Justice Crenshaw, not the president, and certainly not Pat Brody. But they were all good enough, and unless somebody came up with more than a few secretive meetings with a former Marine buddy, he supposed Thomas Larrigan was good enough, too.

He better be, because now, with the official announcement of the nomination, the president's political future was on the line.

—❧❧—

JESSIE PARKED IN the strip mall across the street from the Motel 8 in Deer Creek, Illinois. From where she sat, she could watch both entrances to the motel. She had put on her sunglasses and her Oakland A's cap.

Not that she didn't trust Jimmy Nunziato.

Well, hell. She didn't. She didn't trust anybody. Hadn't for a long time.

For that matter, she didn't suppose Jimmy would trust her. Nobody could get away with what he'd been getting away with all his life by trusting anybody. Besides, he knew she used to be a cop.

He pulled into the motel lot at seven on the button. Driving a dark green Jeep Cherokee. The bald head, the stub of an unlit cigar in the corner of his mouth. Jimmy Nunziato was a cliché in his own story.

He backed the Cherokee into a space toward the rear corner of the lot so he could keep an eye on the entrances. Jessie smiled. She appreciated his caution.

The two of them could do this dance all night, holding back, watching each other, waiting to see who'd been followed.

She let him sit there for five minutes. Then she picked up her cell phone and called him.

"Hey, Jess," he said. "Where are you?"

Jessie started up her car and drove to the exit from the strip mall with her cell phone against her ear. "What the hell, Nunz?" she said. "You checking up on me?"

"Course I am, pretty girl. You wouldn't want it any different. So where are you?"

"I'll be there in a minute. Hang on." She found a hole in the traffic, darted across the street, drove into the motel lot, and pulled up beside his Cherokee. "Here I am," she said into the phone just about the time he turned his head and smiled at her.

She got out of her car and climbed into the passenger side of his. She leaned over and planted a kiss on his bald head. "So how you been?"

"Good," he said. "Keepin' out of trouble. You?"

"Oh, the same," she said. "Trying, anyway. You got my stuff?"

"Of course," he said. "You got mine?"

"Still three grand, right?"

He shrugged. "For you, sure." He handed her a manila envelope.

She peeked in, then took the wad of bills from her pocket and gave it to him.

He stuffed it into his jacket pocket.

"You gonna count it?" Jessie said.

"No need," he said. "I can always find you. I know you know that."

She smiled. "Anybody ever cheated you, Jimmy?"

"One guy did. That was quite a few years ago. You wanna know what happened to him?"

Jessie rolled her eyes. "No, that's all right." She pulled out the documents he'd prepared for her. Illinois driver's license. Birth certificate. Social security card. Passport. Two Visa cards.

She was now Karen Marie Donato, age 33, of 79 State Street, Chicago, Illinois. Jimmy had done a good job with the picture. Cutting and lightening her hair, making her look several years older than she'd been in the old head shot, the one he'd used when he created Carol Ann Chang. The magic of Photoshop.

"It all looks excellent," she said. "These cards, they're open accounts?"

"Yep. You can use 'em if you need to. Better not to."

"I won't," she said.

"Here." He handed her a cell phone. "Take this, too."

"Right," she said. "Stupid, I didn't think of that myself. Thanks." She flipped open the new phone. "Prepaid?"

He nodded. "Only way to go. I'm number eleven on your speed dial, there, okay? Here, gimme that old one."

Jessie handed her phone to Jimmy. He smashed it against the steering wheel a couple times. The plastic shattered in his big hand. He dropped the pieces out the window. "Take care of that problem," he said.

"Professionally done," she said. "So who's Karen Marie Donato?"

He grinned. "You, that's who."

"No," she said. "I mean, who *was* she?"

"Some girl, she was from Steamboat Springs, Colorado, went missing back in '87."

Jessie thought for a minute. "She was, what, twelve or thirteen?"

He shrugged. "Something like that. You can do the math. All I know is, she's long gone and hard to find and probably dead. So now you're her. It's good, somebody's gonna get some use out of her, don't you think?"

"Missing," said Jessie softly. "She's probably got parents, brothers and sisters, a boyfriend, still thinking about her, praying for her, hoping she's alive somewhere."

"So why don't you go visit 'em?" he said. "Hey, you're her now."

"You're sick." Jessie squeezed his arm. "Well, thanks, Nunz." She unlatched the car door.

"Hey, where you goin'?" he said.

"We're done here, aren't we?"

"You planning to keep driving around in that Civic?"

She shrugged. "I've got to drive."

He pointed at the glove compartment. "In there."

She opened it and took out an envelope. Inside was an automobile registration for the Cherokee. It was registered to Mary Ferrone. There was a title to the vehicle and insurance papers, also in Mary Ferrone's name.

She looked at Jimmy. "So who's Mary Ferrone?"

He smiled. "My Aunt Mary. Died last summer."

"What if I get stopped and they check?"

"These ain't fake documents, Jess. This car really belonged to Aunt Mary. And you really are Karen now. You're a real person. Your license, Aunt Mary's registration, all legit." He hesitated. "Still, try not to get stopped, though, okay?"

"You think of everything."

"I do," he said. "I got to."

Jessie smiled. "So what do I owe you for the car?"

"Gimme the Civic. Fair swap."

"It is like hell."

He shrugged. "Close enough."

They got out of the Cherokee, and Jimmy helped her move her stuff from the Civic to her new vehicle. Then she gave him a hug, got behind the wheel, turned on the ignition, and rolled down the window.

"Thanks, Nunz," she said.

He shook his head. "Don't even think about it. Good luck, Jess."

She reached out and patted his cheek.

"Hey," he said. "When you get to wherever you're going, gimme a call, all right? I wanna know you're okay. Speed dial eleven."

She gave him a thumbs up.

Jimmy smiled. "Good luck, kiddo," he said. Then he went over to the Civic, gave Jessie a wave, climbed in, and pulled out of the lot.

Jessie sat in the Cherokee for five minutes, then drove away, too.

Her eighteen months with Howie Cohen and his crew had taught her that there really was such a thing as honor among thieves, and Nunz was about the most honorable thief she'd ever met, and the most thorough and careful, too.

But there was no sense taking any chances. Staying at the Motel 8 in Deer Creek, Illinois would've just been asking for trouble.

She headed for the interstate, eastbound. She figured she'd drive for another hour or so, put some distance between herself and Deer Creek before she started looking for a place to spend the night.

CHAPTER

13

"It is now Friday, and I have not talked with you for a few days, dear Mac. I have not been feeling well. But you will be visiting me tomorrow, and I wanted to finish this part of my story.

"I was telling you about how it was with Thomas. Perhaps now you understand why it is painful for me to tell you my stories. Perhaps now you understand that these memories are like knives to my heart. They made wounds that will never heal. Throughout my time in Paris and then in Hollywood I was bleeding inside, remembering May, and I still bleed, remembering the foolish dreams that Thomas Larrigan encouraged me to dream. It is better not to have dreams at all than to come to the end of your life and realize they will never come true.

"I told you how he hit me on the head with his gun that rainy day in Saigon. I was badly hurt, Mac. Much of what I am about to tell you was told to me. It is not part of my actual memory. There are still holes in my memory.

"The night that Thomas hit me on the head, Bunny came to my rooms to visit. She found me unconscious on the floor and used her influence with the Red Cross to find a hospital bed for me. I was told that Bunny saved my life. If she hadn't come that night, I would have died. There was bleeding inside my head, and my brain was swelling from where Thomas had hit me. The doctors drilled a hole in my skull. They worried that I would not regain consciousness. They worried that even if I did, my brain would be damaged. Perhaps it was, I cannot tell.

"I was unconscious for many days. When I awakened, I found myself in a hospital. I was tended by Vietnamese nuns in their flowing black habits. They told me that my skull had been fractured and I had been in a coma.

"I was very sick, Mac. My mind was jumbled and dizzy. I had terrible headaches, and I was nauseated most of the time. I faded in and out of awareness. I had frightening dreams. I suppose they were giving me drugs, too. God help me, it was many days after I woke up from my coma before I remembered May. When I asked one of the nurses where May was, if she was all right, the nurse just shrugged and shook her head. I believed then that May was dead.

"I was terribly depressed, Mac. I would have killed myself if I could.

"Then one day Bunny came to see me, and I asked her about May. Bunny sat beside me and took my hand in both of hers. 'I don't know where May is,' she said. 'When I found you, your baby was not there.'

"I began to scream. 'I want my baby! Where is my baby?' I tried to get out of bed and fell on the floor. Bunny helped me back into bed and a doctor came and gave me a shot.

"Several days passed before Bunny came to see me again. Then she said, 'I have news of May.'

"'Where is she?' I said. 'I want to see my baby.'

"Bunny was shaking her head. 'I'm sorry, Li An. May is gone.'

"'Gone? What do you mean, gone? Where has she gone? What has he done with her?' I began shaking and crying, and that made me dizzy and nauseated. I believed that Thomas had taken May away from me.

"Bunny held me and whispered to me. She said that May was all right, and she kept repeating it until finally I calmed down. Then she told me what she had learned. On the day that Thomas hit me on the head, he took May away with him and turned her over to an American agency that cared for Vietnamese orphans. He told them that he had found May abandoned, that he didn't know who her parents were, that it looked like she was the baby of an American soldier and a Vietnamese mother. The agency arranged for such children to be adopted, and that, Mac, is what happened to May. While her mother lay unconscious in a Saigon hospital, little May was given new parents.

"They sold her, Mac. It was corrupt, of course, as everything in Saigon was in those times. May's American parents paid a large sum of money to the agency. She was flown to Paris where her new parents met her, signed some documents, and took her away with them.

"'May is safe,' Bunny said to me. 'She is in a good American home where she will be well loved and well cared for.'

"'But she is no orphan,' I said. 'She is my child.'

"'Think about it,' said Bunny. 'The war is all around this city. There are bombs and fires. People are dying in the streets. There is famine and disease. It will get worse. May is better off.'

"And I did think about it, Mac. I thought that I had no hope for any future, no means to care for a child in Saigon in those times, no reason to expect that I would even survive the war. Oh, I cried for my baby. But gradually I realized that I was crying for selfish reasons, for the love I felt for little May, for the emptiness of my life without my baby.

"Bunny was right. By the time they discharged me from the hospital, I had hardened my heart. May had a better life than I could have given her. She was lucky. I was grateful. Thomas had stolen my child from me. But he had done the right thing. Whether he acted out of kindness to his daughter or cruelty to me, I do not know.

"By the time I left the hospital, my hair had started to grow back, for they had, of course, shaved my skull. I had lost a lot of weight. I was not beautiful, Mac. I had no place to go except to Mai Duc. She was kind to me. She took me in, fed me, gave me some little chores to do for her while I regained my health and my beauty.

"And then she put me back to work, giving comfort to those who would pay for it. No longer was there any joy or satisfaction for me in this. I had allowed myself to have hopes and dreams, and then they were taken from me. There was a hole in my heart, Mac, a place where May had lived. And nothing would ever fill it.

"One day Mai Duc called me to her office. An elderly man, a French diplomat, was there, and Mai Duc told me that she had made an agreement with him, an arrangement such as she had made with Thomas Larrigan. I bowed my head and nodded. It did not matter to me. Nothing that happened to me mattered any longer.

"He was a gentle old man who made few demands on me, and when the evacuation of the city began soon after he purchased me, he told me he would bring me to Paris with him if I wanted. I would no longer belong to him, for he had family there. But he said he felt a responsibility toward me. He would give me money and find a place for me in Paris. He would visit me now and then, but I would have no obligation to him. I was free.

"He knew important people in Paris, he told me. They would help me.

"By this time I had lost track of my dear friend Bunny, who had saved my life. I never had the chance to say good-bye to her or to thank her. Of course, I never did see Thomas Larrigan or his friend Eddie. I always assumed they all were killed. Or perhaps they had returned to America.

"I recently learned that Bunny, at least, survived. That made me happy. I do not know what happened to Thomas or Eddie Moran.

"I visited Mai Duc on the day I was to leave for Paris. I thanked her for caring for me all those years, for being a mother to me.

"'Everything is changing, Li An,' she said to me. 'I am happy that you are escaping our country. I myself hope to be leaving soon. I have loved you as my daughter. I will miss you.'

"'And I will miss you, my mother,' I said.

"She opened the drawer of her desk, removed an envelope, and handed it to me. 'This is my farewell gift to you,' she said. 'Do not open it until you arrive in Paris.'

"I did as she asked. I flew to Paris with my benefactor, and I waited until he had delivered me to the little apartment he had rented for me before I opened the envelope Mai Duc had given me.

"It contained a single sheet of paper. On it was typed a name and address in America, and under that was a note in Mai Duc's hand. 'These are your daughter's parents,' it said.

"Their name was Church. They lived in Chicago. They had given May the name Jessie.

"And that is my story, Mac. I was in Paris for only a short time before my friend arranged a small part for me in a low-budget French film. The people who made the film thought I should have a French name, so they called me Simone Bonet, and I have been Simone ever since. I do not like to think of myself as Li An. It reminds me too much of my years in Vietnam.

"I think that first film was a bad one and I was a bad actress. I was required to take off my clothes and do sex scenes, which did not bother me, because I had no pride and no joy in my life, and nothing mattered. Because I bared my breasts and my bottom, and because my body was considered attractive, I was given more sex roles, and pretty soon I began to get some recognition. You would not consider those films particularly racy by today's standards, but back then they were. I knew that. It did not matter to me.

"After a few years I was invited to America to audition for a part in a Hollywood movie. I accepted, of course. In America I would be closer to my daughter. I dreamed of finding her one day, of revealing myself to her. Or perhaps she would see me in a film and somehow know it was I. That idea inspired me to try to be a better actress and to choose better roles, although I know I was not very good.

"I never did see or hear from May, and after a while I came to accept that. I realized that her life was better than any I could give her, and certainly she would not want to learn that her mother was a prostitute from Saigon and a French porn star. So I let her go. I had her new family's name, Church, and I knew they were, or had been, living in Chicago. But I did not try to find her. I let that selfish idea die. May was better off without me.

"I have enjoyed believing that my May grew up to become a beautiful and successful young American woman with loving adoptive parents. I like this dream. It contents me.

"Then just a few weeks ago I saw a photograph in a newspaper. It was Jessie, my May, although the name she was using was Carol Ann Chang, from San Francisco. I know in the center of my heart, the way only a mother can know, that the young woman in that photograph is my child. She is a beautiful young woman, Mac. I can see both myself and Thomas Larrigan in her features.

"It seemed as if fate had delivered my daughter back to me. And so I wrote to her. Now I wait to see what will happen. It has been several weeks now, and she has not replied to me, and I am beginning to wonder if she is my May after all. I will not allow myself to abandon that hope, although it is hard sometimes. That hope gives me the strength to fight against my disease and to tell you my stories. As I have told you before, I tell these stories in the hopes that one day May will read them and learn who she is.

"I will speak of Hollywood another time. I am very tired now, and I want to be alert and beautiful when I see you tomorrow."

—◦◦—

As NEAR AS Eddie Moran could tell, the main industry in the little hamlet of Beaverkill, New York, was trout fishing, and it appeared that the month of May was prime time for it. The commercial center, such as it was, was clustered around a crossroads at the only traffic light in town. The parking spaces were filled with vehicles— most of them SUVs—with more license plates from Massachusetts, Pennsylvania, New Jersey, and Connecticut than from New York. They sported Trout Unlimited and Federation of Fly Fishers decals on the windows and aluminum rod tubes and chest-high waders and tackle bags in back.

Moran counted four shops apparently devoted to fly fishing, three restaurants, two hole-in-the-wall lunch counters, and one high-end camping and outdoor-clothing store. There were several motels and a couple of run-down old hotels and a diner on the outskirts of town. The sign in front of one motel read, "Fishermen Welcome."

Moran drove around until he found the Beaverkill town offices in an old Victorian building on the road heading east just out of town. He put on a pair of oversized horn-rimmed glasses and a necktie, grabbed his briefcase from the backseat, and went inside.

It was a big open room with tall windows and high ceilings and fluorescent lights. A waist-high counter ran its length, front to back. On the left side of the room behind the counter were desks and work cubicles. On the right side were some offices with the doors ajar. They appeared to be empty.

The heavyset white-haired woman behind the counter, the town clerk's secretary, barely glanced at the business card he showed her. It identified him as Charles C. Metcalf, Water and Natural Resources Commission for the State of New York in Albany. Eddie Moran had a card for every occasion.

He asked to see the current listing of property assessments. She asked him if there was something specific she could help him with. He smiled, said no, thanks anyway, he could take care of it, trying mainly to remain as bland and bureaucratic and forgettable as possible behind his big glasses.

A minute later she plopped a thick loose-leaf notebook on the counter and pointed to a wooden table where he could spread out and do his research.

The damn thing was arranged alphabetically by street name, so it took him over half an hour to find Simone Bonet's name listed at 1049 Mountainview Road. She owned twenty-two acres. The home and property were assessed at $345,000.

The white-haired woman seemed to be ignoring him, and aside from a couple of younger women he'd noticed sitting at desks in the open area behind the counter, there was nobody else in the Beaverkill town offices on this Friday afternoon in May. Moran figured everybody was probably off trout fishing, which was all right by him. The fewer people who might remember him, the better.

Back in his Explorer, he pulled out his *DeLorme Atlas and Gazetteer* for the state of New York, turned to the quadrant that included the town of Beaverkill, and found Mountainview Road. It went south to north for the entire length of the town, an old state highway, probably, more or less parallel to the interstate. A winding river ran between Mountainview and the interstate.

Fifteen minutes later, Moran was driving slowly along Mountainview Road. Every mile or so there was a little pull off where the road touched the river, and in every pull off two or three cars were parked. Fishermen, he supposed.

The dwellings were widely separated. There were a few farms with picturesque barns and cows or horses in the pastures, and some small ranch-style homes. Mostly, it was fields and trees and brooks and streams. In places a dirt roadway disappeared into the woods. Some of them had mailboxes at the end, some didn't.

There was no mailbox in front of the driveway leading in to number 1049. Moran located it by the process of elimination. There was a mailbox bearing the number 1021, then a driveway with no mailbox. The next mailbox had the name Hewitt, and the one after that had the number 1065 on it.

Half a mile past Simone's driveway, at a dip in the hilly road, was one of those fisherman's pull offs. Two cars were parked there. Moran stopped, got out, and checked the vehicles. They didn't seem to be displaying any special permits. Just some fishing junk in the back and decals with pictures of fish or trout flies pasted on the windows. Moran guessed that you could leave your vehicle in one of these pull-offs for as long as you wanted. Around here, where trout fishing was the main industry, nobody would hassle a fisherman.

The gurgling of water rushing around boulders and over gravel filtered up to him, and through the trees he could see the glint of the afternoon sun on the water.

It was nice. Peaceful. Eddie Moran was thinking he ought to take up trout fishing. He needed a hobby.

Well, maybe some day.

He got back into his car and continued along Mountainview Road. It was nine miles to the first store, one of those mini-marts with gas pumps out front and candy bars and hot coffee and cigarettes inside. He stopped there, filled his tank, and paid the kid at the register with cash.

From there he turned and headed back the way he'd come. He noted the mileage from the end of Li An's driveway, then continued into town. Twelve miles. Nothing between here and there except a few houses and plenty of fields and woods and trout streams. So if she had to go somewhere, it was twelve miles one way and nine the other to get anyplace at all.

Back in town, he parked his truck, put the clunky horn-rims back on, and went into the first fishing shop he came to. It was empty except for one guy, somewhere in his thirties, sitting at a table tying a fly. He glanced up at Moran, said, "How ya doin'?" and returned to his work.

Moran nodded to the guy, then pretended to be interested in the store's wares. In the middle of the room a big wooden display case sat on a table. It had dozens of small compartments, and each compartment held bunches of trout flies. Racks of rods and aluminum tubes hung on one wall. There were chest waders and hip boots and fishing hats. There were freestanding displays of feathers and fur and fishhooks in plastic envelopes that Moran figured were used for making flies. There were shelves stacked with books and videos. There were landing nets and sunglasses and knives. There were racks of shirts and jackets and vests.

Finally on a table piled with calendars and postcards and souvenir ashtrays and mugs Moran found what he was looking for—a stack of oval decals picturing a trout opening its mouth to eat an insect and the words "Catskill Anglers, Beaverkill, New York" printed around the circumference.

He picked up a decal and took it to the guy at the fly-tying table.

The guy looked up at him. "That it?"

Moran nodded.

"Need some tippet material? Got all the flies you need?"

"I'm all set for now, thanks."

"Buck and a half, then," said the guy.

Moran paid him and left before they could engage in any memorable conversation.

He got back on the interstate and drove north. He put two towns between himself and Beaverkill, then started looking for a motel with the VACANCY sign lit.

In the town of Joshua he rented a room for five nights, paid cash, and signed the name Robert Flaherty. He left the section asking for automobile information blank.

He took a booth in the diner down the street from the motel and had the pot roast special, which he ate with a newspaper propped up in front of him, and a slice of apple pie for dessert. It was pretty good. Eddie Moran liked diners.

The last thing he did before he went into in his motel room that night was to stick his new fish decal on the rear window of the Explorer.

_____

DURING JESSIE'S TREK across the continent she learned that the motels and gas stations and restaurants on the interstate highways were more expensive than the ones on the less-traveled state highways or secondary roads near smaller towns. She found the cheaper ones more congenial, too. The people were friendlier. It was a trade-off, though. She felt more anonymous interacting with people along the interstates, where strangers came and went all the time and nobody paid much attention to you.

So she'd mostly stuck close to the interstates. This trip was not about economizing.

Now that she was in the middle of Illinois with a new identity and a new car, though, Jessie felt that she could stay anywhere, mingle with people, let her guard down, just be herself—whoever that was. For the first time in as long as she could remember, she felt safe.

She knew it was a dangerous feeling. She'd have to resist it.

After she'd swapped cars with Jimmy Nunziato, she continued along Interstate 74 to Bloomington and then, without thinking much about it, hooked onto 55 North. Interstate 55 led to Chicago, thence to Evanston.

Jessie felt her hometown tugging her.

She'd grown up in Evanston, the daughter, the only child, of Michael and Ellen Church. Kindergarten, elementary school, middle school, high school. She'd played softball and field hockey, gone to proms, made the honor roll, worked at the ice-cream stand in the summers, dated nice boys, kept her virginity.

It was a good childhood.

From the beginning, Michael and Ellen had talked to Jessie about the fact that she was adopted. They didn't know anything about her biological parents, but that was irrelevant anyway. The point, they kept emphasizing, was that she was the one they'd picked to be their daughter. That made her special.

Jessie had always accepted that. She felt loved and safe with Michael and Ellen Church. She did feel special. As far as she was concerned, they were her parents and she was their daughter. Being adopted didn't mean anything to her one way or the other.

Her mother died of ovarian cancer when Jessie was a freshman at Northwestern. It happened fast. Her father called her at her dorm in October and told her Mom was in the hospital for tests. He called her again in March when Jessie was studying for midterms to tell her that she better come home right away.

Just like that.

Two years later, on a snowy night in February, Michael Church was murdered in the parking garage at O'Hare airport. Three nine-millimeter bullets in the chest from short range. They found his Nissan Pathfinder parked in a lot near Wrigley Field five days later.

The police figured it was a simple, random robbery. Whoever shot Jessie's father took his wallet and his watch and his vehicle. People got mugged in Chicago every day.

But there were undercurrents of suspicion that didn't escape Jessie. Michael Church was an executive with a computer company that had contracts with several Asian and Middle Eastern governments. He did a lot of traveling. He might have been a government spy. Or a drug importer. There were whispered stories to explain his murder. More interesting stories than just getting mugged in a parking garage for his car and the contents of his wallet. Stories that somehow made Michael Church the villain.

Nothing was ever proven, and the stories died fast. But Jessie never forgot them.

Many people who thought they knew Jessie assumed that she went into law enforcement because of her father's murder. It was one of those simplistic, easily understood, pop-psych explanations, and Jessie never bothered to correct it.

But the fact was, she'd wanted to be a cop ever since she could remember, and she was already working toward her degree in Criminal Justice when Michael Church was gunned down.

It took Jessie nearly four years of part-time detecting to figure out who'd killed her father. His name was Artie Toomer. Toomer was a small-time crack addict who mistook Michael Church for somebody else. By the time Jessie tracked him down, Artie Toomer was already dead, shot twice in the face by his girlfriend while he was passed out on her couch. She explained that she was sick of being slapped around.

So Jessie had been cheated out of her revenge. Hardly a day went by when she didn't think about it, and every time she did, it pissed her off all over again.

On this Friday night in May, Jessie Church found herself in a motel off one of the Interstate 55 exits north of Bloomington, Illinois, near the town of Cooksville, just a morning's drive to Evanston. She wasn't certain why she'd come this way, except that she'd been thinking about her childhood and her parents and, for the first time in a long time, she was wondering where she'd really come from.

She'd left San Francisco because she had to. She headed east because that's where there was space to lose herself, and because she needed to hook up with Jimmy Nunziato along the way. She'd made Beaverkill, New York, her destination because it seemed to be the kind of place where no one would ever think to look. It was a tentative destination. The note from S. Bonet, who claimed to be her biological mother, had given her the idea, that's all.

This was not a quest for her identity. Jessie had not set off on this cross-country journey to find herself or to discover her past or to seek her roots.

She was just trying to shake Howie Cohen.

Now, though, in Cooksville, Illinois, on this Friday evening in May, with a new name and the documents to back it up, she figured she was just two or three days of easy driving from Beaverkill, New York, and she found herself trying to imagine actually knocking on S. Bonet's front door, having this woman open it, seeing her face, and realizing in some flash of recognition that Jessie couldn't begin to imagine, maybe some deep-buried memory suddenly bulling its way to the front of her consciousness, that, yes, this woman had given birth to her.

Jessie found the note that she'd stuck in the pages of the Joyce Carol Oates novel she'd been reading. "I have reason to believe that you are my daughter by birth," S. Bonet had written in green ink. "I would like to verify this. I can only assume that you would like to know, too. I beseech you to respond."

Jessie lay back on her motel bed and closed her eyes. "Beseech" was a strong word.

She wished S. Bonet had not written this note. It was like getting a phone call that your father was murdered. You couldn't ignore it. It changed everything.

Jessie picked up her cell phone and dialed the number on the note.

It rang four or five times. Then a young-sounding woman's voice said, "Hello?"

"Is this Ms. Bonet?" said Jessie.

"This is Jill. I'm sorry. Simone's sleeping. Who's calling please?"

Jessie glanced at the clock beside her bed. It would be nine-thirty in New York. "It's, um, this is Jessie," she said. "Jessie Church."

"Oh. Jessie." There was a hesitation. Then Jill said, "Please hold on. I'll wake her up."

Jessie said, "No, wait. Don't." But she realized that Jill wasn't listening.

A minute later Jessie heard the sound of Jill's muffled voice, as if she was holding her hand over the telephone receiver. She heard Jill say, "Simone." The rest was unclear.

Then: "Jessie?" It was a soft, low-pitched, sleepy voice, and even in that one word, her name, Jessie detected a faint accent. French, probably. Bonet looked like a French name.

Jessie sat there with her back against the headboard of her motel bed pressing her telephone hard against her ear.

"Jessie? Jessie Church? Is that you?"

Jessie realized she'd been holding her breath. She let it out in a long sigh.

Then she disconnected.

14

Eddie Moran's mental alarm clock woke him up at four o'clock on Saturday morning. He dressed quickly—sneakers, blue jeans, brown shirt—then stuffed his backpack with a day's worth of supplies. Three bottles of water, three Hershey bars, two apples, binoculars, the digital camera with the long zoom lens, flashlight, knife, insect repellent, notebook, two pens, black sweatshirt, and lightweight green windbreaker.

He was in his car at 4:15 and turning into the pull off beside the trout stream a half hour later. He nosed his Explorer against some hemlocks at one end of the area to leave room for the other fishermen who might want to try this place. He figured, it was Saturday, looked like it was going to be a nice spring day, and there'd probably be a lot of fishermen out. He regretted that he didn't have any equipment stowed in the back, but he figured his new decal would announce him as just another out-of-state trout fisherman if anybody bothered to look twice at his vehicle.

The sky was just beginning to fade from black to purple as Eddie Moran crossed the street and ducked into the woods.

He picked his way through the scrubby oaks and evergreens parallel to Mountainview Road until he came to her driveway. He followed the driveway, keeping inside the woods, and after about five minutes he saw her house. He crept closer, crouched there on the edge of the opening, and surveyed the setup.

The driveway ended in a turnaround in front. A big SUV was parked there. Judging by the size and the squarish shape of it, it was an old-model Jeep, one of those huge Wagoneers, he guessed, but it was still too dark to see clearly. The building itself was your basic New England farmhouse—two stories high, a couple of dormers on the roof, open porch across the front, with a new-looking glassed-in addition on the back, and beyond that a wooden deck. Behind the house the ground sloped away into a valley, and some low hills rose up in the distance against the dark western horizon.

From where he was kneeling in the woods, Moran could hear the gurgle of water. It seemed to come from the valley in back of the house. Another trout stream, he guessed.

He moved around to the side of the house, keeping inside the line of trees, until he found some high ground. It was a little wooded knoll from which he could watch both the front and the back of the house. It was on the edge of the field that abutted the side yard, and a clump of big hemlocks grew there. It was about fifty yards from the house—close enough to see everything with the binoculars, far enough to remain safely hidden.

Moran crawled under the hemlock boughs and sat experimentally with his back against the trunk. The ground under the tree was a pillow of old hemlock needles. It was more luxurious than he had any right to expect.

He took off his backpack, fished out his big bowie knife, and cut away some branches that blocked his view of Li An's house and yard. Then he looped his binoculars around his neck, spread his windbreaker on the ground, sat on it with his back against the tree trunk and his pack within reach, and settled in to wait.

It would be a long day, but Eddie Moran had spent a lot of long days waiting in the woods, and none of them had been as comfortable and relaxed as this one promised to be.

For one thing, he didn't expect there to be other men sneaking through the woods who'd kill him if they found him and if he didn't kill them first.

A mosquito buzzed in his ear. He squirted some repellent onto his palm, rubbed his hands together, and coated his face, neck, and hands. Then he dug under the layer of old hemlock needles, grabbed a handful of damp dirt, made mud of it between his oily palms, and rubbed it on his face and the backs of his hands. It adhered nicely to the slick insect repellent.

He ate an apple.

Overhead, one by one, the stars winked out. The purple sky faded to pewter. Birdsong filled the woods.

Eddie Moran sat there under the hemlocks, watching and waiting.

─◦◦◦─

"Good morning, Mac. I want to tell you about something that happened last night. I need to talk about it for a minute. It is not in the sequence of my story. I do not know if it is—or will ever be—part of the story. Maybe. Maybe it will be how our story ends. It would make a lovely ending.

"I had just gotten into bed when the phone rang in the other room. Jill answered it. I heard her speak, I heard a strange tone in her voice. When she brought me the phone, she had this odd, concerned look on her face, as if she had heard that somebody I loved had died and that she feared I would be terribly sad. Then she said it was Jessie on the phone.

"I will not tell you the whole story about how I figured out that May, Jessie Church, that is, my dear daughter, is living in California using a different name. As I've mentioned, I wrote her a note several weeks ago asking her—begging her, really—to call me or write to me, but she never did.

"Now she was calling me. She was there, on the telephone. But when I spoke her name into the phone, she said nothing. I heard her breathe for a moment. Then she hung up.

"It must have been May. Jessie. I'm sure it was. Who else could it be? And because she called me—even though she hung up without speaking to me—it must mean that she thinks I am her mother.

"At first I was very sad that she hung up when I spoke her name. I cried. But Jill pointed out that this was really a reason to rejoice, a cause for hope, and I have decided that she is right. It is a very big thing to speak to your mother after a whole lifetime. Jessie needs to understand this and what it means. I am hoping that she will call me again, and that this time she will speak to me.

"So I went to sleep with this feeling of hope that Jessie will call again, and that I will be able to see her and hold her hand and tell her our story before I die.

"I confess that when I awoke this morning I felt less hope. The mornings are not good for me. But now I can feel my hope returning. And I will see you today, Mac. That is another cause for happiness.

"So I am happy today after all, dear Mac. I will see you soon."

* * *

AFTER AN HOUR of driving with Katie beside him, it occurred to Mac Cassidy that they only had one subject of mutual interest to discuss. Of course, neither of them mentioned it. They never did.

Instead, he asked her the standard questions about school—how did she like her teachers, what was she reading, did she get any tests or papers back lately, questions he supposed he asked her every evening—and she answered them fully, with none of the impatience or evasion that you'd expect from a normal fifteen-year-old girl.

Even when he asked her about boys, she didn't roll her eyes. She didn't care about boys, she said. They were so immature. She'd been asked out a few times, but she told them no.

What she didn't say to Mac Cassidy, but what he suspected, was that she didn't go out with boys because she didn't dare to leave her father alone.

He wanted to just blurt it out: "Honey, let's talk about Mom, what do you say?"

No, that wasn't the way to approach it.

He could say: "I miss Mom every day. How about you?"

What he really wanted to say was: "It wasn't your fault."

Except the next thing he would say would be: "It was *my* fault."

He knew Katie was lugging around a load of guilt. He was certain that she knew he was, too. And neither of them could talk about it, not to each other, not to anybody.

So Mac and his daughter devoted themselves to worrying about each other and avoiding the subject that preoccupied them both.

Freud said you were "normal" if you were able to love and to work. Mac was back at work now, and he knew that once he started actually writing the book, he'd be able to lose himself in it. As for love, if love for your daughter counted, then Mac Cassidy was a master of love.

Love for a woman? He hadn't thought about that kind of love since that March evening over a year ago. He didn't know if that made him abnormal or not.

As for Katie, her job was school, and she excelled at that, so he supposed that meant she was able to work. He understood that Katie's version of love was consoling and taking care of and worrying about her father, playing the role of surrogate wife, obsessed with the fear that he, too, would suddenly die. You didn't have to be an expert to know that was not even close to normal.

He wondered what would become of them.

―∽∾―

JESSIE DECIDED TO follow the back roads the rest of the way from Illinois to Beaverkill, New York. She wasn't so sure that she'd end up there anyway. Meanwhile, she wasn't in any hurry. She liked seeing the countryside, the farms and the newly planted fields and the lime-green foliage of the springtime leaves.

After she'd hung up on S. Bonet, she'd lain back on her bed with her eyes closed, letting her mind fly free. She remembered that Jill had spoken the name "Simone," and then she connected the woman's first name with her last.

Simone Bonet. That was her name.

Jessie had heard of Simone, usually that way, that one name. Simone, as though she didn't need any last name, like Cher or Madonna. Jessie didn't know anything about Simone except that she had been some kind of cult movie icon.

She'd done nude scenes that were considered daring for her time, Jessie seemed to remember. She didn't think she'd seen any of Simone's films. If she had, they weren't memorable.

Jessie wondered if this Simone Bonet was that movie Simone.

Simone Bonet, whatever Simone she was, believed that she was Jessie's birth mother.

Jessie wasn't at all sure she wanted to find out whether it was true. She had no particular curiosity about it. It had taken a while to get used to the idea that both of her parents were dead.

And yet she found herself drawn to Beaverkill, New York, and she figured she'd keep driving in that general direction until she got there. Then she'd decide what to do next.

―∽∾―

"YOU OKAY, DADDY?" said Katie.

He glanced at her and smiled. "Just daydreaming, I guess."

They were on Route 84 in the southern part of Connecticut. They'd been on the road a little over two hours. More than halfway there. Katie had tuned the car radio to an NPR station when they left Concord, and when it began to fade, she'd surfed the dial until she found another NPR signal, and she'd kept doing that, looking for the serious talk or the classical music, skipping past the fast-talk stations and the classic rock stations and the easy-listening stations and the hip-hop and rap and other contemporary music stations.

Mac Cassidy figured she was doing that out of consideration for his tastes, although he wouldn't have minded listening to some classic rock.

It was disturbing. Teenage girls were supposed to be selfish about car music. They were supposed to get sulky if they couldn't listen to their own stations. Or else they brought their own iPods with them—Katie had one—that they played so loud into their earphones that other people could hear the noise leaking out.

That's what Katie used to do, back when she rode in the backseat with her two parents up front.

Now she had found some classical music from a station out of Danbury. Cassidy didn't recognize it, but it was melodic and he liked it.

"So what're you daydreaming about?" said Katie.

He glanced at her beside him in the front seat. She was looking out the window, acting almost too casual. He tried to read her body language. He wondered if she could read his mind. He wondered if she wanted him to initiate a conversation about Jane. He wondered if she wanted to talk about guilt and responsibility, about grieving and healing, about moving on.

She gave him a quick, perfunctory smile, and he decided that she was just making conversation, so he said, "Oh, nothing. Sorry. My mind was wandering, that's all."

Then she turned and looked hard at him for just an instant, and he thought he saw in her eyes that she knew. *You were thinking about Mom,* he could practically hear her say. *You were blaming yourself.*

He found his response actually forming in his mouth. The words were right there. He could feel them on his tongue. All he had to do was say them. *It wasn't your fault, honey. It was just an accident. Please don't blame yourself. If you'll stop blaming yourself, I won't blame myself anymore. Deal?*

But he couldn't make himself speak those words. Instead, he smiled at her and said, "We've got to stop for gas pretty soon. Keep an eye out for a place. We can get something to drink."

―⁂―

A LITTLE AFTER ten-thirty, a tall blonde woman pushed a wheelchair out onto the wooden deck on the back of the house. Through his binoculars, Eddie Moran could see that the blonde was somewhere in her thirties, quite good-looking in a slender, muscular way. She was wearing shorts and a tank top. Nice tan. Good skin. Strong arms and legs. If he hadn't been working, Moran supposed he wouldn't be able to prevent himself from thinking about her sexually, imagining her shucking off her shorts and wrapping those long tanned legs around his hips, him cradling her hard round ass in his hands . . .

But now he *was* working, so he banished those thoughts as quickly as they came into his head. He'd learned a long time ago that sex and work didn't mix, unless the sex was part of the work the way it had been with Bunny.

Maybe the time would come for him and the blonde, but not today.

He shifted his binoculars to the figure in the wheelchair. It was Li An—she might be called Simone now, but she was still Li An to Eddie Moran—and she was apparently an invalid.

He studied her face. It was amazing. She looked just the same. He supposed her body had gone to hell—why else would she be in a wheelchair with a blanket spread over her legs?—but her face . . . she still looked about fourteen, the way she looked back then. That same smooth bronze color, those amazing cheekbones, those big almond-shaped dark eyes, skin like silk, no wrinkles, not even around her mouth or eyes, even after all these years.

The blonde went back inside. Li An had a book opened on her lap, but after about ten minutes, her chin slumped onto her chest, and Moran figured she'd gone to sleep.

Around noon the blonde came back out with a tray. It held a teapot and a couple of silver pitchers and two teacups. She put the tray on a table, then leaned close to Li An and spoke to her.

Li An lifted her head. Moran saw her smile, and then the blonde cradled Li An's face in both of her hands and kissed her on the mouth.

Moran found himself smiling. So that's how it was.

He watched the two women sit there sipping their tea and holding hands. After a while the blonde went inside, and Li An started reading her book again.

Moran had been taking notes in his notebook, keeping track of the time everything happened. He didn't know how or if any of it would be useful. It was his habit, and he knew it was a good habit. Keep track of everything. Plan carefully. Be more alert than the enemy. Anticipate the worst.

Do all that and you might survive for one more night.

_⟶⟵_

A GREEN SEDAN—a Toyota Camry, several years old—pulled up beside the old Wagoneer at ten minutes before two, according to Eddie Moran's watch. He noted the time in his notebook.

A tall bearded guy and a girl, looked like a teenager, got out. A minute later the blonde came out of the house. She shook hands with both the man and the girl, and from where he was hiding in the clump of hemlocks, Moran could hear their voices, although he couldn't make out their words. It sounded as if they all knew each other and were happy to see each other.

They went into the front door, and a minute later they emerged onto the deck behind the house. The bearded guy sat beside Li An and gripped her hand in both of his for a minute. The girl went and stood in front of Li An's wheelchair, and Moran could see her bend a little and speak to her.

Then the guy said something to the girl, and she went into the house.

Moran picked up his camera, zoomed in on the guy with the beard, and snapped a few shots. Then he turned the camera onto the green Camry. The way it was parked he could see the rear license plate, although it was at an angle. He couldn't read the plate, but he knew he could manipulate the digital image on his computer and get the numbers, so he snapped a couple of shots.

A little while later the blonde and the girl came out with trays piled with sandwiches and drinks.

They all sat there on the deck and ate.

Eddie Moran snapped a few more photos. Then he found an apple and a Hershey bar in his backpack, and he ate, too, and washed it down with a swig from one of his water bottles.

—◦◦◦—

TRYING TO BE entertaining and upbeat exhausted Simone, and by the time the four of them had finished eating their lunch out there on her sunny deck, she was spent. Having Mac and Katie for company, however, and thinking about their book energized her, too.

Katie helped Jill pile the lunch dishes and glasses onto the tray and the two of them went inside. Jill was going to take the girl with her on her afternoon errands, leaving Simone and Mac alone for an hour or so to give them a chance to talk about their book.

Katie was an adorable girl. Smart and poised and innocent, devoted to her father. Also profoundly sad, deeply troubled. Simone guessed Katie was a little older than Simone had been when she had given birth to May.

Simone heard Jill's car start up and drive away. Mac was sitting beside her. They were both gazing off toward the distant hills. Simone's eyelids were growing heavy.

"It's very peaceful here," Mac said.

Simone blinked her eyes open. "I'm lucky to have found it," she said. "I will live out the rest of my life here."

"How have you been feeling?"

She hesitated. "I think we should try to finish our book very soon." Then she told him about Jessie Church, without revealing the details of her birth. He would learn about that in the tapes. She needed him to understand now, as they sat together, that she had a daughter out there somewhere with whom she felt an urgent need to share her story, to reconnect with before it was too late.

Mac looked at her for a moment, then nodded.

"I have made eight tapes for you," she said. "I know you want to take them home with you. I tried to include everything, but I'm sure when you hear them you will have questions. Next time you come to see me, you can ask them. It was very painful for me, but I did it. The next parts will not be so difficult."

"I look forward to hearing them." He hesitated. "I've been reading about your disease."

"You want to write about it, do you?"

"It's part of your story. Maybe it will give inspiration to others who have it."

"I doubt if I will inspire anybody," she said. "I don't want sympathy. Many people who have my disease are no doubt more courageous and . . . and more tragic than I am. But I have no secrets from you, Mac Cassidy. You may ask your questions."

***

THE BLONDE AND the teenager drove away in the old Jeep Wagoneer at 3:12. While they were gone, Simone and the tall guy sat on the deck and talked. Eddie Moran watched them through his binoculars. He wondered what they were talking about. It looked quite intense.

The Wagoneer returned at 4:27, and the blonde and the kid got out. Each carried a paper bag into the house.

One hour and fifteen minutes, exactly. Moran thought about the distance from this house to the nearest . . . anything. Mini-mart in one direction, and the center of the little town in the other direction where, besides the fishing shops and restaurants, there was a market, a post office, a hardware store, a library. Nothing was closer than twenty minutes away. He figured anytime the blonde left, she'd be gone for at least an hour.

When she left, she'd either take Li An with her—he guessed she drove that big old Wagoneer because it was easy to load a wheelchair into—or she'd leave Li An home alone in her wheelchair.

Either way would work for Eddie Moran.

At 4:58 the man and the girl exchanged hugs and cheek kisses with Li An and went around to the front of the house. The blonde went with them. She and the girl hugged each other. She shook hands with the guy.

Moran noticed that the guy was carrying a white plastic shopping bag. He wondered what was in it.

⌒⌒

MAC HADN'T SEEN Katie so animated and enthusiastic since . . . well, since before that fateful March night over a year ago. Simone was "so interesting" and Jill was "way cool."

"Did you realize," Katie said, "that they don't have a TV in their house? They don't even get a newspaper. They listen to music and read philosophy and religion and poetry, and they meditate and eat organic. I think that's so admirable."

And Katie went on in that vein for the first fifteen or twenty minutes of their drive back to Concord.

Then, abruptly, she stopped, blew out a breath, and muttered, "Well, anyway . . ."

Mac didn't want it to end. "So what else did you and Jill talk about?" he said.

"Simone," said Katie. "She's dying."

Mac glanced at his daughter sitting beside him. Her face was turned to the side window. He guessed she was crying.

15

Eddie Moran was back in his hemlock cave before sunup on Sunday morning. Except there was no sunup. Gray clouds blanketed the sky, and around the time the sun should have come up, a soft rain began to drizzle down.

He stayed there all day. It was dry and snug under the hemlocks. As long as he kept his back against the trunk, only an occasional drop of rainwater fell on his legs.

He ate his apples and candy bars, drank from his water bottles, and blanked his mind against the passage of the empty hours. Now and then he peered into the windows of the house through his binoculars. He'd stayed after dark the previous evening so he could watch the house when the inside lights were on. He thought he had a pretty accurate picture of the layout. Li An's bedroom was downstairs in the corner room. The blonde had the room next to it. Saturday night, at least, each woman slept in her own room.

He sketched the floor plan, including the location of the interior and exterior doors, in his notebook. It appeared that the women left all the outside doors unlocked except, possibly, when they went to bed. Unlocked doors. That was more than he had any right to expect.

At 2:23 in the afternoon, the blonde, wearing a yellow slicker with the hood pulled over her head, came jogging out of the house, climbed into the Wagoneer, and drove away.

She was back at 3:51 and trotted into the house with a plastic shopping bag in each hand. She'd been gone about an hour and a half this time. This was the second time in two days that the blonde went out in the afternoon for about an hour and a half.

When darkness fell, Moran stuffed all his gear into his backpack and wended his way back through the wet woods to his Explorer. There were still a couple of other vehicles parked there by the stream. It made him smile. These trout fishermen, out there all day in the rain, and they didn't even know enough to quit when it got dark. How much fun could that be?

He'd eaten his dinners at different diners each night. He liked diners. They served good, plain food, and they were cheap. Even though Larrigan was covering his expenses, Moran had no interest in extravagance.

There were a lot of diners in the area. Moran guessed that fishermen favored diners for their fast, cheap food and their long hours. This time he stopped at a place that he'd spotted off the highway about halfway back to his motel. He sat in a booth and had the meatloaf, mashed potatoes, mushroom gravy, peas, and a slab of cherry pie. Minimal conversation with the waitress. Not too friendly, not too grouchy. Wearing the horn-rims. Keeping his nose in the newspaper.

No reason why anybody should ever remember him.

Jessie drove all day Sunday, following secondary highways in a northeasterly direction through Illinois and into Ohio. The land was lush and green but flat and uninteresting, and the miles burned away under the big solid Cherokee. She had decided to follow the lakeshore route—Lake Erie through Ohio and Pennsylvania, then Lake Ontario along the northern border of New York state. It was a part of the country she'd never seen.

Eventually—maybe—she'd turn south into the Catskills and find the town of Beaverkill. She'd come this far.

She had to give it serious thought, though. It seemed like a big thing, meeting the woman who might have given birth to you after not knowing her all your life, and not caring to.

In the late afternoon she found a motel outside of Cleveland. She showered and changed and had dinner in an Italian restaurant, shrimp and risotto and two glasses of Chianti.

When she got back to her room, she flopped down on the bed and thought about calling Simone Bonet again. It had been rude, hanging up on her like that the other night.

But she guessed that if she called again, she'd probably hang up again. Jessie wasn't quite ready for this. Not yet.

—⁂—

Monday turned out to be a warm, sunny day, a few puffy clouds, just the barest whisper of a breeze. Eddie Moran had already been sitting under the hemlocks for about three hours when the blonde, wearing tight-fitting, low-cut blue jeans and a little pink T-shirt, displaying a delicious glimpse of her trim midriff, wheeled Li An out onto the deck. It was 9:03.

The two of them ate breakfast out there. When they finished, the blonde stacked the dishes on a tray and took it inside. A few minutes later she came back out holding a rectangular black object about the size of a cigarette pack. She placed it on the table at Li An's elbow.

Through his binoculars, Moran could see that the object was a mini tape recorder.

Li An and the blonde talked for a few minutes. Then the blonde flipped the recorder open and inserted a cassette tape. She handed a little microphone to Li An. It was attached to the recorder by a wire.

The blonde kissed Li An's forehead and went inside. Moran could see that Li An had begun talking into the recorder.

⁓

"HELLO, DEAR MAC. I promised you I would talk about my movie life, and I will try to do that, although I know you will be disappointed. It was nowhere near as scandalous or glamorous as all the rumors about me would make you think.

"It was so lovely to see you again and to meet your darling Katie. She is a dear girl and oh, so bright. She is very sad, though, as you know. As you are yourself, dear man. I am sure time will heal you both, but if you and Katie could just find somebody you trusted, somebody to talk with, somebody experienced with grief and skilled at listening . . .

"I apologize. I should mind my own business. Jill was very charmed by Katie, you know. She suggested we invite her to come and stay with us for a while. I can't imagine that you'd allow her to do that. Anyway, it probably wouldn't be a good idea. With my illness, it just wouldn't be much fun for a teenage girl, as much as we would selfishly enjoy it.

"I think Jill gets lonely sometimes. I don't know why she stays with me.

"I didn't even try to make a tape for you yesterday. It was a rainy Sunday. A bad day for me. Why is it that so many Sundays are rainy? I was feeling quite blue all day. I can't always tell whether it's my disease or other things like the weather that affect my moods, but yesterday my medication wasn't much help.

"I was thinking about Jessie, of course. My May, my daughter. I woke up feeling gloomy and pessimistic. And yesterday was so gray and rainy that the feeling never really left me. Perhaps it was spending time with your Katie. It made me realize that I have missed my daughter's entire life.

"I am better today. The sun is warm out here on the deck, and the birds are singing, and I plan to stay out here all day long. I believe Jessie will call. Maybe today, but if not today, sometime. I believe that.

"You see? I can only think about Jessie, and I am not telling you the story of my life. It seems so inconsequential. Who would ever care enough to read our book?

"Well, you are the writer. Maybe you can make it sound interesting.

"Dear Mac. I intended to tell you stories and recite names and dates and interesting Hollywood facts, and I shall, I promise. But not right now. My mind is on May. Jessie, I mean. Now I am tired. A little nap will refresh me, I'm sure."

<hr />

AFTER SIXTEEN MINUTES by Moran's watch, Li An put the microphone down on her lap, and a minute or so later her chin slumped onto her chest.

The blonde came out immediately, as if she'd been watching and waiting for Li An to go to sleep. She moved the microphone onto the table, turned off the recorder, adjusted the blanket on Li An's lap and knees, then bent down, touched her face, and kissed her cheek.

An hour later the blonde came out again, this time with a glass of juice or something. She woke up Li An and sat there watching her while she drank.

Then the blonde pushed Li An in her wheelchair off the wooden deck. Moran had observed that a flagstone walkway completely encircled the house, and now he saw its purpose. The two women went slowly, stopping often to point into the gardens, which were blossoming with flowers of many different colors. A couple of times the blonde picked a flower and gave it to Li An, who held it to her nose. From where he was hiding, Moran could hear their voices, and sometimes a little burst of laughter. The blonde kept touching Li An's face and hair and hands, and the way Li An looked up at her, it was pretty obvious that they really loved each other.

They finished their circuit at 12:39, and the blonde pushed Li An up onto the deck and then into the house.

They came back out at 12:56. Moran figured Li An had to go to the bathroom or something.

At 1:14 the blonde brought out sandwiches and drinks on a tray. The two of them ate their lunch together, and Moran took that opportunity to eat a Hershey bar and have a swig of water. After two and a half days of watching and remaining still and being stealthy and taking notes and peering through his binoculars, he had it figured out. Eddie Moran knew better than to move prematurely. His patience never wore thin. But now he was ready. He was looking for the right time.

It came at 2:06, when the blonde got into her Wagoneer and drove out of the driveway. Li An was dozing out on the deck.

He'd keep it to fifty minutes. It took at least twenty minutes to get anywhere, and twenty minutes to get back, and even if she only bought gas or picked up the mail or bought a gallon of milk, that would take another ten minutes at least. Fifty minutes would be safe.

So as soon as the Wagoneer disappeared down the driveway, Eddie Moran put his flashlight into his pocket and crept out of his clump of hemlocks. He left the rest of his stuff right there. He'd be back for it.

He followed the edge of the woods around to the front corner of the house. From there, he could see that Li An was still sleeping on the deck. The way she was sitting, she had her back to the house. It would be best if she stayed asleep, but if she woke up, the way she was facing she wouldn't see him, and in her wheelchair, she couldn't come inside to interrupt him.

So he darted out of the cover of the trees, went to the front door, and turned the knob. It swung open, as he expected.

The door opened into a single big room that encompassed the living room, the dining room, and the kitchen. Eddie Moran didn't know much about art, but he liked the stuff hanging on the walls. And he liked the looks of the furniture, and the colorful rugs on the wood floors, and the feeling of space and light.

He noticed those things, but he wasted no time pondering them. He had work to do.

He went upstairs first. If he should be interrupted, if the blonde should return earlier than he expected, he'd be able to slip away easier if he was downstairs. So he wanted to get the upstairs out of the way first.

There were two small bedrooms and a bathroom up there. It was pretty obvious that they were hardly ever used. A thin layer of dust covered the windowsills and bedside tables. Moran opened the drawers of the tables, careful not to disturb the coating of dust. They were empty. He rifled through the dressers and found only women's clothes and mothballs. The closets held winter-weight jackets and pants. Sweaters were piled on the shelves. He rummaged around and shone his flashlight into the corners. No shoeboxes filled with old photos. No shoeboxes at all, in fact.

He guessed these were guest rooms, and the two women didn't have guests very often. It appeared that they only used the upstairs for storage. Anyway, Li An couldn't go upstairs. If she had the photos, they'd most likely be someplace where she could get at them.

There was nothing in the medicine cabinet or the linen closet in the bathroom except medicine and linens.

Moran crept downstairs. He was wearing sneakers and soft clothing. He could move anywhere in complete silence. He could slither and slink invisibly and noiselessly though buildings as easily as through forests and jungles. He would have been an excellent burglar if he'd chosen that career path.

Well, come to think of it, that's what he was doing. Burglarizing Li An's house. As he had Bunny's.

He went directly to the rear corner of the first floor where, based on his observations, he would find her bedroom.

The first thing he saw was the snapshot propped up against the base of the lamp on the table beside her bed. He picked it up. He had seen it before. This photo had been in the shoebox in Bunny Brubaker's closet in Florida. It was one of the dozen or so photos he had come here to retrieve.

He looked at it. The four of them. Larrigan and Li An, Bunny and Eddie. Plus the baby. Larrigan was holding the baby.

Jesus, they looked young.

It wasn't Eddie Moran's nature to waste a lot of time pondering the past or speculating about the future, and especially not when he was in the process of searching a house and time was of the essence. But still, he couldn't help thinking about how things changed. Now Larrigan was about to become a Supreme Court Justice. Li An was in a wheelchair, and Bunny was dead.

Eddie? Well, Eddie was still doing what he was good at, what he'd been trained for.

He wondered whatever became of the baby. Doubtful a baby would have survived what happened in Saigon.

He stuck the photo in his jacket pocket.

He found a handwritten note and a photocopy of a newspaper clipping—but no more photos—folded up in an envelope in the bedside table drawer. The note was from Bunny. It didn't mention Larrigan directly, but it confirmed that she'd sent Li An the photographs. The clipping had a photo of a woman kneeling beside a man's body. He skimmed the story quickly. Something about an assassination attempt. The woman had a Chinese name. He could read it later.

He folded the note and the clipping, put them back in the envelope, and stuck them in his pocket along with that single photo.

Then he began a methodical search for the other photos that Bunny had mailed to Li An.

It took him thirty-two minutes to cover the two bedrooms, the bathroom, the living room, and the bookshelf-lined den. The other photos were not there. Now forty-one minutes had elapsed since he'd entered. He had just nine more minutes.

He thought it was interesting that there was no TV in the entire house. Lots of books, though.

He found the portable tape recorder on the counter in the kitchen. Moran popped the recorder open. There was a cassette tape in it, and it appeared to be half full.

He put the tape in his pocket.

There was an open twelve-pack of cassette tapes on the shelf. There were three left in the pack. He took one out, slid it into the recorder, and snapped it shut. He hoped they wouldn't notice that now there were only two cassettes left in the pack, and he trusted that when they went to play back the new tape that he'd put in the machine, and found it empty, they'd figure that Li An had just forgotten to turn it on, or had accidentally erased it.

A twelve-pack of tapes. Three left in the pack, one in the recorder. That left eight tapes unaccounted for.

Moran thought of the bag the bearded guy drove away with. Could've been eight tapes in that bag.

He looked for the rest of the photos in all the kitchen drawers and cabinets. No luck.

He eased out onto the glassed-in sunporch. From there he could see Li An in her wheelchair. She was facing the valley and the distant hills. She appeared to be still asleep.

There were some bookshelves and a big oak desk on the sunporch. Moran went to the desk. In the top drawer were files holding bills and tax returns and some legal documents. He rifled through them quickly, aware of the time. The photos were not there. Maybe some of that other stuff was relevant, but he didn't have time to read everything, and he didn't dare steal them. What he wanted was those other photographs that linked Larrigan with Li An, that connected him to that time and place and those secrets.

It was troublesome that she didn't have them. It meant that somebody else did.

In the bottom drawer he found a gun. It was wrapped in an oily rag. Without moving the gun, he pulled away the corner of the rag. It was a square, short-barreled little silver automatic, looked like a .32 caliber. As Bond would say, a lady's gun. Moran smiled. Why not? A couple of women living way the hell out in the sticks ought to have a gun in the house. You never knew when some burglar was going to open the front door and walk in.

He closed the drawer. He was done. The rest of those photographs were not in the house. Eddie Moran would stake his reputation on it.

Aside from taking that single photo, Bunny's note, the newspaper clipping, and the half-filled cassette, he left everything exactly as he'd found it.

Li An would miss the photo as soon as she went into her bedroom. She obviously kept it propped up beside her bed because it was important to her. She'd figure it must have fallen under the bed or something. The next morning she'd probably ask the blonde to help her look for it, and the fact that they couldn't find it would be puzzling. But these things happened to everybody, and judging from the way Li An slept all the time, he guessed she was taking medication that would confuse and disorient her and make her doubt her memory.

She'd notice the missing envelope, too. Maybe not right away, though. She might not even connect it to the missing photo. Either way, she and the blonde would be baffled. They'd look everywhere. They'd blame the cleaning lady or poltergeists. Each would suspect the other of misplacing it.

It would end up being a mystery.

The last thing that would occur to them would be that they'd been burglarized. Especially when the burglar was as neat and efficient as Eddie Moran. And nothing of any value was missing.

He looked at his watch. His time was up. He moved quickly into the living room and peeked out the window. The Wagoneer was nowhere in sight.

He slipped out the front door and was back under his hemlocks in two minutes.

Twelve minutes later he heard the now familiar rumble of the old Wagoneer coming down the driveway in low gear. He didn't bother watching through the binoculars or recording the time in his notebook this time.

Eddie Moran was done here.

And so, waiting for night to fall, he settled back against the trunk of the hemlock and allowed himself to think about how good the blonde looked in her cropped T-shirt and snug, low-slung jeans. Maybe some day . . .

∽ᴑᴥᴑ∾

AFTER DINNER, SIMONE sat out on the sunporch to watch the darkness arrive. Almost immediately her eyelids grew heavy. She fought against sleep. She feared sleep—or, more accurately, she feared waking up. She was sleeping more and more. Her daytime naps came more frequently, and they lasted longer, sometimes two or three hours. She was going to bed barely after sundown now that the longest days of the year had arrived. She tended to awaken early, and in those vulnerable early moments of consciousness, in the gray half-light of the day's first hour, she invariably felt in her heart an overpowering weight of dread and despair, and behind her eyes lingered the images and emotions of awful dreams.

Some days, the bleakness never went away. It was not fear of death. Simone had reconciled herself to death. It was . . . emptiness. Her life, she believed, had no meaning. She had contributed nothing. She would be remembered, if at all, for being one of the first actresses to reveal a glimpse of her pubic hair in a movie.

What a legacy.

But now there was Mac's book. Her book. And now there was Jessie Church. Her own daughter. Simone had much to live for, she told herself. She had goals and purposes. She had things to do and events to anticipate.

So why did that overpowering weight of dread and doom continue to press on her heart?

Well, the irony was not lost on her. Now, after an aimless, useless life, she'd finally found hope and purpose, a reason to want to live. And now she was dying.

"You better take me to my room," she said to Jill. "I can't seem to keep my eyes open."

Jill wheeled Simone into her bedroom and, with an arm around her shoulders, helped her move from the wheelchair into her bed. She fussed with the blankets and Simone's pillow, then bent and kissed her forehead.

Simone lifted her hand and touched Jill's face. "I love you," she said.

Jill nodded. "I love you, too." She kissed Simone softly on the lips, smiled, then turned and left the room.

Simone lay there staring up at the ceiling, trying not to cry. After a few minutes, she rolled onto her side to turn off the lamp on the table beside her bed.

It took her a moment to realize that something was missing. The photo, the one she'd taken from the batch that Bunny sent her, that she'd been keeping propped up against the base of the lamp—it was gone.

Probably fell off the table, she thought. The movement of air from pushing back the blankets and fluffing the pillows and getting into bed would do it. It got blown onto the floor, maybe under the bed. She'd have to remember to ask Jill to look for it in the morning.

Simone lay awake longer than usual, worrying about her photo, knowing it was irrational but feeling in her stomach that awful dread, the feeling that something terrible had happened. Or maybe it was a premonition that something terrible was going to happen.

─◌◌─

MORAN WAITED UNTIL dark to slip out of his hemlock cave and head back to his Explorer. This would be his last night on this particular job. Actually, the job was over. He decided to treat himself to a nice dinner.

He deserved it. It was a job well done. True, he hadn't recovered all the photos that Bunny had sent to Li An. But he'd verified that they weren't there to be found. He'd found one of them, and he'd found the note that Bunny had written. He had the tape that might or might not mean something, and in his camera he had digital pictures of the man who'd visited on Saturday along with his license plate numbers.

Larrigan would not be thrilled that the photos were still out there somewhere. But Moran figured that as long as Li An didn't have them, the judge was in pretty good shape. The photos without Li An's explanation of them wouldn't prove anything, and Li An's story without the photos for evidence wouldn't be worth much, either.

Moran remembered seeing a steak house in the town of Beaverkill amid all the fishing shops. Normally he didn't like to eat in restaurants. A single man by himself blended in at a diner but was more likely to be noticed in a restaurant. But tonight, the hell with it. He'd be long gone and hard to find in the morning, and there would be no reason why anybody would want to try to remember him.

He even thought about picking up a woman and bringing her back to his room, now that the job was done. But finding such a woman in the little hamlet of Beaverkill, New York, would not be simple, if such a woman even lived in the town. A couple drinks, a thick steak, medium-rare, a good night's sleep. That's all he needed.

He ended up eating at a booth in the lounge, where his presence didn't seem to be noticed by anybody except the waitress. Eddie flirted with her halfheartedly. She wasn't very attractive, and she didn't even smile at his mildly suggestive comments. He figured she heard them all the time. She'd instantly forget him, just as he'd forget her.

He had a couple of Old-Fashioneds followed by a medium-rare ribeye, baked potato with extra butter, big green salad, house dressing, then coffee and lemon meringue pie.

A big TV sat on a shelf over the bar. It was showing a base-ball game. While he sipped his coffee, Eddie watched. He liked the symmetry of baseball, the geometry of it, the precision of the distances, the importance of numbers and percentages, the compli-cated rules. He really liked how there were long stretches of time when nothing happened, and then sudden moments of quick, intense, important action. He didn't have a favorite team. He didn't know the players. He just liked to watch.

He left the waitress a big tip to make up for his comments. He was glad she hadn't responded to them. She didn't appeal to him at all. He was tired, and now he was pleasantly full and a little buzzed from the Old-Fashioneds, and all he wanted to do was go to sleep knowing he didn't have to wake up before he was ready to.

By the time he got back to his motel, he was yawning. He grabbed his backpack from the backseat and slung it over his shoulder. He patted his jacket pocket where he'd put the photo and the envelope and the cassette he'd taken from Li An's house. They represented the fruits of his three-day labor.

Then he fished out his key, unlocked the door, and stepped into his dark motel room.

As he reached for the light switch, a deep male voice said, "Please don't, Eddie. Don't turn on the lights."

CHAPTER

E ddie Moran pulled his hand away from the light switch. He didn't say anything. There was nothing to be gained from speaking.

"Please drop your backpack on the floor, Eddie," the voice said.

Moran slid the pack off his shoulder, bent down, and placed it carefully on the floor. His camera was in the backpack. That camera had cost a lot of money.

"Thank you," said the voice. "Please don't try anything foolish, Eddie. That would be regrettable. Your silhouette is outlined against the doorway. I'm holding in my hands a twelve-gauge shotgun. It's a semiautomatic with five shells in it, and it will fire as fast as I can pull the trigger. It's loaded with double-ought buckshot. This shotgun has a twelve-inch barrel and an open choke and it's aimed at the doorway. You understand why I'm telling you this?"

Moran stood there, waiting.

"Answer me, please," said the voice.

"Sure," said Moran. "I understand."

"Good," said the voice. "Now, Eddie, take one step forward, please."

Moran did as he was told, and that's when he sensed the other presence in the room. This one was behind him.

"Meet Mr. White," said the voice. "You can call me Mr. Black."

Moran nodded but said nothing.

"Hold still for Mr. White, now, Eddie," said Mr. Black. "He wants to bind your eyes with duct tape. I know you appreciate the significance of this."

Moran understood, and he did indeed appreciate it. If they blindfolded him with duct tape, it meant they didn't want him to see them. If they cared about his seeing them, it meant they didn't intend to kill him.

Or at least it meant that they hadn't decided whether to kill him or to let him live. Either way was a plus under the circumstances. It was more than he deserved for being so sloppy. He should never have had those two Old-Fashioneds.

The second man, Mr. White, moved up behind him. "Close your eyes," he said.

Moran closed his eyes, and Mr. White wrapped duct tape over them. He continued the tape all the way around his head, four turns, bound tight. He'd lose his eyebrows and some hair when he tore the tape off. He didn't want to think about what would happen to his eyelids and lashes.

Mr. White smelled faintly of cigar smoke. Anybody with Moran's training should've noticed that smell before he entered the room. He was trained to notice things like old cigar smoke. He was obviously losing it. Getting old and sloppy.

He sensed that the man taping his eyes shut was a big man. But light on his feet. He moved so quietly that Eddie Moran, who was trained to notice subtle sounds, had not sensed that anybody was inside the door when he opened it. A man that stealthy was a dangerous man.

He heard the door behind him close and the lock click. Then there was a second click, which Moran recognized as the light being switched on. Even with his eyes shut under four layers of duct tape, he detected a subtle difference in the darkness.

"Put your hands behind your back," said Mr. White, standing behind him and speaking quietly into his ear. Moran listened for an accent or a regional twang of some kind. He heard none from either Mr. Black or Mr. White. Their speech was utterly generic and bland. This meant that the natural individuality that all people carry in their voices and speech patterns, the distinctive articulations that enable a trained ear to identify their country or region of origin, in many cases right down to the city or even the neighborhood, had been eradicated from these two.

CIA, maybe. Or FBI. Probably former agents. Mavericks, maybe. Rogue agents for hire. Or maybe not. Maybe they'd been recruited, or just borrowed, from one of those organizations to execute special operations for another agency.

It was all about Larrigan. Moran had a pretty good idea who these two worked for.

"Put your hands behind your back and press your wrists together, please," said Mr. White.

Moran did as he was told, and his wrists and forearms were quickly bound together behind his back with duct tape.

Mr. White patted him down. He took the envelope and the photograph and the cassette tape from his jacket pocket.

A hand gripped Moran's shoulder, steered him across the room, turned him around, and pushed him backward. He fell into the fake leather reclining chair beside the TV.

A minute later he felt Mr. White wrapping duct tape around his ankles.

"Now, Eddie," said Mr. Black, who seemed to do most of the talking, "it would be helpful to know if you're going to cooperate with us."

"I don't seem to have much choice," said Moran.

"You could lie," he said. "You could be a hero. You could refuse to talk."

Eddie laughed. "I won't lie, don't worry about that. I'm no hero."

"Okay. Good. I'm going to ask you a number of questions. Mr. White is quite skilled at persuading people to tell the truth, but we can forgo that if you provide full and truthful answers. How does that sound to you?"

"Fine," said Moran. "Ask away."

"I already know the answers to many of the questions I'm going to ask you," said Mr. Black. "It's sort of like a lie detector test, see? How you answer the questions will tell me if I can trust you. If I can't trust you, Eddie, then I have no use for you."

"I get the picture," said Moran. "Don't worry. I'm not big on loyalty. On the other hand, I'm totally committed to saving my own skin. I'll tell you what you want to know."

"Excellent," said Mr. Black. "That's what I hoped. We have big plans for you, Eddie, assuming we can trust you."

"What kind of plans? What do you want me to do?"

Mr. Black chuckled. "Nothing you haven't done before."

❧

MORAN WAITED UNTIL he was certain that they had driven away. Then he waited some more, just to be on the safe side. In the disorientation of not being able to see, it was hard to keep track of the passage of time.

Before they left, they'd removed all the tape except what they'd wrapped over his eyes. Mr. Black said: "Give us ten minutes, Eddie. You wouldn't want to see our faces or our vehicle."

He figured he'd waited fifteen or twenty minutes. Then he peeled the tape off his eyes. A lot of hair came off with the tape. It hurt like hell.

He had answered all their questions. He didn't lie about anything. This was about saving his own skin, not Larrigan's or anybody else's.

They already knew that he was working for Larrigan. And they knew he'd been spying on Li An.

They didn't know about Saigon. That's what they were after.

So Eddie Moran told them all about it.

They'd emptied his backpack onto the floor, and they took his camera and his notebook. He wouldn't miss the notebook, and they wouldn't find anything useful in it anyway. It just had the notes he'd been making in preparation for entering Li An's house. But taking his camera, that was really unnecessary. They could've just removed the memory card and left the camera. It was practically brand-new, state-of-the-art, very expensive. He loved that camera.

About the only interesting things they'd get out of the camera were the pictures of the guy who'd visited Li An on Saturday, along with his license plate numbers.

And they took the tape that Eddie had taken from the recorder at Li An's house. He hadn't had a chance to listen to it, so he had no idea if it would help these guys.

After they'd looked at all his stuff and asked him all their questions, they told him what they wanted him to do.

The last thing Mr. Black said to him was: "Do a good job, Eddie. Everything depends on it."

—◦◦—

SIMONE OPENED HER eyes. Her room was dark. She lay still. Something had awakened her. There was a presence here. Someone was in her room. The sensation was powerful.

She listened. Was that breathing? She wasn't sure. The sound was soft, barely audible.

She darted her eyes around, trying to see without moving her head. She saw nothing. Just the still darkness.

Then she realized what it was. It hadn't been a sound. It was an odd mingling of smells—Jill's familiar soapy scent that lingered in the room long after she'd left, mixed with a faint, but sharp and acrid odor. This was an odor foreign to her room but not to her memory. Testosterone mingled with male sweat.

"Who's there?" she said. She was startled by how loud her voice sounded. "Jill?"

She heard the rustle of clothing, just the smallest sound such as would be made by the flexing of an arm or the bending of a leg.

"Who is it?" she said again.

Without warning, the ceiling light went on. Simone squeezed her eyes shut against the sudden glare.

When she opened them again, she saw that Jill was sitting on the chair beside her bed with a man standing close behind her. The man was holding a gun against the side of Jill's head. It looked like the little gun she and Jill kept in the desk drawer. Jill's eyes were very wide, and Simone realized that her beloved friend was crying silent tears.

Simone stared at the man. "Who are you? What do you want?"

He smiled. He was somewhat older than she was, Simone thought, but he had a boyish smile. "You don't recognize me, Li An?" he said.

She hadn't been called Li An for over thirty years. She looked at the man again, and then, behind his leathery, creased, time-worn skin she saw the face of that devilish boy.

"Eddie?" she whispered. "Eddie Moran? Is that you?"

"It's been a long time," he said.

"What do you want? Why are you here?"

"I'm sorry," he said. "There's something I have to do."

"What? You have to do what?"

"I'm really sorry about this," he said.

Simone thought she could actually see regret in his eyes.

"Sorry about what?" she whispered. "What are you doing here, anyway? Why—"

There was a muffled cracking noise, and Jill's head suddenly slumped down on her chest. She was very still. Her eyes were half open. After a moment, blood began streaming down her face and dripping off her chin.

It took a moment to register in Simone's brain. Then she whispered, "Oh my God. Oh God. Oh." She felt the panic of slow realization rising up in her throat and filling her head, a great pounding pressure behind her eyes and in her ears. She looked up at Eddie Moran. "What have you done? What did you do? You *killed* her?"

"I'm sorry, Li An," Eddie said.

"You killed her," she said again. "Why did you have to kill her?" Simone realized she was crying. She closed her eyes, seeking her calm place. "Why? Why did you do that, Eddie? Jill never did anything to you. What do you want?"

"I've been thinking a lot about old times, Li An," he said. "We used to be friends."

Simone found herself nodding through her tears. "Friends," she said. "Yes."

"Remember?" he said. "The four of us? We had a lot of fun, huh?" He shrugged. "Oh, well. Things have a way of changing, don't they?"

And Simone watched as Eddie Moran raised the little square silver gun and pointed it at her chest.

17

At eight o'clock on Tuesday morning, Roberto Martinez pulled into the driveway, parked next to Jill Rossiter's Wagoneer, climbed out, and went around to the back of his old Dodge pickup. He dropped the tailgate and laid out the pair of two-by-twelve planks for the ramp. Then he hoisted himself up into the truck bed and backed his John Deere lawn tractor down the two planks.

He looked at his watch. Right on time. The ladies liked to have the section around the deck finished by nine so they could enjoy the outdoors in the morning without the racket of the tractor.

He topped off the gas, climbed onto the seat, got the mower started, and began cutting the side lawn. Usually Ms. Rossiter, the blonde lady, Jill, she came out and waved to him while he was mowing. She always left a pitcher of lemonade or a glass of juice or a cold Coke on the deck for him.

Sometimes Jill would push Ms. Bonet out in her wheelchair as he was finishing up the side section, and Ms. Bonet would wave and smile. Roberto felt bad about her disease. When he first started working for her, she'd been an energetic, fun-loving person. Now she needed the wheelchair to get around, and she seemed sad most of the time.

The grass was growing fast. This time of year, especially with all the rain they'd been getting, many of Roberto's customers wanted to be mowed twice a week. But the ladies said once a week was plenty, which was fine by him. So he showed up every Tuesday morning at eight o'clock. He mowed the grass and trimmed the edges, and if Jill had anything else for him, he did it. She liked tending the gardens herself, but sometimes she wanted him to spread some mulch in the flowerbeds or cart away some dead branches or bags of leaves. Roberto kept the fruit trees pruned and fertilized and, in general, looked after their yard.

Roberto Martinez's grandfather had started up his little landscaping business to serve some of the old Catskill resorts. When the resorts closed down, he'd kept the business alive by taking care of wealthy people's yards.

Roberto didn't think Jill Rossiter and Ms. Bonet were particularly wealthy. But they had a nice place, and they didn't mind paying him to keep it looking good.

He finished mowing the side lawn a little before nine. Jill still hadn't come out onto the deck to wave and smile and leave something to drink. He hoped she wasn't sick or something. Ms. Bonet needed Jill to take care of her.

He finished the mowing and did the trimming. By then it was about quarter after eleven.

He needed to know if they had anything else they wanted him to do today. Usually Jill came out on the deck to tell him, but he hadn't seen her. So he went to the front door and rang the bell. When Jill didn't come to the door, he started to get a bad feeling.

It didn't make any sense. She had to be home. Her Wagoneer was right there in the driveway.

Roberto started imagining terrible things. Jill slipping in the shower and banging her head, or falling down the stairs and breaking her leg, or getting food poisoning or something, not being able to take care of Ms. Bonet, needing help herself. Maybe both ladies were bedridden with the flu, and Ms. Bonet, without Jill to bring her medicine or water or to help her to the bathroom, was stranded in her bed or her wheelchair.

He walked all the way around the house and tried to peer in through the windows. The shades were drawn in the bedrooms. There was no sign of life in the living room or kitchen or on the sunporch. The house had that empty, deserted feeling.

He ended up on the deck. It didn't look like anybody was home. He supposed there were plenty of good explanations. Except in the nine years that Roberto Martinez had been taking care of their place, Jill and Ms. Bonet had been there every single Tuesday morning. Not once did he find them not home, even back in the time before Ms. Bonet was in her wheelchair.

He tried the door that opened from the deck into the sunporch. It was unlocked. Roberto was quite sure that if the ladies had gone away for a few days, they'd have locked up the house.

He poked his head inside and said, "Hello? Jill? Are you home?"

He waited, and when Jill didn't appear and nobody called back to him, he yelled louder. "Jill? Ms. Rossiter? Ms. Bonet? Are you there? Hello? Is everything all right?"

He hesitated. He didn't feel right about walking into somebody's house, even people he knew as well as he knew the ladies. But now he was definitely worried, and he felt that it would be irresponsible of him to just drive away. He'd feel terrible if both ladies were really sick or if Jill had had an accident or something. If they needed help, Roberto should give it to them.

So he stepped inside. He called their names again. No answer. He moved from the sunporch into the kitchen. He saw no evidence that the ladies had had breakfast. No juice glasses or cereal bowls in the sink. No coffee in the electric coffeemaker. Jill always had a coffee mug in her hand in the morning.

He called "Hello?" once more, and when there still was no answer, he went down the short hallway to the bedrooms.

The first one was empty. Judging by the clothes that had been dropped on the floor, this was Jill's room. The bed had been slept in. The covers were thrown back as if she had gotten up suddenly. As if there had been some kind of emergency, Roberto thought. His mind was now swirling with all kinds of terrible scenarios.

He found both ladies in the other bedroom. Jill was lying on her side on the floor beside the bed, as if she'd toppled sideways off the chair and gone to sleep right there.

Ms. Bonet was in a half-sitting position in her bed. Her head was slumped on her chest. A big dark blotch covered the front of her.

Roberto Martinez stood there looking at them. It took a minute before he comprehended what he was seeing.

He swallowed back the bile that rose up in his throat. Then he took a deep breath, crossed himself, mumbled, "Holy Mary, Mother of God," and went for the telephone.

WHEN MAC GOT home from the post office on Tuesday afternoon, Katie met him at the back door.

He took one look at her face and said, "What's the matter, honey?"

"You had a phone call. Some sheriff from New York. Sullivan County. That's where Simone and Jill live. He said he had to talk to you. He said it was important. He wouldn't tell me what he wanted."

"Did he leave a number?"

Katie nodded and handed Mac a slip of paper.

"I'll call him right now," he said.

He went into the kitchen, took the phone off the hook, and pecked out the number Katie had given him. He sat at the kitchen table as it rang. Katie sat across from him. She put her elbows on the table and her chin in her hands. She was watching Mac with big, solemn eyes.

On the third ring someone picked up and said, "Norris. Who's this?"

"It's Mac Cassidy, returning your call. Is this the sheriff?"

"It is," he said. "Sheriff Roland Norris. Appreciate you getting back to me, Mr. Cassidy. We've got ourselves a situation here, and—"

"Where's here?" said Mac.

"Township of Beaverkill. Sullivan County, New York." He cleared his throat. "We appear to be looking at a double suicide here, sir, or more accurately, a murder-suicide, and we found a business card with your name on it tacked up here beside the telephone, and we were wondering—"

"Wait a minute," said Mac. "Hold on, please." He covered the phone with his hand. "Honey," he said to Katie, "this is private, okay?"

She narrowed her eyes at him for a minute, then got up and left the room. He heard her trot up the stairs, and then her bedroom door shut with a click.

He sighed, then spoke into the phone. "Sheriff?"

"I'm here, Mr. Cassidy."

"What about a double suicide? You said double suicide, or a murder-suicide. What the hell does that mean?"

"We got two bodies, sir, and it looks like—"

"Whose bodies?" Mac said, although he knew the answer.

"Simone Bonet and Jill Rossiter."

Mac slumped back in his chair and blew out a long breath. He couldn't think of anything to say.

"Mr. Cassidy?"

"Yes. I'm here."

"I'm wondering if you can shed any light on this for us."

"What do you mean?"

"Why did they have your business card tacked up beside their telephone?"

"I'm working with Simone on a book."

"A book?"

"Her autobiography."

"You're working with her, you say?"

"I'm writing it, actually. I'm a writer. A ghostwriter."

"That's interesting," he said. "So she's famous?"

"Sort of, yes."

"I didn't know that," said the sheriff. "So when did you see these ladies last, Mr. Cassidy?"

"Saturday," Mac said.

"Working on the book, were you?"

"Yes."

"How did they seem when you saw them on Saturday?"

"You mean, were they suicidal?"

"Just your impression."

"I don't know them well enough to form an impression. I've only met them twice. I've spent most of my time with Simone."

"You're writing a book about her and you don't know her very well?"

"We only just got started a couple weeks ago."

"You must have some impression."

Mac thought about it. He'd probably have more insight after he'd listened to the tapes, but he'd decided he wanted to have all of them before he started so he could listen to them straight through, get a feel for the big sweep of Simone's life, rather then getting her story in pieces. It's the way he'd done it with all of his ghost-writing.

"Simone," he said to the sheriff, "has—had—a devastating disease. She was dying. She was pretty depressed."

"You *know* she was depressed, or she *seemed* depressed?"

"Both, actually. She told me she was taking medication for depression."

"Okay," said the sheriff. "What about Jill Rossiter?"

"I don't know. She seemed . . . normal. But really, I spent very little time with her. She took care of Simone. She was a nurse, I think. Can you tell me what happened, exactly?"

"I don't see why not," said the sheriff. "What apparently happened was, Ms. Rossiter got Ms. Bonet's registered handgun and pulled up a chair beside Ms. Bonet's bed and shot her twice in the chest, then pressed the gun against her own head and killed herself."

"Was there a note?"

"No, sir. No note."

"Doesn't that bother you?"

"It bothers me some," said the sheriff. "No note is why I'm calling you. It's a loose end. Loose ends bother me. So I'm wondering if you can shed any light on the situation."

Mac hesitated. Then he said, "Suppose I came out there to talk with you?"

"I don't see how that's necessary, Mr. Cassidy. But thanks anyway."

"No," said Mac. "I mean, I want to. If you wouldn't mind. I'd be grateful for a little of your time."

"What for?"

"Sheriff," said Mac, "I'm writing this book. Now my subject is dead. This, what happened, will most likely be the last chapter."

"You want to come out here, talk to me, like interview me, for a book?"

"That's right," said Mac. "I'll need to have the whole story if I'm going to write about it. I'll need the truth of it. I'll need to interview you. I'll need to see where it happened. I'll need your help, sheriff, if you're willing to give it to me."

The sheriff paused, then said, "I don't see why not. Maybe you can help me clear up some things, too."

"Yes," said Mac. "I wouldn't be surprised."

"When did you have in mind?" said the sheriff.

"How's tomorrow?"

"Tomorrow's fine."

"I'll be there around noon. Would it be all right if we met at Simone's house?"

"Oh, I don't know . . ."

"Is it a crime scene?"

"We got a murder as well as a suicide here, Mr. Cassidy. That definitely makes it a crime scene."

"Right," said Mac. "I'd really like to meet there, though."

"Well, I guess so. We can do that."

Mac disconnected with Sheriff Roland Norris, reached up to the wall hook, and hung up the phone. He remained seated at the kitchen table and thought about it. He decided that he was surprised but not shocked that Simone had taken her own life. She'd told him that she was on medication for depression, and it didn't seem to be working very well. She knew her time was limited. The doctor had told her that the disease would progress rapidly. She knew exactly what to expect. It wouldn't be pleasant, not for Simone, and not for Jill, either.

Still, it had seemed to him that Simone had hope, that she believed she still had a lot to live for. She was enthusiastic about their book. She was hoping to meet Jessie, her daughter. She liked being outside in the nice weather, watching the gardens bloom, hearing the birds sing. She and Jill loved each other.

Mac hadn't gotten much of a sense of Jill. She'd seemed devoted to Simone. That was about it.

The sheriff had called it a pact. That made sense. Simone deciding it was time, Jill agreeing to do it for her, then going with her, joining her.

Or maybe Jill did it on her own, seeing Simone depressed and in pain, not being able to bear it, deciding to put her out of her misery, shooting her while she was sleeping, then herself.

Either way, they were both dead. He knew that at some point he'd have to figure out what it meant for their book. If there could still be a book.

Mac shook his head. The hell with the book. He'd worry about the book another time.

Right now he was thinking about Katie.

Katie seemed to have connected with the two women, and especially with Jill. For the first time in a long time, she had seemed, however briefly, almost happy.

And after what happened to Jane, now this?

He went upstairs. He heard music coming from behind the closed door to Katie's room. Wagner, if he wasn't mistaken. Heavy, melodramatic music. You had to be in a certain mood to listen to Wagner.

He tapped on Katie's door. A minute later the music abruptly stopped, and then the door cracked open and Katie peered out at him. Her forehead was furrowed as if she hadn't known who might be knocking on her door.

"Can we talk?" Mac said.

She nodded and opened the door wide for him.

Mac went in. Katie sat on her bed with her hands clasped on her lap and looked up at him.

"That was the sheriff in New York where Simone and Jill live," he said. "He—"

"What happened?" said Katie.

He shook his head.

"They're dead, aren't they?"

"Yes, honey."

"So what happened?" She was sitting there on the edge of her bed, perfectly still, looking up at him without expression.

"They, um, it looks like they committed suicide."

"Both of them?"

He nodded. "I don't know any details. Just that they're both dead. I'm going out there tomorrow."

"Why?"

"To talk with the sheriff. To see what happened."

"But why? If they committed suicide . . . ?"

Mac shrugged.

"For your book?"

"I want to know what happened."

Katie looked at him for a minute. "They wouldn't do that," she said.

"Simone was pretty depressed," he said. "She had a terrible disease. She knew she was dying."

Katie shook her head. "She was expecting to hear from her daughter. It meant everything to her. It gave her something to live for. Jill told me all about it. Jill was sad about Simone's disease and all. But she was prepared for it. Jill never would have killed herself, no matter what Simone did. She had plans. She was interested in a lot of things."

Mac nodded. "That's pretty much what I would've thought, too. But we didn't know them that well."

"What if they were murdered?"

"Who'd want to murder them?"

Katie looked up at the ceiling. "I don't know."

"I don't, either," Mac said. "Maybe I'll know more after I go out there."

Katie looked up at him with big round eyes. "I don't get it."

He nodded. He didn't know what to say.

After a minute, she said, "I know what you're thinking."

He smiled. "You do?"

"Yes. You're thinking that I'm blaming myself for what happened."

"How could you blame yourself?"

She looked at him. "It's my curse. The curse of Katie Cassidy."

"Do you believe that? Do you blame yourself?"

"I don't know," she said softly.

Mac went over and sat on the bed beside her. He put his arm around her, and she tilted her head to the side and rested her cheek against his shoulder.

"Are you okay, honey?" he said.

He felt her head shake. "Not really."

"You liked them."

She nodded.

"They liked you, too. Simone told me. They liked you a lot."

Katie found Mac's hand and squeezed it.

He took a deep breath. Then he said, "Does this—what happened to Simone and Jill—does it make you think about Mom?"

He felt her go stiff and motionless, as if she was holding her breath. He was afraid she'd try to pull away from him. If she did, he thought he would keep his arm tight around her. He'd hold onto her, insist that she allow him to hug her. He'd hug her with both arms. He'd refuse to let her go. He'd make her know that he would always hold onto her whether she thought she wanted him to or not. He'd always be there. He would never walk out some evening and not come back.

After a minute, he felt her relax. "I think about Mom all the time," she whispered.

"Do you want to talk about it?" he said.

"Not now."

"Sometime, though," he said. "Sometime soon. We should talk about Mom. Talk about what happened. Okay?"

"Okay."

"Okay," he said. He kissed the top of her head, then stood up.

Katie looked up at him. She'd been crying, and she made no effort to hide it from him. Mac took that as a good sign.

"You coming downstairs?" he said.

"In a minute."

"Do me a favor?"

"What, Daddy?"

"No more Wagner today."

"Okay," she said. "I'm not in a Wagner mood anymore, anyway."

—⌒⌒—

JESSIE HAD BEEN more or less following the Great Lakes northerly and easterly. She'd been taking her time, feeling oddly reluctant to end her odyssey and the sense of independence and anonymity it gave her. She stopped at antique shops and art galleries, driving secondary roads through Ohio and Pennsylvania into New York State, tracking the Lake Erie shoreline up to Buffalo, then along the Canal to Niagara Falls. She'd stopped at the falls to take a look. It was amazing how human beings could commercialize the beauty right out of something so spectacular. She'd felt the same way the first time she saw the Grand Canyon.

She skirted the cities of Rochester and Syracuse, and on Tuesday afternoon she found herself in a town called Pulaski, which seemed to have a disproportionate number of motels and inns and lodges and restaurants for its size.

She took a room at a motel, and when she asked the woman behind the counter to recommend a place to eat, she learned that the locals pronounced Pulaski "*Plask*-eye," with the emphasis on the first syllable, and that the main source of income in the town was from out-of-staters who came here to go fishing in the lake and the river that ran into it. Apparently at certain seasons fishermen from all over the northeast flocked to Pulaski, New York.

Mid-May evidently wasn't one of those seasons. There were plenty of vacancy signs, and Jessie didn't have to wait for a table at the mostly empty Italian restaurant, where she had a nice antipasto and some decent veal scaloppine and two glasses of red wine.

Back in her motel room, she took out her cell phone. She'd been thinking about it for the past few days, ever since Friday night when she heard Simone Bonet's voice and chickened out. She thought about it in the daytime while she drove, thought about it while she waited to fall asleep at night, thought about it when she woke up in the morning.

Jessie guessed she was becoming obsessed.

She had to do it. She had to find out. Then she wouldn't be obsessed anymore.

She took out the note that Simone had written, unfolded it, hesitated for just a minute, then dialed the number.

It rang four times. Then there was a click, and a woman's recorded voice answered. It sounded like the woman who had answered when Jessie called before. "Hello," said the voice. "We're not here now. Please leave your name and number and we'll get back to you."

Jessie pressed the "end" button on her phone and dropped it on the bed. She flopped back onto the pillow and looked up at the ceiling. It was disappointing. She'd spent all that time working up her courage to call, and now nobody was there.

Maybe she should have left a message, given her cell phone number. If Simone Bonet was as eager to talk with Jessie as she'd said in her note, she'd return the call.

But Jessie didn't want to be surprised. She needed to control this situation. She would call at a time when she felt ready to talk.

She figured she was less than half a day's drive from Beaverkill, New York.

Pat Brody typed in his password and saw the blinking icon indicating that a new e-mail was waiting. He retrieved the encrypted message and instructed his computer to translate it.

It was from Bellwether. The subject line read "Patchman Report."

Blackhole reports Patchman married underage girl, Saigon '74, never divorced. One daughter, abandoned or sold, present status unknown, possibly named Jessie. Eye injury not, repeat, not line of duty. One witness, not yet eliminated, potentially useful. Verification documents, tapes, photographs, not recovered. Advise. Time of essence. Bellwether.

Brody read it again, letting the implications sink in. He found himself nodding. He'd had a bad feeling about Larrigan all along.

So the judge was a pedophile and a bigamist and a hypocrite and a fake hero, and there was proof of all of it, but the proof, the documentation, had yet to be recovered.

Jesus.

Bellwether wanted instructions. Brody had to make a decision. The first and obvious choice was to call the whole thing a big
mistake and try to minimize the fallout. Go to the president and
tell him he had to withdraw Thomas Larrigan's nomination—or,
better, convince Larrigan to make up some excuse and withdraw
himself—before it was too late.

No good. Politically speaking, it was too late, especially given
the decision the president had made to link himself with Larrigan
in a personal way and announce his nomination before they'd had a
chance to complete their investigation.

Pat Brody blamed himself. He'd had no information, but he had
a bad feeling, and even though it was clear that the president had
made up his mind to go public, it was Brody's responsibility to step
up and speak out, to do his job as advisor.

All too often, this president made it clear that he didn't want
advice. He was full of enthusiasms. He was impetuous. He was like
a big kid. To some voters—the majority of them in the recent election—this translated as vigorous, active, energetic, lovable.

Sometimes, though, it translated as stupid and heedless and just
plain wrong-headed, and according to the polls, this was how it had
been going with increased frequency lately.

Larrigan was Pat Brody's mistake, and he was certainly prepared
to take the fall for it, if that would solve the problem. But Brody
knew that the president's reelection chances would be considerably
diminished if his poor judgment about the Larrigan nomination
ever came to light. If Larrigan withdrew, regardless of what explanation they could concoct, the press would never let the president
off the hook. If Blackhole could come up with this devastating
information, sooner or later some Woodward or Bernstein would
get the story, too. Probably sooner.

The judge's eye was not a war injury? His wonderfully jaunty
eyepatch, his trademark, the emblem of his heroism—it represented
a thirty-year lie?

In a way, a self-serving lie was as bad as pedophilia and bigamy and baby-selling.

All in all, just devastating.

According to Bellwether there were photographs and tapes and documents to confirm it all. If they weren't recovered, sooner or later they'd come to light. They'd be worth hundreds of thousands of dollars to the tabloids.

Christ. It would be the worst kind of scandal. This wasn't some complicated financial scam that Mr. and Mrs. Average Voter couldn't understand and wouldn't care about. Just publish a photograph of the man with the black eye patch. Anybody could understand this story.

This story had human interest. More than that. Human fascination. Larrigan was the president's personal choice for the seat on the Supreme Court. They played golf together. Their wives were college classmates. The president could never distance himself from the judge. The time had passed for that.

The media would find out, and they'd milk it, and it would be one more example of the president's bumbling, another source of jokes for Letterman and Leno, front-page news for the tabloid and supermarket trash mongers, an excuse for even respectable reporters to poke and probe into the backgrounds of other presidential appointees.

At best it would be a distraction from the business of the nation, a drain on energy and money and manpower. It would further erode the already shaky credibility and authority of the president and his administration both at home and abroad.

At worst, it would destroy the president's chances of getting reelected. That was intolerable.

Pat Brody couldn't ask the president what he wanted to do about this. Pat Brody couldn't ask anybody. He was absolutely OYO on this one. On your own. That's why he was called a trusted advisor.

He turned back to his computer, read Bellwether's cryptic message one more time, then clicked on "reply."

Bellwether: Instruct Blackhole imperative recover all evidence, neutralize all witnesses. Emphasize all. Agree time of essence. Meet usual place 23:00 Wednesday. Read and delete. Shadowland.

Then Brody opened a blank mail document, typed in Blackhole's code, and wrote "Instructions" on the subject line.

Blackhole: Bellwether instructions forthcoming. Emphasize finish job soonest. OYO as always. Meet usual place 23:00 Wednesday. Read and delete. Shadowland.

Brody read over his two emails, clicked on "send," then deleted his sent-mail and received-mail files.

And so, just like that, it was done. Pat Brody had fulfilled his responsibility. He'd made the decision, and now it was out of his control.

Experience had taught him that in this job, it was important to worry about the things over which you had even a small degree of control. But it was equally necessary to forget about the things which were beyond your control. Otherwise the job would devour you.

So now it was in Blackhole's hands.

~•~

JESSIE TRIED THE number again from her motel room at a little after eight the next morning. Again it rang and rang before the answering machine picked up. And again Jessie hung up without leaving a message.

She couldn't figure out why this bothered her. She didn't even know this woman who thought she was her mother. Why should she care that nobody answered the telephone? Why did it give her an empty feeling? Why did this woman have to write that letter and bring this complication into her life in the first place? Before she'd received that letter, she never thought about her birth mother, never wondered about her, never cared.

So where the hell was Simone Bonet, now that Jessie was ready to talk to her?

She unfolded her New York road map and spread it out on her bed. Pulaski to Beaverkill. As near as she could tell it was between 200 and 250 miles southeasterly. She could take 81 due south into Pennsylvania, then cut east on 84. That would be the fast way.

But she'd been avoiding the interstates since Illinois, and she saw no reason to change. She enjoyed the secondary roads. She liked seeing the countryside, skirting the population centers. Besides, she felt safer driving the uncrowded two-lane state highways. And still there lingered that reluctance to arrive anywhere, to end this long cross-country journey, to begin the next part of her life.

So she figured five or six hours by the back roads. Get some breakfast, hit the road by nine, she'd be in Beaverkill in the middle of the afternoon.

She crammed her stuff into her backpack, left the motel key on the bedside table along with a five-dollar bill for the maid, and went out to her car, which was parked right in front.

She unlocked the back door and tossed in the backpack.

That's when she saw her duffel sitting on the passenger seat, where it had spent the night.

Jessie made a fist, punched her palm, and muttered, "Stupid!" She'd been sloppy. She should always have a gun within reach. Until last night, she'd been lugging the duffel into whatever room she was staying in, and she'd been sleeping with the Sig nine under the pillow beside her.

Last night she fucked up, and it could've killed her. She had to think that way. Always.

This mother shit, it was distracting her, making her careless.

You survive by assuming that Howie Cohen has somebody on your tail, that the guy in the truck behind you plans to shoot you, that the middle-aged woman sitting by herself at the bar works for Cohen, that the guy in the business suit who pulls up to the gas pumps next to you has been sent to assassinate you.

You've got to think that way all the time.

Relax and you're dead, Jessie thought.

She'd been lucky this time. She couldn't let it happen again.

—ౖ౭ం౭—

A STATE POLICE cruiser was parked behind Jill's Wagoneer in the turnaround in front of Simone's house. Mac saw a uniformed officer sitting behind the wheel. A man in gray suit was leaning against the fender talking into a cell phone.

Mac pulled in behind the cruiser, got out, and went over to the man in the suit. "I'm Mac Cassidy." He held out his hand.

The man snapped his phone shut and shoved it in his jacket pocket. "Detective Alberts, state cops," he said. He held out his hand.

Mac shook his hand. "I was expecting the sheriff. Sheriff Norris."

"This is no longer a local investigation," said Alberts. "Norris told me you were coming."

Mac shrugged. "Okay. Did he tell you why I wanted to meet him here?"

"He thought you might be able to help us." Alberts was a tall, slightly stooped guy, with thinning blondish-brown hair. Somewhere in his forties, Mac guessed.

Mac nodded. "I'll try. And maybe you can help me. I'm writing a book about Simone. What happened here, it's got to be part of the book."

"Pretty cut and dried," Alberts said. "The Rossiter woman shot the Bonet woman twice in the chest, then turned the gun on herself. Murder-suicide."

Mac found himself shaking his head.

"You don't buy it, Mr. Cassidy?"

Mac shrugged. "What do I know?"

"You knew these ladies. I mean, you're writing a book."

"I didn't know them well. We really had only just gotten started."

"But you spent some time with them. Here, at this house. Is that right?"

"That's right."

"Ms. Bonet, she was famous?"

"She used to be in movies. You didn't know that?"

Alberts shrugged. "I don't know anything about either lady. I understand they pretty much kept to themselves. People respect each other's privacy around here. So Ms. Bonet was a movie star?"

"Not really a star. More like a cult figure. She was in some *avant garde* films in the eighties. She did nude scenes."

"Nude, eh?" Alberts looked away, and Mac wondered if he was offended.

"She was mysterious," Mac said. "Had secrets. Didn't reveal much. People were interested in her. She was a kind of Reagan-era cultural icon."

The detective gazed up at the sky. "Does it surprise you that these ladies would carry out a suicide pact, Mr. Cassidy?"

"I don't know. Maybe if I saw how it looked."

"I can tell you how it looked. Ms. Bonet was half sitting up in bed with two bullet holes in her chest. A lot of blood. Ms. Rossiter was lying on the floor to the left of the chair, a bullet hole in the right side of her head. Not much blood at all. Powder burns on her hair and scalp. Looked like she had the gun pressed right against her head. The gun, a little .32, was lying on the floor, three rounds gone. It was registered to Ms. Bonet. Gunpowder residue on Ms. Rossiter's right hand and wrist."

Mac shrugged. "Sounds like a murder-suicide, all right."

Alberts narrowed his eyes at him. "But . . . ?"

Mac shook his head. "But nothing. I guess they probably committed suicide, just the way you say it looks. But let's say that's not what happened. The only other explanation is, somebody killed them both and tried to make it look like suicide."

Alberts nodded. "And?"

"Okay," said Mac. "If somebody killed them and set it up so it would look like Jill shot Simone twice in the chest then turned the gun on herself . . . which, you say, is exactly what it does look like . . . but if somebody did it . . . killed them . . . tried to make it look like suicide . . . the question is why."

Alberts nodded. "And who."

"Well, sure," said Mac. "Who, too. The who and the why go together."

"That's a pretty wild scenario," said Alberts.

"But just for the sake of argument, let's say that's how it happened," said Mac. "What about a motive?"

Alberts spread his hands. "Near as we can tell, nothing was taken from the house. There's money and jewelry and silverware and art. A lot of stuff that looks pretty valuable. It's all still there. This wasn't a burglary."

"What about . . . ?" Mac let his voice trail off.

"No sign of sexual assault on either woman. Nothing like that."

"Can you think of any other motive?"

Alberts shrugged.

"So it must've been suicide."

"We talked to Ms. Bonet's doctor, Dr. Mattes," said Alberts, "and he said she was dying of multiple sclerosis, that the disease was progressing rapidly, and that she'd been pretty depressed about it. He prescribed something for her, but in her situation, he said it wouldn't necessarily do much for her depression. The doctor also believes that these two women were, um, lovers, very devoted to each other. He thought it was entirely possible that Ms. Bonet would decide she wanted to die." Alberts spread his hands. "Murder-suicide."

"You're comfortable with that?" said Mac.

Alberts nodded. "Sure. You're not, huh?"

"I'm surprised, that's all," Mac said. "I know Simone was depressed and sick, but she had things she was looking forward to."

"Like what?"

"Like finishing our book. Like getting together with her daughter."

"She had a daughter?"

Mac shook his head. "I don't know much about it. Just that Simone had a daughter who she gave up for adoption when she was a baby. She'd be a grown woman now. They'd recently had some communication. Maybe I'll know more when I listen to the tapes."

"What tapes?"

"Simone has been telling her life story on tapes for me. For our book. I haven't listened to them yet."

"I'd like to hear those tapes," said Alberts. "They could go a long way to clearing this whole thing up."

Mac smiled. "You think there's something to clear up?"

He shook his head. "Nope. Not really."

"Well," said Mac, "if Simone talks about a plan to commit suicide on tape, I'll let you know, okay?"

"Good deal." Alberts shrugged. "You want to go inside, have a look?"

"Can I?"

"Sure. You can tell me what you think."

⸙

JESSIE CROSSED THE Delaware River a little before noontime. Now she was getting close. She'd been driving on the winding two-lane roads, definitely country roads, with sandy shoulders and continuous bends and rises and dips. They wound through woods and past fields and over little rocky brooks, and there weren't many signs of civilization. Hardly any other vehicles on the road. Here and there a mobile home or a hunter's cabin nestled among some trees. That was about it.

After a while she turned into a grassy pull-off and looked at her road map. As near as she could tell, she wasn't more than an hour's drive from Beaverkill.

She picked up her phone and got out of the car to stretch her legs. She hit redial as she paced around. Simone Bonet's number was the last one she'd tried.

It rang three times. Then a man's voice picked up and said, "Yes?"

Jessie hesitated, then poked the "end" button.

She hadn't expected a man to answer. It threw her.

She took a breath and thought about it. Okay, so Simone was married, or living with a guy or something. Why should it matter to Jessie?

She decided it didn't. She hit redial again, still pacing around beside the road.

Again a man answered. She couldn't be sure, but it sounded like a different voice.

"May I speak to Simone Bonet, please?" Jessie said.

"Who's calling please?"

"Is she there?"

There was a hesitation on the other end. Then the man said, "Jessie? Is that you?"

State Police Detective Alberts fished a key out of his pocket, stuck it in the lock, and pushed open the front door. Mac followed the cop into the living room. It looked the same as it had the last time he'd been there.

"Don't touch *anything*," Alberts said.

"There was no sign of forced entry?" Mac said.

"No," said Alberts. "Mr. Martinez, the gardener who found them, said the door was unlocked so he walked in. That was the side door off the deck. We're keeping the house locked now, but I would guess the ladies didn't lock up at night."

Mac looked at him. "Really?"

"This is the country, Mr. Cassidy. Most folks don't bother locking their doors. People feel safe around here."

"Yeah," said Mac. "I can see why."

Alberts shot him a glance. The lieutenant led the way to the bedroom. He stopped outside the open door. "This is how we found it," he said. "Except, of course, there were two bodies here."

Mac stood in the doorway. He hadn't been in this part of the house before. There wasn't much to see. A straight-backed wooden chair was pulled up beside the bed. The bed itself looked like it had been slept in. The pillows were bunched up against the headboard and the blankets were turned down.

He saw no bloodstains or bullet holes. It was just an empty bedroom.

"Maybe you see something I don't see?" said Alberts, making it a question.

Mac shook his head. "No. I don't think so." But something was nagging at him.

Right then the phone beside the bed rang. It sounded loud and sudden in the hush of the empty house.

Alberts let it ring a couple of times, then picked it up and said, "Yes?"

He held it against his ear for a moment, then shrugged and put it back on its cradle.

"Nobody there?" said Mac.

He shook his head. "Hung up on me." He hit a couple of buttons on the phone, put it to his ear, looked up at the ceiling, then shrugged. "No luck. Cell phone probably." He waved the back of his hand, dismissing the subject. "Anyway, what were you were saying?"

"Nothing, I guess," said Mac. "You asked if I noticed anything. I don't know how I could. I mean, I've never been in this room before. But still, I've got the feeling that something is . . . I don't know . . . wrong. Off. Out of place or something."

"You saying—?"

The phone rang again.

Mac said. "Let me. Okay?"

Alberts shrugged. "Be my guest."

Mac picked up the phone and said, "Hello?"

There was a hesitation. Then, "May I speak to Simone Bonet, please?" A woman's voice.

"Who's calling, please?"

"Is she there?"

"Jessie? Is that you?"

Mac heard a quick exhalation of breath. "Yes," she said. "Yes, it is. Who are you? How did you know?"

"I'm a friend," he said. "Simone talks about you all the time."

"So put her on the phone." Mac thought he heard panic rising in Jessie's voice. "I want to talk to her."

"Where are you?" Mac said.

"I'm standing beside the fucking road in the middle of nowhere getting aggravated."

"What state are you in?"

"State? New York."

"Do you know what town?"

"Jesus," said Jessie. "I'm not lost. Near as I can tell, I'm less than an hour from Beaverkill. That's where I'm headed. I want to see Simone Bonet, and that's where she lives. But if she's not there . . ."

Mac was thinking that if he told Jessie that Simone was dead, she wouldn't come. He wanted to tell her in person. He wanted to meet her. He wanted to help her if she needed help. He realized that for some reason he felt obligated to Simone to finish what they had started. To get her story told. If Jessie was Simone's daughter, she had the right to know it. He figured they could get the story from the tapes Simone had made.

"Why don't you come to the house," he said. "Do you know how to find it?"

"Yes, I've got GPS. I just wanted to make sure she's there," Jessie said. "That's why I'm calling. Assuming she still wants to see me."

"I'm sure she would," he said. He gave her the landmarks for the driveway.

"Tell her I'll be there in about an hour," said Jessie.

"Good," said Mac.

He hung up the phone. Alberts was looking at him. "Who's Jessie?"

"Remember I mentioned Simone's daughter?"

"That was her?"

Mac nodded. "She's about an hour from here. She's on her way."

"Where does she live?"

"California."

"She came all the way from California?"

"Looks like it."

"Does she know anything about this?" Alberts waved his hand at the bedroom.

Mac shook his head. "I don't see how she could know anything. Simone gave her up for adoption when she was a baby. They just got in touch with each other recently."

"And now it's too late," said Alberts. "Too bad." He looked at his watch, then at Mac. "I'm afraid we're going to have to call it a day. I've got to be somewhere."

They walked.

"So the daughter is on her way?" Alberts said.

Mac nodded. "I'm going to wait for her here, if that's all right."

Alberts shrugged. "Do me a favor, though. If she has any thoughts or insights or theories, make sure I hear about them."

"Of course."

"And if you—"

"Wait," said Mac. "I remember now. Something Simone told me the first time I was here. She gave me a batch of old photographs and documents for the book, and she told me there was one photograph from the batch that she was keeping on the table beside her bed."

"A photograph?" said Alberts. "A photograph of what?"

"I don't know," said Mac. "I didn't see it. Was there a photograph beside her bed?"

He shrugged. "No, I don't think so."

"I mean, when you first went into the bedroom? Maybe somebody took it for evidence or something?"

"Nobody took any photograph."

"So she probably moved it. Or maybe I'm not remembering right." Mac shrugged. "Anyway, I feel better. It bothered me that I couldn't think of it."

"Happens to me all the time," said Alberts. "Trust me, it only gets worse." He handed Mac a business card. "Ask Jessie to give me a call, would you? And if you think of anything else . . ."

"Sure." Mac took out a card of his own and gave it to the detective. "If you need me for anything."

_⸙⸙_

THE DARK GREEN Jeep Cherokee pulled up behind Mac's car and Jill's old Wagoneer. It was five minutes of two. Mac was sitting on the front steps of Simone's house. He stood up and started toward the Cherokee.

The door opened and Jessie stepped out. He saw the resemblance instantly, even though Jessie had short blonde hair and her skin was fairer than Simone's. The eyes and the mouth, the shape of her face, the jawline and cheekbones, were the same.

She was tall and willowy, wearing shorts and a sleeveless jersey. She had athletic legs, muscular shoulders. Her skin seemed to glow with fitness and strength and health.

Mac realized he was staring at her. It occurred to him that he hadn't looked at a woman that way—the way he realized he was looking at Jessie—for a long time. Hadn't been much interested in how a woman looked.

"Hi," he said. "Jessie?"

She nodded. "You're Cassidy?"

"Yes," he said. "Mac."

She slammed the car door, then turned to face him. She put her hands on her hips and smiled. "So do I pass?"

"What?"

"You're staring at me."

"I'm sorry." Mac smiled. "You look like Simone."

"Really." A statement, not a question. Sarcastic. Skeptical.

"Yes. Your eyes especially."

"She's Asian?"

"You don't know anything about her, do you?"

"Nothing whatsoever," said Jessie. "Just that she saw my picture in the paper, and based on that, she thinks she gave birth to me."

"And you drove here all the way from California to find out if it's true?"

Jessie narrowed her eyes at him for a moment. Then she nodded. "Sure. Why not?"

Mac shrugged. "It's a long drive."

"So where is she?" Jessie said. "Why are you meeting me out in the driveway like this. Who the hell are you, anyway? You her boyfriend or something?"

He didn't know how to say it except to say it. "Simone is dead, Jessie."

She frowned. "What?"

"She's dead. It happened Monday night."

Jessie went over to the front steps and sat down. "What happened?"

Mac sat beside her. "Suicide, apparently."

"What do you mean, apparently?"

Mac told her everything he knew. As he talked, Jessie peered intently into his eyes. He found it unnerving. It was as if she could see right into his brain. He thought she was the kind of woman he couldn't lie to or keep a secret from.

As he approached the end of his story, Jessie started shaking her head. When he finished, she said, "And you believe it?"

"What? That they committed suicide?"

"Yes."

"I guess so. That's what it looked like."

"Never mind how it looked," she said. "Just from what you know about her. Your sense of her. Your instincts. Would she do this? Can you imagine her and her friend actually doing this? Planning it? Agreeing to it? Carrying it out?"

Mac shook his head. "Not really. But—"

"She said she wanted to meet me, right?"

"Oh, yes," he said. "It was very important to her. It's what kept her going, I think. When you called the other night—when Jill answered and you hung up on Simone—she was thrilled. She was convinced you'd call again, that you wanted to learn about yourself, that you'd come to meet her. She thought you were just shy. She thought that's why you wouldn't speak to her. That you were bashful."

Jessie looked at him out of the sides of her eyes. "I am. I'm extremely bashful."

He wondered if she was flirting with him.

"So why would she do this," Jessie said, "if she had things she was looking forward to?"

"There are reasons. Her disease, her depression . . ."

"Tell me what you think, Mac."

He nodded. "Okay, I find it hard to believe they would do this." He liked the way she said his name. He liked the way she held his eyes with hers. "Simone was deeply involved in our book. She was committed to it. I don't believe she wanted to quit before it was finished. She was telling her story for me on tape. I think it was hard for her. I think she had a lot of painful memories. But she wanted to get it done. She said she was doing it for you. So you'd know all about yourself."

"Look," Jessie said. "We don't even know if I *am* her daughter. I mean, so I've got Asian eyes and I'm the right age, and I happen to be adopted."

"Your name, too."

"Church," said Jessie.

Mac nodded. "Simone knew the name of the people who adopted you."

She was looking at him. He found it hard not to look away from her eyes.

"All that," she said softly. "It sort of adds up, doesn't it?"

"It does," said Mac.

"My parents," she said. "They told me I was adopted right from the beginning. It was one of the first things I knew about myself. They told me it was something I should be proud of. Like they picked me out. It made me special. But they never told me anything about my . . . my origins."

"I know that you—her daughter—were about the most significant thing that ever happened to her."

Jessie jerked her head toward the house. "I want to go inside."

"It's locked," said Mac. "The police have the key."

She nodded. "I could get in."

"Bad idea," he said.

"I'd just look around. See what kind of stuff she had. Books, paintings, you know? Get a feel for her. For Simone. If she was my mother . . ."

"Better not," said Mac.

She looked away from him for a minute. Then her eyes swung back. "They murdered her," she said.

"Who?"

"I don't know," said Jessie. "I don't know who or why. But I understand this scenario. It's easy to set up if you know what you're doing."

Mac was shaking his head. "What do you know about . . . scenarios?"

She smiled. "I was a cop. A detective. I had a lot of special training. I learned to observe and to visualize. I worked undercover for a year and a half. I can think like a criminal."

"That's comforting," said Mac.

She didn't smile. "How you described it, one man could do it, since she couldn't get around on her own. Easier for two. Convenient, she kept a gun in the house. But if not, they would've used one that wasn't registered, couldn't be traced. So they make Jill sit in the chair beside Simone's bed, and the guy with the gun presses it against Jill's head and pulls the trigger. Then he shoots Simone in the chest. Then he puts Jill's hand around the pistol and he aims it at Simone and shoots her again. Then he lets Jill fall onto the floor with the gun in her hand. They don't take anything. They probably wear latex gloves. They leave no clues. In and out in fifteen minutes."

"Jesus," Mac whispered.

Jessie shrugged. "Piece of cake."

"Maybe they did take something," he said.

"What?"

"She told me she kept a photo beside her bed. From when she was young. Now it's not there."

"That's it, then," said Jessie.

"Okay," said Mac. "Except—"

"Except why?" she said. "What's the motive?"

He nodded.

"You tell me."

He shrugged. "The cop who I talked with said it wasn't burglary," he said. "And it wasn't sexual. What's left?"

"The fact that we don't know the motive," she said, "doesn't mean there isn't one."

"I didn't mean that," Mac said. "But maybe it was just random and crazy. No motive."

"No such thing," she said. "There's always a motive, even if it appears to be random and crazy. Nothing's really random. Crazy people have their crazy reasons."

"What about a serial killer?"

"Doubtful," said Jessie. "Serial killers almost always leave something behind. At the crime scene. On the body. How they arrange it. Or how they mutilate it. They don't try to disguise what they do. They're proud of their work. They expect to get caught. They want to get caught. They want the world to know how important and powerful they are. Anyway, the cop, he didn't mention other murders similar to this one around here, did he?"

Mac shook his head. "No."

"So," she said, "process of elimination, there's some logical motive."

Mac nodded. It all made sense. "You really understand this stuff. Oh. Detective Alberts, he'd like you to call him. I have his card."

Jessie shrugged. "Maybe I will."

Mac smiled. "Meaning, maybe you won't, huh? Anyway, meanwhile, we don't know anything. It could have been suicide."

Jessie shook her head. "It wasn't. They were murdered. We'll figure it out." She fixed him with that penetrating look. "Do you want to figure it out?"

"Yes. Of course."

"For your book?"

"Sure. I guess so. For Simone. She deserves the truth." He looked at her. "What about you, Jessie?"

"I'd rather you didn't call me Jessie," she said.

Mac frowned. "How come?"

She shook her head. "Long story. Call me Karen, okay? For now, I'm Karen Donato."

He shrugged. "Sure. Okay. So are you with me on this?"

"Getting the truth?" she said. "Listen, I drove all the way from California. At first this was just a place to head to because I had to get away from where I was. But I kept thinking about it, and the closer I got, the more I wanted to meet her, to know for sure whether or not she was my mother, to find out about myself. It started to feel really important to me. So now, yeah, I am significantly aggravated. I drive all the way across the country, and then somebody kills her and prevents me from meeting her and talking with her and figuring it out? It pisses me off. I want to know why."

"I've got an idea," said Mac.

"The tapes," said Jessie.

He nodded.

"Let's listen to them," she said. "I've got a bunch of questions."

"Like?"

"Like, for starters, if Simone was my mother, who was my father?"

—⟨⟩—

LARRIGAN WANTED TO use the parking garage again, which was all right with Eddie Moran. The way they did it, Eddie parking on a different floor, walking down, the garage dim and dank, easy to tell if you were being followed—it was pretty secure.

Of course, Eddie could never be sure when those guys who called themselves Mr. Black and Mr. White were following him or when they'd try to contact him again or what they intended to do next.

It was pretty obvious they weren't done with him yet. Guys like that, they killed you when they were done with you.

Eddie Moran intended to remain useful to Mr. Black and Mr. White for as long as possible while he tried to figure out how to prevent them from killing him.

He'd killed Li An for them. Somehow he doubted if that would be the end of it.

The judge's car was parked where it had been the other time. Eddie opened the passenger door and slid in. "Semper fi," he said to the judge.

"What's up?" said Larrigan. "I don't like this."

"What don't you like?"

"Sneaking around," he said. "Meeting this way."

"You want to reserve a table for two at the Four Seasons, wear neckties?"

Larrigan blew out an exasperated breath. "So what've you got for me?"

"How about, your troubles are over?"

"What do you mean?"

"Li An. She's dead."

"Dead?" Larrigan turned and glared at Moran with that one blue eye. "You're saying you—"

"Suicide, judge. Her and her girlfriend. Both of them. A suicide pact."

"Jesus," said Larrigan. "You killed her."

"Read my lips," said Eddie. "It was suicide."

"Bullshit," said Larrigan. "I know you."

"Why would I kill her? You think I just go around killing people? We just got lucky here, that's all. She was sick and depressed, and she did it."

Larrigan laughed quickly. "How lucky can you get, huh?"

"Yeah. Pretty lucky."

"What about those photographs?"

"She didn't have them."

"What do you mean?"

"I mean," said Eddie, "Li An didn't have the fucking photographs. They weren't in her house. I looked everywhere."

"You went in and searched?"

Moran nodded. "They weren't there. Trust me."

"Where the hell are they, then?"

"I don't know," said Eddie. "But I don't see that it matters. Without somebody to tell the story, verify who's in those pictures, explain what they mean, they're harmless. And besides you, me, Bunny and Li An, there is nobody else, right?"

Larrigan smiled. "And now it's just you and me."

"Anybody sees those pictures, they wouldn't recognize any of us. You, looking like a damn hippie, no patch on your eye. All of us just kids. Li An was a baby, for Christ's sake."

"I wish the hell you got them, though."

"Well," said Eddie, "I didn't. They're gone. It's over, and I'm done with this whole damn thing. You're in the clear, okay?"

Larrigan smiled crookedly. "Okay."

"So congratulations, Justice Larrigan." Moran held his hand out.

Larrigan grasped it. "Justice Larrigan," he said. "That sounds pretty good." He pulled an envelope from his jacket pocket and handed it to Moran. "We should probably steer clear of each other for a while."

Moran stuffed the envelope into his pants pocket. "Call me if you need me," he said.

Mac was headed home to Concord, and Jessie was following him in her green Cherokee. Mac kept an eye on his rearview mirror, and whenever Jessie fell behind or a car got between them, he slowed down until she was there again. They'd exchanged cell phone numbers in case they got separated.

He waited til quarter of four to call Katie.

It rang four or five times before she answered with a breathless, "Hello?"

"Honey, it's me."

"Oh, hi, Daddy. Sorry. I was outside. I meant to bring the phone out with me."

"That's okay. What were you doing outside?"

"I thought I'd pull some weeds. Our flower gardens are a disaster."

Jane had liked gardening. Said it relaxed her, gave her a creative outlet. She'd done all the weeding and planting. To Mac, gardening was just backbreaking work. He'd been happy to leave it to her.

Katie had showed no interest whatsoever in yard work. No interest in any kind of work, for that matter. Katie had been a normal teenage girl.

But that was when Jane was still alive.

When Jane tended the flower gardens around the house, they always looked good. But in the year since she died, nobody had paid any attention to them. So this sounded like another way that Katie was trying to replace her mother. Mac didn't think that was a good thing, but he didn't know what to do about it.

"Don't pull all of 'em," said Mac. "Leave some for me."

"That's a deal," said Katie. "Where are you?"

"On my way back from Simone's. I should be home around six-thirty."

"Did you find out anything?"

"Not really," he said. "It looks like Simone and Jill committed suicide. I'm sorry."

Katie was silent.

"What do you say we go out to eat tonight?" he said.

"How come?"

He hesitated. "We're going to have a guest. I thought it would be nice if we went out."

"Who's the guest?"

He thought he detected wariness in Katie's voice. Maybe it was his imagination. "It's Simone's daughter," he said. "Her name is Karen. She arrived when I was there."

Katie said nothing.

"Honey?" said Mac. "Did you hear me?"

Katie cleared her throat. "Yes. I was just thinking . . ."

"What?"

"Nothing, Daddy. Want me to call for reservations?"

"Good idea. How about that new Thai place?"

"Okay. What time?"

"Make it seven." He paused. "Karen will be staying with us for a few days."

"I'll make the bed in the guest room."

Mac was trying to interpret Katie's tone. He wondered if she was thinking how Jessie—Karen—had lost her mother just as Katie had. Or if she was resenting the idea of another woman staying in their house.

"See you soon, then," he said.

"Drive carefully."

"I always do. Love you, kiddo."

"Me, too."

He hit the "end" button and dropped the phone on the seat beside him. He was beginning the think this was a bad idea.

He'd asked Jessie if she wanted to listen to Simone's tapes, and she said she definitely did. Jessie said something about finding a motel room, and Mac said, "That's silly. We've got an empty guest room. You can stay with us."

And Jessie shrugged and said, "Sure, okay, that would be nice, thanks."

He hadn't considered Katie, how she'd react to a strange woman sleeping in their house.

He picked up his phone and pecked out Jessie's number.

"That you, Mac?" she said.

"Yep. How you doing back there?"

"I'm not letting you out of my sight."

"Oh, oh." He laughed. "I just talked to Katie. She's calling in reservations for us. There's a new Thai restaurant not far from our house. I've heard it's pretty good. I hope you like Thai."

"Sure," she said. "Thai is great."

"We'll get home in time for you to get cleaned up before we eat."

"Oh, dear," she said. "Am I dirty?"

"I didn't mean—"

"I'm joking, Mac. It sounds great. I'm looking forward to meeting Katie."

"She is, too," he said, wondering if it was true.

—ↄ·ↄ—

THE MINUTE JESSIE walked into Mac Cassidy's house she knew something was off.

There were ghosts here. It was haunted. She could see it in Katie's eyes.

They were standing in the kitchen. Jessie had her backpack slung over one shoulder. Mac had brought in her duffel bag, the one that held her weapons.

Katie had met them at the door. She gave Mac a big hug, and now her arm was hooked through his. Possessively, Jessie thought.

She was a pretty teenager. Mature-looking for her age. Mac had told her Katie was fifteen. She didn't look much like her father that Jessie could see.

She seemed to be making a project of looking anywhere but at Jessie.

"Uh," said Mac, "Karen, Karen Donato, this is Katie."

"Hey," said Jessie.

"Hi." Katie was looking at the floor.

"Did you make the reservations?" said Mac.

"All set," she said.

"Seven?"

The girl nodded.

"Honey," said Mac to Katie, "will you show Karen where the guest room is?" He handed the duffel to her. "She'd probably like to get freshened up before dinner."

"Okay, sure." Katie took the duffel and headed for the stairway. "This way," she said. She still hadn't met Jessie's eyes.

Jessie leaned toward Mac. "I think this was a bad idea," she said.

"She'll be okay," he said.

"You're not telling me things I should know."

"You're right," he said. "Sorry. I will, but—"

"She died, right?"

He blinked.

"Your wife. Katie's mother."

He nodded. "Yes. A year ago last March."

Jessie rolled her eyes. "I figured you were divorced. If I'd known—"

"It'll be okay," he said. "Really. I'm glad you're here."

Katie poked her head back into the kitchen. "You coming, Karen?" She was looking at Mac, not Jessie.

"Coming," said Jessie. She shook her head at Mac, then followed Katie up the stairs.

The guest room was at the end of the hallway. Jessie noted that the master bedroom was directly across the hall. Katie's room was at the opposite end, near the top of the stairs.

There was a queen-sized bed, a dresser, a small desk, and a television on a table in the corner. A set of four watercolor prints hung on one wall. They depicted various waterfowl in flight. On another wall, a window looked out into the leafy side yard.

The room was neither masculine nor feminine. It was clean and neat and pleasant and devoid of personality.

"You've got your own bathroom," Katie said, "through there." She pointed at a doorway. "Closet, there. The TV's on cable, and the remote's in the drawer. We get a million channels." She gave Jessie a quick polite smile that didn't reach her eyes. "Anything else I can get you?"

"Nope," said Jessie. "Thanks. I'm good."

"We should leave for dinner in like fifteen minutes." Katie turned and started for the door.

"Hey, Katie?" said Jessie.

Katie stopped and looked at Jessie.

Jessie shrugged. "Nothing. I'm all set."

⁓∽∾⁓

As soon as Blackhole had returned from the Beaverkill job, he had sat at his computer. He'd summarized the encounter he and Mr. White had had with Eddie Moran, what Moran had agreed to do for them, and how smoothly he had done it. The police had apparently bought the murder-suicide scenario.

And Blackhole wrote down everything that Moran had told them about the woman and her importance. Blackhole had an excellent memory, and Mr. White had done a good job of making sure that Moran held nothing back.

Blackhole had listened to the audiotape they took from Moran, the one that the woman had made. It gave him two names that Moran didn't know. Mac and Jessie. Just first names. Jessie was the woman's daughter. Mac was the one to whom she was speaking when she made the tape.

This tape also told him that there were other tapes, and that this Mac had them. Moran had been interested in photographs.

He had described what was in those photographs. It was clear why he wanted them.

Blackhole needed to recover both the tapes and the photographs.

He transferred the digital images from Moran's camera onto his computer. The interesting ones showed a bearded man, a rugged-looking guy about forty. Had to be the one named Mac. Some shots, he was sitting with Simone, the two of them talking intently. Some, he was with a girl, looked like a teenager. Some, he and the girl were walking toward his car, him carrying a plastic bag. Some, close-ups of the license plate on the car, clear enough to read the numbers. Massachusetts plates.

Blackhole figured the girl was Mac's daughter.

He ran the plate numbers. The car was registered to Edwin MacArthur Cassidy, lived in Concord.

MacArthur. Mac.

Quick Google search. Mac Cassidy had ghostwritten the autobiographies of several famous people.

Simone—Moran had referred to her as Li An—turned out to be a semi-famous former movie actress named Simone Bonet. A recent item in *Publishers Weekly* announced that Mac Cassidy had signed a contract to ghostwrite Simone's autobiography.

That was before she became the *late* Simone Bonet.

Blackhole thought the whole picture was pretty clear. Cassidy had the tapes, and he guessed Cassidy had the photographs, too. So Mac Cassidy and the daughter, Jessie, were the only ones left who could cause a problem. Not counting Eddie Moran, of course.

Blackhole had submitted his report to Shadowland. Twelve hours later he had met with Bellwether. He had received his instructions.

Now it was time to get started.

At midnight precisely he picked up his cell phone and pecked out a number. He hit the send button, put the phone to his ear, let it ring once, then disconnected.

He put the phone on the table and waited.

At precisely seven minutes after midnight, it rang twice, then stopped.

Blackhole dialed a different number.

A muffled voice answered. "Mr. Black?"

"Hello, Mr. White," said Blackhole. "We have more work to do."

~∽∾~

As FAR AS Jessie was concerned, dinner at the Thai restaurant didn't end soon enough. Poor Mac had a struggle, Jessie observed, trying to be warm and friendly to her, and at the same time trying not to be *too* warm and friendly lest he upset Katie.

Katie didn't speak during the entire evening unless she was asked a direct question. Then she was polite and monosyllabic. Mostly she looked down at her plate.

When they got back to the house, Katie gave Mac a hug and Jessie a perfunctory smile and said she was heading up to finish her homework and go to bed.

After Katie went up, Jessie said, "I'm going to leave tomorrow," she said. "Get out of your hair. Let you and Katie get back to your lives."

Mac nodded. "I'm sorry. I guess it wasn't such a good idea. It's pretty tense, I know."

Jessie shrugged. "I'd like to know what happened."

"My wife, you mean."

She nodded.

"She was run over by a train," he said.

Jessie slept fitfully, and when she woke up, she felt unrested and jittery. But alert and focused, too, the way she felt when something important was going to happen. There were powerful emanations in this house. A lot of negative vibes from Mac and Katie. Ghostly vibes from his dead wife, her mother.

Run down by a train.

He'd told her the whole story. He blamed himself. She figured Katie blamed herself. At the same time, in some way that neither of them was able to recognize, they blamed each other, too.

Sunlight streamed in through her bedroom window. She looked at her watch. It was after eight o'clock. She never slept that late, but then, she usually managed to fall asleep more easily than she had last night.

She showered quickly, pulled on a pair of jeans and a T-shirt, and padded downstairs on bare feet.

She found a full coffeepot in the kitchen, poured herself a mugful, and went looking for Mac.

She found him in his office in the back corner of the house, peering at a computer monitor.

Jessie stood in the doorway. "Hey," she said.

He swiveled around and smiled. "Hey, yourself. Found the coffee, I see. How'd you sleep?"

She combed her fingers through her hair, an old habit from when it was long. "Okay. Fine." She went over and sat in the leather chair in the corner of the room. "Can we listen to the tapes?"

Mac nodded. "Simone told me that the main reason she agreed to do the book was so that you could hear her story. Your story."

"Assuming I'm her daughter," said Jessie.

"Simone was convinced that you were."

Jessie shrugged. "Let's do it, then."

Mac inserted a cassette into his recorder. "This is a dupe," he said. "I Fed-Exed the originals to my agent for safekeeping. There were some photographs and documents, too. I photocopied them and sent the originals to Ted also."

Jessie shrugged. "Makes sense."

For an hour she sat there with Mac and listened to Simone's voice describe her horrifying childhood in Vietnam. She had a low-pitched, sultry voice and a faint accent that Jessie couldn't place. A mixture of French and Vietnamese, she assumed.

When she tried to think of this woman—whose voice she was hearing but who was now dead—as her mother, it caused pressure to build behind her eyes.

She watched Mac as the tapes played. Now and then he scribbled a note on a yellow legal pad. He seemed unaware that Jessie was there, and she understood that he was working.

And then Simone's voice said, "And so it was done. I belonged to Thomas Larrigan. I was, as near as I can figure it, about thirteen years old."

Mac lurched at the tape player and punched the pause button. He looked at Jessie. "Holy shit," he whispered.

Jessie frowned. "Huh?"

"Do you know who Thomas Larrigan is?"

She looked at Mac. "You think it's *that* Thomas Larrigan?"

He nodded. "I bet it is."

"Do you realize what you've got here?"

He nodded. "A different kind of story from what I thought, for sure."

"Yeah," she said. "A dangerous story."

"Let's hear the rest of it."

It was after three o'clock in the afternoon when they finished listening to the last tape. The pressure behind Jessie's eyes had been building as Simone described her love for May, her daughter, and her enormous sadness at losing her, and how she longed to see her again, and now, when Jessie realized it would never happen for mother or daughter, the tears broke through.

Mac looked at her. "That must've been hard."

She wiped her eyes on the back of her wrist and smiled. "I'm okay." Jessie cleared her throat. "Are there more tapes?"

He shook his head. "That's it."

"You think it's me?" she said. "You think I'm May?"

Mac shrugged. "It fits, doesn't it?" He hesitated. "I'm sorry, Jessie. I know that's important to you. But I'm thinking about something else—the implications of these tapes. I'm thinking that Simone—"

"She was murdered," said Jessie. "She and Jill. I know. I apologize. That's way more important. They were murdered to keep them quiet, right? To keep this story from getting out. Do you think she knew who Thomas Larrigan is?"

Mac shook his head. "There's no indication of it in these tapes. Simone and Jill didn't have a television. I'm not sure they even had a radio. I never saw a newspaper or even a magazine in their house. It's got to be the same Larrigan, though."

"No question," said Jessie. "She talks about shoving that broom into his eye. Our Judge Larrigan has a patch over his eye. He's the right age. He was in Vietnam. Didn't you say you kept copies of the photos Simone gave you?"

"Plus the documents," he said. "From what Simone said, there's a marriage certificate and a birth certificate." He frowned at her. "*Your* birth certificate. Very powerful evidence."

"Let's look at the photos."

Mac fumbled through a stack of folders on his desk and pulled out several sheets of paper. Jessie got up and went to his desk. She put a hand on his shoulder and leaned against his back to look.

He moved a magnifying glass over the faces in the photos. They were a little blurry and faded, but there was no mistaking Thomas Larrigan even thirty-five or so years younger than he was now and with long hair and two functioning eyes. Jessie had seen the Supreme Court nominee's picture on TV and in the papers several times recently. This was definitely the same man.

Simone was terribly young and scrawny, Jessie thought, but she had a beautiful face. The other woman in the photos—Bunny Brubaker, according to the tapes—looked a few years older. She was also quite pretty. The other man—Eddie Moran—looked like a teenaged Huckleberry Finn, a rebel type with a fuck-the-world grin that the girls probably found irresistible.

In a couple of the photos, Simone—Li An, back then—was holding a baby. Jessie shivered at the realization that she was that baby.

Jessie said, "Why don't you see what you can find out about Eddie Moran and Bunny Brubaker."

"You think because Simone—?"

"Eddie Moran and Bunny Brubaker were there, too," she said. "They probably know everything Simone knew."

"Good thinking."

Mac went to Google and a few minutes later he clicked on a story about a woman named Bunny Brubaker getting robbed and murdered in a motel room in Davis, Georgia. According to the story, the police believed drugs were involved. Ms Brubaker's killer had not been apprehended. There was no picture of the victim with this or the two other short news items that he found.

"You think that's our Bunny?" said Jessie.

Mac shrugged. "It fits. Unusual name. She's about the right age."

He then did a search for Eddie Moran—Edward, Edwin, Ed—and came up with dozens of hits, none of which seemed to be quite the right age or background.

He leaned back in his chair and gazed up at the ceiling. "They killed Bunny Brubaker, too," he said.

Jessie nodded. "I'm thinking that if they—whoever they are—if they killed Simone—they probably know about the tapes and the photos and those documents."

He nodded. "I've been thinking about that, too." He looked at her. "If they know that . . ."

"Then they know about you," said Jessie.

⁓᭬᭬⁓

WHEN TED AUSTIN answered the phone, he said, "I was going to call you. What the hell is going on?"

"You heard about Simone," said Mac.

"Yes. Suicide. That's terrible."

"I don't think it was suicide, Ted."

Austin was silent for a minute. "You're saying . . .?"

"I'm saying that what Simone knew got her killed. You haven't listened to those tapes I sent you, have you?"

"No," Austin said. "Should I?"

"No," said Mac. "But you should know that they're dangerous. The photos and documents corroborate what's on the tapes. I hope they're in a safe place."

"They're safe," said Austin. "You better explain."

Mac summarized Simone's story as succinctly as he could.

"Wow," said Austin. "So let's see if I got this right. Judge Larrigan got his eye patch from a fight with his wife, making him a phony war hero. He had a baby with a fourteen-year-old girl, making him a pedophile and a statutory rapist. He married the girl and probably never divorced her, meaning he's a bigamist. He abused his young wife and then deserted her. He may have sold his baby." Austin paused. "This is the man who's going to sit on the Supreme Court?"

"No way he'll make it to the Court if the media get wind of this."

"If the media hear about all this," said Austin, "there'll be more hell to pay than that."

"I expect that great efforts will be made—have already been made—to keep this story from the media."

"Killing Simone," said Austin.

"Right."

Austin was silent for a moment. Then he said, "This is a helluva story, Mac. A much bigger story than we bargained for."

"Don't think that hasn't occurred to me," said Mac.

"We can't, um, go to the authorities, I guess."

"I don't think so."

"Because these people, these killers . . ."

"Unless I'm mistaken," said Mac, "these killers *are* the authorities."

⌘

WHEN JESSIE CAME downstairs later in the afternoon, she found Katie in the kitchen.

"Can I help?" said Jessie.

Katie was at the stove stirring something in a big pot. She didn't turn around. "No, Karen. Thanks. Everything's under control."

Jessie got a Coke from the refrigerator, then sat at the kitchen table. "Smells great," she said.

"Hope you like marinara sauce." Katie still hadn't looked at Jessie.

"I do," said Jessie. "So how was school?"

"Did he send you in here to make friends with me?"

"He?"

"My father," said Katie. "He likes you, you know."

Jessie hesitated. "What makes you say that?"

"It's so obvious."

"Look," said Jessie. "I'm only going to be staying one more night. I'm sorry if I make things uncomfortable for you."

"What makes you think I'm uncomfortable?" Katie turned to face Jessie. Her cheeks were wet.

"Oh, honey," said Jessie. "I'm sorry."

"You probably think I'm like jealous or something," said Katie. "It's not that. I just wish he could be happy. I try, but . . ."

Jessie got up, went over to Katie, and put her arms around her. Katie let her arms hang at her side, neither resisting nor participating in the hug.

"You can't be responsible for somebody else's happiness," said Jessie softly. "Nobody can do that."

"My mom made him happy," Katie whispered. She dropped her forehead onto Jessie's shoulder, but her arms remained rigid at her sides, as if she was fighting the urge to return Jessie's hug.

"Nobody will ever take your mom's place," Jessie said.

She felt Katie stiffen. She was afraid that the girl would pull away from her. But after a moment, Katie said, "Was Simone really your mother?"

"I think so."

"I met her," said Katie.

"I wish I had," said Jessie.

"She was really nice."

Jessie nodded.

Katie was silent for a moment. Then, in a whisper, she said, "So how does it feel, having your mother die before you even got to meet her?"

"It makes me sad," said Jessie.

Katie put her arms around Jessie's waist, gave her a quick, tentative hug, and then pulled away. "I've got to stir the sauce," she said. She turned to the stove.

"What can I do to help?" Jessie said.

"You can set the table if you want."

That, thought Jessie, *is progress*.

———✦———

THAT EVENING AFTER dinner Jessie sat on the bed in Mac Cassidy's guest room and took out her cell phone. She realized she'd forgotten to call Jimmy Nunziato. He worried about her, which was sweet, and he wanted her to call and tell him she was all right.

Speed-dial eleven, he'd said.

It rang four or five times before it clicked over to voicemail. Then a recorded female voice said, "We are sorry. This person's mailbox is full. Please try again later."

Jessie hit the *end* button. Hm. That was totally unlike Jimmy Nunz. He deleted all his messages as soon as he heard them. In his business, any kind of record was risky. Nunz was extremely careful. His clients depended on it. He carried his cell with him and answered it when it rang. If for some reason he couldn't answer, he retrieved the message as soon as he could and then erased it.

She tried it again, and got the same message.

She bunched the pillows up and lay back with her head propped up on them. She tried to understand it.

She didn't like what she was thinking.

She went to her duffel bag, took out her laptop computer, and put it on the little desk where there was a cable hookup. Five minutes later she was Googling the name James Nunziato.

There were way more James Nunziatos than Jessie had ever imagined. She narrowed it to "Chicago" and found the item she expected—and feared—from Sunday's *Tribune*.

"Chicago Printer Murdered," the headline read.

Her eyes raced over the brief story. James Nunziato, age fifty-seven, found Saturday morning in his print shop on West 16th Street. He'd been shot twice. According to the police, it appeared that he'd interrupted a burglary.

Jessie hugged herself.

Interrupted a burglary. Right.

Bullshit.

She had Dave Aronson's cell phone number stored in her computer.

He answered on the third ring. "Lieutenant Aronson," he said. "Who's this?"

"It's Jessie," she said. "Jessie Church."

"Jesus," said Aronson. "Jessie. Where the hell have you been? You okay?"

"Dave, listen. I've got a question for you."

"Yeah," he said, "me, I'm fine, the kids are both doing good, growing up, you know, and the wife, she's okay, tryin' to lose some weight, and my mother had that stroke, but she's hanging in there, thanks for asking."

"Aw, hell," said Jessie. "I'm sorry. I'm just kind of frantic here."

"Sure, Jess. Don't worry about it. What can I do for you?"

"Jimmy Nunziato. What happened?"

"You knew Jimmy Nunz, right?"

"Yes," said Jessie.

"Then you know what he did for a living, who he associated with."

"I know all that, yes. And I see that he got killed. What can you tell me about it that I didn't read in the papers?"

Aronson hesitated. "There was one thing."

"What's that?"

"This is between us cops."

"Sure," she said. "Of course."

"They, um, did a pretty good job on Jimmy before they shot him."

"You mean . . . ?"

"Nunz knew something, and by the looks of him they used a knife, Jess. It wasn't pretty."

Jessie took a deep breath. Then she said, "Okay, Dave. I was hoping it was something else, but it's what I needed to know. Thanks a lot. Give my best to your wife and kids and mother, okay?"

"Any time, Jess."

Jessie lay back on the bed and closed her eyes.

Howie Cohen, she thought. *You son of a bitch*.

Then she thought: *I've really gotta get away from here*.

22

Jessie stared up at the ceiling in Mac Cassidy's guest room. Aside from the bluish glow of her laptop computer screen, the room was dark. Ghostly shadows danced across the wall, leafy tree branches swaying in the breeze, backlit by a streetlight. When she was a kid, night shadows like that scared her. She supposed they still did.

What happened to Jimmy Nunziato was her fault. She had no doubt about that.

She knew it would forever be on her conscience. She should never have involved Nunz. It was sloppy and inconsiderate and ultimately fatal. She should've known that Howie Cohen would latch on to him sooner or later. Jimmy was an old friend. That was no secret. And what he did for people who wanted to disappear was widely known. It was a simple deduction for Cohen to figure out that Jessie would go to Jimmy Nunz, and it was logical for him to send a couple of his men to find out what Nunz knew.

Knowing Jimmy Nunziato, she was sure he'd held out as long as he could. But eventually he would've had to tell them what he knew. No matter how brave he might've been—and Jimmy Nunziato was as tough as they came—a man can tolerate only so much cutting.

So Cohen would now know that Jessie's new name was Karen Marie Donato, that her hair was short and blonde, that she was driving a Jeep Cherokee with Illinois plates registered to Mary Ferrone.

What Cohen didn't know, because Jimmy Nunziato couldn't possibly have told him, was Jessie's destination. She'd been careful to drop no hints when she'd been with Jimmy. She might be heading east. That's the most he could've said.

Sooner or later, Howie Cohen would track her down. He had nothing but time—the rest of his life in a federal prison in Maryland, to be exact. He'd sent that man Lesneski to the Muir Woods to kill her, and if he hadn't done it already, pretty soon he'd send somebody else to Concord, Massachusetts . . . or wherever she ended up. And if she changed her appearance again, and got a new identity, and found some out-of-the-way place to hide, it would still only be a matter of time. Something would happen, like her picture finding its way into a newspaper.

Men like Howie Cohen never gave up.

After Jimmy fixed her up with her new identity, her new car, her new cell phone, Jessie had begun to allow herself to feel safe. She should've known better. It was a dangerous illusion. The first rule in undercover work: Sooner or later, feeling safe would kill you. Thinking you were out of harm's way was fatally harmful.

She'd let Mac take her to that Thai restaurant where she'd been noticed, no doubt, by people who knew Mac, knew what had happened to his wife. His neighbors and acquaintances, people around town, they'd remember her. They'd talk about her, a little harmless gossip over the back fence. That poor Mac Cassidy, lost his wife a year ago? He had a date the other night. What do you think of that? A pretty blonde, Asian eyes, looked a bit younger than him. Never saw her before. Katie, his daughter, poor child, she was with them . . .

Who knew how many neighbors had spotted her and had noticed the Jeep Cherokee with Illinois plates that was parked in Mac Cassidy's driveway?

And who knew what Katie might've told her friends, and her friends might have told their parents, and on and on, about this blonde woman with the Asian eyes who just appeared out of nowhere, who was staying in their guest room, who her father seemed to have a crush on. Her name was Karen Donato.

No longer would that name hide Jessie's true identity from Howie Cohen. If she wasn't safe, then as long as she was in Mac's house, neither were he and Katie. She needed to put as much distance between herself and them as possible. With a sense of dread, she thought of Simone's killers. Mac and Katie were already in danger. Jessie was one of the few people who could protect them. If she stayed, they were at risk, if she left they were at risk. Either way, she lost.

Jessie went back to her laptop and checked the train and bus schedules leading out of Massachusetts. Even without a credit card or an automobile, you could get to anywhere from anywhere in this vast country if you had enough cash.

She had plenty of cash. All she had to do was pick a city, an absolutely random city where she had no friends or connections of any kind. A city where Howie Cohen would never think to look for her. A city where she could get a fresh start.

Or maybe it was time to put that passport to use. Just get the hell out of the country once and for all. Portugal, maybe. Or Thailand. Those were two places Jessie had always wanted to see.

───❦───

JESSIE WOKE UP early, but she waited in her room until she heard Katie leave for school. She wanted to keep this as simple and uncomplicated as possible.

She pulled on jeans, T-shirt, sneakers. She took her little Colt Mustang automatic out of her duffel bag and made sure it was loaded. She dropped the gun, along with a baseball cap, a pair of sunglasses, and her cell phone, into her shoulder bag, which already held a roll of twenties and fifties, a can of Mace, a whistle, a pair of handcuffs, a Swiss Army knife, and a roll of duct tape—the standard precautionary items that she'd been carrying with her since the beginning of her days with the cops.

She found Mac downstairs in his office peering at his computer monitor. She stood in the doorway and cleared her throat.

He turned, looked her up and down, and smiled. "Hey. Good morning. Going somewhere?"

"Yeah," she said. "I've got some things to do. I'll be back later to pick up my stuff, and then I'll be on my way."

He nodded. "You going to need money or anything?"

"I'm all set with money," she said, "but when I get back, I need you to do me a favor. You'll be around?"

He shrugged. "Sure. No problem."

"Okay, good, thanks." Jessie smiled. "Well, okay. Gotta go." She gave him a quick wave, turned, and got the hell out of there.

She realized, with a little shock, that she was sorry she wouldn't have the chance to get to know Mac Cassidy better.

⁓

JESSIE DROVE HER Cherokee toward Boston. She'd been to the old city several times, and she liked it. It had personality, not to mention great restaurants. Boston had the same neighborhood feel to it as San Francisco. What she mainly remembered about it, though, was the confusion of the streets, how they were laid out so haphazardly, how most of them were narrow and one-way—almost always the wrong way, no matter where you were trying to go—and how the people who'd been driving her around always seemed to get lost, even though they were supposedly Boston natives.

Well, this time Jessie didn't care where in the city she ended up. Her mission was simple.

She took Route 2 eastbound from Concord, and pretty soon she found herself on Storrow Drive heading into the city, with the Prudential and John Hancock buildings towering off to her right and the Charles River on her left. It was a sunny June day. Sailboats and skulls skimmed over the water, and joggers and inline skaters and cyclists were cruising the pathways along the riverbank, and young people were sunbathing on the grass. It gave Jessie a pang to see how carefree they all seemed to be.

She couldn't remember a time when she'd been carefree. She had no idea what it felt like not to have worries and problems and pressures.

She turned onto Charles Street so that she wouldn't have to negotiate the bridges and ramps and exit options that she saw looming ahead of her. Charles was narrow and one-way, of course, with cars parked densely along both sides. It curved around the bottom of Beacon Hill.

She took the first left off Charles, a one-way street that climbed steeply up the hill. It was narrow and quiet and leafy and lined with brownstones and townhouses. Very few cars were parked at the curb. Jessie read one of the signs: Tow ZONE. RESIDENT PARKING. PERMIT ONLY.

Perfect.

She pulled the Cherokee against the curb right under one of those signs. She emptied the contents of the glove compartment—Mary Ferrone's registration, a few road maps, a couple of gas receipts—into her bag. She looked under the seats, front and back, and assured herself that it was clean.

She left the key in the ignition.

Then she got out, took her cap and sunglasses from her bag, put them on, and walked down the hill, heading for the subway station she'd noticed at the end of Charles Street.

She figured if the Cherokee didn't get stolen first, it would accumulate parking tickets for a couple of days before some resident complained. Then the traffic police would have it towed to a lot somewhere in the city, where it would wait for its owner to come and bail it out.

She didn't know what would happen when nobody claimed it. Maybe they'd try to get in touch with Mary Ferrone, in whose name the car was registered in Illinois. Maybe it would just sit there and rust.

Jessie didn't care. She was rid of it, and Howie Cohen couldn't use it to track her down.

She had more things to do before she could get her new life underway. But dumping the car was an important first step.

As she walked down Charles Street, she came upon a hair salon between an antique shop and a French restaurant. She peered in the window and saw that two hairdressers were standing by the front counter talking. All the chairs seemed empty.

So Jessie went in, and they took her right away. Turned her into a redhead. Gave her curls.

When Jessie looked at herself in the mirror, she grinned. She liked it. She'd never been a redhead before.

The Boston subway system seemed to be about as haphazard as the layout of its streets, but eventually Jessie made it to the North Station, which was the terminus of the metropolitan commuter train system.

The next train wouldn't get to Concord until 3:25 in the afternoon. By the time she walked from the station to Mac's house, it would be close to four.

She had hoped not to have to say good-bye to Katie, but she figured the girl would be home from school and it couldn't be avoided.

She liked being with them. She felt sort of motherly with Katie. And with Mac . . . ?

She wished her life were different. She wished she could be ordinary, just be Jessie and not Carol Ann Chang or Karen Marie Donato. She wished she could just relax and allow herself to love a man. Maybe to love this sweet, sad man, this Mac.

But she couldn't.

⁓᠎⁓

MAC SPENT THE morning on the Internet, collecting and storing in his computer everything he could find about Judge Thomas Larrigan.

He learned that the man was a paragon of righteousness, a doting father, a loyal husband, a respected, even-handed judge, a community leader, a war hero.

He began to wonder if the Thomas Larrigan that Simone Bonet described in her tapes could possibly be the same man.

Had to be. The old photos showed a younger version of this Supreme Court nominee. The man's service time in Vietnam matched Simone's recollection. The story of the eye patch. Everything matched.

Mac Cassidy was sitting on a gigantic story—not just the scandalous truth about the president's choice for the Supreme Court, but also the truth about two murders—Simone and Jill Rossiter—and most likely a third—Bunny Brubaker—that had been committed in an effort to keep the story from being told.

And now Mac knew those truths. And there was no reason to doubt that anybody who was willing to murder Simone and Jill, and who was clever enough to make it look convincingly like a double suicide, and who'd kill Bunny Brubaker and make it look like a botched drug deal . . . they would certainly be equally willing to murder Mac Cassidy, and anybody else who happened to be in the way.

Jessie was leaving. That was good.

He hadn't figured out what to do about Katie.

⁓᠎⁓

HE SKIPPED LUNCH. He had this other story in his head, and he needed to get it written down. Not the true story detailed in Simone's tapes. Now he was interested in the imagined story. It was about the consequences of Simone's story. It was how he connected the events of the past few months, the way he thought they might have unfolded.

First Thomas Larrigan is tapped to succeed Justice Lawrence Crenshaw on the Supreme Court. Larrigan's name, along with several others, is mentioned in newspaper articles speculating about Justice Crenshaw's retirement.

Then Bunny Brubaker sends an envelope full of old Vietnam photographs—most of them pictures of Thomas Larrigan as a young soldier—to Simone Bonet.

A day or two later, Bunny is murdered in a crummy motel room in Davis, Georgia.

Then comes the president's formal Rose Garden announcement of Larrigan's nomination.

At about the same time, Simone Bonet calls Ted Austin about having her autobiography written.

So Ted calls Mac Cassidy, and Mac goes to Beaverkill, New York, to meet Simone.

Simone gives Mac some photos and documents. She begins telling her story onto tapes.

A couple of weeks later, Mac collects the tapes.

Then Simone and Jill Rossiter are murdered. It's set up to look like a double suicide.

Coincidentally—or maybe not—about that time Jessie Church, Simone and Thomas Larrigan's daughter, shows up.

That was the story so far.

There was a lot Mac didn't know. He didn't have much evidence of anything. Just Simone's tapes plus his own logic. He was speculating, noticing how the dots appeared to be connecting.

He was reading through what he had written, thinking it was a great story, although at this point devoid of evidence and utterly libelous and unpublishable, nothing more than fiction hung on a few disconnected facts plus a dead woman's memories, when he heard the back screen door into the kitchen open and then click shut. He glanced at his watch. Katie was home from school.

A minute later she appeared in the doorway to Mac's office.

He smiled at her. "Hi, honey," he said, as he did every afternoon. "How was your day?"

This was when she always came over and gave him a hug and sat in the chair in the corner with her legs tucked under her and told him all about her day at school.

But this time she remained standing in the doorway. She blinked a couple of times. Then tears began spilling out of her eyes.

"Oh, sweetie," said Mac. "What's the matter?"

He started to stand up to go to her when she lurched into the room. Directly behind her stood a man. He was gripping Katie's left arm just above the elbow. In his other hand he held a square black automatic handgun. He was pressing it against the side of her neck.

"Please, Mr. Cassidy," said the man. "Sit down and relax."

"Get your hands off her," Mac growled.

"There's no need to raise your voice," said the man. He had an earpiece hooked around his left ear.

"Who the hell are you?" said Mac. "What do you want?"

"You can call me Mr. Black."

"Whoever you are," said Mac, "you better let go of my daughter."

Katie tried to twist away from the man, but he was gripping her arm tightly. He kept the nose of the gun pressed against her neck.

The man who called himself Mr. Black smiled. "You don't appear to be in any position to issue threats, Mr. Cassidy."

CHAPTER

It was a hair under two miles from the Concord train station to Mac Cassidy's house on the tree-lined suburban street across the river on the north side of town. Jessie had checked it out on her way into the city. She shouldered her pack and took off at an even lope. About halfway to Mac's house, she picked up the pace. She wanted to be there *now*.

She turned onto Mac's street and jammed to a halt. A large, gray SUV was parked in front of a heavily wooded area four lots down from Mac's place. This struck her as an anomaly. In the couple of days she'd been there, Jessie had never seen any vehicle parked on the street. All the residents left their cars in their garages. Visitors and UPS delivery trucks and other business vehicles all pulled into the driveways.

That didn't mean nobody ever parked on the street. But still. It *was* an anomaly, and cops were trained to spot anomalies and to take them seriously.

She strolled past the van, trying to appear casual. From behind her sunglasses she tried to see into it, but she couldn't. It had tinted windows.

Massachusetts plates. Nothing remarkable about it.

Except . . . who had left it there? Where were they now? And why hadn't they parked in a driveway like everybody else?

She supposed she was being paranoid. Okay, good. A long time ago she'd learned to trust her paranoia. Paranoia kept you alive.

Jessie slipped into the empty lot. All of the houses on Mac's side of the street had backyards that merged into thick oak and pine woods. She stayed inside the woods and sneaked past three backyards. She realized she was probably being silly, but so what? No one had seen her, and aside from a few mosquito bites, no harm done.

A screen of hemlocks separated Mac's yard from his neighbors. Jessie skulked behind them as she approached the back of his house. She felt alert and fine-tuned. She didn't understand how it worked, but she'd had this feeling before, and it had never been wrong.

The man was crouching in the shadows behind some rhododendrons near the front corner of Mac's house. He was watching the driveway and the street. An earpiece was hooked over his left ear. He wore a dark windbreaker and dark pants. At his hip there was the small bulge of what Jessie assumed was a gun under the windbreaker. Why else wear a windbreaker on a warm, sun-drenched June afternoon except to hide a gun?

This didn't surprise Jessie. It was about what she'd expected when she first saw that SUV.

This guy was the lookout. His partner had to be inside.

Mac was in there, and Katie was probably home from school by now.

Jessie slipped her Colt Mustang out of her shoulder bag, then adjusted the bag so that it rested out of the way against the small of her back.

She'd try to get close enough to disarm him and disable his microphone before he said anything. At least his gun was holstered, so that if he spotted her, she'd be able to shoot him before he could bring his weapon into play.

He seemed intent on watching the front of the house. Jessie slipped quickly across the driveway, and by crouching low she was able to keep the foundation plantings between herself and the man in the windbreaker.

She'd snuck to within about ten feet of him when he lowered his chin and mumbled something. A message to his cohorts, who Jessie assumed were inside.

She was just a few feet behind the guy now. He'd finished talking—relaying the news that all was clear, she hoped.

Now!

One quick step and she had her a forearm under his chin. She braced her hip against him and levered him back, using all her strength, holding back nothing, the way she had done with the Lesneski man back in the redwood forest about a hundred years ago. Her forearm against his throat was cutting his wind, preventing him from yelling, from even gagging. With her other hand she jammed the muzzle of her gun into the soft place under his ear. She had her mouth close to his face. "Don't say a fucking word," she hissed. "Don't even clear your throat, or I'll blow your head off, I promise. Okay?"

He nodded. No panic from this guy. He was a pro.

Jessie pulled him backward, dragging him behind the screen of bushes that grew along the side of the house, then turned him around and forced him onto his stomach. She sat on the backs of his thighs and jammed the muzzle of her gun against his rectum.

She bent over and put her face close to his ear. "Not a peep," she whispered. "Pulling the trigger right now would be my pleasure. Understand?"

The left side of his face was pressed against the ground. His right eye looked back at her. He nodded.

She plucked the earpiece out of the guy's ear, held it to her own ear, heard nothing but static, and threw it into the bushes on the other side of the driveway. Then she took his handgun from the holster at his hip. It was a nasty square 9mm automatic. She popped the clip and dropped the gun and the clip into her shoulder bag.

"Okay," she said. "Put both hands behind your back."

He did. Jessie fished the handcuffs from her bag with her free hand and snapped them on the guy's wrists at the small of his back.

Then she got out her roll of duct tape and, using her teeth and one hand while she held the Colt with the other hand, she wrapped the man's ankles all the way up to his knees. Only then did she feel safe putting her gun on the ground beside her. She used both hands to wrap the man's face and head with duct tape. She covered his eyes, mouth, nose and ears, leaving just his nostrils exposed. Then she taped his hands, wrists, and forearms together, right over the handcuffs and all the way up to his elbows.

Jessie sat back on her heels and looked critically at what she'd done. The man might be able to squirm and worm his way along the ground. But he wouldn't get very far very fast, and she guessed that he wouldn't be able to tolerate much exertion since the tape prevented him from breathing through his mouth.

She patted him down. Car keys, pocket knife, some change.

No wallet. No identification of any kind.

That, all by itself, identified him.

Jessie knelt beside the guy on the ground. She jabbed her gun into his crotch, put her mouth close to his taped-over ear, and whispered, "Can you hear me?"

He nodded.

"Did Cohen send you?"

He shook his head.

She gave the muzzle of Colt a hard shove. A gurgle came from the guy's throat.

"If you're lying," she said, "you can say good-bye to your testicles. Was it Howie Cohen?"

Again he shook his head.

She sat back on her heels. If these guys hadn't been sent by Cohen to kill her, it meant they'd come for Mac and the Larrigan tapes. How did she fit into that?

The smart thing to do would be to walk away right now. Head for the bus station. Continue what she started back in Muir Woods a couple weeks ago.

Disappear.

Not likely.

"Okay," she said to the man in the duct tape. "You better be telling the truth. I will not hesitate to blow your balls off. I've done it before, and I enjoyed it. Nod if you believe me."

He nodded.

She figured she didn't have much time. Whoever was inside the house was depending on this guy to submit periodic all-clear messages. When Mr. Outside failed to report on time or to answer a call, Mr. Inside would know something was wrong.

So Jessie slipped around to the back porch and crept up the steps to the door, holding her Mustang down alongside her leg. The outside screen door was shut, but the inside door was open. She could hear the grumble of male voices coming from somewhere inside. She couldn't understand what they were saying. One of the voices, she was quite sure, was Mac's.

She took a breath and tried the screen-door latch. It opened with a click that sounded like a gunshot.

Jessie remained motionless for a moment, holding the door ajar.

The murmur of voices continued.

She pulled the door open and slipped quickly into the little foyer where Mac and Katie hung their coats and hats and kept their boots. She eased the screen door shut behind her and latched it silently.

She listened. The voices sounded like they were coming from the other end of the house, past the kitchen and the dining room and down the hallway. They were in Mac's office, she figured.

She slid along the wall of the foyer and paused at the archway into the kitchen.

She darted her head around the corner and quickly pulled it back, then studied the image of the kitchen that had registered behind her eyes like a snapshot. In that mental photograph, the kitchen was empty.

She listened. She heard nothing. No scrape of a shoe on floor tile. No soft inhale or exhale of breath.

Nobody took a shot at her.

She waited for about a minute, holding her weapon in both hands beside her face, ready to shoot. But there was nobody to shoot at.

She slipped into the kitchen, paused again, listened, then started for Mac's office, where the grumble of voices seemed to be coming from.

She eased herself around the corner from the kitchen into the dining room . . . and that's when a hand clamped over her mouth and yanked her head back, and at the same time, something sharp pricked her neck just under her right ear.

Oh, shit.

"Drop the weapon, Miz Church," a deep male voice growled into her ear.

Jessie let her little Colt automatic fall from her fingers. There was a thick carpet on the dining-room floor, and the gun made a muffled thump when it landed.

"The bag," he said. "Drop it."

She shrugged off her shoulder bag and let it slide onto the floor.

He shoved it aside with his foot.

The man had his hand over her mouth. It felt as if her face was in a vise. He pulled her backward so that she was pressing against him. His mouth was right beside her ear, and now the knife was on her throat. He moved the blade and it sliced the tightly-stretched skin under her chin.

The pain was sudden and sharp.

He smelled of stale cigar smoke and Old Spice.

Jessie felt a trickle of warm blood dribble down to the hollow place at the base of her throat. One more ounce of pressure on that knifeblade and it would cut through her tendons and ligaments and cartilage and arteries.

He moved the blade away from her throat, and then she felt the point of the knife prick the skin at the base of her spine. He let go of her face. "Put your hands on top of your head," he growled, "and lace your fingers together."

Big mistake. Jessie whirled, ducked, and kicked all in one blurry motion, a hard kick with all of her strength and all of the momentum of her pivot behind it, and her instep got the guy square between the legs.

He let out a quick, sharp breath, a combination of a sigh and a groan. He dropped his knife, grabbed his crotch with both hands, fell forward onto the carpet, and curled into a fetal position.

Jessie was on him in an instant. She picked up his knife and jabbed its point in the soft place under his chin. She bent close to his face, so close her nose almost touched his. "One word and I'll kill you," she hissed. "Stand up."

The guy rolled his eyes and shook his head.

"Now," she whispered. "Stand up or I'll cut your throat."

The guy managed to get onto his knees, then push himself to his feet. He was bent over and kept one hand cradling his balls.

Jessie stepped behind him, locked her forearm around his throat, and pressed the knife blade against the side of his neck. "Let's go," she said.

She walked the guy through the dining room and through the archway that separated it from Mac's living room.

It wasn't at all what she'd expected to see.

Mac and Katie were sitting on the sofa. Mac had his arm draped around Katie's shoulders. Katie had her legs drawn up under her. They both looked almost relaxed.

A man she'd never seen before was in the leather chair across from them. He had blondish-brown hair. He wore a blue shirt and khaki pants and white sneakers and a black earpiece. One ankle was crossed over the other leg, and his right arm was dangling over the side of the chair. He was holding an automatic handgun in his right hand. It was pointing at the floor.

They all looked up when Jessie pushed the guy into the room.

Katie, she noticed, had been crying. Her eyes were red, but now they were dry.

Mac nodded and smiled at Jessie.

The man in the leather chair bowed his head. "Ah, Ms. Church," he said. "You are quite good, aren't you? Please. Join us. Mr. White, you look like you'd like to use the bathroom. Let him go, Ms. Church. He won't harm you."

Jessie moved the knife and took her forearm away from the man's neck. He mumbled something and staggered out of the room.

Jessie went over and sat on the sofa beside Mac. "What's going on?" she said.

"We're negotiating," Mac said. He touched her throat, then showed her his fingertip. It was red with shiny blood. He pulled a handkerchief from his pocket and gave it to her.

She pressed the handkerchief against her throat. "These guys with knives and guns," she said, "they're here to negotiate?"

He smiled. "I don't think that was their original intent."

"Allow me to explain," said the man in the chair.

"Yes, please," said Jessie.

"My name is Mr. Black," said the man. "That man you escorted in here is Mr. White. I assume you met Mr. Green outside."

Jessie shrugged. "What are you negotiating?"

"Mr. Cassidy has kindly agreed not to publish his very interesting story, or to release any of his documentation, or, in fact, to make public any details about it whatsoever for eighteen months." He looked at Mac. "Eighteen months, we said, right?"

"A year from next December," said Mac.

"We, for our part," said Mr. Black, "have agreed not to kill Mr. Cassidy, or young Katie, here, or you, either, Ms. Church."

"Sounds like a good deal all around," said Jessie.

Mr. Black smiled. "You are a cynic, Ms. Church. But a realist, I'm sure. So you must see how well this will work out for everybody."

"And why didn't you kill us?"

Mr. Black gestured with his gun toward Mac. "Tell her, Mr. Cassidy."

"Simone's tapes," he said. "If anything happens to any of us, I have left instructions that they should immediately be released to key representatives of the media, along with the photographs and documents plus my summary of the facts contained in the tapes."

"And if nothing happens to us?"

"The tapes will stay where they are—in a safe in a lawyer's office in New York City."

"For eighteen months," said Jessie. "That's a year from December. A month after the next presidential election."

Mr. Black smiled. "Smart girl."

"It would be unreasonable," said Mac, "to expect us never to publish Simone's story. On the other hand," he added, "if we were to leak any information before a year from December, if we didn't keep up our end of the bargain . . ."

Mr. Black raised his gun, pointed it at Katie, and said, "Bang, bang."

Katie, Jessie observed, had squeezed her eyes tightly shut.

"So it's a stalemate," said Jessie.

"It's a fair deal all around," said Mr. Black.

Jessie arched her eyebrows. "Is it?"

"Excuse me?" he said.

"What do I get out of it?"

"You get to live, Ms. Church."

"I mean," she said, "Cassidy, here, he ends up publishing his story, making a bunch of money, buying his daughter a car, putting her through college. You, you get the time you need to do whatever it is you have to do. So what about me?"

Mr. Black smiled. "Is there something we can do for you, Ms. Church?"

"As a matter of fact," said Jessie, "there are a couple of things."

Judge Thomas Larrigan slouched in his leather desk chair. He had his feet propped up on his desk and his necktie pulled loose, and he was gazing out of his big office window at the Boston Inner Harbor. It was one of those sultry early-summer afternoons. Sailboats and motorboats skittered over the water, and fishermen armed with surf rods were silhouettes perched on the rocks out at the end of the jetty. Larrigan thought they looked like black insects with long feelers.

He was feeling pretty relaxed, for a change.

The slanting rays of the sun glinted off the water, and a breeze had sprung up, riffling its surface with little whitecaps. Thick thunderheads were building on the horizon.

There were no trials scheduled for the next day, which was the Friday before the long Independence Day weekend. Judge Larrigan intended to drive down to his summer place in Orleans on the Cape to join his wife and kids that evening. He already had his overnighter packed and stowed in the trunk of his car along with his golf clubs. He planned to have a leisurely dinner at the club and leave for the Cape around eight, after the rush-hour traffic had thinned out.

It would be good to get away from the courthouse, where even the other judges had begun looking at him and speaking to him differently. It wasn't "Tom" anymore. Now they called him "Judge." He wasn't one of them anymore. He was the next Supreme Court Justice.

Not that he minded. In fact, he loved it.

It was really going to happen. All the impediments had been removed.

Larrigan smiled. "Justice Larrigan," he said aloud, savoring the sound of it.

He smiled, took a sip of water, and checked his cell phone again.

He still had that one damn message.

It was from Eddie Moran.

He'd rather ignore it. Moran had served his purpose, and he'd been paid. Things were square between them, and Thomas Larrigan didn't want anything to do with Eddie Moran anymore.

But, of course, it wasn't that simple.

He replayed the message. "We need to talk," Eddie said. "It's important. The usual place, six-thirty."

The usual place was the parking garage off Summer Street.

Larrigan glanced at his wristwatch. It was almost quarter of six. He better get going. He had forty-five minutes to pick up his car in the courthouse garage and drive to Summer Street where neither he nor his car would be recognized. He'd give Eddie Moran five minutes. Justice Thomas Larrigan had more important things to think about.

—◦◦—

LARRIGAN PULLED INTO the parking garage at six-twenty-five. He found an empty slot next to a concrete pillar on the third level. A big SUV was parked beside him, and on the other side of the pillar was some kind of van.

With his side window rolled down, he could hear the rhythmic *blip-blip* of water dripping into a puddle on the concrete floor. Now and then distant footsteps echoed hollowly, followed by the muffled sound of a car door slamming and then an engine starting up. The place was dim and dank and shadowy. The weak yellow light from the bulbs in the ceiling just seemed to exaggerate the darkness and sense of isolation in the garage.

Suddenly the passenger door clicked open and Eddie Moran slid in beside him.

"Jesus," said Larrigan. "I didn't see you coming. You don't have to be so damn sneaky." He glanced at his watch. Six-thirty on the dot. "And do you always have to be so damn punctual?"

"Can't help it," said Moran. "I'm just a sneaky, on-time kind of guy, you know? Blame the United States Marines. So how you doin'?"

"Good," said Larrigan. "Excellent."

"Well, that's terrific," said Moran. "Me, I'm good, too."

Larrigan shrugged. "I'm glad." He was looking out the side window at the big concrete pillar right beside the car. Somebody had spray-painted "Yankees Suck" on it with red paint.

"I wasn't sure you cared."

"Of course I care," said Larrigan.

"You and me," said Moran, "we go way back. Our fortunes are linked, you might say."

"You've been a loyal friend," said Larrigan. "I appreciate everything you've done." He noticed how the paint had dribbled down off the bottoms of the red letters. It looked like they were bleeding. "So what's up, Eddie? What's on your mind?"

"Like you say," said Moran, "I've been loyal friend. I'm glad you realize it. But you know, when it comes down to it, loyalty only goes so far. For example, you'd betray me in a minute."

"Jesus, Eddie, I wouldn't—"

"It's okay," said Moran. "That's how it is. I understand. I guess about now you're thinking it's time to separate yourself from your old war buddy, who's a pretty crude character, hardly a suitable friend for a Justice of the Supreme Court."

Larrigan turned to look at him. "I wasn't—"

"No," said Moran. "It's good. I wouldn't hang around with me, either, if I was you. You gotta take care of number one. Nobody blames anybody for doing what needs to be done. It's all about survival."

"I'd never betray you," said Larrigan. He turned away to gaze out the side window, looking at the big pillar, reluctant to look at Moran's face. "I'm truly grateful for everything. But in a way, you're right. There comes a time when . . ."

He shrugged, sighed, and turned again to face Eddie Moran. And that's when he saw the big square handgun that Moran was holding on his lap.

"What the hell is that?" said Larrigan.

"It's a Marine .45. You still got yours, don't you?"

"No." Larrigan shook his head. "So what's with the gun?"

"For one thing," Moran said, "I never felt right, lying about your fucking eye so you could get a medal." He shrugged and raised the gun.

A .45 was serious overkill, Moran was thinking. It made a dime-sized hole just in front of Larrigan's right ear where Moran had pressed the muzzle. But compared to the other side of the man's head, the entry wound was a pinprick. The whole left side of the judge's head was pretty much blown away. Splashes of blood and clots of brain and pieces of hair and bone were splattered all over the inside of the car. Droplets of blood were even spattered on the concrete pillar outside the open window.

Eddie Moran had taken the Marine-issue sidearm from the body of a buddy of his. It happened over there about thirty-five years ago. Their squad was walking single file along a jungle path. It was nighttime, moonless, dark as death.

Carlos was his name. Carlos . . . something Hispanic. He was a private. What the hell was his last name? Anyway, Carlos was the man directly in front of Sgt. Moran, and so he was the one who happened to step on the mine and get both legs blown off.

Sanchez. That was it. PFC Carlos Sanchez. Had an Anglo girl-friend. A pretty blonde, wore a cheerleader's uniform in the picture Sanchez carried inside his helmet. Sanchez was barely eighteen. He died fast. Just bled out right there beside the path.

The .45 could never be traced. It was an unregistered standard-issue Marine sidearm from that old war. It could've been Thomas Larrigan's gun.

Moran's ears were still ringing. A .45 made a head-splitting explosion anyway, but inside an automobile in a concrete parking garage it sounded like a bomb went off.

What was left of Larrigan's head was thrown back and sideways. The whole front of his jacket and shirt and necktie was soaked with blood.

It would've been best if he somehow could have convinced the judge to write down how depressed he'd been, left something that would pass as a suicide note, but Moran figured there were people—his wife, his secretary, some of his colleagues, probably—who'd say how the judge had been tense and stressed lately, under-standable with the big nomination and everything, and they would mention it to whoever did the investigation.

Yes, they'd say, *ever since the president announced the nomination, Thomas hasn't been himself. Certainly not his usual upbeat, outgoing self.*

Still, I can't believe he'd go and do something like this. You never know, huh?

Moran picked up the spent cartridge, stuck it in his pocket, and replaced it with a fresh bullet in the gun's clip. Then he picked up Larrigan's right hand and wrapped it around the handle of the big automatic. He wedged the dead man's forefinger inside the trigger guard, and then, holding the judge's hand with both of his own, Moran pointed the gun out the window and aimed it up toward the top of the wall at the distant end of the garage. Then he turned his face away, mentally braced himself for another ear-splitting explosion, and pulled the trigger.

Pretty much the way he did it with the blonde when he shot Li An. As far as he knew, it worked that time.

If they did it right, forensics would find the empty cartridge case from the second shot on the floor of the car where the gun had ejected it, and they'd test Larrigan's hand and the sleeve of his jacket for gunpowder residue. Moran knew that they didn't always do it right. But the suicide of somebody like Judge Larrigan—especially a suicide without a note—would most likely get investigated pretty thoroughly.

He let Larrigan's arm fall to his side. The .45 slipped out and dropped onto the seat of the car, and Moran left it right there.

Moran hooked his little finger around the inside handle, shouldered the car door open, and slid out. He shut the door with a shove of his hip, then rubbed the palm of his hand over the outside door handle, leaving it smudged. Didn't want to wipe it clean. That would raise questions.

He stood there for a minute, listening. No voices. No echo of footsteps. No distant siren.

Moran walked to the stairway, went up to the fourth level, and got into his car. He turned on the dome light and checked his face in the rearview mirror. A few coagulated drops of Larrigan's blood speckled his forehead. He spit on handkerchief and wiped them away. There was some blood splatter on his shirt, too. He pulled on the nylon windbreaker he kept in the backseat and zipped it to his throat.

He put on his thick horn-rimmed glasses and screwed a Red Sox cap onto his head. Then he drove down to the lower level and then he was out, free and clear, job done, obligations fulfilled, debts paid.

Eddie Moran had done everything Mr. Black's way, and now they were even.

—ᴄᴏ᷉ᴏ—

HOWIE COHEN WAS sitting at his desk in the prison library, as he did every morning. He figured that by the time they let him out—in twenty-two years, four months, and eleven days, if he behaved himself, which was easy enough, and managed to live that long, which was extremely doubtful—he might complete the changeover from the card catalog to the computer.

Most mornings Cohen enjoyed entering the data. He found the library a pleasant place. It was quiet there, and everybody left him alone. The work required his full attention. It passed the time. It was kind of gratifying, too. He liked to be able to measure what he'd accomplished. Now he was working on the fiction, which was alphabetical by the author's last name. He was up to the letter K. He'd been working in the library for seven months. He was taking his time with it, working slow and steady, getting everything just right. Howie Cohen had nothing but time.

This morning, though, he hadn't gotten anything done. He kept looking at those five disturbing photos that he'd laid out on his desk. Photos of his grandchildren. Howie Cohen had seven grandchildren.

One shot was of Hannah, Cohen's oldest grandchild, David's firstborn. You love them all, of course, but Hannah was Grampa's favorite. She was almost twelve now. In the photo, she was sitting cross-legged on the ground in her maroon soccer uniform. She was sucking on a lollipop with a thoughtful expression on her pretty face. Such a smart little girl. Looking quite grown-up in the photo. You couldn't help noticing that she was becoming a young woman. Soon she'd be having her bat mitzvah, which Grampa wouldn't be allowed to attend. Cohen used to read Winnie-the-Pooh stories to little Hannah when she was just learning to read. He remembered the warmth of the little girl sitting in his lap, how she seemed to radiate heat and energy. She called him Pap-Pap. He would point to the words on the page, and she'd repeat them and giggle, and he'd give her a big hug.

In another photo were David's twins, Joshua and Jacob, almost eight now, wearing fielders' mitts, playing catch on a ball field. This shot had been taken with a wide-angle lens so that you could see there were no other children nearby. Just the two boys, all by themselves.

There was a shot of his daughter Ruthie's first baby, Rosanne, just two, wearing nothing but a diaper and toddling around in what Howie Cohen recognized as Ruthie's fenced-in backyard in Bethesda.

Then there was a picture of Kimee, Ellie's youngest, just four, squatting beside a weedy pond, poking at something in the water with a stick.

And finally there was a shot of Ellie's boys, Aaron, nine, and Lester, six, seated on a park bench. A man, a stranger to Howie Cohen, was sitting between them. The man had an arm around the shoulders of each of the boys. He was staring directly into the lens of the camera, and both boys were looking up at the guy in the photo. Clearly, this photo had been posed for Howie Cohen's benefit. The message wasn't very subtle.

Ordinarily a grandfather would treasure these recent photos of his beloved grandchildren—if, for example, his wife or one of his kids had taken them and sent them to Grampa.

But these photos had been shot by a stranger. They had arrived in a manila envelope with no return address. It had been mailed from Washington, D. C. In the envelope along with the photos had been a folded-up newspaper clipping with a headline reading "Muir Woods Body Identified."

Any dummy would get this message, and it made Howie Cohen tremble with fear and outrage.

The envelope had arrived three days ago. Cohen hadn't slept a wink since then, waiting for the next move.

He put the photos and the clipping back in the envelope and stared at his computer monitor.

An hour or so later one of the guards came into the library and walked over to Howie Cohen's desk. "Come with me," he said.

Cohen stood up. "What is it?"

"You got a phone call."

"From who?"

The guard shrugged.

"They're letting me take a phone call now?"

"Looks like it."

The guard led him down the hall to an empty, windowless room. It wasn't much bigger than a closet. It contained a small wooden table and a straight-backed wooden chair. A telephone sat on the table. The guard pointed at the phone. The receiver was off the cradle. The guard gestured Cohen into the room, then closed the door.

Cohen sat on the chair, picked up the phone, and said, "Yes?"

"Mr. Cohen?" It was a man's voice. He didn't recognize it.

"Who's this?"

"Call me Mr. White. Did you get the envelope I sent you?"

"Who are you?"

"Oh, I'm just an amateur photographer. They say a picture is worth a thousand words. Have you heard that?"

"What do you want?"

"Your grandchildren are adorable, Mr. Cohen. They're precious to you. You like to have them visit you, yes?"

Cohen said nothing.

"You like knowing they are safe, living in nice houses in pretty suburbs, attending fancy private schools, supported by the fruits of Grampa's career in crime, am I right?"

Cohen was clenching his jaw.

"Answer me, Howie."

"I cherish my grandchildren, yes. What do you want?"

"Does the name Leonard P. Lesneski ring a bell?"

"I saw that clipping."

"You're a smart man," said Mr. White. "You tell me what I want."

"You're threatening the lives of my grandchildren?"

"So what do I want, Howie?"

"This is about Jessie, isn't it?"

"What's my message?"

Cohen hesitated. Then he said, "I understand. Her safety for my grandchildren's safety."

"Exactly. And how will that work?"

Cohen said nothing.

"Do you know how it works, Mr. Cohen?" said Mr. White.

"Of course," he said. "If anything happens to Jessie . . ."

"What? Say it, Howie."

Cohen blew out a long breath. "I don't want to say it. It's too awful to say."

"I've got to hear you say it."

Howie Cohen's throat felt tight. He swallowed several times. "You want me to say that if anything happens to Jessie Church, something will happen to one of my grandchildren."

"Or maybe to more than one of them," said Mr. White.

"Jesus."

"You are responsible for Jessie Church's safety. Do you understand that, Howie?"

"Yes."

"Say it."

"I am responsible for Jessie Church's safety."

"Good."

Howie Cohen heard the click at the other end as Mr. White disconnected. He sighed, pushed himself up from the chair, and knocked on the office door.

The guard, standing out in the hallway, opened it. "What?"

"I need to make a phone call," Cohen said.

The guard nodded. "They thought you might. Go ahead. Dial nine, then the number."

Cohen went back into the office. He closed the door, sat at the desk, and dialed Bernie's cell phone number. They'd probably trace it. Didn't matter. They already knew all about Bernie.

He assumed they were listening in. He hoped so.

It rang just once before Bernie picked up. "Yeah?"

"It's Howie."

"Hey. How you doin'? Everything okay?"

"Call it off."

"Huh?"

"Jessie Church. I changed my mind."

"You wanna explain?"

"No. Just do it."

"Call it off?"

"Yes."

"Okay. You're the boss."

"Right. And don't ever forget it."

EPILOGUE

By the second week in September, six inches of snow had fallen on the dirt road that climbed through the woods to Eddie Moran's cabin in the foothills of the Maligne Mountains in western Alberta. But even with the bed mounded with another load of firewood, Eddie's big four-wheel-drive Ford pickup had no problem with the snow and the mud.

Somebody had told him that Maligne meant "bad luck" in French. Eddie didn't buy it. He'd been having nothing but good luck lately. Things were working out. He'd finally found a life that felt right. He liked cooking and heating with firewood. He liked reading at night with a Coleman lantern. He liked pumping water by hand. He even liked shitting in his outhouse.

He liked driving the back roads in his truck with his dog, a black mutt, predominantly Labrador, riding shotgun. Eddie had named the dog Sniper. Sniper liked to fetch chunks of wood from the river, and he growled at strangers. He was good company.

Eddie liked the rugged Canadian weather. It tested a man. He was looking forward to winter. He liked the thick woods and the rough mountains and the big dangerous sky. He liked the elbow room and the solitude.

He'd spent the afternoon with his chainsaw at Emil LaBouche's woodlot, felling and limbing dead trees, cutting them into four-foot lengths, and loading them into his truck. Back home he'd dump them in the side yard where he'd cut them into stove lengths and split them at his leisure. He already had six cut-and-split cords of two-year-old Canadian maple stacked in his woodshed, enough to keep his tight little two-room cabin comfortable all winter.

But Eddie planned to keep cutting, lugging, splitting, and stacking wood as long as he could get around in his truck. You could never have too much firewood. Besides, working with wood was excellent exercise. Since he'd come to the Canadian Rockies three months ago, Eddie had become as sinewy and leathery and lean as he'd been when he was in the Marines. He'd never felt better, and that was the truth. He went to sleep when it got dark and woke up with the sun. He cut wood, he patched his roof, he ate fresh cutthroat trout and aged Alberta beef, he read novels.

Eddie even had a girlfriend. Her name was Stella Wilson. Stella was a waitress at the Wolf Creek Cafe in Hinton, out on the Yellow-head Highway. The cafe was over forty miles from Eddie's cabin in the woods. But in that part of Alberta, people drove forty miles each way for a pack of cigarettes.

Stella was divorced—or she was getting divorced, or maybe she'd never been married in the first place, it wasn't quite clear. She was about twenty-five years younger than Eddie, but that didn't seem to bother her, and it sure didn't bother him. She was a tiger in the sack, she liked to cook for him, and all she asked was that he bring her a bottle of Early Times or a carton of Marlboro Reds once in a while.

Life was good. He hardly ever thought about Thomas Larrigan anymore. All that seemed long ago and far away. Eddie Moran had a new life, and it suited him.

There were still a couple hours of daylight left, so he pulled off the road, let Sniper out of the truck, and grabbed his spinning rod from behind the seat. Sniper ran ahead of him as he skidded down the embankment to the creek where the water came curving out of the woods. Here it funneled between some big boulders and then spread out into a long flat pool. Eddie chucked the little gold spinner into the current at the head of the pool. He gave the reel a couple of turns and felt the tug. He lifted his rod to vertical, cranked on the reel, and a minute later a foot-long cutthroat trout was splashing at his feet.

Eddie backed the treble hook out of its mouth, stuck his finger in its gills, snapped its neck, and dropped the fish on the muddy bank behind him. Sniper lay down beside the fish and lapped the slime off it.

Three casts later he caught another trout.

Two was enough. He took out his folding knife and quickly slit the two trout from anus to gills. Sniper sat there and watched. He pried out the fishes' innards with his forefinger and dropped them on the bank for the minks and porcupines and crows, then rinsed the trout and his hands in the stream. He'd fry up some potatoes and onions and bacon to go with the fish. Heat up a can of beans. Wash it all down with a couple glasses of red wine. Let Sniper lick the plate. Find some rock and roll on his battery-powered boom box. Get started on that Tim O'Brien paperback.

Maybe tomorrow night he'd go see Stella.

Life was excellent.

He cut a stick, left the crotch of a branch on it, and strung his two trout on it, in through the gills, out through the mouth. He rinsed his knife off in the river, dried it against his pants, and put it in his pocket.

When he turned to head back to his truck, there was a redheaded woman standing there. She looked about thirty. Olive complexion, dark Asian eyes.

Sniper, standing beside him, was wagging his tail at the woman.

Moran smiled at her. "Hey. How you doin'?"

"Good, Eddie," she said. "I'm doing very good."

He frowned. "Do I know you?"

"I'm Jessie Church," she said. "Tell your dog to sit down."

"Sniper won't hurt you," he said, but he said, "Sit," to Sniper, and the dog sat.

The woman was standing at the end of the pathway that wound down the slope to the bank of the stream. She was wearing tight jeans and a hip-length sheepskin jacket. Her hands were tucked into her jacket pockets.

She was a pretty, sexy woman. Moran had always been partial to redheads.

He frowned. "Jessie Church?" He shrugged and shook his head. "Sorry. If we met sometime, I guess I forget." He took a step toward her, wiped his hand on his pants, and extended it to her. He smiled. "Good to see you."

She took her hands from her pockets. One hand was holding an automatic handgun. Looked like a nine. A Sig Sauer, if he wasn't mistaken. She held it at her side, pointing at the ground. She did not offer to shake Eddie's hand.

"Hey," he said. "What's that for?"

"My parents," she said.

"What'd you say your name was?"

"Church," she said. "Jessie Church."

"I don't know anybody named Church."

"Look at me," she said.

He shrugged. "Yeah, you're sexy, all right. So?"

"You killed both of my parents. Figure it out."

He narrowed his eyes for a minute. And then he got it. "Li An," he said. "And Tommy Larrigan. Christ. I knew you when you were a baby. Baby May. I'll be damned."

"Good," she said. "I wanted to be sure you understood." She raised her hand, the one holding the gun, and pointed it at his face. He was pretty sure it was a nine, now that he was looking down the muzzle.

"Don't do this," said Moran. "Nothing I did was personal. You know that, right?"

"It's personal for me," said Jessie.

"Christ," he said. "I held you in my arms when you were about a month old."

Jessie moved the Sig so that it was pointed at Sniper.

"Hey, come on," said Eddie. "Not my dog."

Jessie gave Eddie a hard look, then aimed the gun at Sniper's forehead, squinted down the barrel, and said, "Bang, bang," in a conversational tone.

She lowered the gun to her side, gave Eddie Moran a long, steady look, then turned and walked back up the path with the big Sig nine dangling from her hand.

After a minute, over the muffled roar of the river, Moran heard the sound of an automobile engine starting up, and he stood there and listened until it faded into the distance.

He knelt down beside Sniper and put an arm around him. "It's okay," he said. "She's gone."

For now, anyway, he was thinking.

Two o'clock in the afternoon; Columbus Day, the national holiday. Bankers and mailmen and Wall Street brokers and schoolteachers all got the day off.

Mac Cassidy didn't resent them. But he was working. Writers never got holidays, although if you asked most people, they'd probably say that the writer's life was one big happy holiday of book tours and *Oprah* interviews.

Mac was doing what he did every day—sitting in his office chair, sipping coffee, and staring bleakly at his computer monitor.

Some days, all too rare lately, the words came flowing.

Most days, like today, he had to pry them loose with a mental crowbar.

No matter what kind of day it happened to be, though, Mac Cassidy planted his ass in his chair and forced words to appear on his screen. Eight hundred words a day, through sleet and snow and flu-like symptoms. That's how books got written. Not in great bursts of inspiration. You wrote a book one painful sentence at a time. Eight hundred words a day, which was a lot of sentences, whether it took an hour or ten hours. Either way, it was exhausting.

But after 125 days—four months, a third of a year—if you did it every day, you had 100,000 words. That, more or less, was the first draft of a book.

When Jane died, Mac had quit writing.

Now he poked the keys that instructed his computer to count the words he'd composed in the five hours since he sat down in the morning.

Still 478. Less than one hundred words an hour. Pitiful.

He had to come up with another 322. He knew what he wanted to say. He had his outline and his notes. But the words themselves had dug in their heels.

He'd been wrestling with this book for a year now, and he still hadn't found his rhythm. He didn't know whether it was this particular book, or it was him. Maybe he'd lost it. Maybe he'd never write anything publishable again.

The phone rang.

Mac grabbed it the way he'd grab somebody's hand if he were falling into a bottomless crevasse. Any excuse not to write.

"Mac Cassidy," he said.

"It's Ted," said Ted Austin. "You're not working, are you?"

"Of course I'm working," said Mac. "And since you're calling me, I assume you are too. Or is this a social call?"

"Have I ever made a social call?"

"Not to me," said Mac. "Not yet. So what's up?"

"I got good news and bad news. The bad news is worse than the good news is good. Let's get it out of the way."

Mac swiveled around in his desk chair so that he could look out the window. The autumn sun was streaking through the crimson maples. "I have acquired a certain perspective on bad news," he said. "You don't need to soften it for me."

Austin cleared his throat. "Beckman's pulling the plug on the Simone project."

Mac found himself nodding. "Did he say why?"

"No. But we can surmise."

"I'm on schedule. We've abided by the contract."

"Sure we have. It's not your fault, Mac. He's not blaming you. What you've shown him is good stuff."

"The Larrigan material is dynamite," Mac said.

"Yes." Austin hesitated. "Exactly."

"Oh." Mac laughed quietly. "I get it."

"Somebody got to them."

"Threatened them, you think?"

"Who knows," said Austin.

"Look," said Mac after a minute. "If you want the truth, it's a relief. I don't like this book. With Simone dead, it's not right. I've been struggling to get a handle on it."

"Then it's not such bad news after all."

"Not that bad." Mac hesitated. "So what's the good news?"

"You can keep your advance."

"That's it?"

"It was a generous advance."

"Yes," said Mac, "it was."

"There's a kicker," said Austin. "It's this. If you publish this book with somebody else, you've got to return your advance to Beckman."

"So I can *not* write it for a nice advance," Mac said, "or I *can* write it and forfeit the advance."

"Yes," said Austin. "Well, you'd probably get some kind of advance, assuming we could place the book. Doubtful it'd be as generous as Beckman's."

"Tell you the truth," said Mac, "I don't want to write it. This book doesn't want to be written. It's been fighting me every inch of the way. I wouldn't feel that bad about keeping the advance."

"I told Beckman we wouldn't make a fuss about it," said Austin. "We could, but we won't. He's grateful for that. He wants to hear other proposals. I've got some ideas."

"You know what?" said Mac. "I'm tired of writing other people's stories. Maybe this would be a good time to try something different."

"Like what?"

Mac was shaking his head. "I don't know. A novel, maybe." He hesitated. "Something from my own heart, not somebody else's."

"Well, Mac," said Austin, "if you write a novel, I'll try to sell it for you. Please keep in the back of your mind, though, that what you're really good at is ghostwriting." He paused for a moment. "We'll talk some more. Happy Columbus Day. Enjoy the holiday. Do something fun."

"Maybe I will," said Mac.

He hung up the phone, stood up and stretched. *A novel*, he thought. *That might be fun.*

He walked through the house and out onto the back porch. Katie and Jessie were working side by side with wicker grass rakes, dragging fallen maple leaves into big piles on the lawn. They hadn't seen Mac step out onto the porch. From where he was standing, they could have been sisters—Katie looking older than her age and Jessie looking younger than hers. Each was wearing cut-off jeans and a big floppy T-shirt and dirty sneakers, with her hair pulled back in a ponytail, laughing together in the slanting afternoon sun, raking crimson and golden autumn leaves into piles in Mac Cassidy's backyard.

— THE END —